OHIO
BRIDES

OHIO BRIDES

THREE-IN-ONE COLLECTION

CARA C. PUTMAN

BARBOUR
PUBLISHING

A Promise Kept © 2009 by Cara C. Putman
A Promise Born © 2009 by Cara C. Putman
A Promise Forged © 2010 by Cara C. Putman

ISBN 978-1-61626-118-4

All scripture quotations are taken from the King James Version of the Bible.

Cover design: Kirk DouPonce, DogEared Design

Published by Barbour Publishing, Inc., P.O. Box 719, Uhrichsville, Ohio 44683, www.barbourbooks.com

Our mission is to publish and distribute inspirational products offering exceptional value and biblical encouragement to the masses.

ecpa Member of the
Evangelical Christian
Publishers Association

Printed in the United States of America.

Dear Readers,

I'm so excited that you have selected *Ohio Brides* to read. These books are near and dear to my heart because they tell the stories of three siblings living in Ohio during my favorite time period. World War II was a time that highlighted our country's ability to come together with great unity to fight common foes.

A Promise Kept is a truly unique story because it begins with the wedding of Josie and Art and continues through the challenges of their first year of marriage. The challenges are large, and often leave Josie wondering where God is in the midst of her life. I know I've been there—no matter how solid my faith is, I can find myself questioning and wrestling with God. Add in a distant English cousin being evacuated from London and sent to live with them, and you'll catch an early flavor for how the European war had begun to impact the United States in late 1939.

In *A Promise Born*, I got to explore a top-secret war project. While not the Manhattan Project, I nearly jumped up and down when I learned that the project to solve the Enigma codes occurred in Dayton. Mark works for the company that is tasked with breaking the code and has to deal with the Navy even though he hasn't enlisted. This story also allowed me to look at the role the women in the WAVES played as they supported the Navy. And how can you beat a closing scene at the White House as the Christmas tree is lit?

For the final book, *A Promise Kept*, I turned to Kat, the youngest sister, who shows up in the other books. Kat had made it clear to me that she needed a truly unique story that would allow her spunkiness and drive to shine through. Enter the All American Girls Professional Softball/Baseball League. At a time where Major League Baseball lost many of its players to the war draft, Mr. Wrigley in Chicago created a crazy idea to start a women's league. *A Promise Kept* is set during the inaugural season of the league. Add in a jaded reporter as hero, and the story was a ton of fun to write—and hopefully a joy to read.

It is my hope that *Ohio Brides* sweeps you back to the days of World War II. Life was hard, but their faith in God pulled them through. I hope through these books you will have a fresh sense of how much God loves you. He will never leave you or forsake you no matter what struggles you face or questions you confront. Please visit my Web site: www.caraputman.com to learn more about my other books and to send me an e-mail. I'd love to know what you think about *Ohio Brides*.

Blessings,
Cara C. Putman

A PROMISE
KEPT

Dedication

To my husband, Eric. We've walked through so much together, but I can't imagine traveling this road with anyone else. I love you.

Special thanks to Sue Lyzenga for reading this book for me literally as it scrolled off the printer. Your eagle eyes caught many errors. And to Tricia Goyer, Sabrina Butcher, and Gina Conroy for helping me fine-tune the beginning.

Prologue

November, 1939

The tick of the second hand rounding the face of the grandfather clock jarred the sudden silence in the small church anteroom. Josephine Miller stared at it, praying it could somehow speed up. Her wedding would start in a matter of minutes. The thought was wonderful. Why did time slow and each second seem to take a minute when all she wanted to do was sweep out of the room and race down the aisle?

In the middle of these crazy, uncertain times, Art Wilson had swept her off her feet and made her feel cherished in a way that blocked out everything.

She turned to look in the mirror standing against the wall; her fingers fidgeted with the pleats as she scanned her appearance. Her white gown flowed around her like a dress designed for a princess. Mama had managed to tame Josie's hair into a sleek upsweep, so different from how she looked most days. Her mother sighed, and Josie caught her gaze in the mirror's reflection.

"You look so beautiful." Mama smiled and pressed her handkerchief to the corners of her eyes. "The gown fits you perfectly."

Joy bubbled around the butterflies filling Josie's stomach. The day she'd longed for had arrived. Only one thing would make her joy complete. If only they'd make their first home in Dayton.

Her smile faltered in the mirror. How she wished Art hadn't accepted a position miles from Dayton and home. She knew the job would provide a strong start for them, an opportunity Art hadn't found in Dayton. Her dreams they'd start life in a small apartment near Mama and Daddy had evaporated. Instead, they'd head to Cincinnati. She'd longed for an adventure, and this move fit the bill. The chance to launch their life on their own was reality. While it might not have been her initial dream, a tingle of excitement edged the glow of anticipation she felt when she thought about her new life with her husband. *Husband.* She rolled the word around in her mind again and again. Heat flushed her cheeks as she thought of everything the word meant. God had blessed her!

"Josephine Miller, you'll be late to your own wedding if you don't move." Her younger sister's sharp words pulled Josie from her thoughts.

Josie cleared her throat. "Isn't that Mama's line, Kat?"

Mama laughed as Josie fiddled with the bottom of her lace jacket. It topped a floor-length, lace-covered gown that made her feel like a movie star or wealthy socialite.

9

Kat stood in the glow of colors flowing through the stained-glass window. They accented her athletic form and the bruise she'd acquired in her latest game with the boys. Josie shook her head. Clothing Kat in a dress didn't make the girl any less of a tomboy. Kat caught her stare and rolled her eyes. "Fine. Just remember I'm the one who told you Art was interested."

The door groaned on its hinges as it pushed into the room, making way for Carolynn Treen. Carolynn had done an amazing job pulling together the wedding of Josie's dreams. Josie's breath caught at the thought.

Carolynn shut the door behind her. "Are you ready, Josie? The organist is waiting for her cue."

"She's ready." Kat played with Josie's small bouquet before placing it back in the vase. "She can't stop fidgeting."

"I've waited a long time for this moment." Friendship followed by a courtship. Josie had known before Art asked that he was the kind of man she wanted to marry. His firm character and commitment to God made him the one she could imagine spending the rest of her life with.

"Only a few more minutes." Carolynn laughed and motioned her hand in a circle. "Twirl, Josie. Let me absorb your beauty."

Josie lowered her chin demurely as she obeyed.

"Hmm. Art is a lucky man." Carolynn squeezed Josie and squealed. "Can you believe it? You're getting married!"

A lopsided smile stretched Kat's face. "About time. Now I get my own room."

"When you put it that way, I'm surprised you didn't push me out sooner." Josie tried to make her expression match her stern words, but couldn't. Tickles of joy pulsed through her.

It was here.

Her wedding.

The tickle turned to full-fledged, gut-splitting happiness.

She'd dreamed someday she would find a man like Art Wilson. But with the war consuming Europe, matters like love seemed trivial. She'd tried to be content helping Mama take care of the house and Daddy, Kat, and her older brother, Mark. Then she'd met Art at church. . . .

Kat snorted. "Ugh. You're thinking about him again. Let's get this wedding over. You are way too focused on him."

Oh, to be thirteen again with unlimited wisdom.

Carolynn's sweet laugh filled the room as she ruffled Kat's curls. "Someday you'll understand. You won't be thirteen forever."

The look on Kat's face telegraphed she sincerely doubted she'd ever be as crazy about someone as Josie was for Art.

Carolynn tugged a corner of Josie's veil. "There. You look perfect. Well, I'd better get back out there and let them know you're ready."

Josie hugged Carolynn then brushed the top of the comb holding the veil back in place. Artificial pearls dotted the top, hiding the stems of the baby's breath lining the veil.

The first notes of "Amazing Grace" filtered through the door. Mama tucked her handkerchief in her sleeve and smiled. "I'd best head in. Let them usher me to my place." She kissed Josie on the cheek and hugged her lightly, the sweet scent of violets filling the air around her. "Love you, Josephine."

Josie sucked in a deep breath and eased it out as Mama slipped from the room. She loved Art to the very core of her being. She'd been amazed to realize one could know something so important in a matter of days. He treated her like a treasured gift, someone he couldn't believe he'd wooed.

"Where's Daddy?"

"I'm here, darling." Louis Miller strode into the room, looking dapper, if professorial, in his best suit. He buttoned the final button on his double-breasted jacket that eased across his ample belly. "You look beautiful, Josephine. Art is lucky to have won you."

Peace filtered into her heart. Daddy would only give his blessing to her marriage to a man he believed would care deeply for her. "Thank you." She took a deep breath. "I can't believe I'm getting married."

"My happiest days were the day I married your mama and the days each of you kids was born. Serve and love him with all you have." Daddy's Adam's apple bobbed as he swallowed. "My prayer is that you will have a love that transforms your life like my love for your mama has me."

The music changed to the sweet strains of "It Is Well with My Soul." It might not be everybody's idea of wedding music, but every time she heard the tune, the words spoke to her soul. She longed to race through the door and up the aisle of the community church. Art and the minister would stand at the front, waiting for her.

Daddy swallowed; then he offered his arm. "It's time, Jo."

"I'm ready." She slipped her hand through his arm and closed her eyes. When she opened them, Kat slipped past her. Kat's green dress highlighted her pale complexion and the reddish highlights in her hair. Kat had taken after Mama's Irish heritage, while Josie looked more like her daddy's mother. Carolynn squeezed her hand before she moved out the door and to the sanctuary. How could she say good-bye to Carolynn? The friend who had cried and dreamed with her?

Daddy tucked her closer to his side. Together, they stepped toward the sanctuary and her future.

※

The music swelled from the organ, and the pastor motioned for the congregation to stand. Art Wilson marveled at the many people who filled the rows to celebrate his marriage to Josephine Miller. Many were strangers, friends of her family. His family filled one row, and a few of his college friends took another. He tugged at the sleeves of his dark suit coat. Where was his beautiful bride? The ceremony should have started by now, but every minute seemed to stretch.

He'd waited a lifetime for this moment. He bounced on his toes as he tried to see over the crowd and find her.

Just one glance of her dark waves. That's all he wanted. One glimpse that solidified the fact she would soon wear his name.

Josie was marrying him. Arthur Wilson. Man with faith and hope for the future, with some money in his bank account. This new job would only improve their circumstances since it held the opportunity to provide well for her. And any kids God blessed them with. He hadn't thought his grin could get any bigger, but the idea of little Josies running around someday made his heart about explode. Yes, he was a man blessed beyond words that a woman like her could love a man like him.

There she was. He stilled, drinking in every detail. She was a vision in white lace. Her dark hair was pulled off her slender neck, and a sweet smile graced her lips, then moved to her eyes when she saw him. The light of promise filled her eyes. No woman had ever looked lovelier. Mr. Miller looked like he had a slim grip on his emotions. How hard would it be to give away a daughter? He would know someday if God gave them children. Their home would be different from the quiet one he'd grown up in. Their children would know their father's love as he bounced them on his knee. Or he'd throw one into the air just to hear the child echo Josie's delicate laugh.

"Who gives this woman to this man?" Pastor Richmond's deep voice reverberated through the sanctuary.

"I do." Mr. Miller handed Josie to him. "Take good care of her, son."

Art captured her soft hand in his. "I will, sir." He gazed into Josie's eyes. Her lips trembled at the edges as she gazed at him. "I love you, Josie."

"I love you more."

A certainty settled on him. He promised to do everything in his power to make this woman understand how much he treasured and loved her.

Chapter 1

January 1940

The smell of ground beef frying in the skillet filled the kitchen. Josie grabbed a bottle of milk from the icebox and turned to the table.

"Mix the biscuits. Brown the meat." The steps to preparing the meal tripped off her tongue. Tonight they would celebrate their two-month anniversary. She wanted to make the evening special but didn't trust herself to broil steak. If only she'd paid a bit more attention when Mama had tried to teach her the finer details of cooking. Nope, she'd had to focus on housekeeping. The apartment sparkled while she slowly tried one recipe after another with varying degrees of success. She was blessed that Art played the good sport regardless of what she plopped on the table.

Warmth flooded her at the thought of Art's smile as he walked through the front door and pulled her into his embrace. She counted down to the moment he appeared. Each day, it seemed he raced home as if another moment's separation would be too much.

Two months. In her most extravagant imaginations, she hadn't pictured how wonderful marriage truly was.

She glanced around the apartment. It was small, but close enough to Art's job that he walked to the factory on all but the coldest days. While he worked, she added touches to the rooms, turning the space into a home. Grandma's davenport, decorated with a few pillows and Aunt Mary's doilies, sat against one wall in the living room. A tiny round table—nothing like Mama's large one—filled the other corner. Josie had slipped a flowered cloth over it. The matching fabric for curtains sat on the lone chair in the bedroom. Soon, she'd buckle down and hem them. She'd made great strides in the room, but there was more she could do to make it feel like home. She turned on the radio that sat on the floor next to the couch. She'd fill the air with Glenn Miller tunes matching her celebratory mood.

As the swinging music filled the air, Josie spun around the room. She must make quite a picture. Joy bubbled inside and spilled over as she laughed.

"It's only a two-month anniversary."

If she felt this excited now, she couldn't imagine what life would be like when they hit six months. A year. Fifteen years.

※

Art glanced at his pocket watch. It felt weighty and substantial in his hand, like the expectations of the men in his family, particularly his grandfather. He'd never

13

forget the words Grandfather spoke as he had handed the gold watch to Art at his college graduation. *"You may have graduated, son, but the men in this family have each earned their way in this world, and I expect no less of you. With your education, you should do more than the others."*

Do more.

No handouts.

Grandfather couldn't have been clearer. He was a self-made man and expected nothing less from Art. Forget the millions sitting in Grandfather's bank account.

A little money would have been nice as a wedding present. Help him and Josie get started. But that wasn't Grandfather's way. Art could respect that.

Art's thoughts turned back to his desk. He'd finished about as much as he could if he still hoped to get home at a decent time. His accounting job with the E. K. Fine Piano Company was a good position. It built on the eclectic experience he'd gained at a small firm in Dayton. The difference? Now he used his education and training every day. That's what he'd wanted when he took the position.

He looked at the stack of papers and corporate books on his desk. A weight settled in his gut. He could work for two months straight and never complete all the work. The firm had been without a bookkeeper too long. It would take forever to straighten out the mess. Yet Art also knew he should be grateful. Thanks to the weak economy, good jobs were still hard to find.

He stared at the piles of paper, but his thoughts were with his bride. *Josie.* Warmth filled him at the thought of her. Marriage to her exceeded his hopes. Life was richer. Not for one minute did he miss going home to a small, empty bachelor's pad each evening. He glanced at the watch again, deciding to stay a few minutes more. After all, working hard at his job *was* taking care of his bride.

"Wilson, you still here?" Edward Kendall Fine III stopped at Art's desk. The rotund man liked to emphasize the fact he was the third. Art failed to see the significance since he'd never known E. K. Fine the first or second. "Burning the midnight oil, I see. I like that in a man. Willing to work until the job's done."

Art wavered between smiling or groaning. In the few weeks he'd been at E. K. Fine Piano Company, it had become crystal clear that E. K. Fine would squeeze everything from the men in his employ. Every last drop of work.

"Making sure I understand the complexities of the company, sir."

Mr. Fine showed his crooked teeth in what some would call a smile. "See to it you do, Wilson. This is a big company. Lots of issues to stay on top of. Keep those books clean."

Art nodded, then opened his mouth.

"Well, I'm off to see the missus. Good night."

Art closed his mouth. Surely if Mr. Fine was headed home, he could, too. The time on his watch stamped in his mind. Six o'clock. He'd have to hurry his walk or be more than an hour late. Josie would understand, wouldn't she?

14

❄

The dish sat on the stove, ready to pop into the oven the moment Art walked in the door. Josie curled up on the davenport and tried to follow the flow of words as they swam across the pages of the book. Usually, Willa Cather's characters spoke to her, but tonight, every fiber seemed tuned to the door as she listened for the sound of Art's footsteps in the hallway. Her stomach grumbled its protest that it was past dinner time.

She heard the creak of one of the hall floorboards. Josie tossed the book onto the couch and stood. Brushing the wrinkles from her skirt, she hurried to the door. He was finally home! Josie pulled the apartment door open and leaned against the doorjamb. "Welcome home."

Art's hair stood up in all directions, as if he'd carelessly run his fingers through it. A smile tugged the corners of her mouth at the thought. She'd seen him make that gesture so many times.

Fatigue weighed down the corners of his eyes. "Thanks." He brushed a kiss on her cheek and pulled her into the apartment with him. "Another day in the office finished."

"Night, too." She whispered the words under her breath. Maybe he wouldn't notice.

Art stopped and looked at her. "What's that mean?"

"Nothing." Josie slid her arms around his waist. "I wish my groom were home more. It's lonely here without you."

"I miss you, too." He snuggled her closer. She giggled and pulled away. "Let me get supper in the oven."

Art shrugged out of his coat, plopping it over the back of a chair. "Smells good."

Josie crossed her fingers. "Hope it tastes good." She said as she popped the pan in the oven. Tugging him to the couch, she sank onto its cushion. "Tell me about your day."

He leaned against the back, head tipped toward the ceiling. His words about trying to catch the company's books up-to-date flowed over her. She didn't really understand much of what he did, but that didn't matter. What did matter was that he loved what he did. And he loved her. She might be a little lonely when he was gone, but she'd do something about that eventually. Right now, she enjoyed the time to develop their relationship as it explored this new level.

"Did you get out today?"

"Just to the library and the grocer."

Art laughed. "I don't know if that qualifies since the grocer is downstairs."

"The library does. I had to walk almost a mile round-trip." She shuddered in an exaggerated shiver. "It's too cold to do even that right now."

His fingers caressed her cheek. "Are you happy, Mrs. Wilson?"

"You'll have to come up with a harder question than that."

"You haven't answered me."

Josie smiled. "I can't imagine being happier."

※

The conversation lingered in Art's mind long after dinner had been eaten and the dishes cleared. Josie seemed so content in their relationship, but he wondered about her loneliness. He didn't expect Josie to spend her days in the apartment. Yet that's what she'd done since they'd moved. He'd asked her to marry him, then transported her out of the familiar to a new world. She'd always seemed the kind who loved adventure, but maybe the reality of living in a new and different place didn't match the glamour of the idea. Her words indicated she didn't think much about it, but still, he wondered.

After work the following day, he stopped at a bookshop. She loved to read. Maybe a book would be a nice surprise gift. He ambled among the rows, trying not to sneeze through the dust that filled the air and tickled his nose. Which of the many volumes would appeal to her? She read so much, he couldn't keep up with her list. It had taken her mere days to discover the library branch near their home, a find that saved them immense amounts of money. Today, though, he wanted to surprise her with a book that would be meaningful to her. Among the rows of books, he spotted a nice fat tome. *Gone with the Wind*. Maybe that would work. At least it had lots of pages. Certainly, it would fill a few of her hours.

He climbed the stairs to the apartment with a spring in his step. Running to the door, he threw it open. "Darlin', I'm home."

Silence answered. He tossed his briefcase on the floor and roamed the rooms—taking all of thirty seconds—but Josie wasn't there.

He pulled off his suit coat and then loosened his tie. Guess he'd settle in and wait. He looked at the briefcase. Maybe the thick book would work for him, too. He settled on the couch and cracked it open.

The scrape of the key in the lock pierced his mind. He rubbed his eyes and then looked at the thing weighing down his chest.

"Well, fiddle-dee-dee."

Josie swept into the room, cold-kissed roses filling her cheeks. "What was that?"

"Um, nothing." Art ran his fingers through his hair and sat up. "Where have you been?" He winced at the note of censure in his voice. "I was surprised you weren't here when I got home."

"I decided to go out. Explore the neighborhood despite the bite in the air. Eclectic architecture fills the neighborhoods around here. Brick. Wood." She pulled a beret from her head and tossed it on the table. A quirky grin—one of her best features—creased her face. "The birds beckoned me to join them." She flopped next to him on the couch.

"In the snow?" He tried to hide his skepticism, but her raised eyebrows signaled he'd failed. He put his hands up, palms out. "Okay. You've transformed into a snow princess who loves the cold. Snow White with the animals talking to you."

"As long as you think I'm the most beautiful in the land." Her face scrunched in a pout. Art couldn't resist her and didn't need to, so he reached for her and pulled her into an easy hug.

"There's no question." He tucked a loose strand of hair behind her ear. "There's no one else for me. No one more beautiful. No one more silly." She poked him in the side. "And no one else I could love."

Josie leaned her head against his shoulder and sighed.

He pulled back. "What?"

"Nothing."

"No, my princess can't sigh like that without explaining. A prince needs the opportunity to fix his beloved's woes."

Josie giggled and shrugged. "I don't know how to explain." Oh, it hadn't taken Art long to learn those words were often the forerunner to something important. "I love the life we're building together. But some days, it feels like I'm stuck. There's got to be more to this area. If only one of the churches we've visited felt like home."

"We'll find one." Out of all the churches in Cincinnati, one had to feel like home. Someday. Until then. . . "What about ladies at the library?"

Josie crinkled her nose. "They're either old or have lots of kids. I don't exactly fit."

"Why not try?"

"Don't you miss anybody from home?"

"You're my home."

She sat up, and a winsome smile flitted across her face. "I struggle to be as content. I miss my friends. I even miss Mark and Kat. Before we moved, if you'd told me I'd miss Kat, I would have laughed. But I'd welcome her never-ending teasing right now." She wiped a tear away, and Art felt something inside tighten. "I love you, Art." He was so glad to hear those words. "I guess I didn't understand leaving would be so hard."

Art sank deeper into the couch. Someday, he'd give Josie the nice furniture she deserved. No more handouts from family. Until then, he wanted to make her happy.

"What will help you meet people? Make Cincinnati feel like home?"

"I don't know. Maybe I'll live in the library every day. Escape in a book."

Art grinned. He'd known *Gone with the Wind* was the ticket. "I got this for you today." He handed the heavy book to her. Her eyes lit up as she took it from him.

"Ah. Fiddle-dee-dee, indeed." She fanned the pages. "How much have you read?"

"Only enough to know the Tarleton twins don't stand a chance with Scarlett."

"Hmm."

"But I do with you."

She snuggled closer. "Then I think it's time to kiss me, mister."

Art couldn't think of anything he'd rather do.

Chapter 2

Valentine's Day. Art would make it home on time. Something told him it would be important to Josie. Days like this he wished he'd grown up with sisters. Maybe they would have taught him the important lessons on what gals expected. Maybe then he'd better understand Josie. She was an absolute puzzle to him. One he determined he'd solve.

Tonight he'd take her to dinner. Celebrate how much he loved her and how grateful he was she'd said yes. He started to straighten the ledgers and papers overflowing on his desk until they began to resemble piles.

"Ahem." Art turned at the sound of a cleared throat.

"Yes, sir?" He stilled as he looked up at the storklike man standing in front of his desk. He'd heard rumors that E. K. Fine II took bites out of employees with his words as he pecked away at them. The look on the man's face puzzled Art. Why would the second Mr. Fine stand in front of his desk?

"Have you followed the news in England, young man?" Mr. Fine picked up the nameplate from Art's desk. "Mr. Wilson?"

"It's hard not to."

"Yes, yes."

Art squirmed in the growing silence as Fine looked over his glasses at him. "Can I help you with something, sir?"

"We have a small plant in England, you know. I'm concerned about our workers there. Their families."

Art couldn't imagine living with the threat of Germans bombing his home in the middle of the night. Here, the renewed aerial attacks punctuated the head-lines. There, the shock of air-raid sirens wrenched you from sleep.

"Terrible times."

"I've never been more glad to live here."

Mr. Fine nodded. "Any family in England?"

"Distant cousins, I think." Art shrugged. "My mother keeps up on those family relationships."

"Well. I'll leave you to your duties." The man ambled out of the accounting department. Art watched him leave and wondered what the conversation had really been about.

He cleared the surface of his desk and smiled. The workday was over. Art punched out and walked the mile home. The best feature of their apartment was its closeness to work. Most weeks, his vehicle sat off the alley. Josie could use it if she needed, though he didn't think she ever had.

18

After sitting behind a desk all day, he enjoyed the feel of sunshine on his face, even as he hunkered inside his coat against the cold. He squinted at the sinking sun and tried to imagine what it would be like to live with the fear that each time he glanced up he might see an enemy plane headed his way. And all he had to worry about was doing his job well and loving Josie. His Josie. His steps quickened at the thought of seeing her again. Their good-bye kiss this morning seemed days ago instead of mere hours.

✳

Josie pushed a hand into her stomach. It hadn't stopped roiling all day. Well, there had been moments she'd felt normal. Then she'd smell something, and her stomach betrayed her again. She couldn't think of anything she'd eaten that would make her feel this way. She should get supper started but grimaced at the thought and covered her mouth to still the nausea.

Maybe a salad would work. No scents involved there. She opened the icebox door and stared inside. Nothing appealed to her.

The apartment door groaned as it swung open.

"I'm home." Art's boisterous voice filled the small rooms.

Josie took a deep breath and steeled herself before turning around. Maybe if she was stern enough with it, her stomach would cooperate. "Hi, honey. Good day?"

"A fine one. But the best part is we're going out for dinner. The cook gets the night off as we celebrate Valentine's Day with a steak, maybe see a movie, then a kiss." He waggled his eyebrows and smiled, the one that normally sent a flood of warmth through her. Instead, Josie clutched her stomach and tried not to groan at the thought of food. His face fell. "Don't want to go out on the town? I thought you'd enjoy that. We can even see that cartoon *Pinocchio* if you want."

The pout in his voice made her smile. "I would love it."

The smile reappeared on his face.

Josie sighed. "But I haven't felt very well all day."

"Do we need to get you to the doctor?"

Josie laughed. "That's not necessary. Just a touchy stomach. I bet I'm better by tomorrow. Do you mind if we stay in tonight? I'll heat some soup, and then we can spend a quiet evening together."

"As long as you don't pull out one of your puzzles."

"All right. I'll let you read *Gone with the Wind* to me, instead."

"Fiddle-dee-dee." He pushed his hand against his heart and grinned. "Anything to make my lady feel better." He pulled her toward him. "Just don't tell anybody about this."

"And who would I tell?" She snuggled next to him, close enough to hear the steady beat of his heart. "It's our secret." Josie wasn't sure it would make her feel better, but it might distract her. If nothing else, watching all-male Art reading a romance would take her mind off her crazy stomach. And maybe tomorrow they could go out.

19

Art leaned down until his forehead touched hers. He gazed into her eyes as if searching for her very heart. Didn't he know he'd claimed it the moment he swept into the Dayton theater with his grandma on his arm? It had been Christmastime, a showing of the *Nutcracker*. Josie hadn't taken her eyes off him as she watched him guide his grandma through the crowd. He'd been so chivalrous toward the woman. It didn't hurt that his hair was the color of a dark chocolate bar and curled ever so slightly around his ears. Josie must have caught his eye, too, since he'd made his way to her side. That had been the first of their many interactions. Through them all, she'd learned while he was easy to look at, his heart was even better.

An easy smile reached his eyes.

She tried to catch her breath at his intensity. "Find what you're looking for?"

"Um-hm." He leaned in and captured her lips with his.

❀

The next morning, Josie struggled to get out of bed. The warmth of the comforter seemed to push her down. The pillow snuggled against her cheek, making it hard to lift her head. She'd wanted to see Art off to his job with a smile and a kiss, but couldn't find the energy. Her stomach roiled at the thought of doing anything, and fatigue overwhelmed her. Ugh. She had to do something. Sitting in bed wasn't a valid option. Her mother's voice echoed in her mind, telling her idle hands are the devil's tools. Josie had never liked the phrase, but since the move, she hadn't worked hard to stay busy.

Maybe a job would help. Give her a schedule beyond getting dinner on the table for Art. An important task, but not enough to keep her mind engaged all day. Only a few days a week, though. She curled up in the bed and tugged Grandma's quilt to her chin. Her fingers played with the edge of the soft fabric. Some of her earliest memories involved sitting on the floor, playing while Grandma and her friends stitched quilt after quilt. Josie had hoped one day she would receive one. Now she had the one that had graced Grandma and Grandpa's bed for years. The wedding ring pattern testified to the hours of love Grandma had poured into its making. Each stitch was filled with the hope and commitment of the decades Grandma and Grandpa loved. Now, Josie and Art could add to that legacy.

Such a rich heritage.

Josie's hand pressed into her stomach. She rubbed it in small circles, trying to ease the waves of nausea.

Her mind wandered through the reasons she could feel so poorly. It didn't seem like the flu. She hadn't had any fevers—just the uncomfortable sensation. A shivery feeling collided with the butterflies. A pulse of hope and fear. It couldn't be what she thought, could it?

Well, only one way to know for sure. Taking a deep breath, she called the doctor and made an appointment. She considered walking the couple miles to the office, then opted for the trolley. After she climbed on, she decided the Packard would have been a better choice. The swaying and clacking of the trolley kept her stomach bobbing and weaving.

After a few stops, the trolley reached the intersection nearest the office. Josie hopped down and entered the office. Once checked in, she flipped through a stack of *Saturday Evening Post*s as she waited. Nothing distracted her from the only possibility that made sense.

What would she do if the doctor told her she could expect a baby to join her family? She took a deep breath and willed her heart rate to slow. She and Art wanted children. It would be wonderful news to hear that their family would start now. She'd push past the fear of what had happened to Aunt Gertie. If she'd been at a hospital, she and the baby would have survived, and that was years ago. Now things were different. And Cincinnati hospitals were much better equipped if an emergency arose.

"Mrs. Wilson?" The nurse stood at the door. Josie gathered her purse and coat. "This way please."

Josie followed her, unsure why she felt so certain of the answer. Her mother would think she was crazy to come see the doctor over something as simple and routine as a baby. But she needed to know. Was she crazy? Or was her body trying to tell her something?

The doctor bustled into the area. "How can I help you?"

"I think I'm pregnant."

"Congratulations. That's great news." He studied her. "Isn't it?"

"Yes." She took a steadying breath and matched his smile. "How can I know for sure?"

After the examination, Josie pulled her clothes on and collected her thoughts. Waves of excitement pushed aside her earlier fears. It wouldn't be her and Art alone for long.

She returned home, trying to figure out how to share the news with Art. He'd been so eager to start a family, talking constantly about having children from the day he'd asked her to marry him. This moment should be one he remembered, but nothing came to her. It felt like her mind had turned into a blank canvas. She stood at the sink, trying to prepare something for dinner. The water dripped in the dishpan, but Josie didn't notice until drops landed on her foot. She turned off the faucet, grabbed a dish towel, and wiped up the puddle. The front door banged against the wall, and Josie jumped, cracking her head against the sink. "Ouch."

"Is the loveliest bride in the world home?" Art's voice teased as he strode into the kitchen.

Josie rubbed her head and tried to clear the fog.

Art leaned in for a kiss. He stopped before he claimed her lips. "How was your day?"

"Wonderful." A purr slipped into her voice, and she watched his face contort in hopeful confusion. Hmm, maybe she needed to work on how she welcomed him. "But probably not as exciting as yours." If only he knew. . .

"Another day marshalling pages of numbers into order. Love the routine of getting them to line up and flow across the pages." He rubbed his hands together and then stepped back to lean against the table. He sniffed the air. "Want to go out to celebrate tonight since nothing's started?"

A burning sensation squeezed her throat. No. She swallowed and smiled. Tonight they would celebrate the beginning of their dreams. And somehow she'd manage to keep the food down. In time, this too would pass, replaced by the other sensations of a baby. Inside her.

His thumb brushed her cheek. She leaned into his hand. "I'd love to celebrate. Give me a few minutes, okay?"

He nodded and pulled his hand away. She felt a chill and hurried to the bedroom. Josie eased to the vanity and brushed her hair, then touched up her makeup. A fresh light shone from her eyes. She couldn't wait to hear Art's reaction. Something in his only-child upbringing made him hungry for the patter of little feet. She couldn't imagine a better gift to give him. After they pulled on coats, he escorted her down the stairs and to the Packard. "Where would my lovely lady like to eat?"

Josie shook her head. "Oh no. You get to surprise me."

She leaned back and closed her eyes as the Packard rolled over the streets. Art stroked her hand with his thumb. She almost purred all over again. The car slowed, and she opened her eyes. Warm lights spilled from a storefront, surrounded by others shrouded in darkness. The light played off the snow drifts along the sidewalk. Art helped her from the car and led her to the door. A woman met them as they entered.

"Right this way."

Josie settled into a chair that Art pushed in for her. The small dining room was filled with bistro tables and patrons. A spicy aroma wafted from the kitchen. A waitress walked by with several plates of food, and Josie's stomach flipped as the scent got stronger. She swallowed and pressed a hand against her stomach, urging it to cooperate.

Art looked at her, a question in his gaze. "Are you okay?"

Josie nodded but kept her lips sealed, afraid to speak.

"Maybe you need to see a doctor?"

"I did." Heat eased up her cheeks at the thought.

"What?"

"I saw a doctor this afternoon." Josie took a breath. How to make this moment everything he wanted?

Art worried his lower lip between his teeth. "You'd better tell me, Josie. Nothing can be as bad as all this."

"No, this is wonderful news. Art, you know how you always talk about wanting to be a dad?" A glimpse of hope flashed on his face. Josie didn't want to hide her smile any longer. "I'm pregnant." Art's mouth dropped, and a big grin cracked his face.

"Really?"

Josie nodded as tears slipped down her cheeks. Her dream of becoming a mother, having children to dote on, was coming true.

He reached toward her as if to pull her into his arms but couldn't reach her around the table. "That's wonderful news, Josie."

Josie swiped at her cheeks. "I know. I thought we could have some time to be us, but God had different plans. I'll be more excited when I don't feel sick." He shared her excitement, and Josie loved Art all over again. This baby came straight from God's hand. The thought stilled her racing heart. God had decided this was the time for her to be a mommy. Excitement escalated inside her. "I've always loved babies."

Art scooted his chair around the table and pulled her into his arms, resting his chin on her head. "Wow. It'll be great. And you'll feel better soon, right?"

"Yes, Dr. Nathan said likely in a few weeks." That was definitely good news. She couldn't wait for her stomach to settle. The sooner the better. Yesterday would have been great. A smile spread on her face. Soon she'd walk the baby in a carriage. And the cradle could fit in the corner of the bedroom.

"We'll be great parents to the little guy."

If the giddy look on Art's face served as any indication, then she had nothing to fear. The bubble of excitement expanded. They were really going to be parents. She couldn't stop her grin. "What's that about a little boy? It might be a girl."

Art leaned back and looked into her eyes. "Either will be fine, as long as the little girl looks like her mommy."

"I'm going to be a mommy." Her voice shook on the words.

"You'll be wonderful." A feather-soft kiss touched her brow.

Chapter 3

The wind carried the whisper of spring as Josie walked to the library a month later. That morning, she'd woken up and not felt the need to rush to the bathroom. She reveled in the lack of nausea. What a miracle to watch the world wake up with new life around her as a child grew inside her.

Her steps bounced as she walked into the small library. The air was cool and musty. She pulled her coat close and wrinkled her nose against the dust. Why did that combination always make her thoughts turn to learning? Exploring the great books. Traveling to new destinations. Seeing life through fresh eyes. She surveyed the stacks, wondering where to start.

"Good morning, Josephine." Miss Adelaide sat behind the checkout counter, back ramrod straight, face set in proper lines. "How are you this morning?"

"Wonderful."

Miss Adelaide frowned at the loud sound. "Shh, dear." Her eyes scanned the tiny lobby area. "We aren't the only ones here."

"Sorry, Miss Adelaide." Josie tried to rein in her enthusiasm to the appropriate subdued level. "It's a beautiful day outside. Hints of spring fill the air."

"Delightful. Now what can I help you with today?" Miss Adelaide pushed out of the chair and took a step toward the fiction section. "Interested in another Jane Austen novel?"

"No." Heat crept into her cheeks. "I'd like one on baby development."

"Josephine Wilson. Are you in the family way?"

"Yes, ma'am." Josie couldn't keep the smile from exploding on her face—didn't want to. Butterflies of excitement tickled her inside, welcome relief from the unsettling sensations.

"That is good news. Good news indeed." Miss Adelaide hurried as fast as her shuffle allowed toward the opposite side of the room from the one Josie usually perused. "Over against this wall, we have a small section of child development books. Personally, I'm not sure there's much wisdom in them. You'll find all you need in the Good Book."

"Yes, ma'am. I still wouldn't mind checking out a few books, though. There's so much I don't know."

Miss Adelaide ran her arthritic fingers along the spines of a row of books. "Didn't you tell me once that you've got siblings?" Josie nodded, though Miss Adelaide didn't wait for her response. "Then you know everything you need. Babies are simple. Love them, feed them, and keep them clean."

Josie wondered. Could it really be that simple? But Miss Adelaide grew up in a simpler time. Before life became modern. "How many children do you have?"

"Oh, I wasn't granted the blessing of having any. I helped my sisters with their broods. Auntie Adelaide to the rescue. Seventeen times."

"Oh my."

"There were a bunch of nieces and nephews, but I love them as if they were my own." She pulled out a book and handed it to Josie. "Well, here you go. If you need anything, you know where to find me. Congratulations again, dear."

"Thank you." Josie watched Miss Adelaide for a moment then turned to the book in her hand. She really wanted a book that could give her a window to what was happening inside her. Did anyone really know? Or was it a mystery reserved for God alone to know? After spending half an hour flipping through the few books the library's collection held, Josie decided the mystery must be God's.

Maybe she'd grab *Sense and Sensibility* after all.

※

Art couldn't wait to race home and grab Josie in a huge hug. The bigger the hug, the more likely the little Wilson could sense it, right? He would have never guessed he'd become such a sap about a baby. No question about it. He loved the idea of a little one to throw in the air. Josie told him it would be awhile before the baby was big enough. But the images of all the things the two of them would do together already played through his mind. Teaching the baby to fish, solving math problems, and showing the child the wonders of God's world. Maybe even leading the child into his own relationship with the Savior. Art resisted the moisture that tinged his eyes at the thought. A strong children's Sunday school program joined the priority list for their new church home.

Was there any greater trust than having a child?

He couldn't imagine one.

And to think three months ago the idea of adding children to their family had seemed like a distant mirage. Now the anticipation stayed with him throughout the day. It seemed the most natural thing for their growing family.

"Another good day, Art."

He looked up to see Stan Jacobs standing next to his desk. Stan filled the space like an ex-college lineman.

"Yep. Now to race home."

"You should join us for a drink before heading home. Time to join the guys. Hasn't the honeymoon worn off?" A slight leer tipped Stan's mouth.

"Not for me." Art couldn't imagine losing the excitement of racing home to see his Josie after a long day apart. He wanted to hear all about her day. And be back in her arms. Yep, that's where he belonged. Not at Rosie's Bar.

"So you say now. Wait till you have your first real fight. Right, boys?"

Art hadn't noticed the other guys from the office gather round. A couple shook their heads at Stan while they grabbed their briefcases. "We don't have that kind of marriage, Stan."

The man snickered, and Art balled his fists. Where did Stan get the idea he could tell Art about marriage? It wasn't like Art had asked for advice.

"Ignore Stan." Charlie Sloan socked Stan in the shoulder. "This big lug doesn't know the wonders of married life. My wife and I've been married twenty-three years. I'd still rather be with her after a long day at work than anything else. And you're right. Drink never solved any problems."

Stan shook his head and stepped away from Art's desk. "Have it your way. But don't be surprised when I say, 'Told ya so.' She'll weigh you down." He winked at Art, then headed toward the door. "Anyone else ready for Rosie's? Come on." Several of the guys joined him as he left.

Charlie shook his head. "That boy's gonna fall mighty hard one of these days. When he does, the earth's gonna shake."

Art wanted to ask what was going to make him fall: drinking or a woman? It didn't really matter, though. "Any advice for this guy?"

"On married life?"

"Yep."

"Make sure you keep your walk with God first." Art cringed at the reminder. They needed to settle on a church home. "Most of our challenges I created when I forgot to put God first. Amazing how quickly my perspective turned sour." Charlie put a hand on Art's shoulder. "Better get home to the missus now. It's been a long day away from her."

Art grabbed his briefcase, jacket, and hat from his desk. "Sounds good to me."

The week passed in a blur of routine. Life the way he liked it. Work hard while he was at the factory office. Then spend his evenings at home with Josie. Now that she felt good again, they'd walk the neighborhood after dinner when the weather cooperated. He couldn't wait to push the baby's carriage around the block. He could already see the neighbors oohing and aahing over the little boy. Josie kept teasing him that the baby could be a girl, but he knew.

Friday night, he hurried home, ready for a quiet weekend. The moment he stepped through the door, he sensed something wasn't right. Josie lay curled in a ball on the small couch. Her arms wrapped around her middle, a tight look on her face. She moaned, eyes squeezed shut. He dropped his briefcase by the door and rushed toward her.

"Josie, honey, what's wrong?" He studied her face, his concern building when he saw tears on her cheeks. He brushed one away, trying to read her face. Why wasn't she saying anything? Pressure built inside him. Something was wrong. Looking at her face, terribly wrong. "Josie?"

She opened her mouth then screwed it shut. Looking at him, a sob welled from somewhere deep inside her.

"Baby, it's okay. Whatever's wrong, we'll fix it." Somehow he would. He promised himself he would. No matter how much it cost. He'd fix it, since the sight of her like this tore him apart.

※

Josie tried to stop her tears, but they flowed. She'd never known fear like this.

The cramps had started around noon. She hadn't thought much about them, but they grew in intensity. Right before Art got home, she'd felt the rush of blood. She wanted to protect the baby but had no idea what to do. All she could do was curl into a ball and wait for the next contraction. The helplessness crushed her.

Shouldn't she do something? Mothers protected their children.

She groaned as another cramp squeezed her middle. This was not supposed to happen.

"Josie?" Art's voice quivered, far from his usual tone. "Talk to me. Please."

God, where are You?

She needed His peace. Right now. Before she pulled too far inside herself trying to protect something beyond her power and ability.

"Baby?"

Her heart broke at that word. Sobs replaced the stream of tears. Art grabbed her, pulled her tight to his chest. "I'm taking you to the hospital. Now."

She tucked her face against his chest, tried to pretend everything would be okay. But as she felt another gush of blood, she knew it would never be okay again.

❋

Dr. Nathan walked into her hospital room. Sorrow replaced his usual grin. "I'm sorry, Josie. There was nothing we could do."

Tears trickled down her cheeks again as a sense of disbelief vied with certainty. Her baby was gone.

"You should be able to have other children."

The words, intended to comfort, only intensified the pain. The last thing she wanted to think about was other children. Right now, all she wanted was her baby. The one she would never hold. A sob slipped out. She sealed her lips tight against the threat of more.

Art moved his chair closer to the bed, grabbed her hand, and held tight. "I called your mom and dad. She'll see about coming but didn't sound optimistic. Something about your grandma."

Josie nodded. She didn't really expect her parents to come. What could they do? The pregnancy probably hadn't seemed real to them, after all. It had only solidified for her with the doctor visit and recent baby flutters. Art stroked her hair, but she couldn't look at him.

"We'll keep you overnight, and then you can go home." Dr. Nathan looked at her chart, then turned to leave. "I'm sorry. There's nothing we can do in situations like this."

As soon as the doctor left, Art slipped onto the bed beside her. He held her, and she felt tears fall on her. "I'm so sorry, Josie." His words were broken. His dreams, too, had died. What had she done to cause this pain for him? He'd never been anything but excited about having a baby. She wanted to yell at the heavens. Didn't God know? She'd wanted this baby. Now that the baby was gone, desperation filled her. Didn't He understand?

Chapter 4

Even though Josie insisted she could walk, Art swept her up and carried her from the backseat of the Packard into the apartment. After he ignored her protests, she'd gone still, almost listless. They'd lost a child, but now he felt like he was losing her, too. She'd retreated so far inside herself he wasn't sure how to find her.

How could it hurt so much to lose one they'd never met? And with Josie lost in a place she'd created, he didn't have anyone to share the pain with. What should he do? This was virgin territory for him. So he prayed. Surely God knew exactly what they each needed to move forward. There would be other children. Art had no doubt of that. But that didn't erase his pain.

No, if anything, the pain led him straight back to the main question. *Why?* God could have prevented the loss. But He hadn't.

"Here we are, Josie. Do you want to lie down in the bedroom?"

She didn't respond. She burrowed deeper into his chest. He eased onto the couch and settled her next to him. Dr. Nathan had said she'd be back to normal in a few days. Maybe physically, but Art wondered about the rest of her.

In this unchartered water, he desperately wished someone could hand him a map.

※

Josie tried to rouse herself. Art needed her to pull out of the pain. Could she share the depth of where her thoughts took her? Had they lost the baby because of something she'd done? Had she not been excited enough? Not appreciated the growing gift inside her?

Her thoughts were at war. Her head told her it was nonsense. But her heart felt bruised. Josie needed a reason, but there was none.

Dr. Nathan had said it was too early to know whether the baby was a girl or a boy. She'd had dreams of a little girl dressed in pleated dresses, with hair a mess of blond curls. Art had sounded so certain it was a miniature him. It hadn't really mattered, though, because in a few months they'd know. Now she wondered. Was it a daughter or a son she'd never hold? She felt tears fight for release, but she refused to succumb. She'd done nothing but cry since the cramps had begun. She gritted her teeth until her jaw ached, but tears trickled down her cheeks anyway. Yet another sign of her body betraying her.

Art rubbed small circles on her shoulders and upper back. She relaxed against him. She had done nothing to deserve his gentleness, yet he continued to pour out his love on her. So like Jesus, serving others.

"Read me something." The words squeaked out. A plea for something to soothe her.

The kneading slowed. "What would you like?"

"Anything full of hope." How she needed that.

He reached for the Bible on the small side table. She turned her head to watch him flip through the gently worn pages. "How about a Psalm?" Without waiting for her acquiescence, he began reading.

" 'Be merciful unto me, O God: for man would swallow me up; he fighting daily oppresseth me.' " Art's rich baritone reached deep inside her, making her believe because he believed. " 'What time I am afraid, I will trust in thee. In God I will praise his word, in God I have put my trust; I will not fear what flesh can do unto me. . . .' " Oh, how she needed that: the certainty that she could trust in the God she'd praised all her life. Surely He was still there, still worthy of praise even when her heart was broken.

" 'Thou tellest my wanderings: put thou my tears into thy bottle: are they not in thy book? When I cry unto thee, then shall mine enemies turn back: this I know; for God is for me.' "

God *was* for her. What a comforting thought. She could trust that promise. She *would* trust that promise. Despite what her heart felt at that moment in time. God was for her.

" 'In God will I praise his word: in the Lord will I praise his word. In God have I put my trust: I will not be afraid what man can do unto me. Thy vows are upon me, O God: I will render praises unto thee. For thou hast delivered my soul from death: wilt not thou deliver my feet from falling, that I may walk before God in the light of the living?' "

Fresh tears wet her cheeks as she listened to the familiar words of Psalm 56. God held all of her tears. The thought was somehow comforting. He had never promised that her life would be pain free. As she wiped her cheeks, how she wished He had. No, He'd promised He would value each tear she cried. What an amazing—and absolutely humbling—thought. The God of the universe cared enough to watch and collect each tear.

A strange, unexpected peace washed over her. She might not see how, but she knew with a certainty they would make it to the other side of this valley. As Art's voice continued to roll over her in soothing waves, Josie relaxed against the couch and him.

❋

A soft kiss on her cheek pulled Josie from darkness. Confusion swirled through her mind. Where was she? Art must have moved her into their room at some point during the night.

"I've got to get to work, baby." Art leaned over her, dressed, with his tie jumbled around his neck and a hat slapped on his head. "Will you be okay?"

Josie nodded. What else could she do? He had to work. And she'd find a way out of the morass pulling her back to the blackness. Trails of peace that had teased her had evaporated during the night. Art's rough fingers stroked her cheek before he kissed her again.

"I'll hurry home. I love you." He waited a moment, then stood.

She licked her lips then she tried to find her voice. "Love you."

The door closed behind him, and she turned back into her pillow. She prayed sleep would come. She wasn't ready to face the day and her emptiness.

✳

"Hello," a soft voice trilled into the apartment.

Josie looked up from the book she held in her lap. She'd read no more than four pages in the hours since she had crawled out of bed, her thoughts lost in the land of what-ifs.

"I hope it's all right I came in." A familiar older woman stepped into the living room, a smile softening her wrinkled face and a basket hanging from her arm. "That fine young man of yours asked if I'd look in on you. I don't know if you remember my name—I'm Doris Duncan. My husband, Scott, owns the market, and we live below you on the second floor."

The woman had always been friendly, but in the several months they'd lived here, she hadn't ventured up the last flight of stairs to this apartment. Josie stiffened her defenses. She didn't want to spend time with a stranger. "That isn't necessary. I'm fine."

"I'm sure you are. But I brought a light lunch anyway. I love an excuse to get out of my place."

Josie bit back a bitter protest, but the deep growl of her stomach silenced her. Betrayer. The last thing she wanted to think about was food. Yet as Doris pulled items from the basket, a sweet honeyed aroma wafted toward her. Maybe she could eat something. She struggled off the couch and moved the few steps to the kitchen. "Here are some plates."

"Perfect. Here, settle down." Mrs. Duncan placed several small bowls on the round dining table. Finally, she unearthed a cloth-wrapped bundle that could only be sweet rolls, the source of the wonderful scent. "My mama's special recipe. They always comfort me whenever I need an extra reminder of love." Her easy movements stilled as she eyed Josie. "Here. Sit, child. You look weak around the edges."

Josie sank onto a chair and waited. Doris had something to say, otherwise why come? They weren't exactly friends, barely acquaintances, hardly even neighbors. Watching Doris made her want her mama. The hollow in her heart longed for Mama to hold her and tell her everything would be okay. But Mama hadn't made the drive, and the ache remained.

"Where would I find the silverware?"

"The drawer next to the sink."

Doris flitted back to the table and then settled on a chair. She reached across the small table for Josie's hand. "Let's pray first." Without waiting for Josie's response, she bowed her head. "Father, we come before You. You are a holy and awesome God. But You are also the God who experiences our pain with us. As my neighbor walks through this time, I ask that You surround her with Your love and shelter her in Your arms. Give her hope, Lord. And help her believe You have nothing but good plans for her."

Josie stiffened at the thought. If He really had only good plans for her, why this loss? It certainly didn't meet her definition of *good*.

Stillness settled in the room, and Doris did not release her hand. Peace relaxed Doris's face, and she tilted her head to the side as if hearing something special. Josie waited, fatigue settling over her like a heavy blanket. Oh, for some peace. Instead, she wanted to curl up in a ball and pretend the last forty-eight hours hadn't happened. Yep, hiding would solve all her problems. And who was she to think she had problems when bombs fell in Europe? People died, while others lost their homes and livelihoods. She sat in a small, comfortable apartment, with a husband who had a good job. All their needs were cared for, and they even had enough for wants. She should feel blessed. Instead, her arms felt empty. Empty of the child she hadn't understood how much she wanted until the baby was gone.

"You'll pull through this, Mrs. Wilson. You're made of strong stock. You may not ever forget, but you will not live in this place with this loss unless you choose." Doris's voice filled with strength and a knowing.

Josie studied her, then looked at her plate. Even the sweet roll tasted like sawdust. "You've experienced this. . .loss." The word stuck in her throat. It was so inadequate. "Haven't you?"

Doris's faded blue eyes glistened with what looked like tears. She looked out the window, fixing her gaze on nothing Josie could see. "It was thirty-two years ago. We'd been married a year. Both so thrilled to have a baby on the way. Well, the baby embraced Jesus before we held him." A single tear trailed down her weathered cheek. "I won't say I don't still feel the knowing I've missed a lifetime with that child. But eternity is so much longer." She looked at Josie, peace reflecting in the tears. "I will see him on the other side. And we'll have so much to catch up on."

"I don't want to wait." Josie tried to hide her broken heart in the angry words.

"I know. But as with many areas in life, we may never understand the why now. Until then, I trust God." Sadness tinged Doris's face. "It's been thirty-two years, and many of my questions remain unanswered. But I know I will see that child one day. And then this time will seem insignificant in light of eternity."

✳

Art hurried home from work. The day had dragged as his thoughts returned home with worries about Josie. Should he have made an excuse to stay home? He had to work, provide for her, especially at a time when life seemed unfair. Had he done the right thing asking Mrs. Duncan to check on her? He thought so but wondered how Josie had reacted. She could be feisty when backed into a corner. He prayed she hadn't felt that way.

When he reached home, Josie sat on the couch in her nightgown, her hair pulled out of her face, her features drawn. She held a handkerchief against her cheek as she watched him walk in.

"Hey." He sank onto the couch next to her.

She leaned away from him, but he edged closer. She couldn't force him away, not when she needed him. She might not understand it yet, but they would walk through this together. They'd both lost a child.

But they would not lose each other.

Chapter 5

Warmth brushed Josie's face. She cracked open her eyelids, struggling against the weight pushing her farther into the bed. In the days and weeks since the loss, the bed had called her name, urging her to spend daylight hours ensconced there. The fight seemed futile. Rays of April sunshine teased her through a crack in the curtains. If she opened the windows, the scent of hyacinths would filter into the room. Instead, she burrowed deeper under the comforter, practically pulling it over her head.

She reached out for Art, but he was gone. Long enough that his side of the bed felt cold. The aroma of coffee filtered through the door. The scent tweaked her heart. She should have gotten up before Art left for work, should have made his breakfast like she used to. She closed her eyes against the fresh well of pain. His life continued—the normal cycle of work and home.

Yet she felt trapped. Stripped of her dreams. Filled with what-ifs. What-might-have-beens. They echoed through her mind. She knew God had more for her than this, but relief from the thoughts only came as she slipped into sleep.

Minutes passed as she tried to force herself back to sleep.

"Enough." The muffled word didn't carry much force, but it propelled her out of bed. Slipping her robe on, she stumbled out of the bedroom, through the small living room, into the kitchen. Josie reached to tie the robe shut, then stopped as her hands brushed her stomach. Pain cramped through her, and she tried to catch her breath against it. What should be softly rounded remained all too flat. Her hands trembled as she dumped the coffee, then filled the pot with water and set it on the stove. She waited for waves of anger to overtake the pain as it had many mornings. Instead, the ache spread until she could almost feel the weight of the baby she would never hold. Lips compressed tight against the sob wanting to escape, she grabbed her Bible from the counter, where it had collected dust since the frantic dash to the hospital. She fluctuated between resignation and anger-laced questions directed at the heavens.

She stroked the worn cover and sank to the couch, wondering if she dared open it. Josie almost didn't want to know what God wanted to say to her. The words brought such comfort when Art read them, yet marched across the page like angry ants whenever she tried to read.

Maybe she didn't want to hear anything.

Especially from a God who hadn't held her when she needed Him most.

Her thoughts spiraled back to the pain.

He could have prevented the miscarriage.

33

She should feel the flutters of life deep inside her.

The feeling of betrayal wouldn't leave. He was God. He could have stopped it. He should have stopped it. And if He had—she pressed a hand against her stomach, desperate to stop the anger that filled her—things would be so different.

Her pulse raced. He'd disappeared when she'd needed Him. She'd lain on the couch and begged Him to be with her, but instead, she'd spun like a child who'd lost her father in the chaos of a state fair carnival. No matter how she searched for Him, she couldn't find Him.

Breathing in shallow gasps, she knew the fear couldn't be more real. She'd never felt so abandoned.

"Knock, knock." The words trilled through the opening door. Josie tried to scrub the pain from her face as Doris slipped into the room. The soft scent of cinnamon filled the room just as Doris had filled a void in her life. She'd become a constant through the fog of Josie's questions and life-stopping pain. Even when she pushed Josie to focus on Art and what she had, Doris had become a welcome part of Josie's life. Her persistence had edged their relationship from strangers to acquaintances to friends.

Josie had ached for a friend. And then Doris appeared. Art should probably thank Doris for keeping her from completely losing her way.

"How are you doing this morning?" Doris smiled at Josie as if it were the most natural thing in the world to find her in a nightgown and robe with unbrushed hair at ten o'clock in the morning. "I brought over some of my cinnamon bread. Fresh baked this morning. Did the smell tempt you from bed? Nothing smells better to me in the morning. Well, that lilac tree outside our windows might."

Just when Josie wondered if Doris would ever slow down and wait for a response, she stopped and smiled. "Listen to me chatter. I must like the sound of my own voice this morning." She nodded to the book Josie held. "Glad to see you looking at that. The answers you seek rest between its covers."

"You're right." It was easier to admit it than argue with the woman. It wasn't Doris's fault that God has gone conspicuously silent. "Maybe someday I'll find them." Josie slapped her hand over her mouth. "I didn't mean to say that."

Laugh lines crinkled the corners of Doris's eyes. "Of course you did. And that sentiment doesn't surprise God at all. Go ahead and tell Him exactly what you think and feel. I doubt you'll surprise Him."

The lady had a point. "All right." The teakettle whistled, and Josie stood. "Would you like some?"

"Yes. I'll get plates for our bread." As soon as they were settled back at the table, Doris grabbed Josie's hands and bowed her head. After a quick prayer, she looked at Josie and smiled. "As soon as we're done here, get dressed. You and I are going out."

Josie frowned. The last thing she wanted was to leave. Doris tipped her chin and stared her down.

"You're not getting out of this, young lady, so you might as well give in graciously. It's time to get your thoughts off yourself." A smile softened the words' edges. Doris winked at her, then took a bite. A few minutes later, the bread had disappeared along with the tea. "Scoot. I'll clean up the kitchen while you get ready."

It seemed she had no options. Josie stood and headed to her room. She slipped into a gingham dress and pulled her hair into a simple twist. Even those little actions made her feel better, more in control. She slapped a hat on her head and grabbed a purse. Squaring her shoulders, she rejoined Doris.

"Much better." Doris tugged her toward the door. "You'll be glad you came."

"Yes, ma'am." What else could she say? Doris had made up her mind.

They stepped onto the sidewalk, and the sun felt wonderful. It warmed Josie, and a bubble of something sweet filled her.

"Don't analyze that too closely, dear. You'll be surprised by hope on even your darkest days. God has a way of doing that." Doris kept the pace brisk as they walked several blocks. Josie hurried her steps to keep up, watching for signs of spring. The scent of the season of new life, a heady mix of hyacinth and tulips, filled her senses.

"Ah. Here we are." Doris led her into a church. Josie tried to find the name, but Doris pulled her in, much faster than she'd expected the older woman to move. The urgency in her steps pulled at Josie's curiosity. What had her so excited? "This is one of my favorite days of the week. There's something wonderful about God using me to serve others." As she talked, she led Josie along a hallway and then down some stairs. The aroma of something spicy tickled Josie's nose and collided with the smell of unwashed bodies as they walked into a large, open room. Josie struggled not to grimace at the mix of odors and what it did to her breakfast.

"What are we doing?"

"Caring for others. Today's the day my church serves the needy through the soup kitchen. Someday, we may open every day, but until then, we share the need with other churches." As she walked, Doris brushed the arm of a man seated at one of the tables. "How are you today, Bruce?"

"I'm still alive, ma'am."

"That's good, real good. Make sure you get your soup and bread."

"Yes, ma'am."

The next hours flew as Doris put Josie to work pouring vegetable soup into bowls too numerous to count. She tried to ignore the fact that many of the women coming through were large with child. She tried to smile even as a knife cut into her heart. Gritting her teeth, she kept the tears from falling. And as she focused on those in front of her with immediate needs, a dream slowly reawakened in her heart, one she'd shoved into a hidden corner. Images of the times she'd helped her mother in settings like this. When the whole family had pulled together the extras they had to share with the less fortunate. And there had been so many during the hard days of the '30s. While she'd thought those times had passed, today reopened her eyes to the need. Maybe she could play a part in meeting those needs, serving as Jesus instructed His followers. And maybe as she took her eyes off her hurt, she'd move beyond the grief.

※

Art hurried home. Today, the numbers had swum in front of his eyes, not sliding into ordered columns like usual. He tried to take in the song of the birds as they flew about, looking for nest materials. Instead, his thoughts fixated on Josie. It had been weeks since they lost the baby, yet it seemed as fresh to her as yesterday. If he came home to find her still in her nightgown again, he didn't know what he'd do.

Shouldn't he be enough?

He shook his head. He clearly wasn't enough for Josie. The thought pained him. They'd only been married a few months, and already she needed more. He cringed and tried to rein in his thoughts. He knew Jesus was the only One who should be her all in all, but it would have been nice to think he mattered, too.

Art's steps slowed as he approached the grocery store. Mr. Duncan pushed a broom back and forth across the sidewalk. "Afternoon."

"Sir."

"How's the missus?" Scott's eyes softened at the edges.

"She's. . . I don't know. I thought she'd be back to normal." The word didn't quite fit, but he didn't know how else to explain the situation. "Is she home?"

"Doris took her out on a service project, but they've been back for a while." Scott leaned on his broom handle. "Can I offer a piece of advice, advice learned the hard way?"

Art nodded.

"Be gentle with her. This pain you've both had. . .well, it's different for a woman. Seems more personal in ways we can't understand."

"Yes, sir."

"Keep loving her. It's the best thing you can do."

Art nodded and climbed the stairs to the apartment. He almost rapped on his door, just to make sure she knew he'd arrived. "Hey, honey."

Josie looked up from her book and smiled at him. He looked closer. Sadness still edged her eyes, but the smile seemed more real.

"Welcome home." She tilted her head for his kiss, then patted the couch next to her. "How was your day?"

"A little off actually." A frown creased her pretty nose. He hastened to explain. "The numbers didn't cooperate, that's all. I'm sure next week will be better." He took a breath, then ventured forward. "Yours?"

The smile almost reached her eyes. "Did you send Doris after me again?"

"No. Should I have?"

"Maybe. She came and practically demanded I get dressed and follow her."

Art sucked in a breath. That could be bad, but Josie looked alive again. "Where did she take you?"

"To church." A soft chuckle slipped out. Art would have hugged plump Doris if she'd been in the room. A giggle from Josie! "She took me to help serve at its soup kitchen. I think I'd like to go back."

"Next week? That sounds fine." Especially if serving brought Josie back to him.

"No. Well, then, too. But Sunday. For services. Doris said we could walk with her." Her eyes begged him to say yes. "We haven't visited this one. Maybe it will be the right one for us."

"All right. If you want to try hers, we can. Sounds like a good church if they're meeting community needs."

Josie took his hand. "Thank you. I think we could meet some nice people there. Maybe Cincinnati will feel more like home." A wistful look took her away from him.

Squeezing her hand, Art cleared his throat. "Let's take a stroll. Enjoy the day." If they didn't hurry, evening would fall. "Before dinner." He pulled Josie to her feet. Her lips turned up at the corners as he tugged her to the door. He stopped, his breath disappearing in the face of her beauty. She might think she was broken, but he knew better. A strength she didn't recognize filled her.

Josie caught his stare. Softness removed the lines around her eyes. "I love you, Art Wilson." Before he could respond, she stood on tiptoe and stole the rest of his breath with a kiss.

He deepened the kiss, and thoughts of abandoning the walk played in his mind.

Chapter 6

The alarm clock jangled on the bedside table, and Art jerked awake. He groped for the clock. After he silenced it, he lay toying with the idea of sleep. To make it to work on time, he needed to get up and move. Instead, he scooted closer to Josie. A sigh breathed from her lips as he pulled her close. She scooched nearer without opening her eyes.

For this moment, all was right in his world. He could pretend they hadn't lost the baby two months ago. And thank God, Josie was edging her way back to him, slowly returning to the same vibrant woman he'd married a few short months ago.

"Good morning, sweetheart."

A smile teased her face at his words. "Morning." She snuggled close a moment, then stretched. "Let me get you breakfast."

"Really?" He'd enjoy eating her eggs rather than his burned toast.

She slipped out of bed and pulled on her robe. "I'll have it ready when you get out of the shower."

As he hurried through his morning preparations, the scent of bacon reached him. His stomach growled, and he laughed. Time to eat. When he reached the table, Josie had placed two plates of food on it. She sat at the table, Bible open in front of her as she waited.

"Find anything good?"

"Yes."

"I love seeing you like this."

She looked up at him, and her nose crinkled. "Like what?"

"Ready to tackle the day. It's been awhile."

"I know, and I'm sorry."

"I understand."

"Not really, but you try, and I appreciate that. Now I want you to enjoy your eggs." She turned to the stove and poured a mug of coffee before handing it to him.

Art mulled over her words, looking for hidden meaning. Could he address them, or should he leave them be? One thing he'd learned from watching his parents' tense relationship was to tread carefully where a woman's emotions were concerned. Scott had reinforced that lesson with his challenge. Art definitely didn't understand the depths of what moved those emotions. But each conversation helped.

She settled onto the chair next to his. He leaned over and kissed her cheek, pleased to watch a smile play across her lips. If he let himself linger there, he'd never get to work.

He grabbed his Bible. "Let's start a new practice in the mornings."

Josie looked at him, brows crunched. "Okay."

"I'd like to read a Bible passage with you each morning. We could start with Psalms. Spend a few moments connecting with each other and God before our days begin."

"I'd like that." A soft smile creased Josie's face.

※

After devotions, he headed out the door. E. K. Fine Piano Company had operated for decades without his daily presence, but at times, he wondered how. The books were finally falling into an order that delighted him.

The numbers marched across the books in even rows. And the timing couldn't be better.

Mr. Fine had directed the managers to find ways to turn the company's enterprises into militarily useful ventures.

Art's whistle echoed a bird's song as he ambled the blocks to the factory. His mom could tell him exactly which type of bird he echoed, but he had no idea other than the tune pleased him. His steps quickened to match the timing.

After winding through Eden Park, he reached the factory. He glanced up at the large clock tower in the center of the brick building. Five till nine. He'd arrived with a couple minutes to spare, but not as early as he'd hoped. Next time, he'd have to avoid whistling with the birds and get that head start on the day.

Even so, he didn't restrain the smile that tipped his mouth as he waltzed through the main doors. A turn to the left and then the right, and Art worked his way back to the office he shared.

Charlie Sloan looked up from the *Cincinnati Enquirer* spread across his desk. "Morning, Art."

"Morning." Art looked closer. The paper was too easy to read. Charlie had it upside down on his desk. "Good read?"

"Hmm?" Charlie looked down and grinned. "Practicing my upside-down reading skills."

Art laughed. "That's an unusual skill."

"But handy when one's called into Fine's office. The murmurs about the war keep me wondering. How many pianos do you think folks will buy then?"

"Not sure." He could only make an educated guess after working for the company only a few months.

"Not as many as you think. And I wouldn't be surprised if we're put on some kind of ration. I'm sure the government will have a better use for the materials we consume."

The coffee he'd had that morning burned through Art's stomach, leaving a horrible aftertaste in his mouth. Had this been a bad move? Wouldn't the new guy be the first to go if the company retreated?

"Don't let it worry you." Charlie patted a document on his desk. "Fine has a plan."

Art sank into his chair and faced the mountain of work. He tried to focus, but his thoughts circled back to Charlie's comments. What did he know about the piano industry? War seemed far-off for the United States, but a few years ago, it had looked that way in Europe, too. What impact would entering the war have on an economy still recovering from the deep struggles of the last decade? God was in control. He knew that. But as the unspoken questions ricocheted off each other, he fought to cling to that truth.

His steps faltered as he left work that evening.

He'd made the right decision when he accepted the job and moved to Cincinnati. Despite everything happening, he believed that. God would watch over them, and even if the war somehow reached the United States, he'd have a job. The company would get creative, and he'd help with that if necessary.

His briefcase hung from his grip as he trudged up the steps to the apartment. They should have found one on a lower floor. Their third-floor apartment had too many steps to climb at the end of the day. He pushed his hat brim back and pushed onward. The aroma of something warm and chocolaty floated in the air. His stomach grumbled as he hoped it was brownies. If Josie had baked his favorite dessert, then she'd had a good day.

A door groaned as it opened. Sounded like his door. A tired grin tugged his face when Josie poked her head into the hallway. She wore a bright red dress that hugged her curves in all the right places. A fire to be close to her propelled him up the last steps.

"You are a sight for sore eyes."

A smug grin split her face at his words. "Glad to hear it. A man should want to come home to his wife at the end of the day." The words purred as they tickled his ear. Josie snuggled close, her head sliding perfectly under his chin, the puzzle piece that fit him.

He savored the moment. No matter what questions had pelted his mind, she was part of him.

A door squeaked below, and Josie pushed back. "Let's go inside. I don't want to give the Duncans a show."

"We are married, Josie."

She grimaced. "Still."

"All right." He let her pull him inside and shut the door. Tossing his briefcase to the side, he tucked her close again and inhaled the soft scent of something floral in her hair. Lavender? Maybe violets? Whatever it was, he'd have to keep her well stocked. "Did you bake me brownies?"

"Maybe. But first you have a telegram." She waved at an envelope sitting on the dining room table.

"Did you read it?"

"No, silly. It's addressed to you."

He chuckled. "We're married. You can read my mail."

"Remember that when you accuse me of invading your privacy." She crossed her arms and stared at the envelope.

"No worries about that." He picked up the envelope and slit it. Pulling out the sheet, he read the block letters once and then again:

8 Year Old Coming STOP Evacuating with Group from London STOP Should Arrive Early July STOP More Details Coming STOP Winifred Wilson

Josie read the words over Art's shoulder. Did the telegram really say someone planned to send a child? To them? An eight-year-old? In July? The calendar pages had already fluttered to May. Josie gulped as she looked at the words again. This child would arrive in two months. She worried her lower lip between her teeth as she considered how to fit a stranger's child into their apartment. It was comfortably cozy for two. Still, the spare room would have to transform into a bedroom.

Why would anyone send a child to them? Especially this Winifred Wilson, whoever she was?

A furrow had formed along the bridge of Art's nose as he read. He mouthed the words.

"What does it mean?" Josie took a deep breath and tried to push the shrillness from her voice. "Do you know Winifred?"

Art shook his head, a puzzled expression on his face. "I'm not sure. The name's vaguely familiar, but I can't place it. Guess I'll call Mom and get the scoop. She's probably a distant cousin looking for a safe place for her child to live during the war."

Josie rubbed her forehead, where a tight band gripped her. Germany had just invaded France and Belgium, so she could understand the desire to get a child away from the seemingly inevitable invasion of England. What would she do with an eight-year-old? There was no indication if the child was a boy or girl. The thought of a boy running all over the cramped space caused her to catch her breath.

"Do you realize this says the child will arrive by early July? This is May."

A frown creased Art's face as he watched her. "Maybe I should call Mom now."

That sounded like the best thing to do. Maybe she'd have more information. Josie wanted to be available, but the telegram didn't provide enough details.

Art headed downstairs to use the phone in the grocery store, and Josie trailed him. Mr. Duncan waved them over, and soon Art had dialed his parents' home. Josie crowded next to Art and picked at a fingernail while she waited for the conversation to start.

"Mom? Josie and I got a telegram today from Winifred Wilson. Do you know her?" Art nodded and hmmed a bit. "Really? A distant cousin. Do you know how she knew to get ahold of me? . . . Okay. . . She wants us to take their daughter in. From England." Art's brows bunched together as he listened. "Grandfather said that? All right. Have fun at your dinner."

Art hung up and looked at Josie. "Winifred is my third cousin." He shrugged. "Grandfather told her how to get ahold of us. Told her we were the young, vibrant couple that could keep up with her little girl. He's paying her way here."

"Really?" The man was a mystery to Josie.

"Well, I guess we wire back that we'll take the girl."

Josie drew in a deep breath and released it. She glanced around the small store. "I don't know where we'll put a child. . .or what we'd do with one. . .but we'll make it work. It won't be easy, though."

"Probably not, but it's the right thing to do."

Josie rubbed a hand across the ache hitting her head. Art was right, and ready or not, they'd soon be foster parents to an eight-year-old. Josie could only imagine the problems and challenges of a child removed from all she knew and loved.

Chapter 7

Days passed without any further information about the girl. Art's mom didn't know any more than she'd already told them, and no answer had come to Art's telegram that they would shelter the child as long as requested. Josie tired of looking around the apartment, wondering where a girl and her belongings would fit. The second bedroom seemed too small—little more than a closet, really—but it remained the only option.

The more Josie tried to imagine sending a child across an ocean to live on a continent with strangers, the more she wondered at the sacrificial love behind the act. One afternoon as she sat at the kitchen table reading her Bible, it struck her. It was an act of desperation. Desperation to provide for the well-being of a daughter. Desperation to ensure her safety.

In some ways, that act mirrored the despair Moses' mother must have felt when she set him in a basket of reeds and pushed him into the waters of the Nile with no idea or promise of the outcome—merely the knowledge death waited if she did nothing. The act would require such trust and sacrifice. Trust that God would intervene. And Jochebed's willingness to sacrifice her dreams of how life should be. All to save her son.

Josie wanted to welcome the child, not merely endure the intrusion. The stay could be too long to allow it to become simply a duty. It could actually be fun to have the girl join them. It would certainly fill days that bordered on purposeless now.

Summertime in Cincinnati. They could take the child to Cincinnati's amusement park, Coney Island, and to Reds baseball games. Maybe she'd save baseball for a time Kat visited. Kat could explain the game to their guest. Josie had never understood the rules—certainly not enough to make someone who may never have seen a game understand. Maybe Art would fill in those details.

Josie shook her head. There was so much about her husband she still didn't know. Fortunately, God had given her a lifetime to uncover all the details, the likes and dislikes. With another weekend upon them, maybe she should make a point to learn what she could. She could call it a treasure hunt. Search for the nuggets that made Art the man he was.

The mantel clock chimed a new hour. Five o'clock. Time to get ready for Art to come home. Josie hurried to the bathroom and pinched her cheeks before adding a touch of color to her lips. She whipped a brush through her hair and practiced her smile in the mirror. A glow filled her eyes that she wondered at. Her mom often got a soft, doe look around her eyes when thinking about Josie's dad. This was the first time Josie had noticed the same look in her eyes.

The clock eased toward five thirty, and restlessness propelled her out the door and down the stairs. She couldn't stand to wait another moment in the apartment. No, the day was beautiful enough to meet him on the sidewalk. A streetcar zipped down the middle of the street. She cupped a hand at her brow, shielding her eyes from the sun.

Josie scanned the sidewalk, looking for his familiar gait. There. Her breath caught at the sight of him walking her way. His shoulders were pushed back, hat thrust at a jaunty angle on his curls.

She knew the moment he saw her, because a big smile cracked his face and he picked up his pace.

"Josie." He picked her up and twirled her around right there on the sidewalk. "Ready for an evening out?"

She looked down at her plain skirt and simple white blouse. "That depends on where we're going."

"Get on your walking shoes, baby. We're headed to Coney Island."

Josie shrieked and held on tight. "That sounds perfect. But no roller coasters."

"You'll love them."

She wrinkled her nose and made a face. She couldn't imagine riding a roller coaster, even though she'd heard they could be fun.

Art laughed and patted her cheek. "Go on. You've got fifteen minutes to get ready."

"Yes, sir." She kissed him on the cheek, then spun and rushed inside.

A glow filled Josie at the thought of an evening exploring the amusement park. Even if it meant talking Art out of roller coasters. Moonlite Garden could be fun, too, since dancing had been one of the activities they'd enjoyed while courting, but in the months they'd been in town, they hadn't made it to Coney Island or other venues. The thought of finally visiting the amusement park and seeing the famous ballroom and oversized swimming pool excited her.

❋

Art watched as Josie pulled a navy dress out of the wardrobe. Its vibrant color accented the blooms on her cheeks. She looked in the mirror, fingers playing with her makeup doodads. He hoped she realized she didn't need anything to enhance her beauty. *Thank You, Lord, for this gift.* He had a feeling he would never tire of watching her or enjoying her. No, especially when life sparkled in her eyes for the first time in a while. While he hoped it wasn't merely the prospect of a night out, he'd enjoy it. But if a night out brought this response, he'd make sure he planned more.

Josie tucked a strand of hair behind her ear. "Ready?"

He'd been so engaged in watching her that he hadn't done anything else. Art cleared his throat. "All right. Need a wrap?"

"Just a sweater, please."

Art reached behind the door for where she stored them. He ran his hand along the four or five there. "Which?"

"This one." Josie brushed past him and smiled as it slid from the hook into her arms. The fabric felt like a caress. Maybe they should stay in. . . . Another look at her face and her excitement and he decided no. They'd explore the amusement park first. She pulled on her sweater, her face inches from his. She must have read something in his expressions, because a softness claimed her.

"Later." Promise filled the single soft word she breathed. He nodded. He could wait.

He tore his eyes from her mouth and gestured toward the door. "This way, milady."

The Packard served as their steed, and soon they arrived at Coney Island. The lights pulsed from the roller coasters even though it wasn't yet twilight. He couldn't wait to show Josie the sight when the rides stood against a dark sky.

They strolled arm in arm around the outskirts of the park past the Moonlite Gardens. The swinging sounds of "A-Tisket, A-Tasket" reached his ears. He laughed as Josie bopped in time to the music. "Maybe we'll take that in another night."

Her giggle sounded like music, made sweeter by its absence. She stepped closer to him. "The night is perfect just spending it with you."

"I hope you still think so when it's over."

"I will." She reached up, and he stopped. The air came alive with expectation. She leaned in and kissed him. "Thank you."

The wail of a saxophone pierced the air. "Come on. Let's see what rides this place has."

Josie willingly followed his lead as they strolled the park.

※

They walked past a small Ferris wheel, lights lit as it spun round and round. Calypso music tinkled its way from the carousel. The animals rode up and down as it circled over and over. Art made a beeline for the roller coaster next to the carousel. The Wildcat stretched across the back of the park. Josie eyed its length. The ride towered above her, then rolled up and down in a pattern. Art bounced on his toes, and Josie steeled herself. She had to ride that beast. Surely it couldn't be any worse than riding a car through mountain passes. Who was she kidding? Josie gulped and pulled back.

"What?"

"I'm not sure I can ride that thing."

Art looked from her to the roller coaster. "Come on. It'll be great. You'll enjoy it so much I won't be able to get you off it."

Josie highly doubted that. A train rattled to a stop. The folks getting off had big grins stretched across their faces. None looked like they'd fared poorly because of the ride. "All right. I'll go, but we'd better do it now before I change my mind."

Art tugged her toward the line. Before she'd steeled herself, they were climbing into a car and buckling into the bench seat. Josie bit her lip as the car faltered in its steep climb. They crested the hill, and Josie's heart stopped. They towered above the city, and she could see the downtown skyline in the distance. The view was amazing, dotted with the twinkling lights of a city bathed in dusk.

"Maybe this isn't so bad."

"The ride's barely started." Art's words tickled her ear.

"Really?" Josie turned to him, then sucked in a breath as the train plummeted over the edge of the hill. The car jerked and pulled from side to side. Her teeth clacked together, and her knuckles whitened where she clung to the bar. She shut her eyes, but a scream still escaped. Art tugged her to him, and his chest vibrated with laughter. Josie peeked as the train eased its descent. Oh no! They were climbing another hill.

Finally, the ride ended, and they stumbled out of the car. Josie almost dropped to her knees to kiss the ground. "I've never been shaken so hard. People think that's fun?"

"Admit it—you enjoyed it."

"Maybe a tad."

He spun her away from him and grinned. "More than that."

Art looked longingly at the ride, then led Josie down the walkway. An easy silence fell as Josie watched other couples walk by hand in hand.

"What do you wish for?"

Josie stopped and turned toward him. "What?"

※

Art smiled at Josie. The night was going so well. He couldn't wait to hear her answer. Josie's gaze drifted from him to some spot across the crowded grounds. He tried to follow it but couldn't see what had captured her attention. "Let's sit down." Josie tugged him toward a park bench.

They worked their way through the crowd.

"So you haven't answered my question." He hoped she'd give him a glimpse into her heart. Where did her wishes and dreams lie?

She nodded, keeping her eyes fixed on the table. "Have you ever been afraid to wish for something? Afraid that if you speak it, the dream will die?"

"Not that I remember." Where was she headed with this thought?

Josie settled back as if somehow that simple sentence had told her everything she needed to know. "I really want to understand, Josie."

"It's nothing, really." Her mouth twisted as if the words had a bitter taste to them.

Art squeezed her hands and held on until she looked at him. "All I hope is your wishes include me. I only want to make you happy. Give you moments like this."

"I do love you, Art. My life is so much richer with you in it." She hesitated. He opened his mouth to probe further into her dreams, but she rushed to speak before he could. "Someday we'll have children, and then I'll look back and long for these days when it was you and me." A shuttered look fell over her face.

"Are you afraid we might lose another child?" He hadn't considered that.

"It's silly, I know."

"No, I can understand. We'll have a family. At the right time. And then you'll wish for some relief." He leaned back and draped his arm around her shoulders. "I like that dream. Kids."

"Someday." A wistful smile touched her. He didn't know how to comfort her and felt like he had to treat her with kid gloves. "Until then," she added, "we'll serve God as best we can. Take in your cousin."

"Those aren't dreams."

"It's enough for now. Living with you. Spending time together."

He almost believed her. But he also heard the cry of her heart, and he could do nothing about that. He wanted to live in this moment. Instead, the shadow of yesterday and the uncertainty of tomorrow hung between them.

Until someday arrived.

Chapter 8

Josie curled on the couch with a copy of *The Grapes of Wrath*. She set the copy to the side and stared out the window. Miss Adelaide had foisted it on her the last time she stopped at the library. While she'd enjoyed the movie, she struggled with the book so far. When the passing traffic served to hold her interest more than the book, there was a problem.

"Must be me." She shook her head and looked at the book. Maybe the lazy June heat prevented her from comprehending what she read. Josie reached behind her, pushing the lace curtain to the side. Not even the hint of a breeze slipped through the open window.

The thump of steps on the stairs pulled her from her drowsy state. A light knock beat a rhythm on the door. With a sigh, Josie pushed off the couch and walked to the door. "Yes?"

"Is this the residence of Mr. and Mrs. Wilson?" A voice that sounded overly cultured filtered through the door.

"Yes." Josie opened the door.

A slight woman dressed in a neatly tailored suit with a smart hat bobbing on top of her upsweep stood in front of her. The plaid of her suit matched the currently popular ones Josie had seen in catalogs. "I'm Miss Annabelle Rogers. Here to do a home visit in anticipation of you receiving a child."

A home visit for a child? What could the woman mean? Unless it had something to do with the unanswered telegram.

"May I come in?"

"Yes." Josie shook the woman's hand and invited her in. "I have to admit I'm confused about why you're here."

"May I?" Annabelle inclined her head toward the couch.

Warmth filled Josie's cheeks. Where were her manners? "Of course. Would you like anything to drink?"

"Not now, thank you."

Josie sank into the armchair and studied the woman, who couldn't be much older than she was. She pulled files and a small notebook from a leather briefcase, setting them in a precise order next to her on the couch. Her nails were painted a rich red that matched her lips. And her face was pleasant though not beautiful. With her files arranged, she looked up with a tight smile.

"I've been hired by the families sending their children to the United States to ensure the homes are suitable for children."

Josie's back stiffened at the words. Not suitable? Of course, she and Art would make wonderful foster parents.

"You're one of a few families in Cincinnati. Most of my time will be spent in Canton." Josie's face must have reflected her confusion, because the woman rushed to continue. "The Hoover Company is arranging transit for almost one hundred of its employees' children."

"How does this impact us? Art's distant cousin asked us to take a child. We haven't heard anything since answering that we were willing, but surely they wouldn't ask if they didn't want us to have the child."

Annabelle's eyebrows raised, and she shook her head slightly. "You don't have children yet, do you?"

Josie swallowed as she tried to again decide how to answer the question. She did have a child. Just not here in her womb or arms.

"Once you do, you'll understand a parent's need to ensure those caring for their children are qualified." The woman opened a file and made some notations. "How long have you been married?"

The questions spilled on top of each other until Josie felt drained. Annabelle finally asked for a tour of the space. She continued to make notations, leaving Josie exposed. If only she'd had notice and the opportunity to clean. She cringed each time she noticed a cobweb or a dust bunny. Would they not receive this child all because every surface didn't sparkle? She couldn't let the child down like that.

Finally, the woman collected her files and smiled her smug, slightly superior smile. "That should be all. Thank you for your time."

"Is there anything else we need to do?"

"Once I've met your husband, we should be done, unless I have additional questions."

"It shouldn't be a problem to meet Art. We'll get a time from you? When will we learn the date the girl arrives? Do you know anything about her?"

"The children are scheduled to journey over in July. I will meet the group and chaperones in New York and journey with them to Ohio. If Cassandra Wilson's parents agree you are suitable, you can expect to have her join you within six weeks. Time is critical in getting the children away from the war."

Josie nodded. She couldn't imagine not having the child, Cassandra, join them. Sometime during the last hours, she had fully committed herself to welcoming this child. So their lives would need some adjustment. Everything worth doing required a sacrifice. And if they could ease the child's life for a period, so much the better.

"Will you be of assistance once the child arrives?" She cleared her throat. "Once Cassandra joins us?"

"Yes. I'll have ongoing site visits and be available to answer questions. You won't be left alone to figure out what to do." Now that the interview had concluded, it was as if a layer of ice had slid from Annabelle. "I will do my best to ensure that the match is successful for the duration."

"Thank you." Josie stood at the door after Annabelle left. Soon Cassandra would join them. She looked around the room, seeing a thousand items to take care of before then.

※

Art fought the urge to laugh as Josie spun around the rooms in her perpetual motion that hadn't eased since Annabelle Rogers visited a week earlier. She flitted near him, and he pulled her into his lap.

"Here, rest a moment. You'll wear yourself out before another day passes. You need to reserve some energy for the child, you know."

She pouted, lips puckered but sparks in her eyes. "I know. But I refuse to leave one thing for that Annabelle to find fault with. I can tell she'll be a hard taskmaster."

"I thought you said she warmed to you."

"Y–e–e–s." She drew the word out to several syllables. "But I won't make it easy for her to mark us down on her forms."

He chucked her under her chin. "Maybe she's writing us up."

"Maybe. But I don't think so."

"Well, you've made the decision easy for me. Pack an overnight bag. First thing in the morning, we'll load the Packard and head home for the weekend."

Her shriek left him rubbing his ear, hoping he'd hear in the morning.

"You mean it?" He nodded as she squealed again. "It will be wonderful to go home."

"Then we will. Who knows when we'll get away again once Cassandra arrives."

Her kiss was all he needed to know the suggestion was perfect. It would be good to visit family, maybe see some friends.

The next morning, they were up early, Josie pushing to get them on the road. The Packard carried them down the highway. With the windows rolled down, the breeze ruffled Josie's hair and kept the heat from stifling the car. The miles ticked by until they finally pulled into Dayton. Art wound through the southern neighborhoods until they neared the area surrounding the University of Dayton.

Josie's family's home nestled on Volusia Avenue south of the university, where her father taught. Stately trees lined the street where the homes had yards unlike even a couple blocks away where the houses practically touched each other. As he parked, Art braced himself for the barrage that was sure to come. Her family moved at a different pace than his and seemed to have only one gear: fast and loud.

"Oh, I hope they haven't left already." Josie leaned out the window and bounced as she waited for him to open her door.

He rolled his eyes. "It's only eleven. I don't think you have to worry about that."

"You don't know us very well yet." The use of *us* was softened only slightly by the smile on her face. She wasn't part of that *us* anymore. He was supposed to be her only family. He opened the door, and Josie accepted his hand, giving him a dazzling smile in the process. Maybe he'd overlook her words. She didn't really mean them. "Come on, slowpoke."

Josie rushed through the front door as if she'd never moved into her own home. "I'm home. Mom? Dad?"

A squeal that could only come from her kid sister split the air. "Josie!" Clomping feet indicated Kat barreled their way. She was dressed in a baseball uniform and almost knocked Josie down when she slammed into her. "You're here." After a quick hug, she slugged Josie in the shoulder. "Why'd you stay away so long? Did you get married or something?"

Josie giggled and locked arms with Kat. "Do you have a game today? Can we come?"

"Sure. But we have to leave soon. Dad's taking me since Mark says he has to study." The look on Kat's face communicated she didn't believe him. "You'd think he'd want to come."

"Let us come instead. We'd love to. Right, Art?"

He tried to look eager at the chance to sit in the hot sun and watch kids play ball. If he were going to watch ball, he'd rather it be the Reds. But if it would keep Josie happy, he'd do it. He'd take a magazine with him. After all, how well could girls play?

Josie's mom hurried out of the kitchen. A large apron was tied around her waist, but flour dotted her sleeves and face. "Josie." She pulled her daughter into a hug and whispered something in her ear. Josie nodded.

"I'm so sorry about the baby. Are you sure you're okay?"

Josie nodded. "I'm fine, though there are days."

"We're still praying for you." Mom stepped back. "Let's get you a quick bite before the game."

Art and Josie joined Mr. Miller at the game. The team turned out to be coed, thanks to Kat's presence, and Art had to admit that for a girl, and a young one, she played well.

"Where'd she learn?"

"Mark. I think that's why she's hurt he won't come to her games."

"How many does she play in a week?"

"At least two if it's anything like prior summers."

Art shook his head. This girl was unlike others he knew. To be that committed to a man's game. Why hadn't Mr. Miller talked to her about the need to act like a lady? She was approaching fourteen and playing with men after all.

"I'm glad our girls won't do things like that." The words must have left his mind via his mouth because Josie turned on him.

"I would hope that any child of ours who wanted to participate in physical activity would have the chance. If that means organized teams, what of it? You have to admit Kat is good."

She was. And there lay the problem. Some things girls didn't do. Some things were sacred to men.

But he'd never seen anything like Kat nabbing a pop fly and the young men rallying around her.

Saturday passed in a blur with Josie's family. The warmth was a welcome change from the formal atmosphere with his family. While he might not be sure about the ball-playing, he enjoyed the other competition in the family. He and Mark locked wits over a game of chess that left Art scrambling for the advantage.

Sunday lunch with his family was another story. During the formal meal, the clink of silver on china served as the musical backdrop to an awkward silence. Art tried to enjoy his beef Wellington but couldn't as he noticed Josie tense. When Grandfather invited him to his study, Art knew it wasn't for a casual conversation, but couldn't imagine why Grandfather would summon him since he'd ignored them both during the meal.

"Would you like a drink?" Grandfather approached a small cabinet behind his desk and arched an eyebrow at Art.

"No, sir."

"Still a teetotaler, I see."

"Just chose not to drink."

"All right." Grandfather settled in his leather chair behind his massive desk. "So, boy, how's business in Cincinnati?"

Art sipped his beverage and sighed. So it began. "Fine. My employer's trying to anticipate what will happen if we enter the war."

"Tell him not to waste his time. We won't enter. If we did, we'd never recover. Your mother tells me you're taking in one of the British cousins."

"We've been asked to."

"Glad to hear it. Wonder what would make the parents consider you rather than some of the more established relations."

"Mom said you suggested it."

A twinkle filled his grandfather's eyes. "So I did. Delighted you've decided to accept her."

"We're happy to help. Actually, excited about it."

"Harrumph. Don't know that there's anything to be excited about, since I doubt they can pay anything."

"They don't need to."

"Tell me that after you've provided food and clothing for a child." Grandfather shook his head, then took out his cigar box. He selected a cigar and shoved it between his teeth without lighting it. "Mark my words: You'll need help."

"What would you have us do? Leave her in danger when they've asked for our help?"

"No, but watch your pennies. I'm willing to help some, but your grandmother and I won't underwrite her entire stay. In that case, we might as well keep her here."

"That won't be necessary, sir."

"Keep it in mind."

"Yes, sir."

The conversation wandered from there. Grandfather probed him about the company and mood of Cincinnati. By the time they left, Art's mind had wearied of the grilling, and he was relieved to leave the family estate behind and take the highway toward Cincinnati.

Chapter 9

Josie dusted a corner of the knickknack table in the living room. She turned to another surface, but there was nothing to dust. Every surface had been wiped and scrubbed for days.

Her heart sank, and she lowered herself to the couch. They'd only been home a week, but she felt odd. Mark went to school. While she wouldn't want his homework—he had a crazy amount as an engineering student—she would like the direction he had. And Kat lived life with an energy that left Josie longing for a fraction of it. Even Carolynn, her best friend, seemed to have moved on with a verve that left Josie wondering if her presence had mattered when she lived in Dayton.

Everyone seemed fine without her.

Why couldn't she say the same?

Enough moping. She pulled on shoes, grabbed her purse, and headed out the door. The June sun beat down on her, and she wished she'd grabbed a hat to shade her eyes. Instead of going back upstairs to get one, she waved at Mr. Duncan as he swept the sidewalk in front of the store. With a quick glance for traffic, she ran up McMillan Street toward the library. When she reached it a few minutes later, she hesitated. Why had she come? She didn't need any books, since the few she had still needed to be read.

"Come in, dear." She must have hesitated at the door too long since Miss Adelaide had come to her. "I hoped I'd see you today."

"You did?"

"Wanted to talk to you about something. In out of the sunshine first. Can't leave the desk too long, you know." Miss Adelaide shooed her inside, returned to her seat, and smiled in satisfaction. "There now."

"How can I help you?" Josie leaned against the desk.

"I'll be taking a vacation this summer, and I need someone to mind the branch." Miss Adelaide focused on Josie, while Josie's mind rushed in confusion. Why tell her this? "My favorite niece is expecting her first child. There's no way that event can happen without me. There's just one problem."

"There is?"

"Yes. Who will mind the library? The young lady who sometimes fills in for me has left town herself for the summer. And the student who works in the evenings isn't interested in working from nine to nine all summer."

"Surely someone from one of the other branches will step in."

Miss Adelaide's lips curved down. "They could. But they never come here.

They don't have a clue where things are or how we like them done."

"Don't all the branches use the Dewey system?"

"That's not what I mean, and you know it, Josie. No need to get impertinent."

Josie struggled to keep her face placid. No need to add to Miss Adelaide's indignation. "So why tell me?"

"Why, you will take my place while I'm gone." Miss Adelaide said the words as if they were clear to anyone with any sense.

"Me? I have no training."

"Maybe. But you love books, you know the library, and you're my choice." Sitting with her arms crossed and a stern look on her face, Miss Adelaide looked like she believed she could force her will.

Josie sighed. "We'll have a little girl joining us in the next month. I don't know that I can care for her and do something like this."

"Bring her with you."

"I don't know that it's that simple. I'm sure she'll want to do other things." And what would Art think?

"Well, you're my choice. Talk to your husband and let me know if you can do it in the next week."

Almost against her will, Josie nodded. Miss Adelaide might be small, but she had a forceful personality. "Let me look for a book."

Miss Adelaide turned to help a patron without giving Josie another look. As Josie wandered the stacks, the idea grew on her. It could be a nice outlet for a few weeks. And surely Cassandra would like the library. What girl wouldn't?

The evening passed slowly. Josie left supper warming in the oven as she waited for Art. The clock hands moved around its face while she waited. She picked up several books but couldn't escape into any. By the time he made it home after nine, she couldn't talk to him about anything. If she didn't know better, she'd say there was smoke clinging to him. But he didn't smoke.

He'd scarfed down his dinner, then settled on the couch with a paper.

"What kept you late tonight?"

He didn't even look up. "A project, then out with a couple guys afterward."

"I missed you."

"They've been after me for months, so I thought now would be a decent time before Cassandra arrives." The paper slid down so that she could see his face. "I assumed it would be okay."

Josie nodded. "It's fine. I just wondered."

※

Later the next morning, Doris slipped into the apartment, bringing the sweet smell of muffins with her.

Josie smiled when she saw the basket on Doris's arm. "You must think I never eat."

"You are on the thin side." She patted Josie as she brushed by. "I hope Art likes you that way. Scott likes me with a little more padding." Doris worked around the kitchen as if it were her own. "I've got Bible study in an hour. You should come."

Josie tensed. "I won't have anything in common with anyone."

"You don't know that. You bemoan not having friends here, but I don't see you do anything about it." Her eyes narrowed as she crossed her arms. "Time to quit whining and act. Besides, you won't have any of these muffins unless you join me."

"Then what are you doing?"

"Teasing you with the scent and getting your coffee ready. You don't have much time."

Josie considered fighting Doris, but one look convinced her the only outcome was to give in with grace. "All right. When do I need to be ready?"

"Fifteen minutes," Doris stated matter-of-factly, as if it were the most natural thing in the world to walk into someone's home and demand they do something.

Josie shook her head and hurried to her room.

An hour later, she followed Doris into the fellowship room of the church. Several knots of women gathered around the outskirts of the room or in chairs. While she and Art had attended a few Sundays with the Duncans, Josie didn't know any of the women. Several glanced their way, but Doris led her to the coffee table. Setting her basket on the table, she pulled back the towel. The women quickly gathered.

"Are those your famous cinnamon muffins, Doris?" A tall redhead slipped between them.

"Yes they are, Rita. Would you like one?"

"Yes, ma'am. I'd like more, but will have one." She patted her tummy. "Still working on the baby."

Josie considered her, then shook her head. "You look wonderful."

"Tell that to Joey." She sighed dramatically. "It's been a year, and I have a couple pounds left. As long as Doris keeps bringing her treats, I think they'll be permanent residents." She winked at Doris. "Not that I mind." She took a bite of the muffin, bliss settling on her face. "Yes, ma'am, these are delectable." She startled. "Good heavens, I'm being a terrible hostess. My name's Rita Brown. You are. . . ?" Rita extended a slender hand to Josie.

"Josephine Wilson, but my friends call me Josie."

"Josie it is." A woman stood up across the room and clapped her hands. Rita leaned close. "That's the signal. Subtle, isn't it?"

Josie stifled a giggle with her hand. Maybe this wouldn't be so bad after all. But as the women discussed 1 Samuel 1, she reevaluated. Many of the women were Doris's age or older. In all likelihood equally sweet, but not people she immediately connected with. She didn't want a grandma telling her what to do. She wanted a friend who would laugh and cry with her. But many of the younger women were mothers with small children. Even though she enjoyed Rita, pain pierced her heart each time she saw Rita's little girl. By now, her own stomach would have been firmly rounded, and no one would question her state.

It didn't help that the scripture focused on Hannah and her desperate pleas for a child. Josie wondered if she'd ever understand why God allowed the things He did. Why could some women so easily have children, while others remained barren and desperately longing for a babe? Still other children suffered from illness or died at young ages.

She must have sighed out loud, for Rita patted her hand. She leaned close. "You all right, Josie?"

Josie sniffed and nodded. Doris leaned across Josie toward Rita. "This is a hard topic for the girl."

The leader sent pointed looks their way, but Doris and Rita continued to talk over Josie. Josie shrugged an apology to the woman. It wasn't her fault that the lesson hit so close to her heart. Or that her neighbors had decided now was the time to discuss her. She elbowed Doris and frowned.

Doris winked at her and went back to talking about Josie as if she weren't there.

Josie tried to ignore them, but a thought kept flashing through her mind. What if Doris had insisted she come today because of the topic? What if she'd decided Josie needed more than a new forum to meet people? A swirl of emotions played through her at the thought she'd been manipulated. She tried to pull her thoughts back to the passage, but each time she did, another pang went through her.

A woman across the circle wiped moisture from her face. What caused her tears? Had she lost a child, or was she unable to have one? Josie felt pressure build in her nose as she imagined the woman's story. Pain welled up, and she forced back tears that weren't focused on her own loss.

This was crazy! She had enough to handle without adding another's pain to her own. She should get up and leave. Let Doris explain for her. Instead, she pushed her chair back and read the passage.

Hannah had begged for children, longed for them, made vows to God to obtain them. And God eventually heard her. Then He allowed her to have Samuel. The praises overflowed from her heart.

Josie had not longed for children with such a passion. Until she had lost this child, it had been a distant idea, something that would occur in the future. As the conversation swirled around her, she lowered her head.

Father, help me seek Your face in the midst of this. I don't want to forget this life I lost, but I also don't want to linger in the grief. Help me move forward. Bring me to a place that I can rejoice in You again. Not because of what You might give me. Not to entice You to grant my requests. But praise You because of who You are.

Tears streamed down her cheeks as peace filled her heart. For a moment, it seemed God had come down and danced over her. She soaked in His presence, desperate to memorize it. She didn't know how long it would last, but she wanted to capture the feeling for the hard days that would come.

God hadn't forgotten her.

Chapter 10

The noise ricocheted off the ceiling as the men entered Rosie's, the neighborhood establishment. Stan swaggered as if he'd returned home from a long absence. Art grimaced. As far as he knew, that's how Stan felt. Art shouldn't be here. Calling it an establishment did not hide its true nature. While he might drink a Coke, everyone else ordered beers. Why had he allowed Stan to talk him into venturing out with the other guys again? This simply wasn't something he enjoyed.

And if Josie found out. . .

The thought lingered. What would she think? He didn't know, but he assumed she wouldn't be pleased.

He rubbed the back of his neck, felt the prickly hairs. Time to get a haircut. Hadn't he seen a barber down the street? He could still leave and get the haircut taken care of rather than stay with the guys. As he prepared to push off the barstool, the bartender set a mug in front of him. Foam sloshed over the sides. Who would have ordered him a beer?

"Bottoms up." Stan leered at him over the top of a matching mug.

Art scowled. His father had preached the lesson loud and clear. Only fools who couldn't control themselves visited those places. Drinking should be done within the walls of a man's home. Art shook the image from his head.

"Come on, time to loosen up. You're too uptight, even if you are a bean counter."

"Aw, leave him alone, Stan." George Brothers peered behind him, scanning the room.

"Find what you're looking for?" Stan's disgust was clear. "You know she ain't interested in you."

"Sure she is. She just needs to know me."

Unease set up camp in Art's core. He didn't know who they were talking about, and he didn't want to. He needed to leave. Now. These two fancied themselves a regular Abbott and Costello. First problem? They missed the speedy humor of skits like "Who's on First?" Second problem? He couldn't believe he was listening to their vulgar comments.

Stan sat at one side of him, George on the other. Art ran his hands along the top of the long bar. It wasn't smooth as he'd thought. Instead, the wood was dented and battered. His thoughts raced as he looked for a way out.

Okay. So this wouldn't be easy. He should have never agreed to join them a couple weeks ago. When had it become easier and easier to walk in?

He glanced at his watch. Six thirty. Josie wouldn't be happy. She'd noticed his other absences. While she hadn't said anything, he knew that would change. Hopefully, this was one of the days she'd spent time at the library shadowing Adelaide. She might not even notice he was late. "I've got to leave." He threw some change on the bar and stood. "See you next week."

Traffic blared around him as Art double-timed it home. He barely noticed when he almost stepped into the path of a cab. His thoughts remained fogged. He needed to have his head examined. Choosing to spend more time with those guys rather than rush home to his bride. He knew better than to let Grandfather's disapproval settle into his spirit.

Friday night. They had the weekend to spend together. Thankfully, tonight was free.

※

Josie stared at Annabelle Rogers. Where was Art? She'd reminded him this morning the social worker would stop by for a last home visit before leaving to meet the children on the East Coast. He had to be here. It was the remaining step in satisfying Annabelle that Cassandra would thrive with them.

She picked at a fingernail. "Are you sure you wouldn't like something to drink?"

"No. This should be a quick visit." Annabelle cast a pointed look at her watch.

"He really should arrive anytime." Josie hoped her words were true. Lately, Art hadn't rushed home. She didn't know what he did and wanted to avoid being the wife who nagged her husband about his whereabouts every day. Either she trusted him or she didn't. As long as she could, she'd choose trust. Believe the best about him. They'd exchanged promises, and she intended to keep hers.

She tried to make small talk, but the longer they waited, the more difficult the task. Annabelle didn't help things, either.

"I really must leave."

Josie grimaced. "I'm sorry you made the trip for nothing."

"Do you understand that we're out of time?" Her face pinched. "I'm not sure what to tell her parents. I can't vouch for your husband or his character."

"He's definitely a character." Josie smiled but realized Annabelle was too upset to take her words lightly. She cleared her throat. "He's wanted to host Cassandra from the moment we got the telegram."

"Then he should have been here to make sure we completed the paperwork." Annabelle stood and smoothed her skirt. "I may come by Monday night if he will be here."

"He will if I have to go get him myself." Josie followed her to the door. "Again, I'm sorry."

Annabelle strode past her and hurried down the steps. Josie eased the door shut. Everything in her wanted to slam it, but why worry Doris or risk the door? Art would be home soon, and then they'd figure out what was going on.

She paced the living room as she waited, gnawing on a nail. This wasn't like Art. Her heel caught the edge of the rug, and she sprawled against the couch. Her temper flared at the thought of the position he'd placed her in. He'd promised to be home. He'd understood he was required for the home visit. Maybe he'd changed his mind about Cassandra. *Argh.* She needed to talk to him. Understand what he was thinking. Trying to figure it out made her stomach clench.

Art sneaked through the door, as if he thought he could avoid her or she wouldn't notice his late arrival. He froze when he saw her sitting on the couch with her arms crossed. She bit her tongue to keep from saying something she'd regret.

A sheepish look filled his face. "Hi."

She nodded.

"I take it you missed me?" He tried to charm her with his Clark Gable smile.

She refused to soften. At least until he knew what he'd missed. "You're late."

"Yeah."

"Did you forget the appointment this evening?"

The color drained from his face. "The social worker?"

"Yes. She waited quite awhile but had to leave half an hour ago. Especially since I couldn't give her any indication of when you'd arrive."

He sank to the sofa next to her, then raked his hands through his hair. "I'm sorry, Josie."

"We may not get Cassandra now." How that thought pained her.

"She's not ours."

"But we're supposed to provide a safe haven for her. We can't do that until this home study is complete. And that won't happen unless Annabelle meets you." She sniffed the air. It was smoky but not the rustic aroma of wood smoke. "What did you bring home with you? Maybe it's a good thing you didn't meet. You smell like a bar."

He wouldn't meet her gaze. "Why? Why would you start going to bars now?"

"I don't."

She tried to scorch him with her stare.

"Okay, I have a couple times. But I'm not drinking, Josie. I promise."

Could she believe him? She had never imagined that was an option with him. And why now? Had she done something to push him away? She popped off the couch as her thoughts ran wild.

"Josie, calm down. You're acting crazy."

"I'm acting crazy? I'm only trying to make sure we can help your cousin. That's what you wanted. Did something change and you forgot to mention it?" Josie took a deep breath. If her voice got any louder, Doris and the grocer would hear every word.

Art hesitated. Had he changed his mind while she'd fallen in love with the idea of helping the girl?

"My job is getting intense. And you'll be working at the library this summer."

"You said it was okay."

"Sure, I did. It's clear you need an excuse to get out of the apartment and meet people." Art shrugged. "It seemed like a good way to help that happen. It's a lot with taking in a girl we don't know."

Josie gritted her teeth. "It will be fine. And this is a little late to change course. They leave in a couple weeks."

"We shouldn't force this. That's all I'm saying." Art crossed his arms and leaned against the couch. "Maybe I got too excited. Knight in shining armor and all that."

"How's that wrong? We all need a knight to save us from time to time."

"Maybe I'm not knight material." Art looked at his hands, and his voice cracked.

"Why say that?" Josie wrinkled her brow. "You're my knight."

"No. You keep looking at me like I'll fail."

If his eyes weren't dull with pain, Josie would have argued with him. But the longer she looked at him, the more she understood he really believed that. Somewhere, she had gone wrong in the months since they'd married. How could she restore him to his steed?

"Is that why you've stopped coming home after work?"

He hunched over, elbows on knees. The silence grew until Josie didn't know how to break it.

"It's been a hard week. Pressure from work. Trying to ignore Grandfather's voice in my head telling me that I have to work harder than the others and make my way in the world in a way that honors our family name. I honestly forgot, Josie. I didn't do it on purpose." He searched the room as if looking for more words. "I'm sorry, but that's all I can say."

"I'm sorry." Josie searched his eyes, then took a breath. "I hated not knowing where you were or what to do. If you don't want to take Cassandra in, I'll accept your judgment." Somehow she would make her heart agree.

"No, I'll call Miss Rogers and apologize. This is the right thing to do."

Josie tried to stretch her lips into a smile. Their conversation hadn't addressed the bars, but it was enough for now. At least he hadn't been drinking. Though how long could that last? And with an extra body to clothe and feed, there wouldn't be much left over for vices like that.

Art stood and pulled her toward him. She relaxed into him. They would make it through this and much more. The miscommunication would be fixed, and then Cassandra would be on her way.

Chapter 11

A rt paced the train depot's platform, his nervous energy wearing on Josie.
"Can you believe we're picking Cassie up today?"

"Um-hmm." She'd spent the last two weeks getting the apartment ready. Once Art and Annabelle had talked, things had moved so quickly she was still spinning.

She pulled at her glove to see her watch, then scanned the horizon. Anytime now the train should chug into the station, and she'd be a parent. The thought still seemed surreal. Earlier this year, she'd been unsure about having a baby; now she welcomed an eight-year-old.

But when a distant relative asked one to take in a child who was threatened by war, yes was the only correct answer. Who could have foreseen the turn the war would take? That evacuations abandoned last year would restart with the intensified air raids in London? That a relative would search hard enough to find Art?

Josie pulled off a glove and nibbled on a fingernail. Her nerves jumped with each sound.

Annabelle and Art had finally connected over lunch. Josie hadn't participated so hadn't told the social worker she'd taken a temporary job. All that mattered was that after a long lunch, Annabelle had given her approval to the match.

Just like that, they were on their way to pseudo-parenting.

Her stomach gurgled, and she pressed her hand firmly into it. Eight. Old enough to have fun and not require the close care of a smaller child. But also old enough to understand why she'd been sent from home. Josie remembered the abandonment she'd felt when left with her grandparents for a week. This was so much more than that. Could an eight-year-old truly grasp why parents sent them away? Not as punishment, but for protection? The choice must agonize.

Josie prayed they'd get along well. They had to since there was no end to this placement. She pulled in a shuddering breath. She must get her emotions under control before she let fear run away with her. Kat wasn't much older, and she'd see something like this as a grand adventure. Surely Cassandra would, too.

"Are you ready, honey?" Art stopped in front of her and grabbed her hands, running his fingers along her jagged nails.

She tried to smile but felt it quiver on the edges.

"Chin up. This will be great."

"I know."

"This is what you've worked so hard for. Helping this little girl."

"I don't know how little she'll be."

Art scooped her up and spun her around until she giggled.

"Put me down before I can't stand." Josie relaxed, grateful for Art's distraction. There was no reason to get so tense. This was what she wanted, after all.

Art resumed his pacing. "Why isn't the train here?"

"Soon enough."

A shrill whistle pierced the air. Art stopped his pacing and turned toward her, a grin splitting his face. The man certainly saw this as an escapade or some grand adventure.

"That's got to be her train."

Josie smiled as the beginning pushes of excitement vied with her questions. What would this child add to their lives? "I'm sure it is."

"I wonder how we'll know her." From his jacket breast pocket he pulled a faded photo that Annabelle had provided. "Surely this isn't how she still looks."

Josie studied the pose again to amuse him. The girl with golden hair hanging in Shirley Temple curls looked about five, freckles dotting her nose above a charming grin. "No. But I don't think it will be hard to find her. How many little girls travel such distances? Her escort will surely look for us as we search for them."

The iron behemoth groaned and squealed as it slowed to a stop. Josie stepped forward and hooked her arm through Art's. "I'm excited to meet your cousin and welcome her."

Art's eyes shone with light. "That makes two of us. Here's hoping we don't overwhelm her."

People hopped off the train, some rushing into the arms of waiting loved ones, others striding into the terminal and out of sight at the clip of people with a mission. Josie scanned the dwindling crowd for two figures wandering, hunting for a contact.

"That must be her." The excitement in Art's voice mirrored his bouncing action. Josie grabbed her hat to keep it from sliding off and turned her gaze to where he pointed. Across the platform, a young girl walked in their direction, carrying a duffel and a lost look. Annabelle walked next to the child, a harried expression on her face and her clothes disheveled and wrinkled. What had happened on the train to leave Annabelle in such a state?

Josie took a step toward the child, unsure how best to approach her. Would the child welcome a hug, or would she find it invasive? Josie should have asked Annabelle such key questions before this moment. Now all she could do was look at Annabelle with a question in her eyes. Annabelle shrugged, exhaustion pushing her shoulders forward.

A whistle sounded, and the child jumped. She dropped the bag, and her sweet face pinched. Josie's heart tightened. This child had lived through things Josie hoped never to see or experience. She let go of Art and hurried to the child's side.

"Cassandra?"

The girl stood still, but a tear slipped down her cheek. Josie knelt in front of her, not caring if her hose ripped with the movement.

"My name is Josie Wilson. You're going to live with us awhile." She touched the side of the girl's head and then lightly stroked her cheek. Only then did Cassandra stir. "Can we help you with your bag?"

Cassandra looked at her, face tinged red and eyes wide. "Sorry, ma'am." Her voice threaded the space between them in a whisper. "Will I live with you then?"

"Yes. We're delighted to have you live with us for a bit."

A wary knowing crept across Cassandra's face. "It's likely to be longer than that."

"Then you'll stay the duration. I promise."

Cassandra considered her a moment. Annabelle nudged her forward. "I hate to do this, but now that you're connected, I must get back on the train. There's one more soul to deposit with his new home. More miles to travel."

Art shook her hand. "Thanks for getting her safely here."

Annabelle nodded, then turned and hurried back to the train. Cassandra watched, a forlorn look shadowing her face. Time to distract her from another lost connection.

"Here. Let me introduce you to my husband, your cousin Art. Then we'll take you home, show you your room, have dinner, get you a bath." Josie bit her lip to stop the flow of words. "Sorry about that. I tend to talk when I'm excited."

"Any other time, too." Art laughed. "You'll be hard-pressed to get a word in edgewise. Cassandra, I'm Art."

Cassandra looked at his hand and then shook it. She was small, wiry. Freckles on her small nose dotted strawberries-and-cream skin.

"A pleasure, sir." She laughed, but it sounded strangled and way too mature for a child. "Thanks for taking me."

"Did you enjoy your trip?" Art walked her toward the exit, her bag thrown over his shoulder.

"Once we were off the boat. We had to wear our life vests all the time, and I didn't like it."

"I see. Did you travel with many children?"

Cassandra chewed her lips, her thin shoulders poking through her dress. "Most of them went to a place called Canton. Do you know where that is? Miss Rogers said she needs to go there after she delivers Bobby. A company is taking those kids in."

"Will you miss the kids?"

Cassandra chewed her lip. "I didn't really know any of them before the trip."

"Would you like to see them again?"

"Maybe." A door seemed to shut in her expression.

"The first order of business is to get you an ice cream. All brave children need a treat." He led the child to the car, and Josie followed a small distance behind. The image of Art helping a little girl that looked like the best of both of them flashed through her mind. Someday. She smiled at the thought and the fact that the pain didn't accompany it. Maybe Cassandra was exactly what Josie needed to finish healing and stop dwelling on her own pain.

Cassandra nodded off in the car before they reached the drugstore, so Art turned the car home instead. The moment they parked, Doris came running out the back doorway.

"You've arrived." She watched Art struggle to pull a sleeping Cassandra from the backseat. "Poor child must be all done in."

Josie nodded. "You would be, too, if forced to travel for weeks into the unknown."

"Well, you have the girl now and can befriend her."

The thought stilled Josie. She'd focused so much on getting Cassandra here that she hadn't considered the fact they were total strangers to the girl. While she'd worked hard to make the way for Cassandra, the child didn't know this.

Art groaned. "Could you close the car door, Josie? I'll get her upstairs."

"Here, let me get the back door for you." Doris chased Art across the backyard.

Josie closed the door, then leaned against the car. *Father, prepare my heart to be sensitive to the needs of this child You've sent our way. Give me insights into her, and help me be her friend. Help me remember she already has a mother.* Such sacrificial love left her blinking in the sunlight.

A window on the third floor opened. Art hung out and waved to her. "Coming, Josie?"

❊

It took several days to get Cassandra acclimated enough to willingly venture out. It seemed the child had brought the war with her. At loud, sudden sounds, she might dive for cover. Under a bed, under a table, the location didn't matter as long as she felt protected. The behavior charmed Josie at first but grew odd as Cassandra repeated it. Then Cassandra explained the air-raid drills. The drills had been consistent but random. Josie prayed that Cassandra would reach a point where she didn't live life poised to hide at a moment's notice.

Josie also struggled to find foods that Cassandra liked. So many things Cassandra asked for sounded nasty, like haggis. Josie hadn't considered the conflict of the different cultures. The British spoke English, after all, but the differences highlighted the early days with their visitor.

A week after Cassandra arrived, they walked to the library branch. Josie needed to get Cassandra out of the house and prayed the sunshine would bring some life to the child. As Cassandra raced ahead, Josie decided this was what the child had needed.

"Cassandra, wait." Josie paused until the bounding child obeyed. While the neighborhood traffic stayed light during the day, cars zipped down the streets.

She could just imagine the wire they'd have to send if something happened to Cassandra. SORRY *STOP* CHILD FLATTENED BY VEHICLE. She shuddered at the thought.

Cassandra looked to Josie and smiled.

"I think you like the outdoors, Cassandra."

"It's much nicer here than in the city."

Josie laughed. "Your city is larger than this one. We'll have to explore some of the parks around here. Get you out more often."

Cassandra grinned at her and grabbed Josie's hand. She swung it back and forth in large arcs until they reached the library. Once there, Cassandra raced up the steps and flung open the door. In a minute, she'd selected three books at random and stood at the checkout table, ready to leave. So much for a quiet time scanning the stacks for a few good reads.

"Can we leave now?" Cassandra's voice ricocheted off the ceiling and walls.

Miss Adelaide leaned forward, lips twisted in a mock frown. "Keep your voice down, young lady. You are in a library and should speak in subdued tones."

"Like this?" Cassandra whispered the words.

"Yes."

"All right," Cassandra shouted, then skipped to the doorway.

"You really must do something about the child before you begin working here." Miss Adelaide shook her head and laughed. "She seems full of vinegar."

"Today, at least. I'm enjoying the child I discovered on the walk very much."

"Good. Just remember to keep a firm hand with her from these early moments. You set the tone of your relationship."

There might be truth to the words, but they seemed harsh. "The child's just arrived from a war zone. I'm sure we'll be fine."

Miss Adelaide shook her head and looked toward the ceiling. "I'll pray you are."

Cassandra stuck her head back in the door. "Can we go find a park now?"

Josie nodded. "Just a moment. I'll see if Miss Adelaide has some ideas for us."

Miss Adelaide quickly checked out Cassandra's books and one for Josie. "There's the beautiful Eden Park on the other side of your home. I'd start there. See you next week."

Josie gathered the child and headed toward home. "We'll try the park on a day that we have a picnic packed. How's that?"

"All right." Disappointment colored Cassandra's words, and Josie determined to get her to a park as soon as possible.

She held tightly to Cassandra's hand as the child skipped next to her. The skipping seemed to loosen her tongue, and the child talked the whole way home. That ease disappeared as soon as Josie started lunch preparations. She stared in the icebox looking for inspiration.

"Do you have anything good today?"

"How about a sandwich? Maybe some chips and fruit?"

"Any fish to go with the chips, ma'am?"

Josie chewed on her lower lip. She didn't care for fish, so never bought it. If it would make Cassandra content, she would run downstairs to see if the grocer had any. No, that was crazy. Better keep things simple. "Not today. Ham sandwiches are the menu. We'll get fish the next time we shop. You'll have to let me know other foods you enjoy, so I can keep them in stock."

Cassandra's nose scrunched. "Can we go today?"

Josie laughed. "No, sweetie. We have to eat what we have first. Waste not, want not."

"Then I suppose ham will do."

"Why don't you go read a book while I get the plates ready?"

The afternoon passed quietly as Cassandra read her books and Josie cleaned. A burble of delight filled Josie. Maybe this experience wouldn't be as easy as she imagined. But Cassandra was filling a space in their small family.

Chapter 12

"Cassandra, time for breakfast."

Silence answered the words. Josie tiptoed down the hall to Cassandra's small room. Cassandra lay on her side, curled around her doll, tears streaming down her cheeks. Josie watched a moment, unsure what to do but knowing she wanted to comfort the poor child. She eased into the room and knelt beside the bed. She stroked the child's tangled curls. "Sweetie. I'm so sorry."

Cassandra's silent tears turned to sobs that wracked her small frame. "I want my mum."

"I know, darling. I so wish you could be with her." Josie struggled for words as tears threatened to overflow her eyes. "You must miss her."

"Awfully." The word shuddered from Cassandra. She scrubbed her face and tried to sit up. "Sorry, ma'am. I'll stop crying." Tears continued to stream, and Josie reached out to swipe one away but stilled when the child flinched.

Josie cleared her throat. "Should we write her a letter today? Let her know how you are?"

The little girl nodded. "I'd like that."

"Let's get you some breakfast. Then we'll get out some paper and pencils. I know she'd love to get mail from you."

"But the post won't deliver it for ever so long."

"Maybe. But we can keep sending letters, knowing she'll read them eventually. And with each letter, she'll be so happy to know what you're doing and that you're safe."

Cassandra frowned. "I haven't done much."

"Then we'll change that."

The conversation played through Josie's mind during breakfast, chores, and the balance of the day. She and Art needed to do something to give the child plenty to fill letters. Even simple outings would fit the bill. When Art arrived home and Cassandra was settled for the night, Josie sat on the couch next to him, ready to plan their attack.

"We really need to do something to occupy her mind. The child is focused almost exclusively on what's happening at home."

"That's natural, I'd imagine."

"Probably true, but it will be easier for her if we can give her things to anticipate."

"Okay." Art pulled at his pockets playfully. "Remember, we aren't made of money."

"I know, but maybe your family would help, especially since Cassandra is part of the family."

"I'd rather not ask."

Josie snuggled closer to his side. "Okay. I'll keep the outings inexpensive."

"What did you have in mind?"

"Things like the Sunlite Pool, movies, ice cream. It doesn't have to be extravagant. The library every day won't satisfy her. She told me she hadn't done anything that she could tell her mom about."

Art laughed as he wrapped an arm around Josie. "Not everyone takes pleasure in libraries like you, darling."

"Definitely their loss."

"Maybe. These other options sound good as long as we spread them out with things like picnics or outings to the parks."

"Then we'll start this weekend. A movie and some ice cream. Maybe we can even find *Pinocchio* playing somewhere." Josie tipped her head and kissed his cheek. He turned and claimed her lips. Josie relaxed into his kiss.

❊

Saturday morning Art woke slowly. It felt good to relax without the pressures of work weighing on him. Mr. Fine continued to put pressure on the white-collar employees to see into the future. If Art could do that, he wouldn't be working for a small company like this. He rubbed hands across his face, trying to brush the vestiges of sleep away.

Josie didn't lie next to him. He'd hoped to hold her for a moment, but she'd bounded out of bed before he could. He turned on his side and considered getting up. A soft sound reached his ears. It was muffled, but clear.

Was this what Josie had dealt with most of the week?

He cringed at the thought of comforting a crying child. What did he know about girls? He waited, hoping Josie would take care of Cassandra, but her footsteps didn't pad toward the door. He gulped and pushed out of the bed. After grabbing his robe, he faltered outside her room. Wails replaced the quiet cries.

Surely she would stop. Without his intervention. She had to. Right?

Tears baffled him.

And there'd been so many in this apartment. He barely knew what to do with Josie's. What on earth was he supposed to do with a little girl he barely knew? Promise her a pony? Give her his car? He considered doing both, then slapped himself on the forehead.

"You're a well-educated man. You can handle an eight-year-old." The pep talk did little to get him out of the doorway.

Cassandra looked up, her face blotchy from the crying.

"Can I get you anything?" The words sounded inane even as they slipped by him. He cleared his throat. "How about I get you a drink of water?"

Her face crumpled. She whimpered, and he looked around her room, desperate for something that would comfort. There. Her doll had fallen under the bed. He knelt before her and picked up the doll. "Were you missing her?"

Cassandra frowned but swallowed hard against her tears. "No, sir. Missing me brother and da."

"Tell me why."

"On Saturdays, we'd always do something together. Hike across a park. Splash in a pool. Play rugby or football."

Art straightened. This he could do. "Josie and I have planned some outings for you, too. How would you like to go to an amusement park today?"

"Sir?"

"You know. A place with rides and roller coasters."

"I don't know about that." She shrunk back into herself.

Art backpedaled. "How about we go to the pool there and you can watch the rides. See if it's something you'd like to try in the future. Think that might work?"

She nodded. "I'd like to try."

"All right. Let's get up then. Josie probably has a good breakfast ready. Then we can prepare for our adventure."

The morning passed quickly as Josie prepared a picnic for them, and they climbed into the Packard. Cassandra remained quiet but took an interest in their surroundings as they drove.

He glanced at her through the rearview mirror. "How's Cincinnati compare to England?"

"It's not as crowded. The folks seem stand-offish."

Josie turned around to look over the seat. "Stand-offish? Who?"

"That Miss Adelaide hasn't warmed to me yet."

"It's your charming personality, Cassie. All that rushing about at the library keeps her on edge."

The banter continued until he reached the park. After paying the entry fee, they ventured into the area around the pool. It was supposed to be one of the largest pools in the country, and looking at its size of two hundred by four hundred feet, Art believed it. If Cassandra wandered off, they might lose her amid the crowd.

"Stay with one of us. No wandering."

Cassandra rolled her eyes as only an exasperated eight-year-old can. "Yes, sir."

"I'm serious, Cassandra. I've heard it holds ten thousand people. I'd hate to lose you so soon after you arrive."

"I'm not an infant." Indignation filled her voice.

"I know. But stay close."

"We're fine, Art. There aren't nearly that many people here." Josie grabbed Cassandra's hand. "Let's explore a bit. Find the best spot to settle down."

Art followed as the girls picked their way through the crowd. He gladly dropped the towels and toys when the gals chose a spot. From here, he could see a wide stretch of the pool. Enough to give Cassandra some freedom.

Cassandra pulled off her blouse and skirt and rushed in her swimsuit into the water.

"I hope she can swim." Josie's voice held a tinge of concern. "Why don't you go with her? Make sure she's okay."

Art nodded. Probably a good idea while they determined her skill level. In no time, Cassandra had talked him into the deeper areas of the pool, and he was roughhousing with her. The girl's giggles reverberated across the water. He could get used to days like this.

❈

The days slid from the calendar, Josie trying to keep up with Cassandra and Art. Those two had settled into an easy relationship since their time at the pool. She was almost as active as Kat, and Josie looked for ways to get her involved in sports or other activities. Josie toyed with the idea of signing up Cassandra for a basketball team at the YWCA. What would Cassandra's mother think if her daughter went home a tomboy? Probably not much, since Cassandra had indicated she played sports like rugby and football. Or was this a way of protesting her placement? Josie was at a loss to know, so did the only thing she could.

"Cassie, how'd you like to join a basketball team?"

Cassandra looked up from the book in her lap. "Basketball?"

"It's an American sport. You run up and down a court and throw a ball into baskets on the wall. My sister likes to play it, and there's a place near here with teams."

"I don't know."

"Kat enjoys it, but she plays baseball, too."

"I'll give it a go."

Josie took Cassandra to the YWCA. After her first practice, the drive passed in silence. When they'd about reached the house, Josie cleared her throat. "What did you think?"

"There's an awful lot of running and throwing the ball."

Josie laughed. "That's right. It's integral to the game."

"I'm not sure if it's for me, but I'll try again if you like."

"I think I do. In fact, I think I'll take a fitness class at the same time."

They'd barely reached the house when Annabelle stopped by. Cassandra had hopped in the bathtub, so Josie led Annabelle to the living room. Once Annabelle had settled on the couch with a Coke, she grilled Josie on how the transition had gone.

"Is Cassandra settled?"

"I think she's adjusting. We're doing all we can to help her." Josie chewed on the jagged edge of a fingernail.

"How?"

"The child never stops moving, so I'm looking for activities for her. We're trying a basketball team at the YWCA. We walk to the library and places like that. Anything I can think of to get us out of the apartment often. I knew the apartment was small but had no idea how one added body, especially one so small, would make it seem tiny."

"The activity is good for her. Should keep her healthy and her mind occupied."

"It does seem to help. While she loved the trip to the Sunlite Pool, we can't afford to do that as often as she'd like."

"Let's find some alternatives then."

The two shared ideas for a bit, and Josie took satisfaction in the fact that Annabelle's list didn't contain anything she hadn't already considered.

"Maybe take walks to Eden Park as a family."

"I don't know that Art will want to walk back through there each night."

"You could meet him on his way home."

"That's a great idea." Josie sipped her Coke. "From her reading and letter-writing, I can tell she'll do fine in school." She clasped her hands around the glass and sighed. "She's starting to relax, but still tends toward formality. Thanking us for every little thing we do."

Annabelle considered her words. "Any flashes of frustration or tears? I'm seeing a lot of that with the children. It's as if they've been trained to be very polite. But the strain eventually burdens them. Their emotions bounce all over."

"There are tears, but not any more than you'd expect for a child who's been separated from her family. Is there anything we can do to help her?"

"Give her time and love. She'll calm."

Josie considered the words after Annabelle left. She just needed to stay the course. But it felt like she should do something more to ease Cassandra's transition. Especially considering there was no planned end date. It could be a long war if Cassandra couldn't settle into their home. If only other evacuated children lived near. She made a note to ask Annabelle the next time they talked.

Regardless of those concerns, she had to get Cassandra registered for school. In fact, the pattern of school coupled with the chance to meet American kids might help immensely. After a morning at the library, Josie and Cassandra walked to the neighborhood school. While Cassandra had attended a private school at home, there was no way Art and Josie could afford to send her to one. No, she would experience the fullness of American life by attending the public school. Cassandra trudged after her, a frown tipping the corners of her mouth down.

"Must I go to school?"

Josie laughed. "Yes, miss. I know your folks would think your education is critical. Parents are funny that way."

"I don't know they'll like me learning American history."

"Sorry, but that's your option here. Guess you'll be ahead of your classmates in that area when you go home."

Cassandra tucked her small gloved hand in Josie's. "Thank you for all the effort for me."

"Happy to. You're good practice for the day I have children of my own." Pain squeezed through her, but she shoved it to the side. "Besides, it will be good for you to meet some children. Make some friends while you're here."

"But I won't be here long enough."

"I hope that's true. Even if it is, think of it as developing pen pals."

Cassandra's grimace made it clear she wasn't buying that argument. "Maybe."

"Stiff upper lip and all that." Cassandra's surprised look rewarded Josie. "I'm learning a thing or two by listening to you."

"Right."

Josie squeezed Cassandra's hand. "Now let's get you squared away. You'll love it."

Chapter 13

W ilson, I need to see you. Now," E. K. Fine's voice bellowed through the room. The others turned to watch his reaction.

"Coming, sir."

Tension stretched across his neck and shoulders. Could anything good come from being called into the boss's office? Art sucked in a deep breath and let it out slowly.

Art barely reached the glass-front office before Mr. Fine started talking. He paced back and forth behind his desk as he talked, using a cigar to punctuate the air.

"Wilson, you've done a fine job with the books. You've marshaled the numbers effectively. Even I can understand them." He chuckled while Art watched, unsure how to respond. "Just a little humor. Anyway, I called you in here for a new project."

Art stood taller. That sounded like good news.

"I'm sending you to Chicago for a series of meetings. There are some manufacturers there who are further down the road for switching to a war economy. I want you to meet with them, see what they did, and determine if any of that can work here. The key to success is to always be a step ahead of all the other companies. There will be a limited number of contracts, and I want us to land at least one. We can't be unprepared."

"Yes, sir. Any particular industry?"

"Use common sense. You'll be fine."

"Anything we can learn from what the company did during the last war?"

"No. Even if there was, that ended twenty years ago. Not relevant to today."

Art nodded. Guess the man didn't live by the maxim that "those who can't remember the past are condemned to repeat it."

"When do I leave?"

"Tomorrow. My secretary has your train ticket."

"How long?"

"Plan on a week."

Art grimaced. Josie would not be thrilled to have him leaving. Especially on such short notice.

"Art? Any problems?" The look on Fine's face communicated the answer should be no.

He'd promised to take Josie to a show tomorrow night. Doris had agreed to watch Cassandra so the two of them could get some time alone. She would be disappointed if that didn't work out. After a steeling breath, Art said,

"I can't leave tomorrow, sir."

"And why not? You should be pleased with the opportunity."

"I am, but I have plans with my wife."

"That?" E.K. waved his hand as if swatting a fly. "That's not a problem. Leave now, pack, take her out tonight instead. The missus will understand."

While a good theory, in practice Art doubted it would hold up. They weren't newlyweds without responsibilities now. Doris might not have the freedom to adjust her schedule and watch Cassandra.

E.K. sat back in his chair, fingers steepled in front of his face.

"I'll get that ticket now."

"Good man. Don't let me down."

Art strode from the room then halted at the secretary's desk. She handed him the ticket with an apologetic smile. "The others will meet you at Union Terminal at seven."

"Yes, ma'am."

"That's a.m."

"I understand." Art grabbed the ticket and returned to his desk. What would he need for these meetings? E.K. couldn't have been more vague if he'd tried. He sank into his chair unsure what to do.

Stan came and stood in front of Art's desk. Leaning against it, he smirked. "Ready for our trip?"

"Are we the only ones going?"

"Nope. Choirboy's coming, too."

While Stan meant that as a pejorative term, some of Art's tension eased at the realization Charlie would join them. Art wouldn't have to deal with Stan alone, and Charlie had the experience with the company to have a good grasp on what it could do if it switched focus. Better yet, it meant reinforcements when standing up to Stan.

"It'll be good to have him along."

Charlie grinned from his desk. "We'll team up on Stan."

"Sure. You think that. I'll keep you hopping."

"As long as it's not from bar to bar."

Art laughed at Charlie's earnest expression. Charlie winked at him. Yeah, this trip would be okay. Josie would be okay. Josie. He was supposed to head home. "I'll let you two handle packing what we'll need for the trip. I'm under orders to go home and see my wife."

"See, that's why I'll never marry." Stan snickered. "Why be tied down to a dame who wants to keep you home and in her lair all the time."

"There are benefits."

"Nothing I can't get already."

Charlie shook his head in disgust. "You are hopeless, Stan."

"Maybe, but at least I'm not tied down."

Art changed his mind. Maybe it would still be a long week with Stan.

✳

"You have to do what?" Josie couldn't believe Art was leaving. Travel wasn't part of his job. What about their night out? She'd looked forward to it all week. And how could he help with Cassandra if he wasn't here? School started soon, which would bring a new set of adjustments to Cassandra's life.

"We can go out tonight, and then I'll pack."

He said it so matter-of-factly, as if plans could change in an instant.

"But we can't leave Cassandra alone. Who can stay with her on such short notice?" She dug her fingernails into her palms to distract herself from the building tears.

Art sighed and pulled her into his lap. "I don't like it either, but the boss made it clear I have to go. If it's important to the company, then it has to be important to us, too. It's only for a week, after all."

"You're right." His arms slipped around her, and she leaned into him. "I can still hate the idea."

"I know."

Josie tried to push up, but he held on. "Let me see if Doris can come tonight."

"She can." His voice had turned husky. "Come here."

She stilled as he reached up to kiss her. She sank into his embrace as the kiss deepened. Art ran his fingers through her hair, and her thoughts muddled.

"Miss Josie?"

Josie startled and pushed away from Art. Patting her hair, she turned to see Cassandra standing in the doorway. "Yes?"

Cassandra's brow furrowed. "Did you say you're leaving tonight?"

"Just for a bit." Josie licked her lips, considering how to ease Cassandra's fears. "Doris from downstairs will come up and stay with you."

"I don't need someone."

"You'll have fun. You know how much you enjoy Mrs. Duncan. She'll probably have you help her with cookies."

Cassandra crossed her arms, chin jutted.

"Come here, sweetie." Cassandra reluctantly walked across the room and joined them. Josie smoothed her curls. "It'll be fine. We'll be back about bedtime."

Cassandra eased next to her. "Promise?"

"Yes." Josie's heart ached at the fear in that one word. She hugged Cassandra. "Now let me get ready. And make plans for tomorrow night. It'll be just us girls, and one of the last nights before school starts."

A wistful smile touched the girl's face. "I'd like that."

Art watched her go. "I hate to leave as school starts."

"Don't worry. We'll suffer through." Josie poked him in the ribs. "Let's get out of here."

✳

Art slipped out the next morning with a light kiss on Josie's forehead. The feathery touch teased her out of sleep in time to watch him leave, and then roll back over. She relaxed into the mattress, the things she needed to do flashing through her mind. Work at the library in the morning and then take Cassandra shopping for some school items. The child's small suitcase hadn't contained nearly enough options. Two outfits, underwear, and pajamas didn't qualify. Josie's part-time pay would help purchase the extra items the child needed, and a small sum had arrived from England to help with the costs.

After a quick breakfast of toast and tea, they headed to the library. Josie saw Cassandra ensconced in a quiet corner before settling herself in at the circulation desk. Cassandra must have found a set of books that delighted her, because she stayed in place for the morning. Josie wandered over to her side.

"What did you find to read?"

Cassandra tugged her gaze from the pages to Josie's face. "*Little House on the Prairie.* Was it really like this?"

"I don't know. Despite what you may think, I didn't actually live then." Josie tousled Cassie's curls. "But I like the way she describes life back then."

Cassandra closed the book and held it to her chest. "May I check it out?"

"Absolutely."

"Okay. May I please go outside for a bit?"

Josie considered Cassandra. "For a bit. But no getting dirty. We have to get your school things after this."

Cassandra placed the book on the circulation desk, then skipped out of the building. Josie stayed busy helping folks find books. Right as she'd begun to wonder what Cassandra was up to, the child came in with a couple of daises.

"These are for you."

"Thank you, Cassandra." The child beamed from the praise. "They look a tad thirsty. Let me find a vase or glass to put them in." Josie found a cup shoved in the back reaches of the desk. "Here. Why don't you fill it with water and wash your hands. Then I think we'll leave."

Cassandra skipped toward the washroom. The sunshine had warmed her cheeks, and the wind had mussed her hair.

After returning home long enough to leave the flowers on the counter, the two drove downtown. Soon she found a parking space near several of the stores she planned to visit. Josie enjoyed browsing, but Cassandra acted overwhelmed by the selections. As they strolled the racks, Josie pulled out option after option.

"Would you like the playsuit or the skirt only?" The red plaid was cheery and played well with Cassandra's complexion.

"I'd rather not have either, please."

"Why not?"

"I don't think my mother would like me to have either one."

Josie stared at the child. "I don't understand why not. You must have clothes for school. And either of these options should work."

"Well, I don't like them." Cassandra turned away from Josie.

"I can't send you to school in one of two outfits. After all, the one at home needs some serious mending, and I can't wash clothes every night."

Cassandra shifted from side to side. "Mum didn't send money with me. I can't pay."

"Sweetie, she wired some for things like this. If it's not enough, it's all right. Art and I are happy to take care of them. Now which one do you like?"

Slowly Cassandra caught the spirit of school shopping and jumped in. Before long, she wanted one of everything and Josie had to rein her in.

Once the shopping was over, Josie smiled at the surprise she'd planned. They stowed the bags in the backseat of the Packard and headed out to the zoo. Cassandra's eyes got round when she realized where they were.

"The zoo? Are we really going in?"

Josie laughed. "Of course we are. One last hurrah before school begins. Besides, someone's waiting for us." Josie parked the car and glanced at her watch. Hopefully, they'd arrived in time to catch one of Susie the gorilla's shows. Miss Adelaide had told her it was quite a sight to watch the gorilla cavort with her trainer. Josie hoped it brought joy to Cassandra.

Josie grabbed Cassandra's hand and walked through the park toward the show. While the gorilla entertained the crowd, Josie delighted in watching Cassandra's reaction. The girl beamed as they strolled through the zoo afterward. And the smile didn't fade as she prepared for bed.

Josie tucked Cassandra in and prayed with her. Several new outfits lined the dresser in Cassandra's room. Cassandra had sparkled as she organized them and lined them up in her room. Now Josie's prayers shifted to finding a friend for Cassandra, someone who could ease her little-girl loneliness.

She walked through the apartment, straightening as she went. Now that Cassandra was in bed, the place felt too quiet. Josie missed Art. His presence made the apartment home. Without him, everything felt a bit off.

There was so much she wanted to share with him—the little details of the day she enjoyed sharing when he came home each night. But for now she would wait.

Chapter 14

The day's meetings had finally ended. Art couldn't decide if this trip constituted a fool's errand. He sat all day with nothing to contribute as folks debated how they could evolve their companies to meet the demands of a war economy. As far as he could tell, there was no indication the United States would actually enter the war. Let China and Japan duke it out in the Far East while Germany and Italy fought the rest of Europe.

"Come on, guys. Time to head out." Stan waggled his eyebrows. "Enjoy the sights of Chicago."

Art stifled a sigh. Each night the same thing: Stan badgering Charlie and him to go anywhere but the hotel. "Your idea of the sights differs from mine."

"You are such dead weight."

Charlie laughed and bumped Stan. "I don't think that's what you mean. You know you're welcome to join us."

"Not my idea of a good time." Stan stalked off.

Art watched him go. Yet again he thanked God for Charlie's presence. "What kind of shape do you think he'll be in tomorrow?"

"The good Lord's the only one who knows." He clapped Art on the shoulder. "Let's grab a bite."

They walked several blocks until they found a tiny Chinese restaurant. The aroma of ginger, garlic, and other things Art couldn't name collided in a way that made his stomach rumble.

"So your thoughts?"

Art looked up from his egg drop soup and blinked. "On what?"

"How we're supposed to keep the company afloat."

"You think E.K. really cares what we think?"

Charlie shook his head. "Doesn't matter. What matters is that if we want to continue to have jobs, we must think creatively."

"I think we're wasting our time. We're not in a war."

"I pray you're right. However, our allies have to get their munitions and other supplies from somewhere. It might as well be us."

"Have you forgotten we make pianos? Do you expect them to start dropping grand pianos as bombs?"

Charlie's rich chuckle filled the air. "That's a creative idea. Might be too expensive and unwieldy. . . ."

"You're nuts."

"Just going with your idea." Charlie paused as the waitress brought steaming bowls of rice topped with different sauces and meats to the table. "But it's time to get serious. Come up with a proactive plan. So when the day—"

"*If* the day. . ." Art jumped in.

Charlie nodded. "Okay. If the day comes, we're ready to help the company that pays our bills compete."

When he put it that way, Art had to agree. "What about plane parts?"

"Maybe." Charlie's wrinkled brow indicated his skepticism. "That's the kind of thinking I'm after. What kind of parts do you mean?"

They spent the balance of the meal trying to come up with ways to use the processes and materials they already had. Hopefully, they'd be ready.

※

Four days later, Art opened the front door and tossed his suitcase on the floor. "Josie. I'm back."

Those words had never sounded so good to his ears. The week away from home had been long. While he hoped it benefited E. K. Fine Pianos, he belonged right here with his girls.

Josie squealed and ran out of the kitchen. In two steps, Art picked her up and spun her around the living room.

"I have missed you so much, gorgeous." He set her down and gazed into her eyes. "I didn't think you could become more beautiful, but you did."

Josie leaned her cheek against his cheek. "I've missed you, too."

He held her a moment, savoring the feeling. The seven days had felt like seventy. But the moment he walked through the door, he'd known. He was home. He kissed her with an intensity that had her leaning into him. Slowly, he pulled back until his gaze locked with hers. A soft smile played across her face. He ran his thumb along her cheek and then turned. "Where's my other girl?"

Josie frowned. "She's downstairs with Doris. We needed a bit of space from each other."

"Things going that well?"

"She's struggling with school."

"In the first week? Is it academics?"

"Nooo." Josie chuckled. "The child has already been bumped up a grade, and it may happen again. No, she's a British child thrust into an American school."

Art scratched his head. Josie meant for him to pick up on something, but he wasn't getting it. Nope. Wasn't coming to him. He shrugged. "You'll have to help me."

"She won't say the Pledge."

"The Pledge of Allegiance?"

"That's the one. She says she's not an American, so she won't pledge to a flag that isn't hers." Josie looked over his shoulder at the door. "I don't know that I blame her, but. . ."

"It does put us in a spot."

"I'm not worried about us. I'd hoped she'd make friends at school, but this

81

isn't helping her cause. At all."

Ah, so that was the issue. "Has she mentioned wanting friends?"

"No, and that's the problem. She puts up this front that she doesn't need any. But you should see her watch the other kids."

Art tugged Josie away from the door. "Keep your voice down. What if she hears?"

"I honestly don't think she'd care." Josie straightened his tie, played with his collar. "Cassandra's a turtle pulling into her shell. She's done so well with us, but this is somehow different."

"She's probably homesick. Misses her school and friends there."

"I know. But she could be here a long time. She's not working to make the best of that."

"Could that be her age? She's only eight."

Josie's sigh lingered as if pushed up from her toes. "These first weeks are critical. If she wants to make friends, she needs to pick her battles carefully. Refusing to say the Pledge isn't the best foot to start on."

The door squeaked on its hinges as it swung open. Art turned, a broad smile on his face when he saw Cassandra. He stepped toward her and hunched to her level. "How's my girl?"

Cassandra's face crumpled then hardened. "I'm not your girl."

She raced past him to her room and slammed the door.

"Welcome to my world." Josie grimaced. "We have to find a way to reach her, Art. I can't stand the thought that the rest of her time here is going to be miserable."

Art agreed. The only problem was he had no idea what to suggest or do. Maybe he should go back to Chicago.

✼

Josie struggled to fight the fog of sleep. The quilt kept her pressed to the bed, even as her brain argued that somebody needed her. A soft mewling pulled at her. She shook her head, trying to clear it. Cassandra? She shook off the blanket, and Art snuffled in his sleep. Faint moonlight lit her steps as she padded to the door.

Through the crack, she heard the soft cries. Poor child.

Heart heavy, Josie eased into Cassandra's room. The girl tossed on the bed, caught in the throes of another nightmare. "Please, Mummy. Please."

Josie perched on the edge of the bed. *Father, surround this child with Your arms. Bring peace to every fiber of her being. Only You can calm her and give her the assurance that she will never be alone and that she is safe.* She leaned down and pulled Cassandra into her arms. The child stirred, then slowly opened her eyes. The tension in her body eased when she recognized Josie.

"I'm not in London?"

"No, you're safe here in Cincinnati."

"What about my mum?"

"I don't know, sweetie. But I'll stay with you for a while. Go back to sleep."

Josie prayed until a soft dawn eased across the early morning sky and Cassandra slipped back to sleep. As she stroked Cassandra's golden curls, tears fell down Josie's cheeks—tears for the child before her and the torment she felt. But also for the child she didn't have. The one that she hadn't even known if it was a boy or girl. While God knew and held that child, Josie wished she'd had a chance—even once—to see her baby.

Instead, she'd pray for Cassandra, the child entrusted to her. That she could do.

By the time Art got up and was ready for the day, Josie had slipped into a simple flour-bag dress and prepared coffee and eggs. He gobbled the food while skimming the newspaper. As she sipped some coffee heavily flavored with cream and sugar, she watched him. Her nose wrinkled as he drank his coffee black. Ugh.

Headlines highlighted the continued intensity of the air raids over Britain. Bombers had dropped their payloads over London. Josie would have to remind Art to take the paper to work so Cassandra couldn't see the headline. Such news could only turn her dreams to more nightmares.

"Any plans for today?" Art's words made the paper vibrate.

"Hmm? Get Cassandra to school. Pray she makes some friends and begins to settle in to the routine. Spend a few hours at the library. Then join Doris for a new Bible study."

"Sounds like a full day."

"I suppose." Now that she thought about it, life was busier, fuller since Cassandra had arrived. Whatever the reason, it pleased her. "I doubt I'll work at the library much longer."

Art looked up from the paper. "Why not?"

"Miss Adelaide has been back for a week now."

"You'll miss the work." It wasn't a question, but a statement that showed how well Art understood her.

Josie shrugged, trying to hide how much it did matter. "If it comes to that, yes. I guess I'll have time to volunteer somewhere else. I've gotten used to having somewhere to go."

"Maybe you'll get pregnant again, and we'll have a baby to keep you occupied." He said the words so casually, while they ripped at the scab on her heart. A stab of fear punctured her at the thought of another pregnancy ending like the first.

She didn't feel recovered from this miscarriage. But clearly, Art had placed it completely behind him. How could he do that? Her nose started to tingle, and she bit on her tongue to distract herself. She wouldn't waste the tears on someone who didn't understand the depths of her pain. Besides, God was piecing her heart back together. Cassandra seemed to fill part of that process.

Art glanced at his watch. "We've got a couple minutes for our Bible reading."

Josie eased onto the chair next to him. She needed this time to connect and find peace before the day erupted around her. As Art read Psalm 91, Josie listened to the words, letting them flow over her.

Art finished, then pushed back from the table. "See you tonight." He paused connecting with her gaze. "I know God has something for you."

As he rushed out the door, Josie fought the surge of frustration. His words sounded trite, an afterthought meant to placate her. That wasn't what she needed. She didn't know what she needed. A manual for how to reach a shell-shocked and bitter child? Instructions on how to create a community in a new city that still felt foreign after ten months?

What she did know? Time to get Cassandra up and walk her to school. And hope the teacher didn't have any other surprise news like the Pledge fiasco.

Chapter 15

"Josie." Doris huffed up the stairs, her words trembling ahead of her.

Josie stuck her head out the door. "Yes, ma'am."

"Thank goodness you're home." Doris stopped and sucked in a breath. "You've got a call downstairs. Said she was your sister."

Why would Kat call her? Josie looked from Doris to the door. "Can I get you anything?"

"Go on ahead. I'll just catch my breath."

"Yes, ma'am." Josie brushed past Doris and hurried to the back room of the grocery store. Someday it would be so nice to have a phone in the apartment for privacy. At least they didn't get many calls. She picked up the receiver. "This is Josie."

The wire crackled and popped. She pulled it tighter to her ear. "Hello?"

"That you?"

Josie could barely make out the words. "Yes."

"This is Kat. We made it to a championship this weekend. You'll come, won't you?"

"Who made it to what?"

The sigh was strong enough Josie could imagine Kat rolling her eyes. "My baseball team, silly. We made it to the big tournament. You have to come."

"I'll check with Art. I don't think we have anything going on."

Kat squealed. "Then you'll come."

Josie laughed. To have the enthusiasm of an "in-betweener.""I'll see what we can do. When do we need to be there?"

Kat filled her in on all the details. "And be sure to bring Cassandra with you. We all want to meet her. Does she have the best accent in the world? Can you understand what she says? What does she think about Cincinnati?"

"You can ask her those questions when you meet her."

"Make sure you're here Friday night, so we can get an early start Saturday. You won't want to miss a game. Bye." Like that, Kat was off and on to her next event.

Josie shook her head. Mr. Duncan stuck his head around the corner. "Everything okay?"

"Yes, sir. Thanks for getting me."

"No problem. Doris enjoys an excuse to hustle up them stairs."

His wry look left her chuckling as she hiked up those same stairs. When she entered the apartment, Doris sat on the sofa, flipping through Josie's Bible. A stab of something, violation maybe, flashed through Josie.

"Find what you're looking for?"

"No. I'm looking for an elusive verse. Ah well. It'll come to me. Probably in the middle of the night, but they always come."

Josie perched on the wing chair. If they spent the weekend in Dayton, she needed to pack. Figure out what they would need at the ball diamonds.

"Well, I'll head back down. Tell Cassandra I'll have fresh cookies for her."

"She'll probably smell them and stop before she comes here."

Doris shut the door behind her. Time to pack.

✳

Art hurried up the stairs. The next place they lived would be closer to the ground. Today he didn't have the energy to charge the steps like usual. He opened the door to a whirlwind of activity. Josie had two bags lying next to the couch.

"Going somewhere?"

Josie looked up at him with a coquettish smile. "How's a weekend in Dayton sound?"

"Honestly? Terrible." All he wanted was a quiet weekend. Maybe take Cassandra for some ice cream. Keep life simple. Yeah, that sounded really good. Until he looked at Josie's face. "I take it we're going."

"Kat's team is in a tournament, and she wants us there."

While there were many things Art didn't know about Josie, it had been clear from the beginning her family took priority. That made them his priority, too. Guess they'd make the trek. "When do we need to arrive?"

"Not sure when the games start tomorrow. Could we drive tonight?"

"Is that why the bags are packed?"

She had the grace to wear a sheepish look. "Do you mind?"

"As long as you're happy, it's fine with me."

The door opened behind him. He turned to see Cassandra, cookie crumbs dotting her chin. "Doris sent extra sugar cookies up with me." She stared at the bags, a frown growing on her face. "What's all this?"

"How'd you like to go on a weekend adventure?" Josie's voice begged her to share the excitement. "We'll stay with my family and watch Kat play baseball games."

Cassandra wrinkled her nose. "You promised to take me to the movies."

"We will." Josie looked at Art before continuing. "In fact, I bet we'll go while we're in Dayton. We can't watch baseball all day. Besides, this is another American sport. You've enjoyed basketball, and I think you'll like this, too. Better yet, you'll get to meet my family."

✳

Art picked up the first couple bags. "Will we eat here first?"

"I've got supper ready."

"All right. I'll load the bags, then we can eat and get out the door." The tournament could be competitive since Kat played on a good team. And Mark might have time to play some games this trip. Josie's mom would dote on Cassandra.

Everybody needed extra mothering from time to time. Especially girls thousands of miles from home.

An hour later, he'd loaded the Packard and they'd eaten. The wheels turned as they made their way to Dayton. Art cracked his window and let the breeze blow through the vehicle. When they pulled in front of the Millers' home around nine o'clock, welcoming lights blazed in each window.

Art parked at the curb. "Do they know we're coming?"

"I'm sure Kat told them." Josie shrugged like it didn't matter one way or another. She was probably right.

The front door bounced open and a flash of checked fabric raced to the car. When it stopped, he saw it was Kat.

❋

"You made it!" Kat's words ran on top of each other, bringing a smile to Josie's face.

"I promised we would."

"No, you said you'd talk to Art. That doesn't mean much until you're here." Kat smiled so big her face almost cracked. "You got here in time to watch my team win the whole contest."

Art laughed. "Nice to see your ego's still intact." He urged Cassandra forward. "I'd like you to meet Cassandra Wilson. Cassandra, this is my sister-in-law, Katherine Miller."

Kat stuck out her hand. "Pleased to meet you, Cassandra. But you can call me Kat. Katherine is way too long of a name to yell across a baseball diamond."

"What are we going to do with you?" Josie pretended to frown but had a feeling Kat saw right through her. Somehow Kat knew the world would revolve around her whims. If that meant playing baseball with the boys, so be it. She'd never let anything slow her down—and she'd just turned fourteen.

Cassandra grabbed Josie's arm and hung on.

"Don't worry, Cassandra. You and I will become friends. Maybe even grab an ice cream cone after the games."

"Could we get a sweet, too?"

"I don't see why not."

Cassandra's face lit up.

"Let's introduce you to Mom and Dad." Kat led a willing Cassandra into the house.

Art slipped an arm around Josie's waist. "Do you think we could have her move in with us?"

"Who?"

"Kat, of course. Other than you, I haven't seen anyone else get Cassandra to trust them that quickly."

Josie leaned her head against Art's arm as they strolled up the walk. "Call it the Miller girl charm." She felt the rumble of his laugh, and it pleased her. "Though you do well with her, too. She lights up when you're home spending time with her. Ready to cheer Kat on?"

"We wouldn't be here if I wasn't." He patted his jacket pocket. "I've got a magazine or two stashed for the dull periods."

Josie pulled away from him and playfully slapped him. "There will be no dull moments."

"Of course not." Art held his hands in front of him. "It's the Boy Scout in me. I like to be prepared for anything."

"On your best behavior, Art. You don't want Kat to hear."

"No, ma'am. Can't guarantee good behavior." His face took on a long pious look.

"Why on earth not?"

"You have to buy my good behavior."

"I don't do it with Cassandra, so why on earth would I do that with a big guy like you?" Josie crossed her arms and stared at him.

"Because it's a small fee really. Just a kiss."

"A kiss?" Josie made a show of tapping her finger on her mouth and thinking about his proposal. She hoped he wouldn't notice the warmth spreading across her cheeks. "All right, but you'd better kiss me good and long."

A slow Cheshire cat grin spread across Art's face, until his dimple appeared on his left cheek. "My pleasure."

※

Once everyone had met Cassandra, Mother showed them to their rooms. Cassandra would bunk with Kat, and Josie and Art had her small room. They slipped into bed so they'd be ready for the morning. Cassandra jumped into their bed as soon as the sun's rays filled the room with light.

"Is it time to leave yet?"

Josie peeked at the child. Cassandra fairly vibrated from where she'd bounced. "I can't wait to watch Kat play."

"What time is it?"

"Seven."

"Let Kat get you breakfast, and we'll be down in a bit."

Cassandra bounced out of the room, then Josie rolled over with a groan.

"What was that?" Art's muffled words drifted out from under the pillow he'd pulled over his head.

"That would be your cousin. We might as well get up and ready for the day."

An hour later, Josie's family joined them for the game. As Mark bantered with their dad, Art settled back, providing Josie a place to lean. Rain the night before had knocked down the dust, and the crowd yelled encouragement and jeers, depending on their loyalties.

After they'd been at the ball fields a couple hours, Josie decided she was thirsty.

"Would you get me a Coke?"

"Sure you don't want to come with me?"

Josie smiled but shook her head. "I don't want to miss a play."

"One Coke coming up. Want to come, Cassandra?"

The girl shook her head, eyes fixed on Kat as she played shortstop. Josie loved watching Kat play that position. Normally, a taller, more athletic guy played there, but Kat played like she had springs on her shoes. Art pouted and pulled Josie to her feet. "We'll be back in a minute, Cassandra."

The girl didn't seem to notice, as she stayed fixed on the action. Mother motioned that she'd take care of Cassandra. Art grabbed Josie's hand and tucked her against his side while they walked.

The line at concessions was several people deep when they reached it. The gent in front of them kept looking over his shoulder and shaking his head.

"Have you ever seen anything so ridiculous?"

Art looked at the man. "Were you talking to me?"

"No, but you'll do. What are they thinking, letting a girl play?"

"Probably that she's good enough." Josie didn't try to keep the snap from her voice. Insolent man to question Kat's playing.

"Nah." The man swatted a paper through the air. "I bet her father's sponsored the team or her boyfriend's captain."

Art shook his head. "Nope. Kat's too young to have a guy. What's your name?"

He stuck out his hand. "Jack Raymond. I'm only here because my editor sent me. Seems he thinks a small tourney like this has a story buried somewhere." A sour expression twisted the young man's face. "I am definitely not cut out for this kind of sports reporting."

"Stick around, Jack, and I'll introduce you to that girl. She could very well be your story."

The thin man clamped a pencil between his teeth. "Maybe, but I can't see it."

Josie bit her lip to keep from making a retort. Kat's play should speak for itself. If the reporter didn't know that by now, then he hadn't watched the game at all.

The line moved forward again and it was Jack's turn to order. Art nodded at the window. "Go ahead."

"Dames aren't supposed to play baseball. Anyone in their right mind knows that." Jack looked toward the field. "Though she is a cute thing."

Josie hoped this Jack Raymond wouldn't take Art up on his offer to introduce him to Kat. Kat wouldn't hesitate in taking on each of his ridiculous comments.

"Well, back to the salt mines. I've got a story to file." He tipped an imaginary hat. "Nice to meet you."

Josie watched him saunter off. An unsettled feeling flared. It was a good thing he wouldn't stick around to meet Kat. She didn't need someone like him telling her not to play with the boys. It brought too much joy to Kat. Yep, they'd all be better served without Kat and Jack meeting.

Chapter 16

Art hurried to turn the corner and tear down the hall. He wanted to yell, "I'm late, I'm late, for a very important date." People stepped out of his way without a word from him. They must have seen the panic that leaked from his mind to his face. He skidded to a stop outside the conference room. It would only make things worse to run in. He steeled himself and opened the door.

When Art walked into the room, E. K. Fine III sat at the head of the conference table. "Nice of you to join us, Wilson."

Uh-oh. Never a good sign when Fine called someone out in front of everyone.

"You're in time to fill us in on your scheme to have this fine company produce airplanes."

How did the man do it? How did he call his company a fine one without cracking a smile? The company was a fine Fine company?

Charlie Sloan patted the chair next to his and removed his notebook from it. As Art took the seat, Charlie whispered, "Focus, Art."

Good advice. Art sucked in a breath. "What would you like to know, sir?"

"Why should this company manufacture plane parts?"

"I don't recommend we transition now. No, we plan, determine what changes are needed to the plant and our process. But for now, continue to craft pianos."

"Know any experts on manufacturing plane parts?"

"No, sir. I'm an accountant. I deal with numbers, not processes or manufacturing." Though the challenge of anticipating the future and plotting a course of action captured his mind. He and Charlie had spent hours elaborating on Art's initial idea. On paper, it looked like the company could transition to plane parts with relative ease. Art excelled at his job when Fine let him focus his energy on accounting. But he knew the company's small reserve of cash would evaporate in a few months if they didn't develop a plan. It wasn't the books' fault the company stood in danger. A well-managed company should be more in the black, but that hadn't happened here. As the reality of the company's situation had emerged, he'd wondered if he should look for another job. Art didn't want to worry Josie, but he also didn't want to run the risk of unemployment.

Charlie jumped in, followed by other employees. Art relaxed as attention was diverted from him. No doubt about it. It was time to look for another position.

✸

"Cassandra. We need to hurry, honey." Josie slipped on an earring and then examined her reflection one last time. When Annabelle had called to see if Cassandra would participate in this October program to raise awareness of the needs of children in England, it had sounded like a great idea. A few children from Canton would participate, making it a good way for Cassie to see some of her compatriots. But now that Josie raced to get Cassandra to the community meeting in time, she wondered.

"Sweetie, we have to leave now or we'll be late." No response. Josie hurried from her room. Cassandra had shut and locked her door. Josie twisted the doorknob a couple times to no avail. She rattled the doorknob, but Cassandra ignored her. "Young lady, let me in your room now."

"No."

"You'll miss the program."

"I don't care." Cassandra's pitch rose with each word. "I don't want to go somewhere where you'll show me off like a prize pet." Panic laced her words.

Josie leaned against the door. "I don't understand, Cassie."

"You want people to think you're an amazing person. 'Look at me, I took in a kid whose parents didn't want her anymore.'"

There was the rub. "Your parents love you. You'll get letters soon."

"No, I won't. I haven't received one since I arrived."

"That doesn't mean they don't love you. Or that we feel like we have to keep you. We also don't want you here so we can show you off. You're Art's cousin, part of our family. We want you with us."

Cassandra's sobs vibrated through the door.

"Let me in. We don't have to go to the program. They'll understand. But you must talk to me."

They missed the program. Josie decided if it were important, there would be future opportunities. Instead, they walked the neighborhood, ending at the library. Miss Adelaide lit up when she saw them.

"My two favorite people in the world. I declare it's good to see the two of you. Where have you kept yourselves?"

Josie shook her head slightly. No need to go backward. "We're doing okay today. Miss Adelaide, how are things here?"

"I'm swamped. Tell me you'll stay and help." Miss Adelaide rested her chin on her steepled fingers. "I can tell the kids are back in school. They all need expert advice on class projects."

Cassandra seemed willing, so they spent a few hours at the library. Cassandra pitched in to help file the books and soon returned to her usual sunny mood. On their way home, Josie gave Cassandra a quarter and let her select some candy at the drugstore.

"Thank you for the sweets."

"You're welcome." If only life's challenges could be solved with a quarter and handful of sweets. Josie absently rubbed her stomach as they finished the walk home. Cassandra ran ahead of her and climbed the stairs to the apartment. Doris caught her eye as they walked by and her eyes softened. She pulled a handkerchief out of her housecoat pocket and pressed it into Josie's hand. Josie looked at the square of cloth, puzzled.

"Thank you, Doris, but why do I need this?"

"Check your cheeks, dear." Her smile seemed watery. "I'll be up in a moment."

Josie nodded, then mounted the last stairs. Each took more effort, and by the time she reached the apartment door, she felt like she couldn't breathe. She felt overwhelmed and didn't know whether to cry it out or stifle the tears. She pressed her hand to her mouth and stared at her wedding ring.

Her throat constricted, and she groped her way to the couch, where she collapsed. A sense of panic filled her. Where had this come from? By the time Doris let herself in, Josie wasn't sure she could breathe anymore.

Doris tsked as she took off her sweater and rummaged through the cupboards. "I'll make some tea."

Josie tried to nod through her tears. "What happened?" The words slipped between hiccups.

"I'm not 100 percent sure, but I think your grief is back."

Josie shook her head. "That can't be. I've been fine."

Doris slipped into the room and settled next to Josie on the couch. "The loss you've experienced comes and goes. Some days you won't cry because of your loss. Other days it will be all you can do to move. Today must be one of your sad days."

"But I was okay until, I don't know, it hit me."

Doris wrapped her in a hug while the tears flowed unchecked. Eventually, Josie became aware that Cassandra stood at the end of the room, fear cloaking her face. Doris followed Josie's gaze.

"Cassandra, how would you like to come downstairs with me and help me bake some cookies? Mr. Duncan keeps telling me he wants some snickerdoodles for the grocery, but I need some help. How about it?"

Cassandra looked from Josie to Doris and back. Josie pushed a watery smile on her face. "It's all right with me. I'll be here whenever you're done."

"Okay. I'd like to come help."

"Be back in time to finish homework."

Cassandra rolled her eyes in the way only children can. Then she skipped to her room and put on her shoes before following Doris down the stairs. Josie watched them leave, then moved to her room. She clutched a pillow across her stomach, as if bracing herself. She tried to identify what she felt the need to brace from, but couldn't. Instead, an unsettled feeling seeped in.

Something was about to change. And she didn't think it had anything to do with her baby. Whatever it was, she couldn't shake it.

She curled up on her bed. Tried to form a prayer. All that came out was, "Father, please help."

Chapter 17

Mrs. Wilson,

Would you please come to school to meet with me tomorrow? We need to discuss Cassandra.

Miss Taylor

J osie stared at the note she'd found under Cassandra's bed. It looked like it had fallen out of her bag and lain there forgotten for a week. Miss Taylor would think she was an uninvolved, uncaring foster parent. She rubbed a hand over the ache drilling her forehead. She wanted to believe the note meant they needed to discuss good things, but the tightness in her stomach warned that wasn't the case.

Each day that passed without word from home, Cassandra pulled further inside herself. While she'd never been the most outgoing child, she'd blossomed in the months since arriving. Now she'd retreated as if protecting herself.

Without letters from home, Cassandra feared the worst. Josie couldn't blame her. Since letters hadn't made it, Josie decided to take a proactive approach. She'd send a telegram and see if Annabelle could pass the word through her work.

Reaching the decision, Josie stood and changed out of her cleaning outfit into a nice dress. She carefully applied rouge and a touch of lipstick. Pulling on pumps and pinning on a hat, she grabbed her purse and headed out the door. Maybe she could catch Miss Taylor over lunch and explain she'd found the note today.

Josie walked the few blocks to the school. She entered the doors and wound through the halls to the fourth-grade classroom. When she peeked through the door, she found the room empty. Books were scattered across the surfaces of the desks, and the chalkboard was covered with division and multiplication problems.

What sounded like hundreds of feet pounded on the floor. Josie looked up to see a class headed her way. None of the children looked familiar until she spotted Cassandra, standing a head shorter than the other children, with the hint of a Mona Lisa smile teasing her features.

Miss Taylor led the way. A thin woman, she struck Josie as a person who enjoyed her charges. Maybe even delighted in her work.

A cautious smile curved Miss Taylor's lips. "Mrs. Wilson."

"Hello." Josie played with her purse straps. "I'm sorry I haven't stopped by earlier. I located the note this morning."

A light—could it be relief—flickered in Miss Taylor's eyes. "Let me get the class settled, and I'll have a minute."

"Thank you." Josie smiled at Cassandra as the children walked into the classroom. The girl avoided her eyes and shuffled after the other children. Josie leaned against the wall while she waited. She had to establish contact with Cassandra's family.

Father, give me insight into her heart. Show me what to do. And give me the same for Art. Something's happening there that I don't understand. She turned over her worries and fears while she waited.

Her eyes were closed when the door opened. Josie pushed off the wall and watched Miss Taylor.

"I've got a few minutes but will have to keep a watch on the students."

"Of course."

"Cassandra's struggling."

Josie nodded. "I've noticed the shadow of a change at home, too. Is she keeping up academically?"

"Yes. I'd move her up another grade, but she's struggling so with the children right now that I don't think it would be best for her."

"Could the problem be that she's not challenged?"

Miss Taylor shook her head. "She is a little girl who is afraid."

"Do you have any recommendations?" Josie nibbled on a nail.

"I'm not a social worker, but something has to happen. Cassandra's miserable. And we have to make a change. I'm concerned she's making enemies."

"Does she still refuse to say the Pledge?"

"No. She's just quiet, and that's okay." Miss Taylor shrugged. "We'll deal with that later. This is more important." Miss Taylor straightened her skirt and turned as if to go back in the classroom. "Maybe see if there are other evacuated children around here that she can get together with. Maybe knowing she's not alone will make a difference."

"Thank you," Josie whispered as Miss Taylor returned to her classroom.

Josie marched to the telegraph office and sent a message to Cassandra's parents, begging them to send some word to Cassie. She walked home and asked to use the phone. While she didn't like asking Annabelle for help—she'd helped raise Kat, after all, and that girl was turning out well—Josie knew she couldn't take care of this situation on her own.

The thought of Kat covered from head to toe in dirt but grinning so big her face just about cracked warmed Josie. Maybe Cassandra needed a good romp in a mud puddle. Art didn't seem to need much from Josie right now. She didn't have a baby. What she did have was an eight-year-old who'd retreated into a world of pain.

Josie dialed Annabelle's number and left a message. She spent the balance of the afternoon praying for Cassie. As soon as the girl got home, she ran to her room and slammed the door. Wails echoed through the apartment. Josie looked at the door, then approached it. She resisted asking what was wrong. Cassie's answer would be, "Nothing," but the slammed door said something else.

"Cassandra, I've got cookies and milk ready for you. Fresh from the oven."

Silence answered her.

"I'll bring some to you."

"Thank you." The muffled words sounded watery.

Josie went to the kitchen and brought a plate with several chocolate chip cookies and a tall glass of milk to Cassie's room. She opened the door. "Here you go, sweetie."

Cassandra looked at her with watery eyes. "Am I in trouble?"

"No. I want to help you. I'm so sorry you're not happy. Is there something I can do to help?"

Cassandra's chin quivered. "I want to go home. I want to see my mum and hug my grandmum."

"I wish I could do that for you."

"It was my birthday yesterday, and nobody knew."

A rock settled in Josie's stomach. How could she have forgotten to learn such an important date?

※

Art sat in the unexpected meeting, curious about why E. K. Fine had called it. His normal pattern was to head home as soon after noon as possible on Fridays. Instead, it was four thirty, and he'd called a full staff meeting of nonplant employees.

"Know what this is about, Art?" Stan plopped onto the chair next to him and crossed his legs and arms.

"No. I bet Charlie does."

Charlie laughed. "I don't have the pulse of the company like that. We'll learn together."

That worried Art. E.K. acting outside his normal patterns seemed a red flag. The guy didn't like to put in one extra minute of work. He enjoyed resting on the laurels of his father and grandfather. Maybe that's why Grandfather had adamantly refused to help Art, wanted to keep him from getting lazy on the money others accumulated.

More employees filtered in until there was standing room only. The air turned stale and hot. Art pulled at his shirt collar. Someone along the wall opened a couple windows, but even the crisp October air didn't help much. More ties and bow ties got loosened.

E.K. swaggered into the room, and Art sat straighter in his chair.

"Attention." The murmur of voices drowned out E.K. He clapped to little avail. Art whistled through his fingers. The piercing sound caused the conversations to die. "Thank you." E.K. placed his hands on the table in front of him. "I've called you here for a quick meeting. Our family has decided to sell this company." Murmuring rose from around the room. E.K. waved them down. "I am pleased to announce that we have a purchaser and a signed agreement. I wanted you to hear from me before rumors circulated. The Wilson Holding Company out of Dayton has acquired us."

Art could see E.K.'s mouth continue to move, but nothing registered. All he heard translated into static. Grandfather had bought the company? Why? The family had never done anything related to manufacturing musical instruments. It seemed far outside the investment parameters Grandfather had developed.

Art knew from working on the books things weren't as solid as E.K. wanted everyone to believe. But this? He tried to relax his shoulders, but he wanted to leave.

This could not be good news for him. Not when Grandfather had made it so clear he was not impressed with Art's choice of employer or position.

"It's my pleasure to introduce the man who will soon own this great company."

Art watched as Grandfather strode into the room. His suit was fully buttoned, and a precisely folded handkerchief was tucked in the pocket. With his silver hair and mahogany walking stick, Grandfather looked ready to take on anything the company could throw his way.

Art swallowed and wished he'd chosen a seat toward the back. There was no way Grandfather would overlook him. Nope. Grandfather located him immediately, his frown lightening a moment before returning.

"Good afternoon." Grandfather's rich voice filled the conference room. "My company is interested in this company because I see great potential here. It will be up to each of you to prove that you have the ability to contribute to its growth. I am not interested in employees who maintain the status quo." His stare bored through Art. "That will be all."

Grandfather turned on his heel and left the room. Art watched him leave. Why not stay long enough to say hi? There must be some event back in Dayton, though Grandfather would be hard-pressed to make it home in time for anything tonight.

E.K. clapped his hands. "That will be all."

Some people left the room as if they couldn't wait to leave. Others gathered in small groups around the periphery. Art remained in his seat until he felt a sharp jab in his ribs.

"What are you waiting for, Wilson? Let's get the weekend started." Stan waggled his eyebrows and made a drinking motion.

Some folks couldn't take no for an answer. "No, thanks. I've got some work to finish, and then it's home for me."

"I'll drink one for you." Stan strutted from the room.

Charlie shook his head as he watched the man leave. "Someday his behavior will catch up with him."

Much as Art might like to believe it, he had a feeling Stan was like a cat who always landed on his feet. "I've got to get a project wrapped up. See you next week."

Art stumbled into the office and sank into his chair. He laid his head against the back, eyes closed, as he tried to wipe fear from his mind. Grandfather had not bought the company just to put him on edge. No, Grandfather was a businessman who carefully investigated potential companies. He'd seen something that made the company look like a good investment, one that happened to employ Art.

Art looked at the stack of ledgers on his desk, then shook his head. No way his mind would focus enough to finish them accurately tonight. Time to go home and forget about work. He had to before he drove himself crazy trying to anticipate what Grandfather would do once he officially owned the company. Art grabbed his swagger coat and bolted from the office.

He needed some space. Grandfather had made it clear the last time they visited that he wanted Art to stand on his own two feet. How did buying the company Art worked for figure into that independence unless Grandfather wanted to teach him something?

Chapter 18

From the moment he walked in the door, Art had mumbled to himself and slammed doors. Josie watched, unsure what to do. He threw his briefcase on the floor, then tossed his coat across the back of the davenport. Tugging at his tie, he stomped to their bedroom.

Cassandra had yet to emerge from her room. Now this.

It would be another delightful evening in their home unless she could get to the bottom of what bothered Art. She determined to control what she could: her attitude. She'd start there and hope it spread throughout the apartment.

"*A mighty fortress is our God.*" She hummed the tune over and over, building to a crescendo before easing into a popular tune. Before long, she transitioned to another hymn. Peace and joy washed over her as she focused on her heavenly Father.

She inhaled. The rich scent of meatloaf and potatoes filled the air. She grabbed hot pads and pulled the pan from the oven. Soon the meatloaf, along with peas, baked potatoes, and bread waited on the table. Art still hadn't returned from the bedroom, so she finished setting the table. She lit a couple of tapers and watched the flames' reflections dance across the surface of the glasses. It had been awhile since she'd decorated the table with care like this, and she liked the effect. Once the meatloaf had a chance to set, she cut it.

Neither Art nor Cassandra exited their lairs based on the aroma, so she went after them. She knocked on Cassandra's door, then slipped it open. Cassandra lay curled on her side, doll tucked under her arm, mouth open as she slept. The girl's cheeks were puffy and streaked with wetness. The child must be exhausted to have fallen asleep already. Josie decided to let her sleep. She grabbed the blanket from the foot of the bed and pulled it over Cassandra.

Josie left the room and opened the door to her bedroom. Art sat on the edge of the bed, dress shirt off, head in his hands. Her heart raced at the sight.

"Art." She hurried to his side. "What's wrong?"

"I don't know for sure."

She frowned. That didn't make much sense. "Are you ill? Did you get fired?"

He kept answering no to her questions, but he wouldn't look at her.

"Art Wilson. You are scaring me. It's time for dinner. Cassandra's asleep, so we can talk over meatloaf." She tugged on his hands until he groaned and stood. She pulled a face. "My meatloaf's not that bad."

He laughed, the sound fractured and edgy, but an improvement. "Lead on, Mrs. Wilson."

"Thank you. I think I will after you put something on over your T-shirt."
Art complied, and they settled at the table. After Art said a quick grace, she
studied him. "What's happened?"

"I'm probably blowing everything out of proportion."

"It's easy to do."

"Grandfather's bought E. K. Fine Piano Company."

Josie's fork clattered to her plate. "Really? Why?"

"That precise question has worried me since I learned it late this afternoon.
Fine isn't the typical company Grandfather purchases. It's not a natural fit for his
portfolio." Art leaned over his plate. "All I can come up with is that he either wants
to monitor me or take this job away from me."

"Art Wilson, that is the craziest thing I've ever heard. Why would your
grandfather wish to see you jobless? He loves you and only wants what's best
for you."

"See, I know you're right, but another part of me—"

"He does care, you know. He shows it through pushing you to be your best.
That works for him."

"But it leaves me worried at times like this."

"You don't need to be. Why not give him the benefit of the doubt? Maybe
he investigated the company after learning you'd accepted the job. . .needed to
make sure it was good enough for you or something. Through that research, he
decided it needed someone who could improve the company. Maybe he wouldn't
normally take any notice, but because you work there, he did."

Art nodded, his fingers tracing the pattern in the tablecloth. "That makes
sense."

"So don't worry about it." Josie placed her hand over his, stilling its restless
motion. "Work hard for him. He'll be pleased." She squeezed, then released his
hand. The meat loaf smelled wonderful, and she served each of them a slice.

Art took a few bites. Josie let him eat in quiet, giving him the time to process
his concerns.

"Mrs. Wilson, you are a wonderful woman."

"I am?"

"Yes." Art scooted his plate back and stretched. "I'd like to take a walk, if you
don't mind."

Josie looked at the table. The dishes and cleanup would keep her busy for a
while. "That's fine with me. Remember, everything will be okay."

※

Art put his coat back on, then headed downstairs and out the door. He walked
with no destination in mind, letting the fresh air and exercise clear his head. He'd
never thought of himself as a fearful man, yet since the move to Cincinnati, he
seemed to keep one eye looking over his shoulder. He should be at ease, enjoying
every moment with his new bride. Instead, he detected her disappointment in
the way he didn't share every emotional valley with her over the loss of their baby.

She couldn't seem to understand he'd grieved and now looked to the future.

And now this wrinkle with Grandfather.

Art's thoughts roiled until he collapsed on a bench in Eden Park. The sky had darkened as he fought his fears. If only it felt like he'd conquered them.

God, help me. That was all he could manage. Over and over the phrase repeated in his mind.

It felt inadequate. He should craft sentences that would persuade God to shift the course of events into a vein that he liked. Instead, that one sentence repeated like a broken record bouncing through his mind, ricocheting off his fears.

He wrestled in the darkness till he felt wrung out.

Finally, he stumbled to his knees. *Father, take this weight from me. I beg You.*

Peace never really flooded. Instead, a trickle dripped over him, giving him the opportunity to choose. So he stood and marched back to his home. God was in control of all the details of his life. He'd released those burdens. It was time to live like the burdens were gone and the future firmly established in God's hand.

A strange car sat in front of the building when Art walked up, but he barely glanced at it.

His place was inside. Climbing the stairs, he slowed when he heard voices from the third floor. Who would be in his apartment at this hour? Then he made out the visiting voice.

The rich voice belonged to Grandfather. Art sucked in a breath, then squared his shoulders. He could recover from anything Grandfather had to throw at him. He'd graduated from college, paid for it on his own, acquired skills, used those skills successfully. He didn't know what else to do to make Grandfather proud of him.

He opened the door and waited for Grandfather to acknowledge him.

"Son." Grandfather nodded from his seat in the shell chair. He treated the seat as if it were his throne.

"Hello, Grandfather."

Josie perched on the edge of the davenport and looked from one to the other. "Your grandfather arrived awhile ago. I was making a pot of coffee. Would you like some, Art?" Her eyes pleaded with him to be nice.

"Yes, thank you." Art stood a moment, then stripped off his coat and settled on the davenport.

"Where's our cousin?" Grandfather barked.

Josie stepped into the doorway. "She fell asleep before dinner. I doubt we'll see her before breakfast. The school week tends to wear her out. They have her in an advanced grade, you see." Josie bit her lower lip in that adorable way she had when she was nervous and talking too much.

"Hmm. Is everything working out with her?"

"Josie has done a wonderful job with Cassandra. She and Cassie have developed a good relationship. We've got a few issues to iron out with school, but even those are improved."

"Glad to hear."

A plate clattered against the counter. Art placed his elbows on his knees and steepled his fingers. "I know you've got a long drive in front of you, Grandfather. What can I do for you?"

Grandfather sighed. "I'm interested in making superior instruments."

Art guffawed. Grandfather's brows knit together at the sound. "Sorry. That's not the answer I expected."

"Obviously."

"Your companies have always focused on consumer goods. Pianos are luxury items."

"Maybe. I think the company is poised to do interesting things or fall apart. Management will play a big role in that success or lack thereof. Consider this an opportunity to prove yourself."

Josie brought in a tray loaded with her china coffee service. "I'm sorry, but I wasn't sure how you liked your coffee."

"Black is fine."

She nodded, then filled two cups with the steaming liquid.

"I have a proposition for you." Grandpa took a sip, all the while looking over the edge of the cup at Art. "I'm buying your company. It's in dire need of visionary management. I think you could provide at least a part of that. But you have to want to. So here's what I suggest. You step up and generate ideas and leadership. Do so, and you can move into management."

Josie gasped, then slapped a hand over her mouth. "Art, that sounds like a great offer."

"I'll have a couple of my most trusted employees at the plant starting on Tuesday. You'll have one month to convince them you're ready to join them." Grandfather eyed him intently as if measuring him. "I'll tell you my decision on Thanksgiving."

"All right. I accept your challenge."

Grandfather gave an approving nod. "That's my boy. Give this challenge everything you've got. I think you're ready to succeed. Wouldn't be here if I thought anything else. I'll see myself out."

Art stood and offered a hand, but Grandfather wrapped him in a quick hug. "Josephine."

"Good night, Grandfather."

After Grandfather left, Art stood by the window. He watched the man climb into the backseat of his vehicle. The chauffeur Art hadn't noticed when he walked up started the car and drove away. Grandfather's challenge echoed through his mind. *Be management-ready in four weeks.* As he considered all that Grandfather expected of his team, Art knew he couldn't prepare in such a short period.

As always, Grandfather had set him up with a chance to prove himself.

Ultimately, as with most challenges Grandfather issued, he had no choice. Sink or swim. Thrive or fail. Grandfather didn't care which.

Chapter 19

Sunday morning, Josie got Cassandra ready for church while Art scrambled eggs. The morning felt relaxed as they ate breakfast and brushed teeth, then pulled on light coats.

Josie inhaled deeply as they stepped outside. The air felt crisp, the kind of day that made Josie think of apple pie with crumb topping. She could almost smell cinnamon in the air. Art linked his arm through hers, and they walked to church. Doris and Scott stood on the steps, greeting people. Cassandra ran to Doris for a hug, and Josie smiled at the sight. No, the child wasn't with her family, but they'd crafted a community for her here in Cincinnati.

The organist played a prelude as Art led them to seats in the back. Josie soaked in the music and the peace. The sweet sense of God's presence stayed with her through the hymns and into the sermon. Art shifted next to her. What brought her peace seemed to agitate him that morning.

After lunch, Art stomped around the apartment while Cassandra curled on the davenport, ignoring him with her nose buried in a book. Lucy Maud Montgomery's tales of Anne of Green Gables had captured the girl's imagination. Josie was glad to see the child engrossed.

"Art, please stop pacing. You're going to worry Doris." Josie blew a curl out of her eyes. "Trust me, you don't want her up here. She's tenacious when she thinks there's a problem." She'd meant the words to tease.

He clomped to a stop. "I don't need you telling me what I do wrong." He turned away, muttering, "I get enough of that at work."

Josie sank into a chair at the dining room table. "I'm sorry. I didn't mean it that way. Want to tell me about work? I tend to assume everything's fine since you don't mention it much."

Art looked at Cassandra, then at Josie. "Can we take a walk?"

"Yes, I'll just knock on Doris's door on our way out. Cassie, we're going outside for a bit. Let Mrs. Duncan know if you need anything, okay?"

The girl nodded, never pulling her nose from the book.

Instead of keeping an eye on the door for Cassandra, Doris headed toward the stairs. "I can relax up there just as well as down here. Go enjoy this beautiful day."

"Thank you. We won't be too long."

"Take your time. There's no rush."

Josie hugged Doris, then followed Art down the stairs. His long stride left her stretching to keep up. After a block, she stopped. Art continued a few feet before he turned.

"What?"

"Wondering if you'd like to slow your steps so I can keep up." Josie smiled at him. "I'd love to walk with you but don't feel up for a run."

A sheepish look cloaked Art's face. "I'm sorry, Josie. Guess I let my thoughts push me." He walked back to her and offered his hand. "Would you like to walk with me?"

Josie held her tongue as they walked another block. She'd learned Art sometimes needed to process what he thought before sharing it. This seemed one of those times. She prayed for him—prayed that God would shower him with peace and wisdom, that whatever bothered him would fall into proper perspective.

Art ran his fingers through his closely cropped hair. "Things are changing at the company. Each day I'm under scrutiny."

"Why do you think that?"

"Grandfather's spies are everywhere, but it's impossible to know what I do that pleases or upsets Grandfather."

"He loves you, Art."

"Probably, but he's always insisted I stand on my own. That was easier to do when he was at a distance. Now he's there. At my job. It's almost enough to make me hunt for a new position."

"You could."

"But I can't surrender before I try. I have to prove I am capable. I can succeed."

"You don't have to prove it to me. I know you're a wonderful man. I wouldn't have married you otherwise." Josie watched him carefully. "Tell me what happened this week."

"One of Grandfather's watchers found a problem with the corporate books."

That could be bad. "Was it your work?"

"No. Several entries made over the months before we arrived. But I didn't find them. Didn't think to look for them. Grandfather will say I'm too trusting. Don't have the bull-dogged determination it takes."

Josie wanted to kiss the lines from his face. Remind him how very much she loved him. "I love you, Mr. Wilson."

He squeezed her hand. "I love you, too."

At the end of the block, they turned to head back to the apartment. Art looked more relaxed, though Josie couldn't pinpoint why. Maybe the act of sharing the burden was enough.

The next morning after Art had left for work and Cassandra was ensconced at school, Annabelle stopped by the apartment. Her sleek blond hair bobbed at her chin, and her tailored clothing had a Katherine Hepburn style. Josie tucked loose strands of hair behind her ears and wished she'd taken a few more minutes on her appearance before the social worker arrived.

"Has Cassandra improved?" Annabelle leaned forward in her seat, gaze locked on Josie.

"We still haven't heard from her family. Cassandra is doing well in school, and keeps her chin up most of the time. But there are times, usually at night, where she thinks about them and worries. I'd hoped you would hear something. Our wire didn't produce anything. Do you have word or another idea on how to reach them? Is there anything we can do to find out if they're safe? I think the not knowing is what bothers her."

Annabelle made a note. "I'll keep trying. I'm not surprised she's homesick. These kids have been taken from their homes and sent too far away. The Battle of Britain is too intense to send them home, though. Then we've got parents like Cassandra's whom we can't locate."

"Does that mean something's happened to them?" Josie didn't think Cassandra could handle that. What child could?

"Oh no. It just means war conditions are in place. I bet we'll hear from them soon, and Cassandra's fears will be quieted." Annabelle flipped a page in the file. "How's she doing making friends?"

"Cassie is a delight with adults. She's showering hugs and seems attached to more than Art and me. But she's isolated at school. She still won't say the Pledge, which doesn't help. It reminds the others that she's different each day, beyond the accent." The teakettle whistled, and Josie jumped up from the davenport. "Would you like some tea?"

"Yes, please." Annabelle didn't look up from her file, where she wrote notes. Josie wished she could see the words.

She slipped into the kitchen and pulled the tea together. Annabelle hadn't come to find fault with them. So why did it feel like the social worker could decide this placement had failed and take Cassandra from them? Her fears were running wild again. This child had entered her family, and Josie needed her. The corner of her heart ready to mother loved caring for Cassandra. And without the girl, the grief might explode again. A shudder coursed through Josie at the thought.

Now was not the time to allow the grief to well up again. After Annabelle left, Josie could fall on her face and beg God for answers. She should have done that first. Annabelle might have ideas, but God would have the perfect solution.

Josie loaded a tray with her grandmother's china teapot, two porcelain teacups, and a plate of snickerdoodles she'd baked with Cassandra that weekend. "Do you like sugar with your tea?"

"Yes, and cream, too, please."

"Ah, you like it the British way."

"I suppose all the time with the evacuees has influenced my tastes."

Josie poured a cup for each of them, adding cream to Annabelle's, then settled back on the couch. "Annabelle, I would like any suggestions you have. Cassandra means too much to me to not do everything I can to help her."

"Could you bring her to Canton for a weekend? Maybe having her around other children from back home would help."

"I'll have to talk to Art about that. It's such a long drive." Josie chewed on a fingernail as she considered the logistics. "We can talk and see if that's something Cassandra would like."

"There are certain times when the Hoover Company has planned excursions for the children. I'll let you know when those come up. I'm sure they wouldn't mind adding Cassandra to the mix." Annabelle blew on her tea before taking a sip. "As long as she's happy here, we're fine. And it sounds like she's doing well overall. On school, see if there's a girl or two she'd like to have over after school. Help facilitate that relationship. It could make a world of difference for her to feel like she has a few friends. I'm sure several of the girls think she's practically exotic coming from overseas."

"Thank you." As the social worker gathered her things and left, Josie felt a surge of energy. Time to help Cassandra make the last transition and find friends her age.

Josie fell to her knees beside the couch. *Father, help me focus on things that will make a difference to Cassandra. I want to be someone You can use in her life. Grant me insight into her heart and thoughts.* Her prayers flowed for a long time until she felt release. Then they shifted to Art and his job.

When she stood, she brushed tears from her face and headed to the kitchen. Time to show Cassandra how much she cared for her.

Minutes before Cassandra would walk in the door from school, Josie pulled a pan of fresh cookies out of the oven. As a child, she'd loved walking into a home that smelled of baking and sitting down to a tall glass of milk and Mother's latest creation. Mark, Kat, and she had often fought over who got the last cookie, with Mark winning. Maybe Cassandra needed the same opportunity to unwind from the stress of school. And it didn't matter that they'd just made cookies that weekend. There was something in the aroma of cookies that helped one unwind.

Maybe during that time, Josie could help steer Cassandra toward appropriate actions.

Dirt and wetness streaked Cassandra's cheeks and clothes when she walked in the door.

"What happened?"

Cassandra tried to walk past her, but Josie stopped her. She placed a hand on Cassandra's cheek and brushed at the grime. "I need to know what happened."

"Nothing." Her shoulders slumped, but anger or tears tinged Cassandra's words. Josie studied her but couldn't tell which caused the veneer surrounding the child.

"Cassie, 'nothing' is not an answer. Something happened, and you need to tell me."

"You're not my mother." Cassandra stomped her foot. Okay, so it was anger in her voice.

"If it involves you, I need to know. Especially since it involves school." Josie put an arm around Cassandra and led her stiff form to the table. "And you're going to do it while we eat fresh cookies and drink some milk."

Cassandra's edges softened. She let Josie lead her, then took a bite of the cookie. Before Josie could stop her, she inhaled four more cookies. The poor child acted like she hadn't eaten a meal in days.

"Did you not like lunch today?" She'd packed a simple lunch of a peanut butter sandwich, apple, and a cupcake.

Cassandra's chin quivered. "I don't know."

"Why not?" Josie feared she knew the answer before she heard it.

"Somebody took it from me." A tear streaked its way through the grime on her cheek.

"Has this happened before?"

Cassandra nodded. "He told me he'd beat me up if I told. Then today, he pushed me on the way home. I scraped my knee." Cassandra held up her knee, and Josie leaned in to kiss it.

"Oh, Cassie. I'm so sorry. Has he pushed you before?"

Cassandra shook her head.

"Good. Did you eat at school at all this week?"

Heat spiraled through Josie's body as the child shook her head. No wonder she'd had some trouble. She hadn't eaten lunch in who knew how long. This she could handle.

"Okay. I'll go to school with you tomorrow and talk to Miss Taylor." Cassandra's eyes got big as saucers. "Don't worry. I won't make you say who is doing this to you, though I'd certainly like to. You shouldn't be bullied."

"If it's not me, it'll be one of the smaller children."

Josie eyed Cassandra. How a child that petite could be concerned about smaller children! "Why did this boy start picking on you?"

"I wanted to play kickball with the boys in the class. He said I couldn't, but others let me on a team. I beat him." She shrugged. "I guess he's not used to losing."

Josie had to stifle a smile. Yet another way Cassandra mirrored Kat.

When Art arrived home an hour later, Cassandra still sat at the table with Josie, working on a puzzle. Josie hadn't wanted to leave the table when Cassandra settled in to spend time with her. Josie scrambled out of her chair. "I'm sorry, Art. I haven't started dinner."

Chapter 20

S o this was what it felt like to have one's future completely outside their control. Art wrestled with the eighty-pound weight that dogged his steps. Most days he could leave it outside the door when he came home. Today, it followed him inside.

The sight of Josie and Cassandra working a puzzle on the table eased the burden.

"How was your day?" Josie's smile warmed his heart.

"Another day at the office."

Cassandra looked up, puzzle piece held in one hand. "Dad used to say that all the time. Before the war."

Art rumpled her curls. "He'll say it again after the British sweep the Germans back behind their borders."

She frowned at him. "Don't lie to me."

"I didn't mean to." When did she become a little adult? "Anyway, I'm starved. What will you ladies prepare?"

"Grilled cheese and soup. Simple is the order of the day." Josie pushed back from the table but laid another piece in the puzzle as she stood. "I think this may yet shape into something. Cassandra, what's your guess?"

Cassandra eyed the misshapen image. So many gaps remained, Art wondered that she even attempted to determine how it would look.

"The Statute of Liberty?"

Art studied the lines of blues and slashes of gray. Maybe she had it.

"Great guess. I told you we'd get there." Josie pulled the puzzle box lid from under her chair. "Maybe this will help us after all."

"Will you help me, Art?" Cassandra's soft brown eyes pleaded with him.

How could he say no?

He settled at the table and watched her a moment.

"You have to do more than watch."

"Of course. But you have to show me the box. I can't do it without a picture. Not the prize puzzle-maker you are."

She laughed and handed it to Art. "Don't show me."

"All right." He studied the photo of the Statute of Liberty and groaned. The colors were so similar. "I have to warn you, I'm terrible at puzzles. Always mess them up."

"How?" She looked as if she didn't believe him.

"Putting the wrong pieces together. My mother always accused me of forcing pieces to match that weren't supposed to." He picked up a red piece and crammed it next to a light blue one.

"Now I see." Cassandra separated the pieces. "Maybe you should watch."

Josie's soft chuckle tickled his ear. He looked up to find her standing next to his chair with a plate of food. "Here are some appetizers for the puzzle-piecers."

"Thanks. I think Cassandra's right." He jammed another couple of pieces together. "My role may be to cheer her on."

"No. I think you should sort them all by color." A mischievous light filled Cassandra's eyes. As he considered the mishmash of pieces, he understood why. It would take someone a year to sort the tiny pieces into the correct piles.

He tweaked her nose, and she squealed.

❋

"So what's with the old man?" Stan rolled his chair closer to Art's desk.

Art tried to ignore Stan and the fact Grandfather strolled the halls of E. K. Fine Piano Company again today. Didn't he have a dozen other companies to run?

"Didn't mean to get you all worked up with that question." Stan put his hand up, palm out, in front of him. "I'll head on back to my desk. My ledgers." His chair wheels squeaked in protest.

After a deep breath, Art pinched his nose and tried to think. He grabbed his mug and took a gulp, then sputtered as the steamy bitter liquid burned his tongue and throat.

Charlie glanced up from the work spread on top of his desk. "You okay?"

Art shook his head as he tried to breathe. Charlie jumped up to help, and Art held up a hand to stop him. "Scorched my mouth."

"All right?"

"I will be." Art set the mug down and watched Grandfather enter the office. "Why do you think he's here again?"

"Determining whether you're ready for more."

Stan snorted. "And pianos are perfectly matched to his investment strategy."

"I don't know. Grandfather usually leaves tours to others." But his grandson didn't work at other companies.

"Here comes the big cheese." Stan sounded a little too chipper. What did he have up his sleeve?

"Good morning, gentlemen." Grandfather's gaze stopped on Art and a faint smile tweaked his face. Art felt Charlie watching him with questions growing by the moment. Grandfather allowed E.K. to introduce him to a few employees. He stopped at Art's desk. "Art. How are Josie and Cassandra?"

"Fine, sir."

"Good. I'll be back after the tour."

It took effort to force his thoughts to the task the company paid him to do, but he eventually marshaled his mind to the streams of data. Soon he was immersed in the numbers, sorting out and anticipating problems.

A shadow fell over his desk and he looked up. Grandfather stood over him.

"I'd like a word with you." While phrased as a request, Grandfather left no question this was not an offer Art could avoid.

"I can take a short break."

Grandfather leaned on his cane a bit as they walked down the hall and into a vacant office. "Sit."

Art sank on the edge of a chair as Grandfather stood over him. "My sources have told me about the projects you're working on. You've done well, but you could do more."

"I haven't been here a year." Art clamped his mouth shut.

"Art, you have the potential to be more than a bookkeeper, but you have to think and act like a manager."

Art wiped a hand over his face. "I expect that will take time. I know I'm new. I'm learning all I can and hope to be promoted in time."

"Humor me. Show me what you can do. Not everyone is willing to work. But that's what's needed to stand out." Grandfather leaned forward. "You got that fancy college education. Put it to work. And not simply by making sure numbers are in the correct column. There's much more you could do."

Art caught the challenge in his grandfather's eyes. "All right. What do you expect?"

"To see how far you'll push yourself. How hard you'll work. Instincts. . .they can't be taught."

Art couldn't make heads or tails out of the innuendo Grandfather expected him to understand. But he saw the challenge and was ready to tackle it. He'd work hard, show Grandfather what he'd learned. And someday, he'd move up.

※

Josie looked at the invitation. With a flick of her wrist, she added a flower to the corner. There. Now it looked perfect.

She'd grown tired of the feeling she couldn't help Art with his job, so she'd decided to do something about it. Charlie's wife, Diane, had jumped in to help her compile a list of the wives of the managers and others in Art's department. Josie thought a tea would serve as an opportunity to get to know them and learn more about the company. While Art had worked there for almost a year, Josie didn't know much about it at all. Now, family owned the company.

She looked at the stack of envelopes and felt excited. She'd loved helping Mama with faculty parties. She should have done this before.

Cassandra and her new friend from school, Ruth, helped her bake cookies and tarts the day before the tea. By the time they finished, Cassandra and Ruth were covered in flour, and the kitchen rang with laughter. The day of the tea, Josie spent the morning making petite egg salad sandwiches. Cucumber would have finished the table, but the season had passed. When Diane arrived an hour before the event, she arranged the treats artfully on plates.

The table didn't look right without Mama's Wedgwood china, but her simple dishes would have to do. Hopefully, the women would come for the chance to get out of the house and meet others rather than to inspect her possessions.

As the clock ticked closer to two o'clock, the butterflies took up residence in her stomach. She pressed a hand against it and moaned.

"Are you okay, Josie?" Diane looked at her, brow crinkled.

"I will be once everybody gets here."

"Even if it's a few, it will be a great start. No one's done anything like this before."

"Leave it to me to lead the way." Ugh, nausea boiled in her throat.

A light knock echoed off the door. Josie hurried to open it. A prim-looking woman in a broad-banded hat stood on the landing. "Are you Mrs. Wilson?"

Josephine smiled and extended her hand. "I am. Please come in." The woman handed over her raincoat. Josie took it and gestured to her petite friend. "This is Diane Sloan."

"Pleased to meet you both." Her gray curls bobbed against the back of her neck.

Josephine opened her mouth to ask who the first woman was, when heels clicked against the stairs. She turned to find a haggard-looking woman huffing to the top of the stairs. "Stars and garters, you should warn a soul about how many stairs there are to climb." She leaned against the doorframe and fanned her face. "I'll think twice about coming again."

The first woman waved a hand in the air as if brushing a snowflake from her nose. "Don't worry about Melanie. She tends toward the dramatic."

"Josie, this fine woman is Mrs. Jonathan Allen." Diane smiled sweetly at the gray-haired woman. "And Melanie is Mrs. Josiah Trumble."

Melanie frowned at Mrs. Allen. "If I tend on the dramatic, she lands toward the cold side of things."

Josie gasped. Had Melanie really insulted her guest? This tea time would implode before it even got underway. She closed her mouth and gestured toward the sitting area. If the verbal sparring continued like this, the apartment wasn't big enough to contain everyone. "Why don't you have a seat? Can I take anyone else's coat?"

With the ease of a woman fully content in her own skin, Diane settled nerves and eased the conversation into politer veins while Josie pulled the teakettle toward the hotter part of the stove. Three more women joined them in time for the tea and treats. While the women filled their plates, Josie pulled Diane to the side.

"Remind me how each woman fits into the company."

"Mrs. Allen is the wife of the vice president. Mr. Allen is a second cousin to the Fine family. Mrs. Trumble's husband is new. He may have come with the new buyer." Diane spoke discretely, smiling serenely the entire time. "Then there's our husbands."

"I think I know what they do."

"Your challenge will be to keep Mrs. Allen happy. Rumor has it, she has the ear of her husband, and he does as he's told."

Josie threw a lemon tea cookie and tiny biscuit sandwich on her plate. The spicy mustard tickled her taste buds, and she hoped it did the same for the others. Quiet murmurs filled the edges of the room as the women enjoyed the snacks. After a bit, the women focused on Josie.

"Why did you invite us over?" Mrs. Allen's tone was light, but an edge carved through the air between them.

"I thought it would be nice to meet all of you. Our husbands work together, after all." A series of blank faces stared back at her. Was it so hard to believe she wanted to meet them? Diane gestured for her to continue. Josie swallowed. She had a good idea. Doris had loved it and encouraged her to take on the project. Surely these women would agree.

"Cat got your tongue?" Melanie squinted at her.

"What? Um, no. Actually, I had an idea." Several women leaned away from her as if to get as far from her as possible. Josie cleared her throat. "A church in this part of town provides relief to many of the city's poor." A couple of the ladies wrinkled their noses. "Many children receive help through meals. But I thought it would be wonderful if we helped by taking on the project of ensuring each of those children receives a Christmas present and stocking."

Mrs. Allen snorted. "That's their parents' responsibility."

"Not if the parents don't have jobs."

A younger woman raised her hand. "I actually think it's a good idea. It would be fun to shop for children."

"And whose money will you use?" Mrs. Allen looked down her nose at the woman. "It doesn't sprout from the ground."

Josie tried to smile around the lump in her throat. "Art and I could contribute a bit, and I think others would, too."

Diane brought a plate of cookies around. "I've already talked to several friends from my church who would like to contribute. The children won't expect anything extravagant, after all."

"You may waste your time if you choose. However, I have other ways to waste my time." Mrs. Allen stood, back ramrod straight. "I'll take my wrap."

Josie scurried to get it for her, then watched in shock as she swept from the apartment. In quick succession, the others left. She stared after them. "What just happened?"

Chapter 21

The threat of snow hung in the air as heavy gray clouds coated the sky. Art pulled the collar of his coat around his throat as he walked to the plant. The first week of November wasn't too early for the first snowstorm, but he wouldn't mind if it delayed. The wind whistled a desolate tune that matched his mood.

The uncertainty at E. K. Fine Piano Company had lessened as Grandfather's managers had stepped in and Fine eased out. The transition should be complete by the new year. Not a moment too soon. Word had leaked he was related to Grandfather. With that came the expectation he knew Grandfather's plans. Nobody believed him when he denied it. If anything, common opinion had evolved to the point his colleagues thought him part of any problem that arose.

He stumbled into the building and shook his coat off. After he hung it on its hook, he sat at his desk. Grandfather might think he should do more than work with numbers, but he really liked it.

E.K. bustled through the door. "A word with you, Mr. Wilson."

Art stifled a groan. He didn't have the reserves to deal with E.K. III before a cup of coffee. He bit his tongue and began to stand. "Certainly."

After a glance around the office, he motioned Art back into his seat. "This won't take long. Some concerns have been raised about the job you're doing."

"I don't understand."

"You're placed on probation."

Art's jaw dropped. "Why?"

"Call it one of my last decisions as president of this company."

Charlie slid into the room and eyed Art.

Fine looked at Charlie then turned back to Art. "I'd encourage you to put your full effort into your position. And tell your wife to leave the other women alone."

"What?" Josie had seemed a bit upset after her tea party last week, but she hadn't said much to him about it.

"She set off Mrs. Allen. Not a wise thing to do."

This time Art couldn't stifle his groan. Of all the women to annoy, Mrs. Allen, wife of the vice president, was a doozy of a choice. "Yes, sir."

"That'll be all." E.K. practically clicked his heels together and scurried from the room.

Charlie leaned back in his chair. "What was that about?"

"Josie's little party." He ground his teeth. "Seems she forgot to tell me the full story."

"Diane didn't mention anything out of the ordinary."

"Hmph." Art couldn't wait to let Josie know that her little party had placed him on probation. What would happen to them if he lost his job? And what about Cassandra? Would she be sent to another home? He couldn't imagine Josie's reaction if she lost the child.

Art's frustration simmered below the surface throughout the day. By the time he reached the grocery, he was ready to boil. *Lord, help me keep my temper in check.* He'd need all the help he could get on that front.

The grocery stood empty, so Art walked through it to the stairs. Cassandra sat on the stairs with a book. She half smiled at him when she saw him. Her tangled curls framed her face, and her dress could use an iron, but she looked content.

"What are you doing out here?"

"Waiting for you, Art." She clutched an envelope in her lap.

A spark of warmth spread through him. "Do I spy a letter? Is it from home?"

She smiled, revealing a gap between her teeth. "It's from my mum. She says everyone's fine." A frown threatened to darken her face. "Though the letter's three weeks old."

"But at least you received one."

"Yes, sir. Oh, Josie wanted to warn you she didn't try to start the kitchen on fire."

Art took a second look at Cassandra. The child seemed completely sincere in her statement. He bolted up the stairs. As he climbed, whiffs of smoke hung in the air. He waved a hand in front of his face.

"Josie?"

"Here." The muffled sound drifted from the kitchen. He laughed when he saw her. She'd tied a towel around her nose and mouth and looked like she wanted to join Butch Cassidy's gang.

"What happened?"

She tried to wave like nothing much, but tears streamed from her eyes. "Bacon got away from me."

He rushed to her side and grabbed her face between his hands. He turned her head from side to side as he examined what he could see of her face. "Are you okay?"

"Feeling foolish. I should be able to cook bacon without this happening." She sucked in a deep breath, then started coughing.

A surge of relief relaxed muscles he hadn't realized were tense. "What if I lost you?" He pulled her close and removed the towel from her face. He leaned down and claimed her mouth with a kiss. She sighed against him. "Please be careful."

Josie relaxed against him a moment, then pushed away. "To think all I wanted to do was make supper."

He settled at the table and watched her work. "I need to ask you something."

"What?"

"What happened at your tea party?"

"Nothing. Mrs. Allen got offended or upset when I mentioned it would be a great idea if we all got behind a drive for less fortunate children." Josie shrugged. "I think some of the others liked the idea, but they quickly followed her lead. Diane and I may try it on our own."

Art scratched his head. He couldn't see the problem in that.

"What's wrong?" Josie eyed him as if trying to decipher what weighed him down.

"E.K. placed me on probation today."

Josie covered her mouth. "Why?"

"Something about being unsure I could do my job, and my wife upsetting Mrs. Allen."

She crumpled in front of him. "I am so sorry, Art." She looked crushed. "I only wanted to help. I didn't know how to help, but my mom always has social gatherings like that for the wives of dad's colleagues."

He put a finger on her lips, and she stilled. In the face of her panic, his frustration seemed so petty. He could understand the urge to do something and not getting it quite right. "It's okay. We'll figure this out."

"What will we do?"

"Not panic. I haven't lost my job. I shouldn't, either."

"But why would your grandfather even let them threaten probation?" Tears streaked Josie's cheeks, giving her the appearance of a child.

"I don't know." He led her to the couch, then pulled her into his embrace.

※

Footsteps echoed off the stairs, and Josie turned to find Cassandra standing in the doorway.

"Are you okay, Josie?" The girl rushed to her side, fear causing her pupils to dilate.

Josie swiped the tears from her face. "Of course." At the child's dubious look, Josie chucked her under the chin and smiled. "Would you help me with dinner?"

The child bobbed to her feet. "Grilled cheese?"

She looked at Art, who shrugged. "Grilled cheese it is."

After dinner, Cassandra pulled out the checkerboard. "Play a game with me?"

"Absolutely. Hope you're ready to lose." Art struck a pose, shaking both fists in the air like he'd already won the round. Cassandra rolled her eyes.

"Last time, I took all your pieces."

"Luck, that's all it was."

Cassandra shook her head. "I'm happy to show you how real checkers are played."

Josie loved the nine-year-old's poise and spunk. She watched Cassandra teach Art a thing or two about strategy. This same spirit translated at school where she'd made a couple of friends in addition to Ruth.

After several games where Cassandra trounced him, Josie looked at the clock. "Off to bed, young lady. You still have school in the morning."

Cassandra groaned before leaving to brush her teeth and change.

"She's blossoming."

Warmth flooded Josie. "I think we've hit on what she needs. The freedom to be scared for her family, but also distractions to keep her from living there."

The week passed, and Josie knew she should heed her own advice. She should have had her baby about this time. As the day approached, the grief that had been lulled to sleep reared its ugly head at random times. She'd feel delight watching Cassandra or talking with Art, then be blindsided by sadness and at times anger.

Her arms ached from their emptiness. And she felt alone in that pain. Doris tried to ease it, but Josie didn't want Doris to understand. She needed Art to understand.

Art pulled her next to him on the davenport. "Want to talk about it?"

"It's complex."

"Most things are."

"I miss our baby." A tear trickled down her cheek, and Art brushed it away. "I'm back to wondering. Why did it happen? Why didn't God prevent it?"

"I wish I had answers for you, Josie."

"I just need to know that you miss the baby, too."

Art wrapped her in his arms. "Not the way you do, but I do. I wonder what he would have looked like, but it's different."

Josie nodded.

"Somehow, God will turn it into something good."

"I know. But it's hard to see that right now. Every time I open the Bible, His promises leap off the page. He collects my tears. He promises to turn what the enemy intended for evil to good." She shuddered. "But my arms are still empty."

"Then fill them with Cassandra and me."

Josie longed to be like Joseph. To be able to look at her heartbreak and see how God had turned it into a wonderful thing. Instead, she felt broken and empty. But Art stood next to her. Her promise to him was worth keeping with every fiber of her being.

In sickness and in health. In good times and in bad. She was committed to Art for the rest of her life. And she would live that love.

Chapter 22

The vocals of Fred Astaire singing "The Way You Look Tonight" swept into the room from the radio. Quivers ran through Josie as she sat at her vanity. She wanted Art to feel about her the way Lucky Garnett had felt about Penny. . .until he noticed her hair filled with suds.

Her reflection bounced off the mirror. She couldn't find fault with it, but a seriousness filled the edges of her face that hadn't touched her when she'd married Art a year earlier.

One year.

So much had changed. She'd experienced a sadness she'd never known. At times, her breath still caught at the thought of what should have been. But God was God, and she had to trust Him. Trust that He had her best at heart. This year, she'd made the decision to live that trust.

But joy had also filled the year. The joy of knowing the love of a good man. She still didn't know how to describe it other than to thank God for him from a grateful heart.

Art was a gift. She certainly didn't understand him yet. But he balanced her in ways she hadn't expected.

She pinched her cheeks, trying to encourage color to bloom on them. He'd be home in a few minutes, and then they would celebrate their anniversary. Cassandra had already gone down to Scott and Doris's apartment, where she would spend the night.

Art had told Josie to dress up, though he wouldn't tell her where he'd made reservations. The long rose gown in taffeta with its bolero jacket looked like something Ginger Rogers would wear in a formal dance scene. Was that what he had in mind?

The door squeaked. She jumped. That must be Art.

"Honey, I'm home."

Time was up. She pulled the dress over her slip and zipped it as he walked into the room. The sight of her working at the zipper brought a smile to Art's face, the kind of smile that warmed her from the inside out.

"Need any help with that?" The twinkle in his eye conveyed his meaning.

"Oh no. I very much want to see this place where you've got reservations."

"We'll have the best seat in the house."

Something about the way he said it made her a bit nervous. "Am I overdressed?"

Art eyed her up and down. He motioned for her to turn in a circle. She

116

complied, then dipped for a curtsy. "I'd say you're perfect."

His approval brought warmth flooding into her cheeks. How she loved this man.

※

Josie looked so appealing with the color flooding her face. He loved the way he could make her blush with a look or a whispered comment.

Would she be pleased when she saw what he had planned? He hoped so. The key was to make the evening memorable in every way. A night she would never forget.

His plan should accomplish that. Her thoughts? Well, he'd have to wait and see.

He looked at his watch. "Ready to go?"

Josie plopped at her little table and frowned at him from the mirror. "Do I look ready?"

How to answer that? She always looked good to him. Even when she lay in bed, rumpled from a hard night's sleep, hair plastered to her face, and sleep softening her expression. But how to explain that she was beautiful because she had chosen him?

Laughter filled her eyes. "Give me a few minutes, and I'll be ready." She picked up her brush and made a motion like she would swat him if he didn't leave. He could take a hint.

The sight of her in her gown should have woken him up. Instead, he felt half asleep and lethargic. Some cold water might do the trick. He turned on the tap in the bathroom and let it run a minute. He scooped water up with both hands and threw it on his face. The blast woke him up but splattered all over his shirt. Not the brightest thing he'd ever done.

He had an excuse, though. It was Friday, and the week had worn him out. The day had taken so many twists and turns at work, he didn't know which way to turn next. E. K. Fine still had clear thoughts on where he wanted the company to go. How it should prepare for the war. He couldn't seem to let go of the company he'd sold. In a few weeks, he'd be gone, but he made life difficult for everyone as he loudly proclaimed his beliefs—beliefs directly opposed to Grandfather's. Art stood in the middle, pulled by both sides of the debate.

A buzzing filled his ears at the thought of the intense argument he'd overheard.

He shook his head. Tonight was not a night to dwell on what happened at work. He could do nothing about that, but he could focus on his bride. She deserved his complete attention.

As she walked out of their room to meet him, he couldn't take his eyes off her. Dressed like that, she deserved his full focus. She'd done something with her hair that made it sweep off her graceful neck. He didn't know what to call it, but he liked it. All she needed was a rose at her ear to be picture perfect. He wanted to smack himself on the forehead. He should have thought of that. What woman didn't like flowers for her anniversary? He certainly couldn't find them in the crisp weather outside. Maybe she wouldn't notice his oversight.

"Shall we?" He offered his arm. He pulled her closer and inhaled the sweet scent of her violet perfume. He could come home to this for the rest of his life. He was blessed among men.

Squeals erupted from the Duncans' apartment as they descended the stairs. He loved seeing Cassandra happy, with a smile that lit up her eyes.

"She's happy, isn't she?" Contentment laced Josie's voice.

Art tucked her arm more firmly through his. "She is, thanks to you."

"I'm just grateful God gave me insight." She sighed. "I wish I'd asked sooner."

Wasn't that the case with so much of life? Art would struggle and wrestle with a problem for days, weeks, or even months on his own. Then he'd hit a point where he knew he couldn't fix or solve it on his own. Finally, he'd acknowledge he needed God's help. What a mixed-up way to approach life.

Art helped Josie into the Packard and then raced around to the driver's side. Quiet conversation floated between them, but Josie never asked where he was taking her. She seemed content to let him surprise her.

This had to be perfect.

He so wanted to honor her tonight. Let her know that he knew what this year had been for her. Show her in a way that he couldn't convey with words.

❈

Art zipped along streets that Josie was pretty sure she hadn't traveled before. He seemed determined to take her on a grand adventure. In all likelihood, it would rival the journey of their first year.

She settled back against the seat, content to let him have his fun. He fiddled with the radio until he found a song. She scooted closer to him as Tommy Dorsey's band serenaded them with "I'll Be Seeing You."

" 'I'll be looking at the moon, but all I'll see is you,' " Art crooned, making sappy eyes at her.

"Hey, you, get your attention back on the road."

He laughed and pulled to a stop. The engine idled as he leaned over to kiss her. She sank into it, feeling the sparks ignite a warmth that spiraled all the way down to her toes.

With a groan, he pulled back, brushing a hand along her jaw with feather strokes. "Have I told you lately how much I love you?"

The words resonated to the core of her being. "I love you more."

"Not possible."

"I think this is a competition we can afford."

His soft chuckle tickled her ear. "Agreed." He leaned away and grabbed the steering wheel. She felt a sudden chill. "Back to the planned activities."

"Spontaneous is good." Did she really purr the words?

Art slipped back into traffic, and after a few more turns, he parked the car. "Here we are."

"Here?" Josie squinted but couldn't see anything she recognized. "Sorry, I have no idea where here is."

He hopped out of the car and then helped her out. "This is the Abbot Observatory."

An observatory?

"Josie, I want to share the stars with you. Here they have telescopes that allow us to see far into space." He led her through some trees to a brick building that looked Greek in its portico style but had a large dome that rose behind the facade.

She bobbled as he helped her up the stone stairs. Once they were inside, she was glad she'd brought her coat. "Why isn't the dome enclosed?"

"The air inside and out needs to be the same temperature, or it distorts the images."

Not only was he handsome, Art remained one of the smartest men she knew. "What?"

"Amazed by your mental prowess."

He tugged her toward the telescope like a kid leading a parent to the candy counter. "Look through here." He pointed at a piece that stuck out from the telescope.

"All right." She ducked a bit and placed an eye on the piece. What had been pinpricks of light in the night sky evolved into brilliant, pulsing lights.

"Isn't it amazing?"

She nodded, then decided he might not see her in the deepening twilight. "Breathtaking."

"Yes, you are."

Heat flushed her cheeks again, but this time she gratefully accepted the cover of darkness. They explored the night sky until she was too chilled to stay out any longer. Art placed his coat around her shoulders as they walked back to the car.

He turned her toward him. "Josie, I don't say this enough. I know this year has been hard. There are things we would change, but I need you to know that you are the only person I would want to share the experiences with. I'm praying the good always overtakes the bad. But even if it doesn't, I am so glad you chose me."

Twin tears perched on her cheeks, glistening in the moonlight. He dabbed at her tears.

"I love you, Art Wilson."

He linked her arm through his and continued the walk to the car. The Packard came into view, and their pace quickened. He settled her into the car, even helping collect her skirt. He searched her face, and she waited.

Finally, he smiled and leaned in.

With a kiss that left her weak in the knees.

To think she had a lifetime to enjoy those.

That had to make her most blessed of women. And by the look in Art's eye, he agreed.

Chapter 23

"A rt Wilson. In my office now," E. K. Fine's voice roared across the room. Art looked up. Charlie gave him a pointed look. Art shrugged. Stan just smirked at him. If he knew what this was about but wasn't telling, Art might have to shake the belligerence out of him regardless of the fifty pounds Stan had on him. Speed and youth had to count for something.

Trailing E.K. to his office, Art kept his eyes and ears open for any information that would be helpful in the meeting.

E.K. barged through his door and headed to his desk. Art stopped as if he'd run into a wall when he entered. Grandfather sat in a chair in front of the desk. Art's spine stiffened, and his senses went on alert.

Would Grandfather allow E.K. to fire him? Art didn't want to think so, but Grandfather had been clear he had high expectations for Art to meet.

"Sit down, Wilson." E.K.'s voice punctured Art's thoughts. Grandfather arched an eyebrow but kept his gaze focused on his steepled fingers.

Only two chairs sat in front of E.K.'s desk. Art sank into the corner of the one opposite Grandfather. Silence settled over the room. Art determined not to fidget but felt like a kid called into the principal's office.

E.K. joined Grandfather in staring at him. Art refused to break the stony silence. They'd called the meeting. They'd have to start it.

E.K. finally cleared his throat. "You're aware I've been concerned about your performance for a while—given you many opportunities to correct deficiencies."

Art clamped his mouth shut until he ground his teeth.

"Mr. Wilson, here, has a proposal he wants to discuss with you. Against my advice, I might add." E.K. stood and huffed out of the room.

Art stared at E.K.'s chair as if the man hadn't left. He could feel Grandfather's gaze. Art turned and met his eyes.

"Well, now." Grandfather leaned forward on the edge of his chair. "Son, I have a proposal for you. I want you to move to Dayton."

"Back to Dayton? Why?" Where was this headed?

"I think you're ready to be brought into the company. Groomed for a position."

Art gawked at him, then spoke with deliberation. "You want me to move my wife again and leave this company?"

Grandfather waved a hand in the air. "As if your wife wouldn't love to move back home. Don't be pigheaded. Come into the business. Learn the ropes. Do well, and you may even become an owner."

Art shook his head. "I can do all that here."

"True, but I'd like a more active hand in developing your career." Grandfather lifted a hand and stopped the refusal that wanted to explode from Art. "I'll leave you to your thoughts. However, I will need an answer by Friday."

"That's tomorrow."

"So it is." Grandfather grabbed his Tyrolean hat and cane from the edge of the desk and walked out of the office.

Words escaped Art. It seemed even his thoughts had abandoned him. He stumbled to his feet, then headed to his office.

Charlie watched him as he grabbed his lunch bag, hat, and coat. "Everything all right?"

Art jangled the change in his pocket as he tried to find his voice. "I'm not sure."

"I'll pray."

Art knew he should respond, but he felt numb, detached from his body. He liked his life well-ordered. It had drawn him to accounting. Work with the numbers long enough, and they made sense. There was a rhythm and pattern to them. One that was often missing when dealing with people.

He didn't know what to think as he walked toward home, the sky dark and heavy above him.

❄

That evening after Cassandra had settled into bed, Josie and Art huddled over the kitchen table. Art held her hand and rubbed his thumb over her fingers. Move back to Dayton? The possibility of moving home excited her. "What do you want to do?"

Art studied her face as if he wanted to search the depths of her soul before answering. "I don't know." He sighed. "Part of me wants to take Grandfather up on his offer. But another part wants to make it on our own. And I know you'd like to move back. . . ." His words trailed off.

"What do you want, Art?"

"I don't know."

"If we weren't married and you could do anything in the world?"

"Then I wouldn't work." The hint of tease in his eyes kept her from smacking him.

"I'm serious."

"It doesn't matter, because I am married to the perfect woman." She began to melt inside at his words. "I'm unsure how to interpret Grandfather's offer. Did he buy the company to watch me work? I can think of easier and cheaper ways to do that."

"It seems like a good opportunity."

"I know." He ran his fingers through his hair. "Let's pray."

Josie relaxed. That's what she loved about this man. He was far from perfect, but he knew where to turn. He held her hands and she listened as his rich voice petitioned God for wisdom and direction. Surely it would come.

✳

Soft snow fell from the sky. From the third-floor apartment it looked beautiful. Peaceful. Serene. At street level, it had brought the city to a halt. Art stumbled outside, intending to walk to work, but the drifted snow left the streets and sidewalks impassable. He wasn't disappointed. The snow gave him time to ponder his answer for Grandfather since Art couldn't get to work.

Art sat at the kitchen table and relaxed with a cup of coffee and the paper. He'd let Josie sleep. No need to wake her since they couldn't go anywhere. Maybe once the snow stopped, they could take Cassandra out to romp in it. Maybe sled down the street.

He sipped his coffee, surprised he'd slept so well. Had to be the result of turning his concerns over to God. But in the light of day, he already felt the struggle to pick that burden right back up.

Lord, help me.

Three small words, but they were all he needed. They might be a never-ending mantra through the day, but that was all right.

"Give it up."

The whisper ricocheted through him. Give what up? He cocked his head, heard nothing else, and went back to the paper.

"The bitterness, your pride. Give it to Me."

Art wanted to pretend he didn't understand. He'd made up the voice. The words came from his mind. But he knew it was a directive. One he needed to heed.

The bitterness and pride froze him in place. He didn't like feeling that Grandfather had manipulated him. Yet he knew that wasn't Grandfather's intent. He'd made a good offer that made sense on most fronts. So why wouldn't his grandson jump at the opportunity? Art needed to have his head examined.

No, he needed to obey.

The thought of forgiving, turning his back on his pride—he could hardly stomach it. But he had to. "Does this mean I have to work for the man?"

"Grandfather?" Josie startled him. He hoped his collar hid the heat climbing his neck.

"Yeah."

Josie smiled, and it went straight to his heart. "Probably."

✳

Several weeks later, boxes lined the living room floor in the corner Josie had envisioned holding the Christmas tree. Even with Cassandra, they'd decided to forgo the decorations while they packed.

Josie stared around the small room, her heart beating erratically. Annabelle had called to say she was on the way. Looking at the piles of household items scattered across the floor, she decided she couldn't feel less prepared. *Father, calm my heart. Help me focus on Cassandra and what's best for her.*

The door opened, and Cassandra and Art stumbled through the door. Cassandra's laugh rang with sweet innocence, and her cheeks were a rosy red kissed by the cold air. Snowflakes clung to her face, probably remnants of a well-aimed snowball. Considering the snow clinging to Art's hair, they'd engaged in a wild snowball fight. Cassandra and Art performed a dance at the door as they knocked trace amounts of snow off shoes and dropped their coats, scarves, and mittens at the door.

"Did you have fun, Cassandra?"

Art didn't look much older than nine himself as he grinned at Josie over Cassandra's head. "Of course she did." He moved as if to tickle her. "She knows she'll be tickle-tortured if she doesn't agree."

Cassandra squealed and turned to run, but Art grabbed her before she could take two steps and threw her over his shoulder. Josie felt a rush of joy as she watched.

"Go get changed, Cassandra. I have a surprise for you when you're dry and warm."

Cassandra perked up. "A letter from home?"

"Maybe." Josie smiled as Cassandra flew to her room and slammed the door. If only that could be motivation every day.

When Annabelle arrived, Cassandra sat covered in a blanket on the davenport, rereading the letter. Josie expected the letter to rip under the girl's intense gaze.

"Would you like some tea? I also have warm milk for Cassandra's hot chocolate."

"I'm fine." Annabelle eyed the boxes. "So it's final. You've decided to move."

Art had grown excited at the prospect of working for his grandfather. Josie couldn't wait to be back in Dayton near family. But she'd realized through the preparations that Dayton wasn't really home anymore. No, that was wherever Art lived.

"Yes, we'll move in a few days at the school break."

"You're sure that will work for Cassandra?" Annabelle arched an eyebrow.

Josie watched Cassandra read the letter another time. "She'll be fine. She's excited about getting to spend time with our families, too. We can't imagine not having her with us for the duration. We made a promise to her family that we'll keep." Just like she'd made a promise to Art to love him through all circumstances for the rest of her life.

Annabelle nodded, then walked over and joined Cassandra. "Do you mind if I ask you a question?"

Cassandra looked up from her letter and grinned. All was well in her world. "Ma'am."

"Are you willing to move with the Wilsons to Dayton? It will mean a new school and home for you."

"Oh, that's fine. My family will still know where I am. And I don't want to be with anyone else."

Josie hoped the new school would give Cassie a chance to start with a clean slate. And Cassandra and Ruth could stay friends through letters, maybe even visits.

As Annabelle prepared to leave, she seemed settled with the idea. She stopped at the door. "You know how to reach me if there are any problems."

"Yes. Thanks for your assistance." Josie smiled at Annabelle. "You've been such a help with Cassandra."

Annabelle nodded. "It's the part of my job I enjoy the most. Don't forget to keep me posted on how things are going. And I'll still stop by periodically." Annabelle chucked Cassandra under the chin. "You've got a great home, kid."

Cassandra's face-splitting grin agreed. Josie showed Annabelle to the door, then turned to Cassandra. Now if she could just get the child to put down the letter and help with the packing.

✳

Art closed up his briefcase. It somehow latched around the pile of items he'd shoved in it. His desk cleared, Art turned to Charlie. "Thanks for everything."

Stan leaned against his desk, arms crossed. "I know you ain't saying that to me."

Art chuckled. "You weren't so bad. Kept me on my toes."

"Here to serve."

Charlie guffawed. "You've got the better assignment, you know. I'm stuck with this guy."

"You can handle him."

Stan rolled his eyes.

The future stretched in front of Art, largely unknown. Had he made a good decision? He honestly didn't know. All he knew was he'd followed God's leading to the best of his ability. And it was too late to change his mind. His replacement had already started, and the house was packed.

He had a feeling Josie wouldn't be too happy if he suddenly decided they were staying.

Grabbing his briefcase, he shook hands with Charlie and Stan. "Good-bye."

His steps were slow as he walked through Eden Park. It might be December, but he didn't want to rush. No, he wanted to carefully consider everything that had occurred in the past months. There had been joy and sorrow with Josie's pregnancy. The uncertainty with his job. The joy of watching Cassandra gain her footing.

God, You are so good.

Those words cycled through his mind, a meditation of praise.

He walked through the door, surprised to find some order to the chaos. Looked like Josie had at least kicked the boxes to the walls. He might walk through without knocking his shins against a dozen boxes.

Josie hurried to him. "Welcome home."

He pulled her in for a kiss, then deepened it. A year, and he still couldn't fathom God's goodness in entrusting her to him. "Any regrets?"

She eyed him carefully, questions replaced by certainty. "Not one. It's been an adventure, Mr. Wilson. One I plan to enjoy for the rest of my life."

As he stood circling her waist with his arms, he believed her. She was a gift from God, and he would treasure her, too. Their promise was one he'd keep.

A PROMISE
BORN

Dedication

Writing books is an endeavor that happens in solitude, but I have been blessed from the beginning with friends who stepped alongside me, believing I could do this and praying for me. To all my friends at Bethel Christian Life Center: Thank you for always encouraging me.

And many thanks to Stephanie Wetli, who asked if she could try editing a book. You didn't know what you were getting into, but your insightful comments have been a blessing. Thanks also to Sue Lyzenga for reading as it scrolled off the printer. I have the world's best neighbors!

And to Jesus: Thank You for looking across time and choosing to offer Your life as the ultimate sacrifice for my sin.

Chapter 1

May 1943

The grinding of brakes straining to bring trains to a stop vied with the final *whoosh* of steam. Even in the early evening, people hustled around the Washington DC Union Station. They darted between the trains lining the tracks, reflecting the excitement filling Evelyn Happ. She didn't know which way to look next other than down the tracks that led to her future. In moments, she'd join sixty-nine other Women Accepted for Voluntary Emergency Service, the navy's WAVES, as they boarded a train leaving Evelyn's home in DC for points west.

The WAVES would get off the train at an unknown destination, assigned to a job contributing to the war effort. That's all she knew. The cloak-and-dagger atmosphere only added to the sense of adventure. Her instructions mirrored that of the other WAVES: Board the B&O's Diplomat. Nothing more. Somewhere down the tracks, they'd get off.

The heels of hundreds of shoes clacked against the cement. Finally, the adventure had begun.

"Come on, Vivian." Evelyn grabbed her friend Vivian Grable by the arm. The waifish girl double-timed to keep pace with Evelyn's strides. "If you don't start moving, you'll miss the train."

"All the activity is fun to watch."

Lonnie Smuthers smacked her gum and rolled her eyes. "Don't push the girl, E. If you walk any faster, you won't need a train. I prefer to ride."

"Why won't the navy tell us where we're going?" Vivian brushed a strand of blond hair out of her cornflower blue eyes.

"War secrets." Evelyn grinned. "Don't worry, Viv. I'll stick close." Sometimes she felt bland compared to these two women. Neither her brunette hair, cut to the government-specified length and curling under her cap, nor her gray eyes stood out in the sea of WAVES.

Viv shook her head. "Fine. Let's get this journey underway. I'm ready for whatever the navy throws our way."

"It's why we joined." Evelyn pulled Vivian down the platform. "Adventure. Service. Intrigue."

WAVES service would be a vast improvement over anything Evelyn had found on the East Coast in the private sector. Few companies had taken her engineering degree seriously. All those hours working through textbook after

129

textbook, studying and cramming didn't amount to anything without someone letting her do the work. She could have traveled to the West Coast and tried a company like Boeing, but she hadn't felt quite that adventurous. Somehow it was easier to head into the unknown in the company of a group of women she had trained with for weeks. Unexpected friendships had developed among them. Friendships that would make the coming unknowns an adventure.

The WAVES: smart uniforms, flexible navy rules. Most of all, the WAVES had a place for her to do something for her country. If she was really lucky, she would get to use some of that until-now-ignored education.

A whistle sliced the air, and Evelyn covered her ears as gals squealed around her. Soldiers hurried past them, all rushing to reach their trains. "There it is." Viv pointed with her free hand to track eight. "Let's hurry."

"Don't worry. We'll make it." Even as Evelyn said the words, excitement quickened her steps. She spotted the Baltimore & Ohio behemoth. The engine's gold lettering stood out against the black paint as it belched smoke. "Ladies, I do believe it's impatient to get us on board."

Lonnie groaned. "I highly doubt that mass of steel has a solitary feeling." She nudged Evelyn. "Get those romantic notions out of your head and climb aboard."

Lonnie's down-to-earth approach wouldn't weigh Evelyn down. No, she had the opportunity to do something meaningful with everything she'd learned while studying at Purdue University.

Finding the dark green passenger cars of the Diplomat, the gals climbed on board. Evelyn led the way down the narrow hallway until she found their sleeper berth. The three women crashed into each other and the walls in the small room until they'd tucked their bags out of the way. Other WAVES boarded, their excited voices fading as they found their berths. Moments later, a jolt shimmied through the train. Evelyn placed a hand over her stomach to stem the excitement. Sometime soon—the navy hadn't given any indication how far they would travel—she'd learn her role.

"We should try to get some sleep, gals." Lonnie pulled her hair into a net and washed her face. "Who knows what the morning holds?"

Evelyn might not know, but she could imagine. As she settled onto the top berth, she let her mind wander through the possibilities. Communications? Aviation? Code breaking? Evelyn doubted the navy would use her in the medical or Judge Advocate General areas because of her training. Regardless, the Allies needed all the help they could get, especially as the Battle of the Atlantic refused to go their way.

"I hope we're not going all the way to California." Viv's soft voice pierced the darkness.

Evelyn had to agree with Viv. She could only imagine how long it would take with the starts and stops to take on fuel and drop off passengers and mail. The suspense about her assignment might kill her during the journey. "Think of the beaches and sunshine. They wouldn't be so bad."

"How's a girl to sleep with all this jostling?" Lonnie growled from a lower berth.

The train threw Evelyn against the wall as it raced around a curve. She rubbed her elbow where it had smacked the side. "Carefully, though most people find it soothing, don't they?"

Viv nodded. "Relax into the berth."

"We could tie you in place, Lonnie." Evelyn kept her tone innocent. She shifted around until she found a comfortable position on her bunk. Evelyn pulled the thin blanket to her chin and forced her muscles to relax. Soon enough, they'd know their destination. She closed her eyes and surrendered to sleep.

※

Too soon, sunlight filtered through the small window, and the conductor came through, banging on the doors. "Breakfast served for forty-five minutes."

Evelyn scrambled to get ready then hurried off while Viv and Lonnie started to dress. Women in sharp WAVES uniforms filled the dining car when Evelyn reached it. She took in the cacophony of voices as they anticipated their destination. Evelyn settled into the only open seat at a small table. "Morning, girls."

Quiet greetings answered hers. The gals at her table were familiar, though she couldn't remember their names. "Any idea where we're headed?"

A dark-haired beauty shook her head, a gleam of adventure in her gaze. "No, but I can't wait to learn our destination."

"Me, either." Evelyn leaned forward, ready to ask more questions, when a whistle cut through the noise. She looked to the front of the car.

"Ladies." Lt. Nancy Meyers swayed gently with the train. "Head back to your sleepers and pack. We change trains at the next stop. The conductor tells me you have fifteen minutes."

Evelyn grabbed coffee and rolls for Viv and Lonnie and hurried back to their berth.

She watched the scenery out the dirty window as her roommates ate their breakfast. Get off? Here? While the thought of getting off the train appealed, she hoped the final destination wasn't nearby. The flat land had been planted for crops and looked entirely rural. She fidgeted at the thought of being stationed near here, though a train change could still send them in many directions. Maybe north or south. Ten minutes later, the train slowed. Lt. Meyers knocked on their door. "Ladies, prepare to disembark."

Energy poured through Evelyn. This was it. Around her, women straightened uniforms and collected personal items. Vivian looked out the window. "We can't have gone far."

"My guess is Ohio." Lonnie shrugged and went back to packing.

Evelyn licked her lips. "Do they have cities in Ohio?"

Vivian laughed. "Sure, but it doesn't matter. If the navy says that's where we're going, that's it." Evelyn kept her knees bent so she could stand throughout the jolts and brakes of the train. The rural landscape had turned to city landscape. Maybe this wouldn't be so bad after all. She saw the sign alongside the tracks: CINCINNATI.

Later that afternoon, after a delay in Cincinnati and a short train ride, Evelyn looked around Dayton's Union Station. This one looked nothing like the one in Washington DC.

Dayton.

She let the name roll around a minute.

"Do they have any bodies of water in Dayton? We are in the navy, after all." She couldn't imagine any place so rural hosting a navy project.

"I'm pretty sure there's not even a coast." Viv shrugged.

Lonnie laughed. "It's as landlocked as a state can be."

Evelyn considered the facts. "Well, I can't wait to learn why the navy thinks we need to be here."

❋

Mark Miller hunched over the plans spread across the table. He ran his fingers through his hair but didn't see anything different. The Bombe should work. Yet each time they ran a code, something happened. The machine refused to operate as designed.

Joe Desch, the wiry man leading the top-secret project, stood at the head of the room and crossed his arms. "The navy wanted this machine operational months ago. What are we missing, gentlemen?"

The engineers filling the room, slumped in defeat. They'd all worked too many hours for too many weeks to endure more dead ends.

"All right." Desch rubbed his chin. "We'll review this again tomorrow. Let's give Adam another test run."

Mark followed the group back to the sweltering room that housed the large computer. It might be a cool May day outside, but the machine raised the temperature to July levels in Building 26. Mark stared at Adam. Would the machine decode the German messages this time or break down in a flash of sparks? Each failure prolonged the stranglehold the Germans had on Atlantic transportation lanes.

The engineers had worked eighty hours a week more often than not since the National Cash Register Company had landed the navy contract to develop the machine. Mark had worked on the project since last September, employed by the brilliant Joe Desch and NCRC. He hadn't anticipated the relentless pressure when he'd returned to Dayton after his studies in Boston at MIT.

The machine clanked then stopped. Mark held his breath and prayed mechanical sounds would replace the sudden silence.

"Again?" John Fields rubbed a handkerchief over his face and shoved it in his back pocket. "Maybe this problem is beyond us."

Grabbing his tools and moving toward the machine, Mark shrugged, refusing to admit defeat. "We'll tear it apart again. Find the trigger."

"Why waste our time? We're making the machine go too fast."

"You know the navy won't lower that requirement." Mark didn't blame the navy. Thousands of German messages were intercepted each day but would remain gibberish until they found a way to break through the scrambling the Enigma machines used to create a code. Without that breakthrough, the convoys sailing the Atlantic continued to be torpedoed by German U-boats. The war couldn't be won when all the men and materials crossing the Atlantic sank to the bottom. "We have to get this right."

"At least you're single. Alice isn't happy with the hours I'm keeping."

As Mark helped remove the front of the machine, he tried to ignore the sting from John's words. He didn't want to be single. He'd love nothing more than to settle down. But none of the girls he knew ever quite fit him. His current girl, Paige Winslow, came closest, but it had only been a few weeks. Too early to know what could develop between them, but he hoped...for what? Someone who would understand him? Someone to put up with the quirks of his job? Someone who supported him as he used his education in the war effort?

That shouldn't be too much to ask.

A sailor entered the room and motioned to Mark, who jolted to his feet. "Sorry, John. I've got to go."

John stared at him. "You're leaving? Just like that?"

"Um...yep. I promised to help transport the WAVES to quarters."

A knowing grin spread across John's face. "I see. Maybe I should join you."

"Mr. Happily Married? Don't think so." Mark slapped John on the shoulder. "See you tomorrow." He reached the door and nodded at the sailor. "Ready for me?"

"Yes, sir." The sailor turned and headed down the hallway, leaving Mark to hurry to follow.

Mark's mother had talked him into helping the WAVES. He'd be one of a handful of men surrounded by seventy women. It might appeal if he didn't have a steady girl. But what kind of woman joined the military? His Paige was the picture of femininity, much like his mother and his sister Josie. Now his kid sister Kat with her love for all things rough and tumble could join the WAVES. He shook his head at the thought. God help the WAVES if she decided to enlist.

Two buses waited outside Building 26. A handful of men loitered next to them. "Was I the last?"

"Yes, sir." The sailor grinned. "Guess you got distracted. If you'll climb aboard, we'll go." He checked his watch. "Their train arrives in ten minutes."

Mark climbed on the nearest bus and settled into the seat behind the driver. What could he do to help these women? Take their bags, stow them, and carry them to the right cabin?

The buses drove through the National Cash Register complex, then up Main Street. The station sat at Sixth and Ludlow, and Mark could hear the *whoosh* of a train's arrival as he climbed off the bus.

"This way." The same sailor led the way to the track.

If these gals traveled with half the luggage his sisters did, Mark would feel it tomorrow. What had he agreed to?

He leaned against the train station wall and watched. Soon a stream of women in navy suits disembarked. One led the way to the sailor. She seemed to have an extra insignia or two on her lapels.

"Are you ready for us, Ensign?"

The ensign snapped to attention. "Yes, ma'am."

"At ease, sailor."

"Yes, ma'am." He pointed back through the station. "The buses are out front."

"Thank you. We're eager to see our new quarters."

Mark worked his way through the gaggle of women to the baggage car. He reached for the nearest bag. A gloved hand touched his.

"I'll take that." He looked up into a composed, weary face. The gray eyes arrested his attention.

"Ma'am, I'm here to help with the bags."

"I'm sure that's kind of you, but I can handle mine."

From the set of her chin, it looked like she'd made up her mind, but this might be her first experience with Midwestern hospitality. Mark tightened his grip and smiled. "I'm sure you're capable, but I'm here to make certain your transition to your cabin goes smoothly. Please let me. I insist."

Her fingers loosened on the handle, but Mark wasn't sure it was because of his charm and welcoming words. He had a sneaking suspicion it was the word *cabin* that stopped her. Interesting. Almost as intriguing as the hint of tears in her eyes.

Chapter 2

Evelyn felt singed by the heat in the man's gaze. He might claim his act was service in the guise of Midwestern hospitality, but it felt like a contest of wills. After a broken heart, she'd promised herself she'd never trust another man with anything important to her. But did she really want to carry that heavy suitcase another step?

Slowly, she released her grip and stepped back. "Thank you."

He continued to appraise her in a way that left heat climbing her cheeks, even as his look remained a far cry from the kind she usually received from men. Maybe her appearance didn't match his expectations. The man secured his grip on the bag, then tipped his head. "It's my pleasure. My name's Mark Miller. Welcome to Dayton."

"Thank you." She tipped her chin. "It will be an experience."

He chuckled and nodded. "That it will. The buses are through the station. Go ahead, I'll be right behind you with your bag."

She turned around and hid her hot cheeks. It didn't appear Mr. Miller intended to make fun of her, but he had no plans to back down on his. . .chivalry.

"What has you all bothered?" Viv's quiet voice pulled Evelyn from her churning thoughts.

"What do you make of that man?"

"The one carrying your bag?"

Evelyn nodded.

"He's handsome and volunteered to help. Relax and appreciate the assistance, Miss Independence."

The girl was right. It was nice to have someone attend to her needs. As Evelyn climbed on the first bus, she reminded herself not to get used to it. The WAVES wouldn't feel spoiled for long. "Guess I'll enjoy the help."

Evelyn turned in her seat and watched out the window as Mr. Miller deposited her case into the bowels of the bus. He made the large case look weightless.

"He is quite handsome," Viv teased.

She had to agree. The man moved with the grace of a weekend athlete.

Lonnie settled into the seat across the aisle from Viv and Evelyn. "Where do you think they'll billet us?"

"Definitely not on a boat," Viv answered.

Evelyn shook her head. "Isn't that a river over there? Maybe they've docked a boat along it for us."

The gals chuckled as the buses pulled out of the station. They drove by a Biltmore. Evelyn knew they wouldn't be lucky enough to stay at a hotel like that. But what could Mr. Miller mean by *cabin*? The image that flashed into her mind was filled with drafty rooms and mosquitoes. The drive wasn't long, and she tried to take in the feel of the small city. After a few minutes, the buses turned into a wooded acreage. Tall trees lined the property with its scattered buildings of all sizes.

"Welcome to Sugar Camp, ladies. Please follow me to your new home." Lt. Meyers ushered them into a large building that looked like a cafeteria. "Go to the front tables to get your cabin assignments."

Cabin? Evelyn's hope that Mr. Miller was misinformed crashed to the ground. "This is a change from basic training." Those dormitories had made her feel claustrophobic. Didn't sound like that would be much of a problem here.

Viv nodded. "You can say that again."

By the time Evelyn reached the front of the line and collected her cabin assignment, she was ready to collapse. Who'd have thought travel would take that much out of a gal? She plodded back to the bus, ready to collect her suitcase and satchel. Mr. Miller stood there, the sweat lining his forehead an indication he hadn't spent the last hour waiting for her.

"Carry your bag for you?" he asked, but the glint in his eyes let her know the expected answer. Frankly, she welcomed the help. She longed for a chance to recuperate from the travel, preferably in a nice, warm bubble bath. "Thank you, kind sir."

She gave him the number of the cabin, and he led the way across the camp. "You're over here."

The cabins looked small. Maybe there were only a couple of people per cabin. But if that was the case, there must be another dozen cabins hidden on the grounds. Mark knocked on the door and opened it. He placed the bag inside and stepped back out. "Here you go."

"This is home?" The thought had Evelyn ready to take her bag, hike right back to the train station, and go home to Washington DC. She hadn't expected the Biltmore, but this—it was ridiculous. The cabin smelled musty with a hint of mold that tickled her nose.

"Good luck." He turned to leave.

"Thank you." She closed the door behind him.

A chill filled the small room. Its walls were uncovered wood paneling. She supposed it held a rustic charm, but not exactly how she planned to live. It looked like original plans called for the room to hold two twin beds with side tables and lamps mounted into the wall. Between them stood a built-in closet. Probably adequate accommodations for two women, but someone had transformed each bed into bunks, suggesting four would live in the small space.

"Do they really expect four. . .here?" The thought of being stacked on top of other people made her stomach churn. She enjoyed people more than most, but this—

"You don't have to look so excited about sharing with me." Vivian poked her head around an inside door and stuck her tongue out. "Here's the bathroom. Looks like it leads to another bedroom." The small woman shivered. "This cabin could use some heat."

Evelyn gazed around the room but couldn't find a heater or radiator system. The blankets lining each bed looked impossibly thin. "Be glad we're here for the summer."

Viv nodded. "That's right. Though it doesn't feel like summer yet."

No, with the clouds ready to drop rain at the slightest provocation, a heavy dampness permeated the area. Evelyn could feel it to her bones.

The main door opened, and two more women entered the room.

"Hey, gals. I managed to change my cabin assignment and am with you after all." Merriment filled Lonnie's eyes as she dropped her bag. She pointed to the gal next to her. "This lovely lady is our new roommate, Mary Ellen. Just met her in the cafeteria."

A woman with dark hair, glasses, and a pleasantly plump build, Mary Ellen walked over to one of the lower bunks, plopped her suitcase on top of it, and without a word began unpacking. Evelyn had to fight the urge to tell the woman to wait until they'd had an opportunity to decide who would live where.

Viv grinned at her. "Don't worry. I'll take a top bunk."

"Thanks." Evelyn watched the activity and had the unsettled feeling she'd been plopped in the middle of a hurricane. Silly girl, she hadn't thought hurricanes reached as far inland as Ohio.

※

The next morning, Mark sat in the weekly meeting, rubbing his aching shoulders. He needed to spend more time on the baseball diamond if that little bit of lifting yesterday had him all tense.

"Time is running out." Admiral Meader's voice echoed through the cold, concrete room. He marched back and forth in front of the assembled engineers and machinists. "Each day that we don't have a working machine leads to more Allied deaths on the Atlantic."

Mark scrunched lower in his seat.

"What do they expect us to do?" John spoke behind his hand toward Mark. "Work 'round the clock."

"I thought we were already doing that."

Meader walked toward them. "Do you gentlemen have anything to add?"

"No, sir," Mark mumbled.

"We're planning an invasion of the mainland, but German U-boat attacks still have our convoys reeling. We have to break these codes. Whatever it takes. If we work around the clock, so be it." He turned back to the rest of the room. "Any questions?"

There were none. The problem came in the lack of solutions.

No matter how many different ways Mark approached the problem, he couldn't see a way to make the machines cooperate.

The Germans had a machine they called Enigma. It scrambled the German messages into gibberish by spinning a message through four different wheels, each spin changing the letter combinations. The British, with the help of Polish scientists, had broken the code when the machine contained three interchangeable wheels. Then the Germans added a fourth wheel, and the code became unbreakable. The United States landed the challenge of breaking the four-wheel code. The Bombes were designed to race through calculations, but so far, the machines only excelled at breaking down or springing oil leaks, not solving codes.

Something had to be done, but no matter where they turned, the problem loomed bigger than any solution.

That wasn't good enough.

Every day, that message was pounded into their heads. Even if Meader and the other navy bigwigs didn't remind them, the newspaper headlines were sufficient.

Some days, Mark wished he'd never accepted the position.

The meeting finally ended, and Mark and John returned to their Bombe.

John eyed the machine. "Adam looks tired."

"Just your imagination."

"Maybe we should give him the day off."

Mark snorted and watched the techs work on the machine. A quick visual inspection indicated the seals had held overnight.

The Enigma machine was small, barely filling a hard-sided valise. In contrast, the Bombe stood a foot taller than Mark and wider than a good-sized davenport. That meant a lot of computing power trying to break a code with possible combinations that ranged in the millions. Astronomical numbers.

The door opened, and Mark looked up. Who could be coming in? He knew everybody who had access.

His jaw almost dropped when he spotted a group of gals dressed in WAVES uniforms.

One of the gals looked around, then took a step back. "I'm sorry. I don't think we're supposed to be here."

John stepped between the women and Adam. "You're right. Only those with clearance are allowed."

An MP, one of the military police stationed in Building 26, hurried into the room, a sheepish expression on his face. "Ladies, you'll need to leave."

Mark watched. Someone would have to learn why no one guarded the door. This was exactly the kind of breach that they guarded against. What were these dames supposed to do other than get in the way and distract the single guys from their jobs? This couldn't be a good idea. No, with the pressure the navy had on them to find a solution yesterday, any distractions here in Building 26 were a bad idea.

⁕

Evelyn followed the other WAVES into the large room. She hadn't expected the silence. She had assumed the hum of the machine would fill the room with a low roar. Then she noticed the men scrambling around the machine, though a couple stared at the WAVES like they'd intruded on sacred ground. This machine looked like a marvel of modern engineering. The magnitude of wiring and components welded and soldered together impressed her.

"What do you make of that?" Vivian gestured to the machine.

"I'm not sure." Evelyn edged closer. She'd never seen anything like it. "They've strung processors together." She longed to analyze the machine. They must be working on something amazingly complex to need such power. Code breaking?

"Ladies, I'm sorry, but we've made a mistake." Lt. Meyers hurried in from the hall. "Please follow me."

"Won't some of us help with these machines?" Evelyn hoped so.

"No, Ensign Happ. Not at this time." Lt. Meyers urged them toward the door. "If you'll follow me, it's time for the rest of your orientation."

The other WAVES turned to file out, but Evelyn stood rooted to the floor. She wanted to understand every element of how the machine was constructed and what it could do. She'd studied all those years for an opportunity like this. Excitement pulsed through her.

This was why she'd joined the WAVES.

"Are you joining us, Ensign Happ?" Lt. Meyers cleared her throat.

Evelyn jerked out of her reverie and found one of the men openly watching her. Mark? Yes, the man who'd helped her yesterday. So he was part of this endeavor. That would explain his presence at the train station, though he didn't look like a valet today. His eyes were guarded. What had happened to all that Midwestern hospitality? She noted his broad shoulders and the dark hair that waved around his forehead and ears. Not the typical engineer build. When he didn't break eye contact, she winked at him, then turned on her heel. "Lead on."

⁕

That night, Evelyn crossed the wooded compound of Sugar Camp from her cabin to the chapel. She followed a steady flow of women filing into the building. Seventy voices quieted at Admiral Meader's command, and the WAVES sat forward on the pews. Evelyn thought they all looked eager to learn more about why they'd come to Dayton. As far as she was concerned, the machines were enough reason, but the other WAVES weren't likely to appreciate them.

Admiral Meader moved to the front of the room, behind a table. A small man with an intense, brooding look sat at the table. Lt. Meyers sat next to him, back ramrod straight, uniform perfect in every detail.

The admiral surveyed the women. "Ladies, you are here to assist with a top-secret military project. You will play a critical role in building parts for the machines, maintaining the machines, and eventually running them.

"But you may never talk to anyone about the job you do in Building 26. Not even among yourselves. If any of you talk, you will immediately be removed to St. Elizabeth's Hospital, where you will serve the rest of the war."

St. Elizabeth's? Where was that? Not that Evelyn was interested in finding out. Everyone treated this project gravely, signifying its importance. "The success of this project is critical to the overall war effort. Accordingly, you must treat it carefully and make sure your lips never become loose about the work you do here.

"If you feel you are unable to do that, tell us now, and we'll remove you from the location immediately."

Vivian leaned closer to Evelyn. "Is he serious?"

Evelyn studied the commander's intent stare and the serious lines around his eyes and mouth. "Yes, I think so."

Chapter 3

J oin us for the night off?" John invited Mark to join a group of engineers and WAVES headed out for a good time. Only a week since the arrival of the WAVES, and already the atmosphere in Building 26 had changed. Mark had known it would happen.

The WAVES might not work in the rooms with the Bombes, but their presence was felt throughout the building. From the rooms where they soldered components to the cafeteria where they spent breaks and meals, the women had men forgetting who they were and why they were in Dayton.

The men were more than willing to give up the routine and mind-numbing chores to the WAVES. Mark had heard more than one man admit he was glad he didn't have to solder any more gadgets and gizmos for the machines.

As soon as Desch told everyone to go home after hitting another wall with the Bombes, several of the guys had hurried off to find WAVES equally ready to hit the town. Now John and his wife planned to join the mix.

The handful of WAVES looked excited, and the men appeared just as eager to show them around. Mark eyed the group, looking for the brunette he'd helped earlier. He hadn't seen her since the detour the day after the WAVES arrived. She had an intelligence and curiosity in her gaze and had lingered so long that he wondered if she understood the machine's purpose. If she were part of the group, maybe he'd join them. What was he thinking? He should spend the time with Paige.

"Not tonight, folks. Have a good time." He'd call Paige. See if she could join him for dinner.

Mark called her from a pay phone on the first floor. He tapped the glass of the booth as he waited for Paige to pick up. It had been too long since they'd had time together during the week. He'd take her to a restaurant, maybe to a movie. After a dozen rings, he hung up. His shoulders slumped, and the evening felt empty. Maybe he could catch the others after all. He hurried from the booth but couldn't find them. Guess he'd go home early tonight. Not the ideal way to spend a rare night off.

As Mark trudged the blocks home from NCR, he felt the nip in the air. He wouldn't mind sunshine breaking through, but it didn't look like it would happen.

Desch had hinted they might get the weekend off if they made a breakthrough tomorrow on the machines. Maybe Mark would get to play a game of baseball with some guys. Kat, his kid sister, would probably tag along, but she'd done that since she was five. She'd been cute then. Now she bordered on a woman who made the men stop and stare. He wasn't sure how he felt about that. Having Josie married off to a good man was one thing. But he couldn't imagine Kat paired off. Fortunately, she lingered on the border of a kid. Sixteen, almost seventeen. Way too young for anything serious.

Yeah, that's what he'd keep telling himself.

He turned up the sidewalk on Volusia Avenue, stately trees shading the avenue and lending substance to the area. A minute later, he stood on his parents' front porch.

The front door opened, and Kat barreled toward him.

"It's about time you got here."

"What?" He staggered back a step as she tackled him.

"I've got news. Big news. The kind of news that will amaze you."

"Really?" Kat lived life at high speed. Mark couldn't imagine what had her so excited this time. "Do I get a sneak peek at the news?"

She shook her head as she pulled him up the steps. "No, you have to wait to hear with Dad. So come on. We're sitting down to eat."

Mark chuckled as she led him down the hallway.

"Mom, I'll wash my hands and be right in."

Kat stuck her tongue out at him and hurried into the dining room. Mark could hear her voice filtering through the door as he washed up. Something had her over the moon.

He strode into the dining room and stopped at his mom's side long enough to kiss her on the cheek. "Evening, Mother, Dad."

He settled into his chair and unfolded the napkin onto his lap.

"Now that you're here, maybe we can hear Kat's news." Dad smiled at his baby girl. "What's going on?"

"I got an invitation to tryouts for the All-American Girls Professional Softball League."

Mark choked on his water and quickly set the glass down. "The what?"

"If you weren't so wrapped up in your job, you'd know. Mr. Wrigley is starting a league. Tryouts are open to anyone, but it's better if you get an invitation. I did. Today. In the mail." She shrieked.

"Congratulations, Kat." Mom took another bite of roast, then asked, "Do you want to accept?"

Kat stared at her, fork in midair. "Of course."

Mom and Dad exchanged a glance. Mark rolled his eyes. This conversation would be very short. By morning, Kat would have permission and pack her bags.

"Girls playing softball? Professionally?" Mark couldn't resist tweaking her nose.

"I've only played since I was six." Kat crossed her arms. "Remember? You took me with you. Taught me to play with all your friends. Kept making me play."

The table erupted in laughter. "Yeah, that's what I did. Forced you to play." He reached across the table and ruffled her curls. "Congrats, kid. If that's what you want, go play with a bunch of girls. It'll be boring compared to playing with me and my friends."

"Yeah. But none of you offered to pay me more than fifty dollars a week to play."

She had a point there.

✳

Evelyn walked across Sugar Camp from the dining hall to her cabin. As she walked, she passed the recreation center, theater, and baseball diamond. Maybe when it warmed up, she'd spend some time at the pool. Anything would be better than the march to Building 26, followed by a long day soldering rotors, the march home, and a meal. The routine was only a couple of days old but already drove her crazy.

There had to be more.

Many of the WAVES had hunkered down in their rooms to avoid the nippy night.

She stopped as she neared the chapel. She'd never spent much time in church. Her family had kept Sundays for sleeping in and the occasional game of golf. In college, she joined a roommate at a small church in downtown Lafayette several times. Peace had always engulfed her there, but she'd leave and rush right back into the cycle of classes and homework. Basic training had been equally busy. Now her life had emptied of busyness—at least of the sort she'd known at home and school.

No, the navy would keep her occupied, but it wasn't a cerebral exercise. Not yet.

Evelyn stopped at the steps to the chapel, hand on the railing. Should she go in? But what would she do? Sit in the cold chapel? Or return to the cabin and curl up on her bed with the blanket wrapped around her shoulders? Neither sounded overly appealing, but she knew what would happen if she went back to her cabin. Nothing beyond reading a book.

She hesitated on the first step, then turned and headed to her cabin. Her shoulders slumped as she trudged to her room. She felt the weight of. . .something. She didn't know what to call it. A presence? All she knew was she felt empty and exposed. Somehow lacking.

She looked over her shoulder, expecting to find someone watching her. She didn't like the sensation. Evelyn tried to shake it. On the next free night, she'd lead the charge for an evening out wearing her dancing shoes, even if she had to wear her navy WAVES uniform. Anything to avoid the inner searching that plagued her tonight.

✳

The next morning, Evelyn hurried through the race to dress. Eight women using one bathroom presented more than its share of challenges. She needed to purchase her own mirror. With four women squeezed in front of the mirror in the mornings, her odds of getting ready without an elbow to the face were horribly slim.

After a near miss with her cheek, she tossed her lipstick down and backed out of the bathroom. "Let me know when it's safe to return."

Giggles flowed from the gals.

"Come on, Evelyn." Viv stepped around the door. "Don't get sore. We're all doing what we have to."

"No problem. Just trying to avoid looking like a clown at work. Too many elbows and bodies crammed in one spot."

"I'll say." Lonnie bounced into the room, every hair perfectly in place and her lipstick expertly applied. "Welcome to life with oodles of women."

Mary Ellen scurried in. "The room's free now."

"Thanks." Evelyn walked into the bathroom and laughed. Her lipstick had disappeared in a sea of toiletries. "Anyone mind if I use their things?"

Three women filled the doorway, giggling.

"Guess we'll get to know each other really well." Evelyn smiled and grabbed a random tube. If she didn't hurry, she'd miss breakfast at Building 26.

An hour later after a quick breakfast in the cafeteria with the rest of the gals, she strode down the hall toward her assigned room. The urge to enter the room with the Bombe pulled at her. She should keep walking. Do as she was told. But when she reached the door, no MPs were present to keep her out. What could it hurt to peek? The engineer in her wanted to see the machine. The woman in her wanted to know if Mark Miller was around. Something about him intrigued her in a way that made her ignore the rules. What did she have to lose anyway? No one was around to stop her. She opened the door and entered, her heels snapping against the concrete floor. Men halted mid-motion. She tried to ignore them as she looked for Mark and then at the machine. Based on the oil pooled at the Bombe's base, it must have sprung a leak overnight.

"Does it do that often?"

"What?" The man she'd broken the rules for stared at her.

"Leak oil." She pointed at the spill.

Mark's mouth pulled down in a tight frown. He studied her a moment. "How did you get in here?"

"Walked in."

He looked her up and down, his frown deepening. "That doesn't mean you can come in. You aren't on the list. The one at the door that someone is supposed to check."

Evelyn struggled to find a response, but her throat tightened until she felt strangled. It wasn't often a man made her even a bit tongue-tied. "Why can't I help? I have the training and background."

"It doesn't matter. Unless you're on that list, you can't be here." He stepped toward her, blocking her ability to step farther into the room. "We're here to troubleshoot. Try to engineer ahead of the problems. That requires access to information, and if you haven't noticed, information is tightly controlled around here."

She raised an eyebrow. The answer seemed too simplistic. All right. She could understand that at one level. The navy made its rules and lived by them without question. So she needed to give him a reason to work with her and push her case to the higher-ups. "How often do these leaks happen?" Wariness swept over the man. "What? Did I say something wrong?"

"We aren't allowed to talk about the machines. Especially with unauthorized personnel." Mark's quiet words carried a punch. "Aren't you supposed to be soldering rotors?"

She didn't want to acknowledge his words, not when she could do so much more. "What if they assigned me to work here?"

Mark studied her closely. "How do you think that would happen? The WAVES brought you here and gave you a position. Seems that's the end of the matter."

"Really?" Evelyn crossed her arms and stared at him. "Does it help to know I have an engineering degree from Purdue University?"

"I'm sure that's great, but that's a small school. Most of us come from MIT. Ever heard of it?" He grabbed her elbow and marched her away from the machine and toward the door.

Maybe mystery wasn't so attractive after all. And maybe he wouldn't take her any more seriously than others had. She squared her shoulders and stared up at him. Even with her pumps, she was dwarfed by him. "I think you may be as shortsighted as most of the men out there. I worked just as hard for my engineering degree as any of you, may have received better grades. And if you think I can't contribute to solving your engineering problems, well, I hope it doesn't delay the success of this project." She bit the inside of her mouth to stop the stream of words and to distract from the stinging behind her eyes. "If you'll excuse me."

Evelyn pulled from his grip and exited the room. She tried to keep her steps steady and slow. It was only when she put distance between the room and her that she allowed herself to run down the wide hallway to the women's restroom.

She shouldn't have believed she could do something special as a WAVES. It appeared these men weren't any more ready to see a woman contribute than the others she'd encountered. She sniffled and fought to pull herself together as she stared in the bathroom mirror. She would not let anyone see how deeply that cut. Somehow she'd find a way to be trusted with this vital project.

Chapter 4

Saturday, Mark couldn't shake the feeling that he'd treated Evelyn poorly. Even as he went through the steps of playing a game of baseball—something that usually brought him pleasure—he thought he'd been too harsh.

He'd seen the tears she'd tried so hard to conceal. Maybe having sisters made him soft, but he hated that his words had caused her pain. It wasn't her fault they didn't know her clearance yet. And if she really did have a degree from a school like Purdue, she might bring a fresh perspective to the challenges with the Bombes. Some of the men didn't like having any women around, thought the WAVES in their uniforms were only there to torment and distract them. But what if Evelyn could do more than the task assigned? What if she could see the problem differently? Bring a fresh approach to the problem?

Did Desch and Admiral Meader have any idea of her background? He should mention it. Make sure they knew.

A ball hit him in the chest, and he groaned.

"You okay, baby?" Paige's voice carried from the bleachers.

"Yeah, Mark, you hurt?" Kat grinned at him from her shortstop position. "You really should get your head in the game or get out."

He had to give it to her. He'd certainly used that line on her a time or two. "Maybe I'll sit out the next inning."

"Good idea." Kat turned back toward home plate, all business.

When the inning ended, Mark scanned the crowd for Paige. She waved at him from her spot, and he jogged to her.

"That looked like it hurt." She ran her fingers along his face, as if searching it for injuries.

Deciding he enjoyed her caress too much, he stepped to the side. "I'm fine. I think I'll watch the rest of the game next to you."

A smile brightened her face, and she slipped her arm through his, anchoring him to her side. "I'd like that. I wish you had more weekends like this."

Mark wanted to explain why his job required so much, but that wasn't an option. She had to live in the dark along with everyone else. "Let's enjoy this one."

The petite woman snuggled next to his side, and Mark wrapped his arm around her shoulders. Paige might be at an outdoor ballgame, but she'd dressed for an afternoon tea. Her short-sleeved dress and fancy hat looked out of place among the crowd. Why would this fashion plate choose to spend her time with him? Paige could have about any man. He didn't know the answer to this question, but he pulled her closer and vowed to enjoy every moment they had together.

She looked up at him, eyebrows raised. "Yes?"

"Merely enjoying your presence, mademoiselle."

A knowing grin softened her face and lit her hazel eyes. "See that you do, sir."

The inning ended, and Mark savored every moment of the sun's rays on his face. It was entirely too rare of a sensation. The wartime schedule might be fifty-four hours a week, but the demands of his job often pushed the workweek closer to eighty hours. Far too much time spent inside. Days like this outside the four walls of some manmade structure were what he needed.

The team played better as he sat next to Paige. Why wouldn't it? It wasn't like he made it to practice. Even this early in the season, he'd been pretty much AWOL.

"Let's get out of here," Paige's voice purred in his ear. When she talked like that, it was hard to tell her no.

"What do you have in mind?"

"Let's walk across the park and go to the theater. Maybe grab some dinner."

Sounded expensive, but he lived at home with minimal costs. Who was he kidding? A beautiful lady wanted to spend her Saturday with him. "Let's run by my house first, and I'll clean up. Then let's see what we find."

After a quick change at home, Mark borrowed his father's car. They headed back downtown and grabbed a bite at a local café before strolling the streets. He tried to focus on Paige's commentary, but his thoughts betrayed him by returning to Adam.

"You're distracted." Her lips pouted.

Mark looked at her hand where it rested on his arm. "It's been a long week."

"But you're with me now. Can't you forget everything else for a while? I don't get to see enough of you."

"I'm sorry. I've tried." How he'd tried. They ambled the block in silence. "What do you see in me?" They stopped walking, and he looked into her eyes, curious to know her thoughts. "I'm an engineer with no plans to leave Dayton. I work a job that demands long hours from me. I practically neglect you because of it. Are you with me only because I'm not in uniform and haven't left to fight the war?"

"There is that." Her smile died under his stare. "For goodness' sakes, Mark, I'm kidding." She turned from him and continued down the sidewalk. "You're a man who's sure of himself and his God. Yes, you're busy and I rarely get to see you, but when I do, you ask crazy questions like this. There's little surface banter." She looked up at him and sighed. "Sometimes I wish there was more of that, but I'll take what you have to offer."

Mark followed her and wondered why her answer wasn't good enough. It felt like she'd pulled out a yardstick and he measured in the "nice but not lovable" category.

He didn't want to be someone's time-filler while they waited for something better to come along. Paige was more than that to him. Beauty infused her from the inside out, she lived patience and virtue teaching children all week, and she chose to spend time with him because she liked him.

What more could he possibly want from a woman?

✳

Saturday afternoon, Evelyn joined a group of women headed to a tea at Mr. Desch's home. The constant dressing like the other WAVES left her feeling unoriginal, so she'd decided to stake her claim on individuality. She pinned a broach on her jacket.

When Viv saw it, she laughed. "Is that the best you can do? A flower broach?"

"One has to work with what one owns."

"Then we need to shop. If you're going to poke at the rules, at least do it with some style that doesn't say, 'This is my grandmother's.'"

"How about colored gloves?" Lonnie tossed a pair at her.

"In the summer?"

"You'd definitely be the only one wearing them."

Mary Ellen looked her over. "I think you need an anchor broach. At least that alludes to the navy."

Evelyn shook her head. "The idea is to tweak this incredibly boring uniform. Add some personality to it. How can one go to a tea looking exactly like everyone else?"

"It simply isn't done." Viv shook her head.

"Exactly." Evelyn caught the glint in Viv's eye and took a step toward her. "Are you poking fun at me?"

"Me?" Viv slipped back. "Never."

"If we don't plan to walk, we need to leave." Mary Ellen stood at the door, chewing on a fingernail.

The ribbing continued until the bus arrived at the Desches' small home. Evelyn didn't mind, especially as others joined in. Maybe they would add their own little statements of individuality. It would certainly make things more interesting.

As soon as they stepped into the backyard, Evelyn could tell Mrs. Desch liked to entertain. A group of women stood next to their hostess near tables loaded with finger foods and drinks. They seemed determined to welcome the WAVES with style. Mrs. Desch looked as if she'd walked off the pages of *Vogue* magazine.

Evelyn couldn't wait to meet the intense man's wife. "I wonder if she's anything like him."

Lonnie strolled next to her, her purse laced across her chest. "I doubt it. Opposites attract."

Mrs. Desch stepped toward them. "Welcome, ladies. We're so glad you could join us. I hope you will enjoy this break from your labors and the opportunity to relax with new friends. There's no agenda other than getting to know each other."

Evelyn looked at her roommates. "Guess that's our signal."

Viv nodded. "Time to mingle and make nice."

Lonnie took off for a table loaded with cookies and other sweets. Mary Ellen trailed behind her.

A smartly dressed older woman approached Evelyn. "Hello, I'm Marjorie Miller."

"Evelyn Happ."

"That's a beautiful name." The woman gestured toward a set of chairs, interest in her eyes. "Would you like to join me?"

"Thank you."

"First, let's get something to drink." The stately woman walked to the beverages. She filled glasses with iced tea for both of them and offered one to Evelyn. Mrs. Miller led the way to the chairs, tugging off her gloves as she settled into her seat. She took a sip of her tea and leaned forward with a smile. "I enjoy meeting new people but always find the first minutes unsettling. It's almost like those first dances one attends as a student. Who will interest me and find me interesting?"

Evelyn laughed. "That description is pretty apt." She looked around the yard. The other women had clustered in small groups. "I'm still finding my way around town."

Marjorie eyed her over her glass of tea. "Then I think I'll adopt you. You need someone to show you around, and you can escape to our home when you need a break from wherever the navy has you stashed."

The offer sounded wonderful. "Thank you, Mrs. Miller."

"Start by calling me Marjorie. Mrs. Miller is my husband's mother. Now tell me about yourself. You're at Sugar Camp, aren't you?"

How did the woman know?

"Don't worry, dear. It's impossible to miss you gals when they close the road and you march to work. That is quite a sight."

In no time, Mrs. Miller had pulled many details from Evelyn and made her feel like she'd known the woman for years. "My son, Mark, works in Building 26 with Mrs. Desch's husband."

"We've met a few times."

The fashionable woman quirked an eyebrow at her.

"He's been quite helpful, though he's protective of his project."

"That's my Mark." Pride bloomed across Mrs. Miller's face. "How do you like your work?"

Evelyn tried to think of a diplomatic way to answer. "It's important."

Mrs. Miller studied her. "But not what you expected?"

"Not really."

The woman patted her hand. "Sometimes God uses the trying times to teach us important lessons."

"Doesn't that require one to actually believe?"

"No. Sometimes the lesson is what attracts us to Him. I've found Him to be a gentle yet persistent wooer." Mrs. Miller smiled, a gentle peace radiating from her countenance. "If you seek Him, He just might surprise you."

Evelyn started to politely, yet firmly decline, when something stopped her. "Maybe I will."

"I'd like to have you join my family for lunch tomorrow. Come to church, too, if you like, or we could pick you up after service. We don't live far from Sugar Camp. Promise you'll join us."

"Yes, ma'am." The cafeteria at Sugar Camp might be open twenty-four hours a day, but its fare couldn't be as good as a home-cooked meal. She'd be a fool not to accept the offer.

Before Evelyn quite knew what had happened, she had agreed to a time for the Millers to pick her up for morning services. Marjorie excused herself to meet some other members of the WAVES. She patted Evelyn's hand as she stood up. "It was so nice to meet you, Evelyn. I look forward to seeing you again tomorrow."

Vivian settled into the chair Mrs. Miller had vacated. "You look a bit stunned."

"You could say that." Evelyn leaned back and absorbed the new dynamic. "Looks like I've been adopted by Mrs. Miller."

"That's nice."

"Umm." Evelyn didn't know which she dreaded more: conversations about a God she didn't know anything about, or more time with a man who didn't see her as anything more than another empty-headed woman.

✳

Sunday morning, Evelyn waited at the entrance to Sugar Camp for the Millers to pick her up. Constantly being in uniform certainly had one advantage: She didn't have to waste time deciding what to wear. Several of her cabinmates had also made plans to attend services but had scattered to churches around Dayton. Soon, a Studebaker pulled next to her, and Mrs. Miller waved her over.

"I'm so glad you joined us." Mrs. Miller introduced Evelyn to her husband, Louis, and daughter, Kat. "Climb in back with Kat."

In no time, the small group hurried up the steps of the Christ Community Church. Anxious thoughts ran through Evelyn's mind. What if she didn't like the services? How could she leave? And what if she didn't like the church? Would she regret depending on others for transportation? Too late to worry now. She set her shoulders and pasted a bright smile on her face as she followed the Millers into the fellowship hall.

Mrs. Miller clasped Evelyn's hands. "My husband will go ahead and grab a pew for us. I'd like to introduce you to some friends."

Evelyn followed Marjorie into the sanctuary, pausing as the woman made sure she met everyone they passed. Mr. Miller had held their seats for ten minutes before they made their way to the front. Kat had stopped to chat with other girls, a quiet but animated discussion.

Someone touched Evelyn's shoulder, and she turned to find Mark Miller standing in the aisle.

"Is there room for me in this pew? The others are filling up."

Evelyn turned and surveyed the room. He was right. She eased closer to Marjorie.

Mark leaned over Evelyn to talk to his mom. "You didn't tell me Evelyn was your guest."

"I forgot to mention it." A twinkle graced Mrs. Miller's eyes. "But if I'd known—"

"I would have done it anyway." Her son sang the words with her.

While she waited for the service to begin, Evelyn examined the stained-glass windows. The images of a man praying desperately in a garden followed by a scene on a cross and the empty tomb intrigued her, but she didn't know what to make of them. No matter how many times she joined a friend at church, the story never made sense to her. Why would a relatively young man in His early thirties allow His life to be taken? Especially if He was truly the Son of God? But as Evelyn listened to the congregation sing and the pastor preach, she longed to understand.

Mark shifted against the hard pew. As he did, his shoulder brushed hers. The warmth of that small connection caused Evelyn to consider leaning closer and prolonging the connection rather than rushing to break it like she should.

What was it about this man that tied her stomach in knots and left her unsure? This one, he was different than others she knew—and in a way that appealed. She eased a breath of space between them and tuned back in to the sermon.

It didn't take long to determine she had daydreamed through too much of it. The sermon made little sense catching bits and pieces. She looked around the sanctuary, her gaze resting on Mark.

He turned and caught her watching him. A knowing smile stretched across his mouth.

Part of her faltered at the way he could read her thoughts.

No one did that. But wasn't that what God wanted to do? Wasn't that why she'd steered clear of church? She didn't want to acknowledge God because that meant He knew everything about her. There could be no secrets or hidden spaces of her heart.

Mark turned his attention back to the front of the sanctuary, and she wondered what it would be like to live life known to the deepest parts of her soul.

Chapter 5

May had almost evaporated, taking Kat with it. Mark hadn't stopped to think how quiet the house would be without his sister stomping around. Somehow, she'd talked her way onto a traveling team, while his life continued in its rut: work, try a new solution, watch that solution fail, work some more.

Some days he felt like an old man way before his time.

He should be grateful, he supposed. At least he was using his education in a way that served the war effort without picking up a rifle. Maybe he'd be more effective with a rifle. Debatable. He'd never hit anything smaller than the side of a shed.

Yep, call him the king of effectiveness.

By Monday, May 31, Mark was ready for something to happen. Adam had to start working, or the project could be over. They'd exhausted all the possibilities and configurations. Today, they'd test the machines yet again, and Mark prayed for a miracle.

Refreshed from the weekend, Mark entered Building 26, eager to take another crack at Adam. A machine was predictable. Rational. When it didn't work correctly, there should be a logical reason. The challenge lay in identifying the breakdown and rectifying it. He brushed by several marines as he made his way to Adam's room. About time they had sufficient men stationed to keep wanderers out. Maybe Evelyn's visits had reinforced the need for a constant presence. After the marine posted at the door checked his name against those listed on it, the guard allowed Mark to enter Adam's classroom.

John and several others stood around the room. It already felt closed in and stuffy. What he wouldn't give for windows.

Mark tossed his hat on the coatrack and hung his jacket. "How'd the test runs go last night?"

John shrugged. "We haven't been debriefed yet. Ready to feed another message through this big boy?"

"Ready as I'll ever be." Much as Mark wanted this to work, he struggled to hold on to the hope that this time would be any different than the thousand other times the Bombe had wrestled with coded gibberish.

"All right." John waved at one of the technicians, who set the wheels to the assigned starting position.

Adam whirled to life. The noise soon reached a deafening pitch as the rotors and gears raced through an almost infinite number of cycles, trying to identify the one that would match that used by the Germans.

By having four wheels with twenty-six settings, the Germans had exponentially expanded the potential code settings. Up to 456,976 initial settings times 456,976 tumbler settings meant the Enigmas had an almost infinite number of configurations. The odds boggled Mark's mind. That impossible problem dominated his work each day. Mark glanced at his watch and saw the machine had already been at it for thirty minutes. This could take hours, if it ever did match the code. Maybe he should get coffee; let John and the others babysit the machine.

"Need anything from the cafeteria?"

John roused himself enough to shake his head. "Nah. I'll grab something when you get back." He looked the machine over. "So far no hitches."

Mark nodded. "But that doesn't mean this time we'll get the breakthrough."

"Oh ye of little faith."

True. But the constant failure had worn him down. Maybe they'd beat their heads against the wall until the end of the war. Never quite reach a breakthrough.

Boy, he'd developed a defeatist attitude. He needed to shake it off and move on. Mark marched to the door. Adam stopped, and Mark stilled. Could this be the time?

Silence almost as deafening as the noise had been minutes before settled over the room. Mark considered banging his head against the door. Another short. They'd have to hunt it down and replace that part. All in an effort to get the machine up and running so it could break down again.

Then Adam backed up and stopped again. Mark and John stared at the machine, then at each other. Silence again filled the room. But a beautiful silence. The kind that meant the Bombe had a match.

They raced to Adam and pulled the printed story with its wheel positions from the machine's side.

Mark stared at the piece of paper. He took the piece to the mocked-up Enigma machine, set the Enigma to the corresponding settings, and entered the coded message. Gibberish printed out the other side. It looked like German, but someone fluent in the language would verify.

Hope pounded through Mark as he looked at the page. Maybe, just maybe, Adam had made a breakthrough.

❋

Evelyn sat at the table, trying to solder the intricate designs on the rotor in front of her. All those hours of fine needlework her mother had foisted on her paid off in the delicate and exacting work. These rotors must be part of the large machines in the guarded rooms.

The work put her mind to sleep, making it hard to stay focused.

Instead, she allowed her thoughts to wander over the people she'd met since arriving. Sunday at the Millers' had been. . .nice. Marjorie served as the perfect hostess, and Evelyn had felt welcome and included. Mark had disappeared soon after dinner when his girl called. Evelyn wondered why this woman hadn't joined them for church and Sunday dinner. The thought felt small. It wasn't her place to be jealous. What did it matter to her if Mark had a girl? It wasn't like she wanted the position.

Did she?

Of course not. She hadn't joined the WAVES to find a man. But if she had, Mark Miller fit the bill. Smart. Good-looking. Kind.

Evelyn shook her head. She needed to focus on gaining experience, the kind that would help her turn her textbook knowledge into practical skills she could use. That was the least she could do to make this time in Dayton valuable.

Dayton certainly wasn't what she'd had in mind when she joined up and left her home in DC.

She'd thought to move from one city to another, but Dayton barely qualified with its 211,000 souls. The District had an urbane flair. Wartime energy pulsed through it. The parts of Dayton Evelyn had seen couldn't compare. And Mrs. Miller's home couldn't compare to her parents' place in Georgetown. During the Millers' Sunday dinners, ambassadors and congressmen didn't surround the table. Maybe that's why the conversation flowed and left Evelyn with a longing to return.

"All right, ladies. We'll take our break now." Charlotte Johnson, the room's den mom, took out her book while the other WAVES relaxed. In a soothing voice, she picked up reading *Little Women* where she had left off at the last break. Her voice had a peaceful quality that lulled many in the room to a restful state. Evelyn couldn't decide whether she liked it or it annoyed her. With each chapter, however, she found herself pulled deeper into the familiar tale. The only problem came when she envisioned Katharine Hepburn as Jo. Before the movie's release several years ago, she'd pictured Jo differently. Now Katharine's face intruded on her imagination.

Evelyn slipped out of her chair to walk to the restroom, her heels clicking loudly against the floor. Sunlight streamed through the windows, warming the walkway that vibrated with excitement. The marines stood at their posts, but others hurried up the hallway toward Adam's room. She followed a few steps behind, wondering if she could slip in and learn the source of excitement.

The marine at the door stopped her. "Your name."

"Evelyn Happ."

He looked at the list but didn't find her name. "I can't let you in."

"Please?" She batted her eyelashes and hoped he'd make an exception for her. He stared at her and moved to block the door. "You aren't authorized."

"Sometimes I wish you all weren't so obstinate."

He looked past her, jaw sharply chiseled as granite.

"Fine." She brushed past him, fighting the urge to stamp her foot in frustration. Something had happened, and she'd probably never learn what. Especially when everyone lived under a vow of silence. She couldn't even talk to the women in her room about what they did. It would take someone with a head full of bricks to not realize the twenty-six points on the rotor corresponded to the twenty-six letters in the alphabet. All she wanted, no, *needed*, was to discuss the project with somebody who understood it.

This was an historic project. It had to be. The computing power in Adam was immense.

✳

Mark and John whooped.

"I can't believe it." Mark ran his hand through his hair as he studied the machine. "Adam found something."

"How can we make sure this isn't a new malfunction?" Wary hope shone on John's face.

"Let's take the message and run it through Eve. If Adam made a hit, so will Eve."

John hurried to Adam and took the original message as well as the stop. He turned to the technicians. "Don't do anything with Adam until we return."

Mark and John hustled into the hallway and followed its labyrinthine path. They turned a corner, and Mark bounced into somebody.

A soft sound came from the woman as she landed on the floor.

"Excuse me." Mark reached down to help her up as John tap-danced beside him.

"Come on, Mark. We've got to get to that room."

"Go ahead. I'll be right behind you."

The gal looked up at him, and he found himself staring into familiar gray eyes.

"Mr. Miller. Do you run into girls often?" Mischief was written across Evelyn Happ's face.

"Only on Mondays." He helped her to her feet.

"My lucky day. Where're you off to in such a hurry?"

He wanted to tell her. She might actually appreciate what they'd accomplished. When she looked at him with such expectation, he wished he could answer. But he couldn't. Answer once, and he could find himself on the Pacific front faster than he could say "GI."

"Sorry." He shrugged. "You know the rules."

Her face fell, renewing the temptation to share his news. "Hopefully the powers that be will let us know eventually."

"Maybe. I'd better catch John."

She nodded, but he found himself reluctant to let go of her hand and break the connection. "Will you join my family for church again this week?"

She paused as if to consider her words. "I think I'd like that. Your mother has been very kind to me."

"She's that sort. She likes to take people under her wing. Show them around. Right now, you're her protégé." He gave her a mock salute. "See you Sunday."

"Yes."

He felt her gaze as he rounded the corner and headed into Eve's room. Tension-filled engineers watched Eve as if their lives depended on her response to the code. Even Desch and Meader had come. Meader stood at ease, while Desch hunched in a chair. The stress and strain of the last months had marked the man bearing the brunt of the navy's pressure.

Mark prayed and paced the floor while Eve gyrated through configuration after configuration. Time crawled, and he wondered if they'd missed something with Adam's stop and reversal. Maybe Adam had simply malfunctioned and they'd failed to recognize the signs of another breakdown. One they'd missed because they hadn't seen it yet. He crossed his arms and leaned against the wall. *Father, please let Eve find it, too.* They all needed the hope some success would bring. Thomas Edison might have said he found ten thousand ways not to make a light bulb before having success, but they didn't have the luxury of time for that many errors.

Men died every day. Others, too. He thought of the children like Cassandra, Josie and Art's foster daughter from England. But the remaining children in Britain couldn't escape the war. The program to ship them to North America had stopped after the sinking of the *City of Benares*, when only thirteen of the one hundred children on board had survived. Maybe the Atlantic would reopen as a means of escape when Adam and Eve succeeded against the Germans' code.

The clock on the wall ticked the minutes away. Tension tightened Mark's neck and shoulders until it felt like they would snap.

Then it happened.

Eve stopped.

Eve reversed.

Eve stopped again.

A cheer erupted as Admiral Meader walked toward Eve. Desch lurched to his feet and hurried to the printed story. He waved Mark over. "Run this through the Enigma."

Mark nodded and walked to the second Enigma. His heart pounded in anticipation. The Enigma would provide proof of their success—or failure. He turned the four wheels to match the settings on the story. A technician brought a message over and typed it into the Enigma. Meader read the paper tape as it slipped from the machine. Mark smiled as once again he thought he recognized some German words. Meader slapped him on the back.

"Gentlemen, we have a jackpot!"

Chapter 6

The cold month of May had given way to June. But the routine of life as a WAVES could drive Evelyn crazy. She needed a change from sitting in the same chair, day after day, soldering rotors. She squirmed at the thought of listening as Charlotte read through another work break.

Yes, the work had value.

Admiral Meader had let them know Adam's one stop in the code had already paid for the project. Good. But she wanted more. She longed to be part of the program that led to more stops. The energy flowing beneath the surface that day had been electric. And she'd watched from the sidelines.

She didn't want to be a small cog in the larger project. While the project needed each little gear and piece to work, she felt cut out of the overall vision. Even Vivian looked at her with disapproval. Why couldn't she settle down and at least pretend contentment? While the other gals relished their breaks and having Charlotte read the next chapter to them, Evelyn itched to dash into the hall, find Mark, and ferret out what else happened while her fellow WAVES stayed locked in their isolated room.

"All right, ladies." Charlotte stood and clapped her hands. "Our day is done. Time to gather with the others for the walk home."

Evelyn joined the women at the door.

Would the WAVES have met her expectations if they'd taken the train all the way across the country to the West Coast?

No. The underlying restlessness stemmed from more than her position. Evelyn knew that as surely as she knew there would be no mail in her slot when she reached Sugar Camp. She marched out of Building 26 with the other WAVES.

"What has you in a funk?" Lonnie strode next to her, marching in time with the others.

The orderly clump of hundreds of feet marching in time drilled into Evelyn's head, adding to the layer of tension pounding her head. "Not sure."

"Join us for dinner. I'm ready to spend time with friends." Vivian turned and grinned from her spot in front of Evelyn. "The kind that like to have fun." She waggled her eyebrows, and Evelyn laughed at the Groucho Marx impersonation.

As soon as they reached Sugar Camp, the three girls locked arms and hurried to the cafeteria. Evelyn allowed the other two to drag her to the mail area. While Vivian and Lonnie hurried forward to their slots, Evelyn hung back.

"Come on. You need to check, too." Lonnie fixed her sternest stare on Evelyn. Evelyn shook her head. "There's no reason."

Vivian pouted. "Just because you haven't had mail yet doesn't mean today won't be your day."

"You don't know my family." Her father was entirely too busy to waste time contacting his only child. Government contacts would keep him in perpetual motion. And her mother would be actively engaged on the social circuit. When one was married to an industrial lobbyist, one must be seen. Letters to a daughter were not seen by the people who mattered. Maybe Evelyn was destined to live a life where the only safe expectations were those that never developed.

"Do you want me to check for you?" Lonnie's offer was sweet, but it wouldn't change anything.

Evelyn approached her slot. Just once. . .

She closed her eyes, took a breath, and reached into the slot. She felt nothing but the wooden sides. "See. Nothing." She forced a smile. "I really don't need to look to know there won't be mail."

Vivian's jaw had dropped, and Lonnie shuffled her feet.

Evelyn sniffed and stepped back. "I need to get something from the cabin. See you guys at supper." She hurried from the building before they could see the tears. Maybe someday, the daily reminder that she didn't matter wouldn't hurt. Maybe.

That night, Evelyn made sure she buried her nose in a book whenever Lonnie or Viv looked ready to engage her. The next morning, she hurried from the cabin and into formation. She needed the anonymity of hiding in a sea of women.

The recent arrival of more WAVES made that easier, but it also indicated the program had accelerated in some way. While she wanted to hide, would the additions make it harder to stand out at NCR? Her skills made her unique from most, but she could be stuck with the mundane job of soldering rotors until the war ended. The thought killed her dreams. Maybe she should have followed her mother's advice and settled for a worthy occupation like nursing or teaching. Instead, she'd risked everything on a gamble to get her father's attention. Ironic, considering he'd be more likely to pay attention if she'd stayed in DC and married a society man.

After she lost count of which rotor she was on, a shadow settled over her.

"Hey, Evelyn."

Evelyn looked up to find Viv standing over her.

"Ready for lunch?"

"Can we leave Building 26?"

Viv laughed. "And go where?"

"Don't you think they have another cafeteria or two on this complex? Maybe the food's better." Evelyn wrinkled her nose. "Would you like Spam casserole or Spam loaf today?"

"You have a point."

Sometimes it felt like more than a railroad spur separated Building 26 from the rest of the NCR complex. Her stomach growled, and Evelyn laughed. "Guess I should settle for any food I find."

The two joined the other employees filtering into the cafeteria. After filling a plate with an egg salad sandwich and bowl of fruit, Evelyn found a table with two vacant seats. Viv settled into the chair across from her and took a bite of some sort of casserole Evelyn had avoided.

Viv pointed her fork at Evelyn. "Join us tomorrow? A group of us are taking a bus to Coney Island in Cincinnati."

"What's that?"

Viv grinned with a glint that worried Evelyn. "Join us, and you'll find out. Quit thinking so much, and come have some fun. All this work is making you a dull girl."

Evelyn took a drink of milk. "All right. I'll join you. Can I help with any of the details?" The last time Viv had planned an event, key details like transportation and meals got overlooked.

"I've got it covered." Viv wrinkled her nose. "That was a one-time occurrence."

"Are you certain? I'd hate to walk all the way to Cincinnati. Sure you don't need me to help?"

"Oh no you don't. I'm redeeming myself. Expect the time of your life." Viv flounced off to join a couple of WAVES at another table.

Evelyn watched her go and chuckled. Tomorrow would be an adventure.

※

The next morning, Viv bounced Evelyn out of bed before the sun had crested over the horizon.

"Come on, Viv. This is my one morning to sleep in."

"Only because you're going to church with that local family."

She had a point. "Still. . ."

"If you're coming with us, you have to get out of bed, sleepyhead. The sun is up, and the bus will leave whether or not you're ready." Viv grabbed Evelyn's blanket and pulled it back. "Come on." She made a motion like she would tickle Evelyn out of bed.

Evelyn launched to her feet, laughing. "You've convinced me."

"Comes from growing up with oodles of siblings. You won't regret it."

Maybe not, but as she raced around her roommates to get ready, Evelyn wondered how comfortable the bus trip from Dayton to Cincinnati would be. In a rush, a group of about eight WAVES piled into Sugar Camp's not-so-trusty woody station wagon.

"Are you sure Woody will last to the station?" Evelyn shifted to get someone's elbow out of her side.

Lonnie twisted awkwardly in the front passenger seat. "If not, we'll have a long walk ahead of us. Let's get this bucket of bolts on the road."

Virginia Jones sat behind the wheel and turned the key in the ignition. After a few stuttering attempts, the engine finally turned over. "Here we go."

Fifteen minutes later, after some starts and stops, she pulled over near the bus stop. Evelyn stood in line with the others to get her ticket.

"There they are." Vivian's voice squeaked. "I didn't think they'd come."

Evelyn followed Viv's gaze and saw a group of men, some sailors and some civilians, headed their way. One or two had a girl with them, but all seemed eager to have a good time. Evelyn scanned the group. It added an interesting dynamic and increased the outing's appeal. She'd kept her head down too much since arriving. Her gaze landed on Mark Miller—with a woman who looked like a movie starlet hanging on his arm. Paige?

※

Mark had welcomed the chance to get up to Coney Island. Without Kat to nag him into taking her every other weekend, this might be his best chance. The summer was young, but with the hours work demanded, he couldn't expect more opportunities to get away to Cincinnati. Paige had jumped at the chance to accompany him and the Building 26 group.

He watched the blond beauty on his arm. She flitted beside him more than she walked, seeming to float with each step, a light touch on his arm.

She wore pants and a colorful blouse and had wrapped a scarf around her hair. Paige shone like a ray of light amid the WAVES in their sports clothes, where most still tended to navy and white like their uniforms. Paige matched what he looked for in a woman. She was beautiful, active in the community and her church, and for some crazy reason liked him.

She must have felt his gaze, because Paige looked up at him. "Mark?"

"Mm-hmm?"

"Are you sure we need to go with the group? Wouldn't it be more fun to slip off by ourselves? I never get to spend time with you." Her voice purred against his neck.

Mark patted her hand but shook his head. "Not today. We'll have a great time with everyone."

"So..."

"Let's start with them, and we'll see what happens when we get to Coney Island. They invited us to join them, not dive off and do our own thing."

Her smile faltered, just at the corners. "Of course. You're right. Forgive me for being selfish."

Mark tightened his hold on her as someone bumped into them from behind. He glanced away and stumbled as his gaze met that of Evelyn Happ. She'd watched them. Caught some part of their exchange. Why did that bother him? She wasn't his vision of the ideal woman. Sure, she looked great, and she understood him and valued what he did in a way that Paige didn't even try to grasp. He stopped his thoughts from continuing down that path. He was here—wanted to be here—with Paige.

Evelyn had an underlying desire for her life to matter, to have a purpose. He'd seen it when she didn't know it leaked out. Sometimes at church, he glimpsed the wariness mixed with yearning.

No, he wouldn't think about her. While she'd joined his family for church and lunch several Sundays, she'd made it clear she wasn't a Christian. As much as he prayed for her, he'd promised himself he'd allow himself to imagine a lifetime relationship only with someone who had committed her life to Christ. He turned to Paige and listened as she talked about her week teaching first-graders.

✳

Evelyn tried to ignore the envy that cropped up as she watched Mark with his girl. He seemed engrossed in every word she said. Evelyn couldn't remember the last time a man had given her that kind of attention. Instead, when she was with men, they'd either wanted to test her engineering ability or keep her entertained with a movie or dance.

Even that hadn't happened in a while.

What would it be like to be a porcelain beauty like Mark's Paige? She'd never know.

She had two choices: mope or ignore it. Ignoring it sounded much more enjoyable. Especially as a damp breeze tickled her hair across her face as she boarded the bus filled with eligible men. Setting her face away from Mark Miller and the promise he represented but could never fulfill, Evelyn turned to the closest seaman and engaged him in conversation. She'd been so frustrated with her WAVES assignment, she hadn't realized how isolated she'd let herself become. She wasn't normally a wallflower, and as she bantered with her fellow travelers, she felt more like herself. In no time, she had the men and WAVES in the seats around her laughing. When they reached the park, she had a man on each arm, urging her to join him.

Viv caught her eye and frowned. Evelyn glanced around and understood. Looked like she couldn't keep two to herself or one of the other gals would travel solo. Not the right approach if she wanted to maintain friendships.

Instead of pairing off, the group stayed together and tried out the various roller coasters and other rides. A smaller group opted to spend the afternoon at the swimming pool, but Evelyn hadn't made the trip to do something she could do at Sugar Camp. She raced from ride to ride, determined to squeeze as many as possible into the few precious free hours. After one too many sodas mixed with cotton candy, her stomach churned, and she laughingly shooed the others toward another ride. She watched them board a car and started to sit on a bench. Instead, she eased onto something soft.

"Ack!" Evelyn jumped up, hand over her heart.

"I can move," a deep voice intoned.

Heat rushed into her cheeks. "I am so sorry." She couldn't look at him.

Mark tugged her hand. "There's room for two. Come on. Sit down."

Evelyn eased next to him, ready to leap to her feet if there wasn't sufficient room. She settled against the wood slats of the bench and cleared her throat. "Where's your date?"

"She decided to rest by the pool." Mark shrugged. "I'd rather watch the fun here. Want to hop on the next car?"

Evelyn looked at the Wildcat, and her stomach rebelled at the thought of the turns and plunges. "How about the Ferris wheel? That's more my speed at this point."

"All right."

They walked side by side across the park. Mark shoved his hands in his pockets. Evelyn tried to keep her gaze in front of her but watched him instead. He seemed content to walk quietly, while she—tempted to fill the silence with words—bit the inside of her cheek to restrain her chattering.

"How do you like the life of a WAVES?"

She considered the question a moment. "What I should have expected. How do you like being an engineer?"

He stopped and looked at her, eyes sparkling. "More some days than others."

"Depending on if the Bombes cooperate?"

His expression closed, and he warily scanned the people around them. "Be careful, Evelyn."

"You're right." She didn't want to end up in some hospital for the rest of the war because she spoke without thinking. "Do you ever feel trapped by expectations?"

"That's an odd question." He purchased tickets for the ride and handed one to her. "I focus on solving problems. My supervisors expect me to solve problems, and I want to keep them happy."

"I suppose."

They settled into one of the ride's cars. The attendant pulled the bar down in front of them. Trying not to brush against Mark, Evelyn looked out across the river as the Ferris wheel started turning.

Mark seemed content to take in the view. "What do you see when you look at the rides?"

"Marvels of engineering designed to give us thrills as we ride them, while hopefully maintaining safety."

"Know what I see?"

Evelyn shook her head.

"I see laws that were established by a Creator who carefully constructed the world and everything in it. Only a mind so much bigger than anything we could do as humans could create the layers of complexity, then reveal the underlying simplicity to human minds to break down and build on. I think that also demonstrates His concern and love for humans. To think of the myriad complications and details and design them in a way to provide for our needs." He shook his head. "It's amazing and humbling."

The ride ended, and they stepped off.

"There you are." A sugary sweet voice made Mark turn. "I wondered where I'd find you, Mark."

"Thanks for the company, Evelyn." Mark put his arm around Paige's shoulders. "I bet it's time to head back to the bus."

The look Paige shot toward Evelyn made it clear the woman believed she hadn't shown up a moment too soon.

Evelyn watched them walk toward the parking lot. Thoughtfully, she looked up, absorbing the sight of multiple rides constructed of wonderful, whirring wheels and gears, now laced with sparkling lights, outlining them against the darkening sky. What if Mark was right?

Someone or something had engineered the underlying rules that she studied and entrusted her life to. Despite conversations with people like Mark and his mother and the occasional visit to church as a child, she didn't understand the complexities of God. She knew the Christmas and Easter stories. Kind of. Maybe it was time to try to break the code. Begin to understand the faith of those she admired. Determine whether God cared about her and her frustrations.

Chapter 7

Adam and Eve had made successful runs but still hadn't achieved the consistency the navy demanded. Mark wrestled with the problem on his walk to NCR and returned to the same conclusion no matter which angle he used. The group needed fresh eyes. The thought wasn't new to him. In fact, he'd gotten quite adept at avoiding it, but that didn't change the facts.

The only person he could think to bring into the project was Evelyn Happ, an unsettling proposition.

But why should it matter if the person who might bring a fresh perspective to the project was a woman? As his mother continued to invite Evelyn over for Sunday church and dinner, he'd gotten to know her, a fact Paige didn't appreciate. But what could he do? Order his mother to end her friendship with Evelyn? That wasn't right. If Paige was nervous, maybe she should spend her Sundays at church with him and come to dinner, too. He hadn't thought that attending different churches was a problem. Maybe he was wrong.

No, Paige overreacted. Evelyn was smart and savvy. He'd seen how quickly her mind worked as she debated his father on all things biblical. The woman seemed determined to examine everything she learned from as many angles as possible. While she still appeared reluctant to accept a relationship with Christ, he prayed her eyes would open. And that it wouldn't affect her ability to analyze the machines.

The only reason not to mention her ability was pride. Such an ugly word. One he didn't like slapping on himself. But what else could he think? At core, he didn't want to risk a woman finding the solution to the Bombe problem.

He opened the doors and walked into Building 26. After passing through the layers of security, he reached Adam's room, ready to get to work. Then he saw her.

"There's a problem with overheating." No hello or other greeting from Evelyn Happ. Straight to the heart of the issue.

How had she worked her way back into the room? He opened the door and checked for the MP. Yep, there he was. "How did you get in here?"

"Walked in like you." She relaxed in a chair, one shapely ankle laced on top of the other. How could a woman make a uniform look that eye-catching? Mark averted his gaze. "Let's focus on the issue."

"The issue is that you aren't supposed to be here."

"No." She placed her feet on the floor and stared at him. "It's overheating. You're working the machines too hard."

"Any first-year engineering student would deduce that." John glared at her, arms crossed and brows drawn together.

Evelyn dipped her chin in acknowledgment. "But why? What's causing it?"

"Believe me, we've applied the scientific method backward and forward to this problem. If there was an explanation, we'd have it."

"Calm down, John." Mark turned toward the woman. "Have any thoughts you'd care to share on how to fix the overheating?"

"Not yet." She chewed on her lip a moment. "How many RPMs is it supposed to cycle?"

"Too many."

She cocked an eyebrow at him. So she didn't like the fact he glossed over actual numbers. Too bad. He wouldn't say another word until he knew she had clearance.

"So what would you like me to do? Since you won't let me engineer the problem?"

"I don't know. If you'll excuse us." Mark turned his back on her and focused on the machine.

"You are an infuriating man."

"That's what my sisters tell me all the time." This reinforced the point that they needed to get her assigned to the room or moved out of Dayton. No matter how she accomplished it, she couldn't keep breaching security. The ease with which she did so made him wonder who else might be able to break in. "Evelyn—"

"Ensign Happ."

Fine. "Ensign Happ, you need to leave."

"Yes, sir. I'll head back to the completely mindless work of soldering rotors."

"It's important work. Without those rotors constructed properly, Adam and Eve and the other machines couldn't operate."

"I know that." Her words snapped into the space between them as she poked a finger into his chest. "Don't treat me like an imbecile."

He stepped back, unsure what she would say or do next.

She deflated, pulling in on herself. "I'm sorry." She took a deep breath. "You're right that carefully crafting those rotors is an incredibly important part of the process." She turned to leave. "But anyone could do that job. They don't need an engineering background. It would probably be better if they didn't."

Mark shoved his hands in his pockets so that he wouldn't reach out to comfort her. "I'm sorry, Ensign."

She waved his words away and continued to the door. "Try soaking the seals in oil."

"What?"

"I said, try soaking the seals in oil before installing them. That should cause the material to swell and prevent future oil leaks." She slipped into the hallway without looking back.

Mark turned to John. "Do you think. . . ?"

"Certainly doesn't hurt to try. I'll hunt for supplies right now."

"No time like the present to test a theory." And if they could actually stop the oil leaks or reduce the number, Evelyn would have proved her worth.

✳

Evelyn had begun to believe the day would never end. After the humiliating episode in Adam's room, she'd slunk to her assigned room as her colleagues wandered in, quiet chatter indicating a readiness to tackle the day.

She needed to stop. She'd pushed too hard, and if she wasn't careful, she'd be shipped out of the navy. Her days at NCR should be spent like those of the other WAVES: focused on a specific task that might not seem important on its own, but when added to all the other pieces, it created an important whole.

Time to stop forcing her luck and accept her lot.

At the close of the day, the WAVES followed their familiar pattern and marched four abreast along Main Street back to Sugar Camp. A Model A roadster eased past them, overloaded with navy enlisted men calling out cadence. Evelyn ignored them along with the other honks and whistles from the stopped cars. She was more than ready to stop feeling like an oddity, a curiosity on the streets of Dayton.

But as she ignored everything else, her thoughts cycled like ruthless rebels back to her failed attempt. And to think throwing out a trite possibility to solve the oil leak problem would make a difference. Surely those men had thought of and tried it. The suggestion had likely only made her look more foolish than her vain effort to sneak into the room.

She should be glad she didn't have to work in that noisy, sweltering room day after day. Soldering might be stationary, repetitive work, but at least she didn't hear the noise pounding in her mind long after her day ended.

Who did she think she was that she could solve problems that had plagued some of the brightest minds in the country for months?

What had her grandmama always said? Something like, "pride comes before the fall"?

If today was any indication, her pride in her abilities had led to yet another fall. Sometime she should choose to do it when Mark Miller wasn't around. It didn't help that she'd see him again on Sunday. It wasn't like she had to join his family, but she enjoyed her time with Mr. and Mrs. Miller. She even appreciated getting to know Mark outside of Building 26's strictly controlled environment.

His family had something special, something that felt like coming home every time they welcomed her. So different from the formal atmosphere in her own home. She didn't want to believe it stemmed from their faith, but that, too, seemed genuine and real to the very core of each Miller. Though she could tell it wasn't their intention, their openness about their faith unsettled her.

No matter how she challenged him, Mark had a ready answer for every question she asked.

How could she know there was a God? Just look at creation. Could anything as complex and multi-dependent as creation simply spring into being without intentional thought and amazing creativity and wisdom? Despite his Ferris wheel speech, she wasn't sure.

She'd asked him, if God existed, why would He care about her? His answer? Because He chooses to. Mark had taken her to the Bible and shown her the early chapters in Genesis. The story of God creating everything and saying it was good. Of walking with the first two people. Evelyn wasn't sure she accepted the simplistic story, but the thought that a God who had created the world would choose to walk on it with His very creation amazed her.

It also consumed her thoughts in the quiet of the night.

What would it be like to know a love like that?

And how could that very same love turn its back on its own Son?

The WAVES passed through the main gate at Sugar Camp.

"Evelyn, join us for the movie in the auditorium tonight." Lonnie pulled her along as the formation broke apart.

"What's showing?"

"Some second-run movie from last year or something. Does it really matter? Let's stay out of our room for a bit. Relax with some of the other gals before the whole process repeats tomorrow." Lonnie spoke with an earnestness that kept Evelyn from laughing.

"All right. Just make sure Viv and Mary Ellen know what we're up to. I won't have anyone feeling slighted."

A bubbly laugh surrounded Evelyn. She turned to find Viv behind her.

"You're the one we're worried about." Viv pulled her hat off. "You know I'm up for a night of not thinking."

"I thought that pretty much described our days."

Lonnie sighed. "Unlike you, Evelyn, the rest of us are pretty content to do what the navy tells us to and forget about it the moment we leave Building 26. There is more to life, you know. Even if that more includes a movie."

Mary Ellen walked up. "Movie? I hope this one includes Cary Grant."

"I'm hoping for James Cagney." Viv pretended to swoon while Lonnie caught her.

"You are too much." Evelyn laughed, glad to leave her worries behind her. "I prefer Humphrey Bogart. Maybe *Casablanca*."

"That film?" Lonnie rolled her eyes. "I can't see anyone liking it. It's so dreary. Why would Rick let Ilsa go? No, give me a real man like Jimmy Stewart."

The banter continued as the women changed into playclothes and headed to the auditorium. Lonnie shrieked when the credits rolled showing the film of the evening was *Philadelphia Story*. Evelyn grinned at Viv and Mary Ellen, and the three promptly fell into mock swoons. Lonnie frowned at them.

"Looks like you and Mary Ellen can both be happy. Viv and I will have to pretend we're seeing our leading men." Evelyn tried to focus on the antics of the socialite and her two beaus, and it worked. . .most of the time.

※

The next morning, Evelyn slipped into her assigned room in Building 26, prepared to settle in and make the most of her assignment. It might not be much, but she would try her best to focus on doing the job well. Especially since she had no other choice.

Charlotte Johnson walked toward Evelyn's seat, a furrow knit into her brow. "Evelyn, I'm not sure what's going on, but Admiral Meader has asked to see you in his office." She kept her voice low, but even so, Evelyn noticed a couple of the WAVES shift in their seats.

"Thank you." Evelyn stood, a sudden swirl of nausea assaulting her. She pressed a hand against her stomach and swallowed. Maybe this was it. Maybe he was ready to send her home or to St. Elizabeth's for pushing her way into Adam's room.

When she reached his office, she announced herself to his secretary. A moment later, the sailor ushered her into his office. Evelyn stopped when she saw Mr. Desch and Mark in the room. Mark smiled, an act which slowed her pulse a trifle. But why would the three want to see her?

"Ensign Happ, please have a seat." Admiral Meader watched her closely.

"Yes, sir." She eased onto the edge of the seat.

"It has come to my attention you are intent on joining the group engineering our machines."

"Yes, sir."

"Why is that?" He leaned forward, elbows planted on his desk.

Evelyn worried her lower lip a moment. How should she answer the question? "I believe I can contribute to the project."

"How?"

She looked at Mark, but he gave no indication where these questions would lead. "I have an engineering degree from Purdue University. I bring a fresh perspective to the machines and may identify solutions and fixes."

"You think our work has been sloppy?"

"No, sir." Evelyn leaned forward until she almost reached his desk. "From the little I've seen of the machines, I think your team has done amazing work." She took a deep breath. If they sent her home after this, there was nothing she could do about that. "I also know that Adam and the other machines still aren't working the way you and Mr. Desch expect and need. I haven't been here through the stages of development. I won't be weighed down by knowledge that this or that has been tried in the past and didn't work."

Admiral Meader held up a hand. "You've convinced me. More than that, your approach to the oil leaks shows me you should be given "an opportunity.""

Evelyn felt like her heart had stopped. Did he just say an opportunity"? She sought Mark, and he nodded slightly. He'd told them her suggestion? She wanted to leap to her feet and hug him, then shriek. Instead, she remained rooted in her chair and tried not to grin like an overeager child.

"Thank you, sir."

"Don't thank me until you hear the extent of your focus."

Chapter 8

Evelyn walked into Adam's room on June 18, wondering what the day would bring. Getting transferred from her old assignment to engineering hadn't resulted in the excitement and sense of contribution she'd expected. While she now sat in Adam's room, she often had to insert herself into the conversations, an exercise that left her drained. She wanted to participate as an equal with the men.

Instead, she watched someone else turn on the machine. If they were lucky, the machine cooperated and ran for a while. If the day was really good, the machine might hit, leading to a jackpot. If the day was a bad one, the machine would break down and take hours to repair.

The challenge was the troubleshooting.

The delicate Bombes liked to break down when under the pressure of the high-speed runs. Then there was the time needed to set them up. It took precision work to get the rotors set properly. She hadn't seen the process, but Evelyn surmised someone somewhere had narrowed down the possible combinations. Otherwise, it would be impossible to know where to start with the billions of potential combinations.

Mark approached her as she placed her purse and hat on top of a file cabinet. "Have you heard?"

"Heard what?" What was it with engineers releasing information in dribs and drabs? Or was that the military influence?

Mark rubbed his head, tenting his hands behind his head. "The navy sent a memo to Desch, ordering him to scrap the Bombes and start over."

"Start over?" Evelyn couldn't imagine doing that. She looked at Adam and the work it represented. "And lose all the hours and improvements you've made? That doesn't make sense, even for the military. What possible reason do they have for ordering that?"

"That's the question, sister." John Fields pulled a chair up and straddled it.

Mark collapsed in the chair next to John. "The brass are infatuated with an electronic machine. It's déjà vu."

Evelyn looked between the two men. Both appeared lost in a fog of disillusionment.

"Didn't we already go through this?" John crossed his arms across the chair's back. "There's nothing we can do to design and build an electronic machine under their constraints."

"You'll have to catch me up. What's the basic problem with this machine?"

John started to give her a come-on look, so she hurried to add, "Beyond breaking down."

"There isn't a problem if we can get it to work consistently." Mark shrugged. "The key problem? The machine is unreliable, and that's unacceptable to the navy."

"But designing a new one will take months."

"Not the way they see it. The original due date for delivery of the machines holds."

Evelyn took the last chair. No wonder the men were so upset. The navy wanted the impossible. "Has it been like this the whole time? Moving targets and changes?"

Mark nodded. "See why we're worn out?"

"Yes." Time to break down the problem. "The oil leaks are under control."

"Well, better since we've soaked the seals."

"What about the rotors?"

"Still skip contacts."

They had to rectify that problem before Adam could work reliably. "Let's focus there."

John guffawed. "Why bother? It's all getting killed by the navy anyway."

"With an attitude like that, maybe. But we can find the solution if we look. That's what I intend to do. You and the rest have spent too much time on this to scrap it now." Evelyn looked at Mark. Would he agree with her or side with John? She didn't know enough about the project at this stage to troubleshoot herself. A thoughtful look cloaked his face.

She needed the help.

The door banged open, and Desch marched in. "You've heard."

Evelyn nodded along with the two men.

"Don't sit there; we've got work to do. I am not about to follow the memo unless there is absolutely no option. The technology isn't ready to produce what those men in Washington demand." The intense look in Desch's eyes left no doubt they'd spend hours today on the hunt for a solution.

Other than when Desch went to the admiral's office to argue his case, the group worked together. Evelyn's pulse raced as ideas and analysis flowed. For once, she experienced what she'd longed for. She was functioning as part of a group engineering an important problem that required her expertise.

If they found a solution, this might turn into the best day of her life.

❋

Mark watched Evelyn as they threw out ideas. Some were terrible, but others had merit. The problem was they didn't have the time to cover old ground.

Desch had them pull out each component and scrutinize it.

"What are we looking for?" Evelyn's words whispered uncomfortably close to his neck.

He slid a bit to the side and shrugged. "We'll know it when we see it."

"I've always hated that statement. So unhelpful."

"But sometimes it's the truth."

She dipped her head in agreement. "You've got a point. Doesn't make it any easier, though." She sighed and rubbed her forehead as if a headache gathered beneath the skin.

Admiral Meader strode into the room. He surveyed the parts strewn over the surfaces. "Find anything?"

Desch shook his head. "Not yet. But we will. We've got some of the brightest minds in this country working on the problem."

"That's not good enough, Joe." Meader sighed. "I've talked to my superiors. Their position hasn't changed. This design of yours isn't working, so they want to move on."

"And waste millions of dollars and all the invested man-hours?"

"They want to stop the bleeding."

Mark looked at Evelyn out of the corner of his eye. She shifted in her seat and fumbled with her hair, brushing it behind her ears. If he had to guess, she wanted to be anywhere but here. Did her hair feel as soft as it looked?

Desch stared at Admiral Meader like he'd gone crazy, and Mark didn't blame him one bit. Desch turned red. "The navy wants us to scrap the Bombe design? Start over? Just like that?"

The admiral nodded, back stiff as a ramrod. "I got you twenty-four hours to find an alternative."

Twenty-four hours? It felt like a grenade had exploded in the room, killing everything Mark had invested his life in this last year. Desch stared through Meader as if ignoring the man's existence.

Evelyn twisted her fingers in her lap, her gaze bouncing back and forth between the two men and the machine. She mouthed, *What do we do now?*

Mark shrugged. That was the question of the hour.

Hours later, he dragged himself home. They hadn't found the silver bullet, but they'd run out of ideas. Desch had sent them off to get a few hours' sleep before trying again in the morning.

His mother met him in the hallway, a letter in her hand.

"Good evening, Mother."

"A rough day?" She pulled her robe tight at her neck.

Mark tossed his hat on the rack and smoothed his hair. "You could say that."

"I have a plate in the warming oven for you." She handed the letter to him, the creases around her eyes cut deep. "This came today. From the draft board."

As if the day hadn't been frustrating enough. "Wonder what this is about. Maybe they'd like to ship me to Antarctica again."

"Sarcasm doesn't become you."

Maybe not, but it made an impossible situation somewhat tenable. No, she was right. A mom's prerogative. "Sorry." He flipped the envelope over. Another summons to come before the board. Explain why he shouldn't be shipped overseas. It should be a simple matter to get his II-A or II-B status, since he was needed for his job. But the board didn't see it that way. Nope, and the top-secret nature of the project made it impossible to explain why he had to stay in Dayton.

The thought of facing those dour-faced men again was like adding lemon to an already bitter day. He didn't know if he could stomach it.

Scanning the letter, Mark discovered he'd have to show up at three o'clock tomorrow afternoon or the police would come for him. Life would be so much easier if the navy would give him some kind of exemption from service. He served but in a way invisible to most of the population. In particular, the draft board.

"Don't worry, Mom. Everything's fine." His stomach growled, bringing a smile to Mom's face. "I think I'll eat that food now."

※

The next morning, the engineers raced against the steadily moving hands of the clock. If he had to guess, Mark would say Desch never made it home.

"Gentlemen—and lady—" Desch nodded at Evelyn, who colored. "We're looking at this problem from an incorrect perspective." He marched back and forth across the room. "You're focused on the theories of engineering. That's all well and good most days. Right now, however, we must apply those theories to the practical world. While all theories indicate these machines should work, reality is that they don't. What practically could cause that?"

John shrugged. "Heat from the RPMs required."

"Certainly, but we've examined that. There's little to nothing we can do about that. What else? Ensign Happ?"

Evelyn swallowed as her gaze raced across the machine. Mark could almost see her mind racing through calculations and maneuvers in her attempt to find a solution. "Sir, I'd consider whether the individual parts withstand the intense pressure exerted against them."

"A worthy objective. Miller?"

"Maybe the problem is with the contacts. Something getting in between the connections and preventing the electrical impulses."

Desch quirked an eyebrow at him. "Nice piggyback to Ensign Happ's suggestion."

The door opened and Admiral Meader strode in. He thrust a paper at Desch. "I've convinced the bigwigs in Washington to proceed with your design. Too much time, money, and manpower wasted otherwise. They're going along. For now. Get these machines working and the production models ready to transport. We still need those on the train to Washington by July 15." The man turned and left without waiting for a response. The weight of imminent failure departed with him.

"Looks like we have a reprieve, but it's only that." Desch turned back to the machine, his pipe poking out of the corner of his mouth. "We have work to do. Back at it."

A bit before three o'clock, Mark slipped out of Building 26 and headed to his draft board appointment. He'd heard tales from colleagues about being escorted to the train station by military police to ensure they boarded the train to their appointments with various boot camps. At the last moment, Joe Desch or someone else from Building 26 had shown up with a letter of some sort and snatched them back to NCR. Mark had avoided such theatrics, but would his luck hold?

Maybe it was time to serve in uniform. Occasionally as he read the paper or listened to news reports from the front, he wondered if what he did truly mattered.

Would the war be better served if he went to boot camp and wherever the army assigned him? Yet the project at Building 26 was important. The navy presence and security made that clear, even if he never knew the full extent of its value.

If he didn't fully understand the project, he couldn't expect to make the draft board understand. Especially with the vow of secrecy he'd taken. The navy left no doubt he'd be shot if he breathed a word about the true nature of his work.

Mark trudged the last block to the meeting and squared his shoulders. He couldn't go into the meeting weighed down by uncertainty. *Father, You're in charge of this. Continue to guide me in the steps You have for me.*

The unsettled boulders resting on his shoulders slowly lifted. Okay, now he could proceed in peace.

Mark walked up to the reception desk. A harried man looked at him, frost in his eyes.

"Mark Miller here for a three o'clock appointment."

"Yes." The man shuffled a few files. "They're waiting for you. Follow me."

Inside the room, four men sat behind a table littered with stacks of teetering files. Mark nodded at them, then sat on the only open chair in front of them. He wondered if he should hunker down for potshots as he waited for the proceeding to start.

A tall man in the middle, dressed in a dapper suit with gold watch attached to his pocket, stared at him. Mark resisted the urge to squirm under the examination.

"Young man, you appear entirely capable of walking without assistance."

"Yes."

"You do not require a medical waiver?"

"No, sir."

"Yet you have not reported for service. You have no dependents to prevent service. You have not requested conscientious-objector status. I fail to see why we shouldn't escort you to the next train."

"As I stated at my appointment last year, my job is of a sensitive nature and requires my presence."

"You work at the National Cash Register Company."

"Yes, sir."

"I am not aware of any projects that prohibit eligible young men from performing their patriotic duty." The man looked at his colleagues, who nodded their agreement. Mark swallowed around a dry throat, visions of an armed guard taking him to boot camp filling his mind.

"I wish I could tell you more, but I can't."

"Why not?" The man leaned forward, a frown etched on his face.

"Because I've taken an oath that prohibits me from discussing the particulars of my job and responsibilities with anyone. Even my coworkers."

"That is patently unbelievable. We are in Dayton, not some top-secret, secure location." The man narrowed his eyes. "Will you report to the train station on Monday morning for transport to basic training?"

Mark closed his eyes. This wasn't going as he'd hoped when he'd prayed, but he had only one answer. "No, sir."

"Then you will spend the weekend in jail until you are escorted there."

A soldier stepped to his side. "If you'll follow me." While posed as a request, the gun at the man's side and the firmness in his stance made it clear Mark had no choice.

"Do I get a phone call?"

The man grunted. "We'll see if we can arrange that."

Mark followed the man into the hallway, a sinking sensation in his gut. If something didn't happen, he'd be on his way to who knew where. He had to get a call out.

Chapter 9

Sunday morning when the Millers picked Evelyn up, Mark didn't fill half the backseat. Instead, Marjorie looked pasty and Mr. Miller greeted her with an unusually solemn expression.

Evelyn slid into the backseat. "Is Mark ill?"

"No." Marjorie's response fell heavy in the car. "He hasn't come home since he left for work on Friday."

That didn't seem like something the oh-so-responsible Mark Miller would do. "He left work early but didn't mention anything."

"He had a meeting with the draft board. We haven't heard from him or seen him since."

"Has this happened before?"

Mr. Miller nodded. "Yes, but he's always explained that his job at NCR requires him to stay in town. It's worked so far."

"Doesn't the navy do anything? Seems they should since he works for them."

"The navy hasn't. And since he can't explain his job, nobody on the board understands it. You know more about what he does than we do, Evelyn." Mr. Miller shrugged, but it looked like the burden he carried settled on his shoulders rather than eased. "Everything's so hush-hush I couldn't do anything to help him even if I knew where they kept him."

Marjorie wiped her eyes with a delicate handkerchief. "I'm sorry we aren't better company."

"Please don't apologize. If today isn't a good day, I will understand."

Mr. Miller turned into the Christ Community Church parking lot. Marjorie leaned back over the seat. "Please don't think that. I have looked forward to spending today with you. A ray of sunlight in a dreary weekend."

Evelyn nodded, then slipped from the car and followed the Millers into the sanctuary. People filled the fellowship area with quiet conversation, that of friends reconnecting after a week apart. The warmth of the interactions still caught Evelyn off guard. No artifice existed among the members of the small congregation. Instead, they cared about each other in a way that Evelyn wanted to experience. After several weeks joining the Millers, she judged the interest and concern in each other's lives genuine. She'd keep watching but thought she might want to become part of something that real.

Person after person inquired about Mark. Marjorie answered quietly, but her posture collapsed a bit more with each kind question.

Evelyn slipped up to her side. "Should we go find a seat in the sanctuary?"

175

"I think our pew will be there as usual."

"You might need the break from all the concern."

With a wry laugh, Marjorie nodded. "I suppose you're right." She sighed. "There's nothing I can do for Mark by talking. Only prayer can help now."

Evelyn followed Marjorie to their usual pew. Marjorie could pray. Evelyn would visit the Desches, make sure Mr. Desch knew the draft board had one of his engineers. Surely he could do something.

The congregation stood to sing a hymn. Evelyn shared a hymnal with Marjorie but listened rather than join in the singing. Familiar words welled in the sanctuary:

> *"Amazing grace! How sweet the sound*
> *That saved a wretch like me!*
> *I once was lost, but now am found;*
> *Was blind, but now I see."*

The words were no clearer now than when she'd first heard them as a child. Sitting through services for several weeks hadn't helped unlock the meaning. Why sing about grace? Wasn't being good sufficient? Why would anyone need grace if they lived a life of service and adhered to society's laws and mores?

Merely sitting in the church hadn't helped. The pastor seemed intent on communicating truth to his congregation, but Evelyn still didn't understand the grave importance everyone put on his words. The Millers clearly lived in accordance with the teachings of their church. But did it make a difference?

The thoughts made her head ache. She shook her head slightly to clear it. If the questions returned, she'd entertain them. For now, though, she'd focus on Mark. His parents had welcomed her as one of their own. The least she could do was work to secure his return.

On the drive to the Millers' home, Marjorie turned to watch her. "What did you think of the sermon, Evelyn?"

"I'm not sure."

Marjorie quirked an eyebrow at her.

"I was distracted."

"By thoughts of my fine-looking son." Mr. Miller winked at her through the rearview mirror.

"Louis!" Mrs. Miller playfully slapped his shoulder. "I apologize for my husband."

Evelyn laughed and felt a release of tension. "He's fine. And actually, yes, your son did distract me from whatever thoughts the pastor attempted to share with us. I'm afraid I wasn't an attentive listener."

"Here we are, ladies." Mr. Miller parked the car.

"Come help me, Evelyn. Lunch will only take a moment to prepare."

Evelyn followed Marjorie back to the kitchen. The windows in the room opened to a view of the landscaped backyard. Marjorie's victory garden filled the back third of the yard, a project Evelyn's mother would assign to one of the staff. "Looks like the garden is doing well."

"Yes. You can help me harvest some of it next week. The beans are getting close." Marjorie slipped on an apron. "Do you enjoy coming to church with us? The reason I ask is I don't want to force you to join us if you'd rather not."

Taking a moment to consider, Evelyn nodded. "I appreciate attending with you. I can't say I understand everything."

"You'd be an exceptional person if you did. I've attended church my whole life and still find much to learn or a fresh way of looking at something. Our pastor is good at highlighting passages in a new way."

"Why does it matter?"

Marjorie looked at her quizzically and handed her a bowl of peas to snap.

"I mean, why does it make a difference whether you go to church or not?" Evelyn picked up a pea and snapped off the ends.

Pulling a meat loaf from the oven to set, Marjorie grabbed two glasses from the cupboard and filled them with water. "It's not the going to church that matters. It's the relationship with Jesus Christ that makes all the difference. I go to church to be encouraged in my faith and challenged to live in a manner that pleases Christ."

Evelyn considered her words. "But what makes Jesus so special? Each week the pastor invites people to give their lives to Him, but why bother?"

"Do you believe there is a God?"

"I suppose."

"Supposing isn't enough." Marjorie gestured out the window. "What do you see when you look in my backyard?"

"An abundance of plants you care for."

"Who made them?"

"Nobody. They just are."

Marjorie cocked her head, crossed her arms, and studied Evelyn. "Really? With all your scientific training, you believe something as complex as a tomato plant simply came to be?"

"The alternative is to believe that something created everything."

"Why would that be harder to believe than spontaneous evolution?"

Evelyn thought a moment. "I guess because your perspective requires faith."

"As does yours."

The quick rejoinder set Evelyn back. "I don't understand."

"No person observed creation. But neither did any person observe this 'just coming to be' that you accept."

Could Marjorie be right? "What does this have to do with Jesus?"

"The Bible tells us that Jesus is the Word of God. God spoke everything into existence through His Word. And Jesus came to die for the sins of the creation He made."

"Why? That doesn't make sense. If He's God, why die for others?"

"Because of love." Marjorie handed Evelyn a glass of water. A comfortable silence settled between them, as Evelyn weighed the words.

"I don't think I've known anyone who loved enough to lay down their life for their enemies." Evelyn shook her head as she tried to fathom that kind of love. "I'll have to think about that."

Marjorie nodded. "It's humbling to think the God of the universe, the Creator of everything, deemed you valuable enough to die for. If you want to explore this, read Genesis 1–3 and the book of John. There you'll find the evidence for what I mentioned."

"I'll do that."

In a few moments, they had the table set for dinner, and Mr. Miller joined them. After the meal was cleaned up, Evelyn slipped away, but not before Marjorie pressed a Bible into her hands.

"Read it if you're curious."

"Thank you." Evelyn carried the volume as she walked up the hill to Sugar Camp. When she arrived, she saw that Woody, the station wagon, sat in its parking slip. She signed out the keys and drove the vehicle to the Desches' home. Once there, she knocked on the door and waited for an answer.

Mrs. Desch opened the door. "Hello."

"Could I speak with Mr. Desch, please? It's about one of his men."

Mrs. Desch stepped back and motioned Evelyn into the home. "I'll go get him."

Admiral Meader walked around the corner. "Ensign Happ, what are you doing here?"

"I have a matter to discuss with Mr. Desch."

"I'm sure anything you have for him can be shared with me."

Evelyn stood at ease. "I'll have to let him decide since this involves a civilian, sir."

"Has the man broken your heart?" Merriment danced in Admiral Meader's eyes. "I'll be happy to assuage any unhappiness."

"No, thank you, sir." She wanted to shake her head. Admiral Meader's reputation with the ladies might be well-founded, after all.

Mr. Desch walked into the room. "Ensign Happ, what can I do for you?"

"I'm sorry to bother you at home, sir. However, I wanted to make sure you knew Mark Miller had a meeting with the draft board on Friday afternoon and has not returned home since. His parents are concerned the board is sending him out on Monday's train, sir."

Mr. Desch rubbed a hand across his forehead. "Admiral, this is exactly why we require papers releasing my men from the draft."

"I can't do that without jeopardizing the project."

Evelyn stepped back. Should she witness this conversation?

"Well, the project will be jeopardized if I lose the minds required to make the project successful."

"You think Miller wouldn't contribute to the war as a soldier?"

"I'm sure he'd make a fine soldier, but his talent would be wasted." Mr. Desch looked at Evelyn. "Thank you for alerting me to the situation." He glanced at Admiral Meader. "I'll see what I can do."

"Good afternoon, sir. Admiral." Evelyn turned to leave, uncomfortable at staying as the men continued to argue. She hadn't realized how tense things were between the two. And the admiral lived there? So much for Mr. Desch's home being his castle. And to think she thought the Revolutionary War had been fought in part to ensure the military wasn't quartered in private homes.

❋

Monday morning, Mark stood at Union Station, surrounded on both sides by military police. He tried to think of something to say to the men but decided there was no use. They merely followed orders and wouldn't have the clout to reverse the draft board's decision. Without a phone call, he hadn't alerted Desch or anyone else to his status. All he could do was go along.

He'd fight after all. Maybe he'd learn to hit something smaller than a shed. He'd have to, or he'd be the world's lousiest soldier.

Funny that, as the war erupted in Europe and spread to the Pacific, he'd never considered himself eligible to fight. He wasn't soldier material.

Guess he'd get to prove he could do it. And he'd have to excel at it like he had his studies at MIT.

"This is our train, Mr. Miller." The sailor to his right took a step toward the train.

"Where are we headed?"

"Chicago."

All right. The big city. They must think he should be in the navy. Ironic, considering he'd dedicated the last year of his life to a top-secret navy project. Even here, he'd keep his vow of secrecy. He'd rather fight than be shot for treason.

"All aboard." The conductor stepped onto the platform.

"After you, sir." The sailor waved him toward the car.

"Mr. Miller."

Mark turned to find the source of the voice. It sounded vaguely like Desch, but he had no reason to be here.

"Mr. Miller." The voice carried again, this time sounding closer.

"Come along, sir." The sailor nudged him in the side.

"Someone is calling me."

"Miller's a common name. No more delays."

Mark took another step toward the train.

"Mr. Miller, stop. I insist." Mark turned and saw Desch huffing toward him. "Good night, man, making me run like that." Desch took an envelope from his coat pocket and handed it to one of the MPs. "This informs you that Mr. Miller is to come with me. Signed by Admiral Meader himself." Desch winked at Mark. "There are limited advantages to having the man live with me. One is obtaining a get-out-of-the-service letter on a weekend. Come along."

"We can't let you take him."

"You will. And if there are any problems, you'll find him at NCR working for me. Good day, gentlemen."

The MP opened the letter and read it as they walked away.

"Thank you, sir."

"Next time let me know so I don't have to pull you from the train itself."

"Yes, sir."

"You've got a young woman to thank for letting me know your predicament. Ensign Happ determined you shouldn't take that train, and I agree with her."

Evelyn?

"Come along. Back to work with you. There's much to be done."

Chapter 10

J oin us for the company ball game?"

Evelyn looked up to find Mark standing over her, a gleam in his eyes. "I don't know. I'm not much into sports."

"Come now. I don't buy that for a moment. As competitive as you are in here, I imagine you're a killer on the field."

Was that a compliment? And did it mean he saw her as one of the guys rather than as a woman? The thought caused her stomach to sink. "I'd hate to kill your impression of me."

He studied her a moment. "I don't think you could do that."

Somehow, when he looked at her, she wanted him to see her as a woman, not as another one of the guys working to solve an engineering problem. The more time she spent with him, the more important that became. There were too few men like him. Intelligent. Kind. Genuine. Handsome. Her thoughts pulled her up short. After so much time wanting to join the engineering group, now she found that wasn't the end of what she wanted after all. No, she needed Mark to see her as a woman.

"Earth to Evelyn." He tapped her gently on the side of her head, then toyed with one of her curls. The look in his eyes softened, and he let go of her hair like it had branded him. "Well, I hope you join us." He backed away from her as if a platoon of Germans prepared to attack.

※

What just happened? A friendly conversation had somehow taken a deeper turn, and Mark felt like he had waded in the deep waters of the Miami River in flood stage.

John walked into the room, then did a double take. "Seen a ghost, Miller?"

"Look that good, huh?"

"Actually, more like you need a chair. What happened?"

Other than touching hair that felt softer than down? Reading a pair of eyes that said so much more than Evelyn probably knew. "Nothing. Guess I'll take a break."

"It's marginally cooler outside than it is in here with that beast. Never thought I'd complain about it running more consistently."

Mark nodded. "Let's get the other fifteen running well; then we'll see what heat is." He hurried from the room. Paige. He needed to spend some time with her. That would undo whatever had just happened with Evelyn. He called Paige's image to mind. She was about as opposite of Evelyn as one could get. Where

181

Paige was blond and willowy, Evelyn was dark and curvaceous. Where Paige worked with children and seemed inclined to motherhood, Evelyn challenged his mind and had never given an indication she dreamed of a family. Where Paige delighted in frills and feminine wiles, Evelyn lived in uniform. One loved the Lord, and the other didn't. That last factor ended the comparison.

He walked across the tracks to the rest of the NCR complex. *Father, I don't know what happened.* That wasn't entirely true. He'd suddenly seen Evelyn as more than another intelligent mind. She was more, much more. *Okay, You see the trouble here. Help me focus on the things that matter to You.*

If his thoughts wandered like this with one touch of the softest curls he'd ever felt, was Paige the woman for him?

The question left him groaning. What a weak person.

And he thought he was strong? No, he was a fool.

❋

Saturday, Mark picked Paige up on his way to Sugar Camp. The company had decided to take the action to the WAVES, and Mark knew he needed Paige at his side to remind him why Evelyn couldn't be anything more than a friend. Albeit an attractive friend. Paige bubbled over with anecdotes from helping in the children's section at the library.

"You should see the adorable children. I could eat them up."

"I'm glad you enjoy it."

"Adore it." She touched his arm with a light, yet electric touch. "Are you okay? You're distant."

"Another long week." He shrugged. "Almost getting shipped off Monday set the tone."

"I'm so glad that didn't happen."

"Would you have missed me?" He needed to know. Was he merely a pleasant diversion? Or more?

"What a question." He caught her studying him. "You know how I feel about you. You're the only man I spend time with, the only one I want to. What more do you want from our relationship?"

That was the million-dollar question. Silence settled over the car as he turned into Sugar Camp.

"Your silence says it all, Mark." She flounced around in the seat.

He parked the car then turned to Paige. He stroked her cheek, and she leaned into his caress. "I'm sorry, Paige. It's a question I need to answer after praying some more." He got out and rounded the car to open her door. "Thanks for coming with me today. I wanted to spend the time with you."

She nodded, a ghost of a smile shadowing her face as she accepted his help

Mark grabbed the blanket and picnic basket his mom had packed from the car's boot. "Shall we?"

They strolled across the lawn toward the recreation area.

"Miller. About time you showed up. We were ready to start the game without you," John yelled across the ball diamond while slapping his glove against his thigh.

"Will you be okay?" Mark situated the blanket on the ground, placing the basket on top.

Paige nodded. "Of course. Go play. I'll cheer from here."

He watched her settle on the blanket, skirt splayed around her like the petals of a vibrant flower. She blew him a kiss.

He grabbed his mitt from the basket, then jogged to the diamond. "Needed me to win?"

John guffawed. "That's right. We needed the all-powerful Miller to ensure success."

The other men laughed.

Mark jogged to the outfield and pulled his cap lower to shade his eyes. This was what he needed. Fresh air. A beautiful woman. And the chance to take out his frustration on a small ball.

※

Cheers carried on the sultry breeze. The cabin that had felt like a freezer when Evelyn had arrived in May now felt like an oven. Since eleven o'clock, cars had pulled into Sugar Camp, bringing an equal contingent of sailors and civilians to her hideaway. Mark Miller worked his magic somewhere in that mix.

Evelyn didn't think of herself as a coward, but still she hid in the cabin. Evelyn Happ. Hiding from a man. Something she'd never done before. But one careless touch had never shifted the foundations of her world.

She didn't want to like Mark.

To him she was another brain. At one time, that had been everything she'd wanted, to be accepted like one of the guys.

Now that wasn't good enough.

And that hand touching her curls, a simple touch, indicated he might if he let himself.

If that was true, why sweat alone in her cabin? She could enjoy the day's events with everyone else. Sweat dripped down her back, punctuating her foolishness. Evelyn grabbed her hairbrush and pulled it through her curls, fighting the tangles. She applied lipstick and ran out the door. The air outside the cabin felt marginally warmer, but at least a breeze stirred the trees.

She hurried to the baseball diamond.

"There you are." Vivian looked up from a blanket where she sat with several sailors. "I wondered if I'd get to entertain these fine men all by myself."

"That would be such a hardship." Evelyn sank to the blanket and smiled at the sailors.

Viv considered the group. "You have a point. Gentlemen, my roommate Evelyn Happ. Don't let her appearance deceive you. She's a brain."

"Thanks, I think." Evelyn shook her head. She settled her legs underneath her, and soon the conversation volleyed among them as she learned about the sailors. She kept half her attention on the field, keeping tabs on Mark. He played some position out in the field far away from the action. An ensign hit a ball so hard the bat shattered. Mark jigged around the field as he worked his way under the ball. Evelyn cheered when he caught the ball and held it up in his glove.

"Out!" shouted the umpire.

Mark's team cheered, so it must have been an important play.

"You still with us?" Viv teased.

"Hmm. Enjoying a moment of the game."

Viv leaned close to her and whispered, "The game or the player?" She winked at Evelyn, and heat flamed Evelyn's cheeks.

"Never mind." She turned to one of the sailors and began to pull his story from him. Anything to get the focus off her.

❋

Mark joined Paige on her blanket when he got relieved during the next inning. "What did you think?"

"Other than that you were a heroic player?"

Her word choice made him chuckle. "I don't know about *heroic*."

"You made the winning play." She raised her eyebrows and stared at him from under the rim of her hat.

"Not exactly the winning play, but it ended the inning."

"See. That's my point." She smiled, admiration filling her face. "You were the hero."

He leaned back on his elbows, uncomfortable with the adoration that filled her gaze. Mark watched the game for a minute and decided the guys were doing fine without him. As two men rounded the bases toward home, he pointed Paige toward them. "See, the team's performing better without me."

"A fluke. That's all. If you were in, they'd score three runs." She pulled a container out of the basket and set it in front of him. "Your mother prepared a feast for us."

"She expects me to feed half the team."

"Really? Well, I want to keep you to myself, young man." She swept her arm around to take in the crowd. "Even if I share with a crowd."

He followed her motion until his gaze landed on the party at a blanket a hundred feet from his. Evelyn sat on it with another WAVES and what looked to be six or seven sailors. The enlisted men were each in positions that made it clear they wanted Evelyn's undivided attention. She didn't appear to favor any one over another, but he suddenly wanted to leave Paige and walk over there and chase the others away. Evelyn needed someone to keep away the riffraff. He started to get up, when a hand touched his sleeve.

"Mark?"

He startled and turned back to Paige. "Yes?"

She smiled, but it looked brittle. "Nothing." She pulled out a packet of cookies. "Here you go."

Mark settled back on the blanket and accepted a peanut butter cookie before eating it in two bites. Paige wrinkled her nose at his manners, but he didn't care. Instead, he wondered why, sitting here with a beautiful woman, he kept thinking of one a hundred yards away whom he could never have.

Paige turned back to the basket, and he sneaked a peek in Evelyn's direction. She laughed at something, the faint sound reaching him.

"You coming back in, Miller?" John stood at the edge of the diamond, glove on hip, staring at Mark.

"Think you need me?"

"I don't know that we'll ever *need* you, but if you'd like to join in, we've got a spot."

Paige pouted when he stood and brushed his pants off. "That wasn't long enough."

"You heard John. Duty calls."

"It always does. And this is only a ball game." She crossed her arms and looked away. Her jaw tightened, then she considered him a moment. "All right. I'm sorry. Enjoy your chance to play."

"I'll be back after this inning." Mark stood, and his gaze collided with Evelyn's. Her smile jolted him to his core.

Chapter 11

U nable to fight back a yawn, Evelyn stretched and noticed the hands of the clock had crept to eight o'clock. Her shift had long since ended, but the work hadn't. So Evelyn found herself listening to Adam race through another run. She must look like a wilted flower after twelve hours monitoring the machine.

"That's all for now, gentlemen." Desch looked around at the few hardy souls. He caught himself when he saw Evelyn. "And Ensign Happ. We'll try again tomorrow."

"Yes, sir." Evelyn tried to shrug off the sting of being lumped in with the men. As the only woman engineer, it happened often, a regular occupational hazard. But at times like this, she wished she wasn't such an afterthought.

Since Mr. Desch had called it quits in the middle of a shift, she couldn't join other WAVES for the walk back to Sugar Camp. She didn't relish the idea of walking home alone, even though this early in July, the sky was still light. Then her stomach grumbled its protest that she hadn't fed it since noon. The thought of eating another cafeteria meal had her swallowing against bile.

She surveyed Adam. The original two machines had multiplied to four and now sixteen. The number made a small dent in the production the navy demanded. The only problem was none of the machines worked consistently.

Mark insisted they'd find a solution. Even quoted the Bible to support that idea, but Evelyn couldn't join him in his confidence. And she'd seen the fatigue and despair that teased him.

She shook her head to clear the thought. The Bombes were the last thing she wanted to think about. She needed at least a few hours' break. As for Mark, she didn't know what to think about him. Her thoughts returned to him too often—especially for a man who chose to ignore the potential fire that flashed between them in unguarded moments.

The door opened and closed, causing Evelyn to look around the room. If she didn't hurry, she'd be left alone. She pinned her hat in place and slid on her suit jacket.

Mark already had his hat and briefcase and stood by the office door.

"Thanks for waiting, Mark." Often he was the only man who lingered or exercised the common courtesies.

"Join me for dinner?" Mark stepped back as if stunned by what he'd said.

She waited to see if he'd revoke the offer. Suddenly, she wanted nothing more than time alone with him.

"In the cafeteria?" Must have decided to stick with his words.

"I'd love to join you, but not the cafeteria. We'll have to eat there tomorrow." She took his arm. "Right now, we're free, so let's find a restaurant."

"One open now?"

"Even if it's pie and coffee. Please?"

"All right. I know the place."

For an unexplainable reason, she felt taller as she walked beside him. It felt so right to be on his arm headed to dinner. "Where are you taking me?"

"It's a surprise. And if we're lucky, we'll catch the trolley downtown."

Mark picked up his pace as they walked down the sidewalk toward the trolley stop. Evelyn double-timed to keep up. No matter how she tried to tease their destination from him, he refused to give it. Maybe the mischievous boy his mother had told her about still existed under all the education and responsibility. A trolley pulled up at the stop. Mark helped her board, deposited coins for their fare, and guided her to a seat. The trolley generated a breeze that felt wonderful. Evelyn considered taking off her hat and letting the breeze ruffle her curls but stopped short when she caught Mark watching her. That annoying heat warmed her neck and cheeks. She could only hope in the fading light he attributed it to the summer heat rather than to his attention.

Mark rolled his neck, waves of fatigue and tension rolling off him. "I'll be glad when this project is over."

"Really?" Evelyn stared at him, trying to fathom feeling that way. "This project is one of the best things that ever happened to me."

The trolley pulled to the curb for the Union Station stop. Mark pulled her to her feet and stepped back to avoid bumping against her.

"Even the long hours? It's a job, Evelyn. There will be others after the war, and maybe those will allow us to work more regular shifts." Mark led her down the sidewalk in front of the station.

"I disagree. This project has allowed me to do something I've never done before."

"What? Contribute? There's more to you than your mind." He glanced at her. "Much more."

If he believed that, why did he continue to hold her at arm's length, never allowing her access beyond a certain point? She'd thought she understood men, but if Mark's behavior served as a proxy for men, she was sorely mistaken.

He led the way to a hole-in-the-wall restaurant that she would have missed in a casual walk-by. "It doesn't look like much, but they serve Mehaffie's pies here. Incredible. Melt in your mouth."

When he opened the door, Evelyn scanned the interior. A single lit candle dotted each bistro table's blue-checkered cloth. A warm, fruity smell caused her stomach to grumble.

Mark grinned as Evelyn pushed a hand against her stomach. "I take it this will work for you."

"I think so." A vacant table by the window beckoned her. "Can we sit there? I'd love to watch whoever is walking by outside."

"Sure." Mark helped her with her chair and settled on the opposite side of the table. "What would you like to try? I'll get it from the counter."

"Counter? I didn't notice it."

"During busier hours, someone comes to your table. But after eight, Antonio makes the patrons do the work."

Evelyn looked around the empty dining room. "That explains the lack of clientele. I'll take a slice of whatever pie you recommend and a cup of coffee."

A few moments later, Mark returned with a precariously balanced stack of two plates with pie slices and two mugs. Evelyn giggled as he bowed his head, announcing, "Your order, mademoiselle. A slice of Dutch apple or Boston cream along with a mug of perfectly doctored tea. They're out of coffee."

"The apple, please." She grabbed the mug from its precarious position and took a sip. The symphony of flavors hit the perfect note. "How did you know how I like it?"

"Let's see. I've worked with you for more than a month and you regularly drink the stuff with my mom. Plenty of time to notice you prefer milk and whatever sweet is available."

Evelyn stared into the mug. What kind of man noticed those details? A man who could work his way into her heart without much effort. She took a bite of the pie, enjoying the blend of apple, cinnamon, and crumb topping. "Much better than the cafeteria."

As they talked about families and childhood, Evelyn realized this was the first time she'd been alone with Mark. Every other time, they'd been chaperoned by his family, colleagues, or a crowd. The Mark she saw now was every bit as wonderful as she'd imagined. Self-deprecating charm mixed with self-assurance. The man knew who he was. Something about his quiet confidence and inner strength called to her.

Their empty plates had sat on the table for a while when Mark glanced at his watch. He shifted in his seat and smiled ruefully. "I need to get you home."

"Yes. We'll have to be back at NCR all too soon." Evelyn grabbed her purse from the corner of the table. Mark hailed a cab and directed the driver to take them to Sugar Camp. After they arrived, he released the cab and walked her to the main gate, Evelyn feeling the spark each time they bumped into each other. "Thank you. For tonight."

"I enjoyed it, too."

Evelyn hesitated, unsure whether to leave him at the gate or wait. She took a step down the path.

"Wait." Mark's voice beckoned her back.

"Yes?"

He chucked her under her chin, and she fought the desire to lean into his touch. Turn it into a caress.

"Evelyn, you are an amazing woman." The shadows couldn't hide the intensity in his gaze. Slowly, he leaned down. Time stilled. When the barest distance separated them, he stopped. Evelyn closed her eyes, breath hitched as she anticipated the connection. He exhaled a breath, and she sensed him pull back. "See you in the morning." His lips brushed her cheek.

She opened her eyes and watched him go, an unsettled sensation cloaking her. She shouldn't have wanted his kiss as much as she had. Not when he belonged to another girl—at least as far as she knew. She closed her eyes against the knowledge. Maybe Mark was no different from the other men out there. Especially the ones she'd entrusted her heart to in the past. The ones willing to kiss any girl who presented herself. Maybe she wasn't so special, after all. How could she be when another woman stood center stage? With a heavy feeling in her stomach, she turned and walked to her cabin.

※

Walking in darkness was the perfect punishment for a man like him. Mark couldn't believe what had happened at Sugar Camp. He refused to look back, even though every fiber of his being wanted to know if Evelyn stormed away or waited.

What had he done?

Though he may have stopped short of kissing her lips, he'd left her with little doubt of where his thoughts lay. This was a relationship he couldn't pursue. And if his actions somehow became an obstacle to her finding Christ. . .

God, forgive me.

The words seemed so insufficient.

And what about Paige? What had he done? He was a fool. That was the truth in stark terms.

He knew better. The Bible was clear. Do not be unequally yoked. That had to apply to all stages of a relationship or it had no meaning at all. He tore his hat off, slapped it against his thigh, and shoved it back on his head.

When he reached home, he hoped he'd escape notice and slip away to his room. But a light in the living room beckoned him. His father sat in his chair, paper in hand.

"Welcome home, son."

"Father." Mark sank into the matching chair on the other side of the fireplace.

Father eyed him over the top of the paper before folding it and setting it to the side. "What's bothering you?"

Mark searched for words. How to explain without his father becoming disgusted with him? "How did you know Mother was the woman you wanted to spend the rest of your life with?"

A wry chuckle erupted from Father. "Does this mean you think Paige is the woman for you?"

"Yes. . .no. . .maybe. . .I don't know." Mark ran his fingers through his hair. "It's complicated."

"Must be. Probably by a certain woman we've come to know."

"Maybe." Mark groaned. "But there's a problem."

"A pretty big one."

"I should focus on Paige, but something is missing."

"Love is more than fireworks, son."

"But shouldn't that be part of it? Shouldn't there be an element of feeling like this woman is the most amazing person in the world and you want to be worthy of her affection?"

Father leaned forward, elbows on his knees. "But if she doesn't share your faith. . ."

"I know." Mark stood and paced with his hands in his pockets as he worked to moderate his voice. "I can't forget that fact no matter how I try. This woman who challenges me and intrigues me doesn't share the most important thing in my life. And I don't know what to do about it."

"I can speak to your mother about not inviting Miss Happ over for Sunday lunches anymore."

"No." Mark shook his head. "I wouldn't rob her of the friendship. She enjoys it too much."

"Your mother?"

"Evelyn."

"What happened tonight?"

"Why?"

"You don't get this upset unless something specific has happened."

Mark blinked, wishing he had a means of escape, but honesty required nothing less than the truth. "Evelyn and I went to get something to eat tonight after we got off. It had been a long, frustrating day. I asked her to join me, and she agreed." Mark sighed. "I walked her home."

"And something more happened." Father patted the chair. "Sit down, son. Let's pray. You're a man and must make your own decisions, but let's bathe those in prayer first."

Mark settled down next to him and listened to the words that washed over him on the way to heaven's throne room. God's grace would cover him. But what would Evelyn do?

Chapter 12

The morning following her catastrophe with Mark, Evelyn seriously considered missing work. Surely a confused and battered heart qualified as sickness. The thought of facing Mark and trying to work with him exhausted her.

Evelyn didn't think she could pretend nothing had happened, even though technically nothing had. Mark hadn't kissed her.

No, he'd just lowered his head within a millimeter of her lips, then retreated to her cheek.

Who was she fooling?

The only reason a man like Mark retreated was if she didn't match his criteria in some way. Or because he still cared for Paige. But how could he after last night? After hours tossing and turning, Evelyn remained unsettled. She needed to ask Mark some tough questions, the kind she'd rather ignore. But her heart wouldn't let her. No, she needed the truth. Did she fail his unspoken criteria, or did he love Paige and had he merely toyed with her? The possible answers scared her, but she had to know.

"Evelyn Happ, snap awake." Vivian stood in front of her bunk and pulled the covers back. "Get up. The government doesn't care why you're moping."

Lonnie walked out of the bathroom. "Next."

"You're right." Somehow she'd face the man. At least machines acted in a rational manner. "Don't worry about me, Viv. I'll be fine."

Viv didn't look convinced. "That settles it. I'm arranging a weekend filled with fun, activities, and dates. You need to get away from Mark Miller for a while."

"Fine." Evelyn didn't have time to focus Viv on something else. She'd go along this weekend. "But right now, I need to fly."

Evelyn hurried through her morning routine and raced to the marching area, arriving in time to join the formation. A moment later, they started the march down the hill to NCR. When a man headed in the opposite direction pulled over and offered a ride to any WAVES who wanted one, Evelyn was sorely tempted. Instead, she kept her eyes locked forward.

If only she could do that the balance of the day and avoid any run-ins with Mark. Then the day would be a success.

※

Admiral Meader marched into Adam's room, a magazine under his arm. Mark braced for the daily barrage of reasons the project wasn't moving fast enough as

Meader slapped the most recent issue of *Life* on the table. Mark winced when he saw the cover. Several soldiers carried a casket draped with an American flag. He knew from reading his mom's copy that the inside contained a list of American dead in the war. He didn't want to think how the list would grow between the early July issue and the end of hostilities.

"Gentlemen, this is precisely why your efforts are not good enough." Meader jabbed a finger on the photo of the coffin. His face was red as he strode to tower over a seated Desch. "You must get the machines working. Now! Any more delays and our efforts will be pulled by Washington. We are out of time." He looked at each person in the room, then spun on his heel and left, leaving the magazine on the table.

Desch picked it up and tossed it to the side. "You heard the man. Back to work."

The words fell heavy in the room.

Evelyn fingered the magazine's pages, cheeks washed of color. "We've considered which parts are most likely to break down under the strain of the speeds you demand. Did we miss any?"

"Of course not." John's voice carried the frustration of months of fruitless efforts.

"Ensign Happ is correct." Desch pulled off his glasses and pinched his nose. "We need to look at this from a different angle. Let's break the machine into the basic pieces critical to its function."

As they had many times before, the engineers itemized the pieces while Evelyn took notes. They broke into small groups to consider how the pieces might factor into the breakdowns. Evelyn practically ran across the room to join the group farthest from Mark's.

Hours later, Desch called them back to his table. A tight smile etched his face. Desch held a rotor and eased sandpaper over it and back. "You see, gentlemen. Sometimes we forget the practical solutions in our focus for theoretical applications and success." Desch pulled a brush from his back pocket and swept it lightly over the surface. "Let's try this."

Mark wanted to believe this would fix the ongoing problem. But could the multiple problems with the Bombes come down to something as simple as slightly uneven rotor surfaces? If it worked, Desch would be a hero.

Desch handed him a rotor. "Get to work, Mr. Miller. You sand while we watch the machine."

"Yes, sir."

"Mr. Fields, here's one for you, too."

John reluctantly accepted the items. "I'll break the rotors."

"That's why when this works, we'll give the sanding to the women with their delicate fingers and control." He smiled at Evelyn. "But for today, I want you to experience what's needed to make these rotors work. Get to it. Gently now."

Mark sanded his rotor cautiously. Desch's theory made sense. At the speeds the machines worked, even tiny variations on the surface of the rotors could cause anomalies.

Evelyn huddled on the other side of the group, chewing on a fingernail, something she only did when stressed or upset. Had he caused that, or did it stem from the pressure Meader had dumped on the room? Her rush to avoid him prevented him from apologizing or fixing the mess he'd made.

All day, he'd been plagued by a simple question. It echoed in the recesses of his mind. *What would Jesus do?* The lingering question stemmed from the book he'd recently finished, Charles Sheldon's *In His Steps*. There was no question Christ hadn't been honored by his actions last night. But He could be honored by how Mark chose to behave from here on out.

That was the rub.

He knew no way to apologize and right his wrong other than to force Evelyn to talk to him. How could that be Christ-honoring? He must proceed cautiously. Especially when Evelyn didn't share his faith. How could he make her understand without coming across as haughty?

And then there was his relationship with Paige. He must resolve how he felt about her. It wasn't fair to waver, especially when a woman like Evelyn could make him forget Paige. He certainly hadn't honored her last night.

So he took the easy road, the coward's path. He worked as hard to avoid her as she did to avoid him.

※

Even though Mr. Desch had given Evelyn permission to leave at the end of her shift with the rest of the WAVES, she felt like a coward as she snuck from Adam's room. Part of her didn't care as long as she avoided finding herself alone with Mark again. Not that he'd given any indication he'd seek her out. No, he seemed as inclined as she to ignore the whole mess between them. The thought of a repeat of last night's stolen moments and kiss caused her stomach to flip.

She hurried to join Lonnie as the WAVES prepared for the walk back to Sugar Camp.

The redhead looked at her, concern pinching her face. "Are you okay? You look pale."

Better not to explain. Lonnie'd tell Viv, and Viv would hunt for someone to distract Evelyn. The woman had already promised to distract her. Viv certainly didn't need the encouragement. Another man wasn't what Evelyn needed. At all.

"Guess I'm tired."

"After your late night, I'm not surprised. When did you sneak into the cabin?"

The WAVES swung into action, marching four abreast out of the building and onto the street.

"Late." Far too late for her battered heart. How would she feel if Mark had actually finished the kiss? Evelyn didn't want to know and didn't want Lonnie probing. She quickly brought up the article about leg makeup in *Life*. Before long, Lonnie launched into a monologue about a USO event she'd attended. Not what Evelyn had in mind when she brought up the topic, but much better than her futile, confused thoughts.

The early days of July ticked by in the routine monotony of work. The Fourth of July fell on a Sunday, so the afternoon was filled with a picnic, speeches, and then fireworks as the night sky darkened. It created a welcome break from the pressure of Washington's deadlines. Evelyn longed for pockets of time to relax and break the monotony. Finally one Wednesday, her shift of WAVES along with the rest of Building 26 was dismissed early to attend a ceremony at Sugar Camp. A ripple of excitement pulsed through Evelyn. This was something different.

She needed a few moments to freshen up with the girls in the cabin before heading to the parade grounds. Chairs for the visitors and VIPs had appeared while she worked. The WAVES and a large contingent of sailors and officers from Patterson would congregate on one side of the field as they prepared to parade past guests and dignitaries. Then they'd clamor for seats, too.

Lonnie straightened her white summer cap against her red hair. Her freckles had popped out in greater numbers since the gals had started using the camp pool. "Do you think all that marching we did in basic training will pay off?"

"Sure. Remember to keep going no matter what happens or who passes out." Viv sat on Evelyn's bed, scrubbing her white shoes. "How do they expect us to keep these silly things clean enough for inspection?" She tossed the cloth to the side. "We're not stopping, right? Just marching across the field?"

Evelyn nodded. "That's what the lieutenant indicated."

Lonnie groaned. "I hope we don't look out of practice. Imagine the brass getting us up in the morning to march."

"More than to get to Building 26 and back?" Evelyn wrinkled her nose at the thought.

"We'll be brilliant." Viv hooked arms with the other two and pulled them out of the cabin and across the parade grounds. "Have you seen all the servicemen here? Some are from Patterson." Her words tumbled over each other. The gal never slowed down in her hunt.

They reached the formation point, and Evelyn wondered which of the seamen in their summer whites was the radioman who would receive the Purple Heart.

Lonnie looked the crowd over. "You know, I think the only reason they're doing the ceremony here is to get more war bonds out of NCR."

"You are incredibly cynical, Lonnie."

The woman shrugged. "Maybe, but watch, they'll turn this into a publicity event." She took a breath and lowered her voice. "This sailor has done his part; now you do yours."

A large group of civilians attended the event. Some Evelyn recognized from NCR. Then she saw Mark. Things remained awkward between them, and she didn't know how to change that. She wanted to ask him outright why he had tried to kiss her. Ask about Paige. But both topics could lead to uncomfortable questions about why she cared. Questions she'd rather avoid.

Evelyn marched in step with the other WAVES past the officers and civilian bigwigs. Even as she marched, she had a heightened awareness of where Mark stood.

The review ended, and Admiral Meader took the stage to present the Purple Heart. The WAVES joined the crowd, Evelyn hunting for a piece of shade others hadn't already claimed.

Lonnie leaned toward Evelyn. "Meader's droning."

Evelyn agreed. "It's still exciting to think this man is receiving the Purple Heart."

"I suppose." Lonnie kept her eyes fixed ahead, but Evelyn could tell she'd stopped listening.

When the ceremony ended, Evelyn waited for the crowd to disperse. No need to push her way through it back to a sweltering cabin. As she lingered, she wondered if Mark would make any effort to approach her. Maybe things would feel different since they weren't in the stilted work environment.

She shaded her eyes with her hand and stood on tiptoe, searching the crowd for him. A lump filled her throat when she spied him watching her, shoulders slumped and eyes heavy.

※

Evelyn's gaze hit Mark with the force of a Sherman tank.

He needed Paige with him, a very visible reminder of why Evelyn could not be the woman for him. Because when he looked at Evelyn, saw the pain filling her eyes, Mark fought to walk away.

If he walked home, he'd pass by Evelyn. He sucked in a breath, then started that way. His mother's words cycled through his head. He needed to settle down. Find a woman who would love him completely. A woman who understood him.

Whenever she talked like that, he got the distinct impression she didn't have Paige in mind.

John waltzed up to him and bumped his shoulder. "Can you believe we got the afternoon off? My wife will be thrilled to see me before dark."

"You'd better get moving." Mark looked at his watch. "It's already four o'clock."

"Don't you have somewhere to enjoy the break?" John grinned. "A date with your girl? Round up a baseball game?"

"I don't know. I've got something I have to do first." Mark squared his jaw and set his shoulders. He needed to confront the problem with Evelyn head-on.

John scanned the crowd, yet seemed to understand Mark meant Evelyn. "Good luck with that, buddy. She's a hard woman to read."

Truer words had never been spoken.

"But you need to get her back on the team. She's been out of it the last week. It'd better not be because of you." John clapped him on the back. "See you tomorrow."

Mark watched him go and found Evelyn again. Her stance challenged him not to back down, hinting she fully expected him to turn and leave. Again.

A few more steps, and he stood in front of her. "Hello, Evelyn."

"Mark." Her tone wasn't cold but missed its usual warmth.

"Do you have plans right now?"

She studied him a moment. "I don't know. Is that an invitation?"

He shoved his hands in his pockets. "Yes. We need to clear the air before it affects our work."

Her eyes hardened. "Can I risk going somewhere with you?"

Ouch. He'd earned that. "Just for a moment. We can stay somewhere very public." And with the sun shining, they'd avoid duplicating the night's dark cloak of intimacy.

She seemed to weigh something in her mind before nodding. "All right. But only for a few minutes."

He tucked her hand on his arm, pausing when a jolt shook him at her light touch. He could not allow himself to go there. She was wrong for him, and surely he had to be for her, too. A fool. He was one if he thought they could find a way to make a relationship work.

"You wanted something?" Evelyn's soft voice pulled him from his thoughts.

"I wanted to apologize. For the other night."

"Which night?" So she wouldn't be easy on him.

"The night we went to the café after work." Her look dared him to admit it. "When I almost kissed you."

"Don't say it." Evelyn tugged away from his arm.

"What?"

"That you're sorry. That it was a mistake. That it never should have happened."

"But it's true."

She shook her head. "No, there's more to us than that."

"There is no us, Evelyn." He ran his hands through his hair and paced in front of her. "I shouldn't have kissed you."

"You didn't." A storm gathered on her face.

"I wanted to."

"And I wanted you to."

"That's precisely why I couldn't." The thought of fighting Evelyn pained him. He stopped, turned to her, and placed his hands on her arms. She tensed as if prepared to run.

❋

Evelyn froze. Dared she take this conversation deeper, or should she leave? She couldn't walk away, not if she wanted to understand what had happened. Suddenly, all she wanted was to force Mark to explain himself and his actions. "I thought you cared for me." She locked her gaze with his and refused to give him quarter.

"I do. But we must act on more than emotion, Evelyn. Much more." Mark sighed, then heaved in a breath.

Evelyn stared at him. "Why? Because of Paige? Do you feel for her what you feel for me?" She bit her lower lip as she waited for his answer.

The color drained from his face, but Mark didn't speak.

"You can't say it, can you? Can't admit your feelings for her. Do you have any?" People turned to stare, and Evelyn fought to keep her voice low. "Or are you no better than other men? Willing to take whatever you can from women. And if that means playing with two, so be it." She choked on the words. "I thought you were different. Better than that. Guess I was wrong."

"Wait a minute. That's not fair."

"It isn't? Then tell me you're no longer dating Paige."

"I can't." He rubbed his hair. "I wish I could sort this out. It's complicated."

"What's so complicated about acknowledging what we have? Why don't your feelings, my feelings, matter?" She held up her hand, blocking the words before he could speak. "Don't tell me something insincere. I deserve the truth. All of it." She wanted to stamp her foot like a petulant child.

Pain filled Mark's eyes. "It doesn't matter what I want."

"That is absurd. Has Paige placed you under a spell? Removed your free will?"

"No. It's not like that."

"What is it? What does she have that I don't?"

Mark's face tightened, and his eyes looked into the distance. Evelyn wanted to hold his face and force him to look at her. Force him to see her.

"You wouldn't understand my reasons."

"Do not decide for me what I can handle. All I want is honesty. If you're going to steal a kiss, you'd better explain why I'm not good enough for you." Tears pricked her eyes, and she batted against them. "I deserve that."

"You don't believe."

What? That was why he didn't want her? She stepped back under the weight of those three words. "Faith? Faith is more important to you than this?" She gestured between them. "That's your excuse." A sob escaped, and she clamped a hand over her mouth. He took a step toward her, but she took another step back and held up her hand, blocking him. "Stay away."

"Evelyn. . ." Mark reached for her.

"No, stay away." She turned and fled.

Chapter 13

For most of the evening, the activity in the cafeteria and cabin distracted Evelyn from her downward-spiraling thoughts. She tried flipping through *Life* and other magazines, but none of the stories held her attention. Even the images from the war couldn't silence Mark's words. Tears battled her anger, until both raged through her.

With nothing else working, Evelyn picked up the Bible Mrs. Miller had loaned her and flipped to her bookmark. Genesis seemed a fanciful tale, but the Jesus portrayed in John—she didn't know what to think about Him. The words might be English, but the meaning seemed deeper, difficult to uncover. *"I am the vine, ye are the branches."* What did that mean? She tossed the book back on the table.

Mary Ellen was the last woman to make it back to the cabin. She held a book under her arm, and peace radiated from her.

"Where have you been?" Evelyn snapped, then shrugged. "Sorry."

"One of the gals in my room at work invited me to a meeting." Mary Ellen shrugged. "It's a book club of sorts."

Viv bounced next to Evelyn on the bunk, hair pulled back and pajamas on. "What are you reading? Maybe I'll join you next time."

"I don't know that it would interest you." She held out the book. Evelyn saw it was the Bible. "We're reading the book of John." She caressed the cover. "I've attended church all my life, but I've never explored it this way. You should have heard the women discussing each verse. They didn't agree all the time, but they respected each other and the book."

Mary Ellen's description intrigued Evelyn. Maybe this was what she needed. And she wanted to understand what Mary Ellen seemed to have found at the meeting. "Could I come?"

"I'd like that." Mary Ellen slipped the book under her pillow, then smiled shyly before heading into the bathroom.

"I knew you were upset, but this?" Viv looked at Evelyn like she'd just suggested joining a convent. "We have got to work you out of this mood."

Viv climbed onto her top bunk, while Evelyn lay down. She put her hands behind her head and studied the underside of Viv's bunk. Prior to arriving in Dayton, she hadn't thought about faith. Life was something to live to the fullest while you could. But if faith mattered to Mary Ellen and the Millers, she needed to explore it more. Not because of Mark's painful words.

No, gaining Mark's approval was the wrong reason to search.

If she participated, it must be for the right reasons. And this book club would give her a way to search without spending Sunday mornings with Mark. She'd miss spending time with Mrs. Miller, but she needed distance from Mark. Working with him was painful enough. No need to force herself to spend her free day watching him and hearing his words over and over again.

The next week, Evelyn walked across the Sugar Camp campus with Mary Ellen. The women allowed silence to settle between them, and Evelyn didn't feel like carrying a conversation. Part of her wanted to run back to the cabin or anywhere else. Why had she thought joining the meeting a good idea?

Every reason abandoned her. Along with her good sense, it appeared.

Mary Ellen led the way to a corner of the cafeteria. "We meet here, then head to the amphitheater or another spot that's open."

Evelyn nodded and followed her to an area where about twenty women had gathered. Not all of the women were WAVES, which surprised her. Then she saw Marjorie Miller. Evelyn turned to leave; she'd explain to Mary Ellen later. She couldn't face Marjorie right now. Not with things so awkward with Mark. She'd avoided going to church and having lunch with the Millers by pleading the need to catch up on her sleep.

"Evelyn." The quiet voice stopped her. She turned to find Marjorie standing behind her, a light in her eyes. So much for escaping. "I'm so delighted you're joining us. Did you come with Mary Ellen?"

"Yes, ma'am. She looked so…happy after last week's meeting, I had to come see what it's about."

"Mary Ellen did seem like a sponge." Marjorie laughed before studying Evelyn. "You aren't avoiding us, are you?"

"Um, avoiding you?" Evelyn felt a pang of guilt.

"Yes." Marjorie led her to a table a few feet away from the others. "Has something happened between you and Mark?"

Evelyn grimaced. She didn't want to have this conversation. Not now. Not with Marjorie.

"Call it a mother's intuition, but when you didn't join us on Sunday, and Mark's lived in his own world, I wonder."

"You needn't worry. Mark has his girl, and I'm only here awhile." Evelyn's fingers fidgeted with the tablecloth, twisting it into rosettes and releasing.

Marjorie leaned forward and placed her hand on top of Evelyn's. She opened her mouth as if to say something, but stopped when a woman called the group to order. She squeezed Evelyn's hand. "We'll talk later."

Tears warred with the thought of running far from this kind woman who genuinely cared. Evelyn's friendship with the Millers had been a highlight of her time in Dayton, but now it felt as awkward as her interactions with Mark. She took a deep breath. She couldn't leave now without disrupting everything, so she settled in. The women sang a song, one unfamiliar to Evelyn. The lyrics settled over her, the women's voices mingling in sweet harmony. After the last note, the leader opened the Bible in front of her on the table. Each of the other women had a matching book. Evelyn felt like sliding under the table. She should have grabbed the one Marjorie had lent her. Marjorie brought her chair around and slid her Bible between them. She pointed to the woman at the front. "Our leader tonight is Patricia Hall."

"Tonight we're in John, chapter three. The chapter begins with a religious ruler stating that Jesus must be the Son of God because of His miracles. In verse three, Jesus responds, 'Verily, verily, I say unto thee, Except a man be born again, he cannot see the kingdom of God.'" Mrs. Hall read from the page in a steady, well-modulated voice.

Mary Ellen raised her hand. "What does that mean, 'born again'? It's not possible."

"That's exactly what Nicodemus said. Look at verse four. 'Nicodemus saith unto him, How can a man be born when he is old? can he enter the second time into his mother's womb, and be born?'" Mrs. Hall's gaze swept the assembled women and settled on Evelyn, who squirmed. "Nicodemus's question seems logical. It's not like you crawl back inside your mother to be born a second time. And the mothers here are grateful for that." Chuckles filtered from a few of the women. "Let's see how Jesus answered him:

" 'Jesus answered, Verily, verily, I say unto thee, Except a man be born of water and of the Spirit, he cannot enter into the kingdom of God. That which is born of the flesh is flesh; and that which is born of the Spirit is spirit. Marvel not that I said unto thee, Ye must be born again.'"

"Ah, that makes it so much clearer." A wry smile twisted her lips.

Mary Ellen and a few others looked at Mrs. Hall as if she spoke gibberish, but others nodded.

"I love a later part of this passage." A woman Evelyn knew only by sight spoke. She carried herself through work with confidence and peace. " 'That whosoever believeth in him should not perish, but have everlasting life.'"

"But what does that mean?" Mary Ellen shook her head. "Each time I begin to think I understand, the language confuses me. 'Born again.' 'Everlasting life.'" Her forehead wrinkled as she ticked off the terms on her fingers.

Mrs. Hall nodded. "Valid points. Christians tend to use strange language. Almost like you need a special dictionary or interpreter."

Evelyn smiled as others nodded.

"I've always wondered." A woman from a back table shrugged. "I mean, why care about everlasting life? It has to be about more than avoiding hell, a place I'm not convinced exists."

Marjorie caught Mrs. Hall's eye and spoke. "I think the key concept is love. Haven't we all yearned for a love that surrounds us, assures us that we're the most treasured person on earth?" Most of the women nodded. "At times, it feels like love of this sort is a creation of Hollywood or books. But we all want more." She flipped a page in her Bible. "That's what this is all about. See verses sixteen and

200

seventeen? 'For God so loved the world, that he gave his only begotten Son, that whosoever believeth in him should not perish, but have everlasting life. For God sent not his Son into the world to condemn the world; but that the world through him might be saved.'

"That's the good news in two quick sentences. God sent His Son for us because of love. Not for one. Not for a few. But for each of us, individually. Because He doesn't want any of us to die and be separated from Him for the rest of our lives. He longs to save us and can because of what His Son did." Marjorie's eyes glistened, and she paused. "Every time I think of it, I'm humbled and amazed. Who am I that I would be deemed worthy of the love of the God of creation? That He would so long for a relationship with me that He would send His only Son to die for me? The Prince of the universe dying for me, dust."

A hush settled over the room as her words soaked in. Evelyn heard the passion in Marjorie's voice. She felt her heart move within her, responding to something in the words. Truth? Was Marjorie right? She spoke with conviction words that stirred Evelyn—she wanted to believe with the same fervor Marjorie expressed.

"There's so much evil in the world." Marjorie wiped a finger under her eye. "So much evil. Yet there is a love that transcends it all. A love that cleanses of wrongs, forgives sins, and makes us new."

Evelyn wanted to experience that love. To understand and have the relationship Marjorie had. Anything less wouldn't be sufficient.

After the meeting ended, Evelyn turned to Marjorie, questions pouring from her. "Can I have what you have?"

"Oh yes." Marjorie focused on Evelyn's questions, answering them with a smile and abundance of patience.

"Thank you. You must think I know nothing about faith."

"I don't mind your questions at all." Marjorie looked past Evelyn, as if falling into a memory. "I wouldn't be able to help you if a woman hadn't first taken the time to share her great love for the Father with me. Sometimes I wonder if she knew how much her kindness and patience would matter in my life."

"And you're sure all it takes is a prayer?" Evelyn couldn't believe it was that simple.

"Think of the prayer as the first step. It gets you on the path to a lifetime of discovery. Every step either leads you closer to the Father or away from Him." She stroked the cover of her Bible. "That's where reading the Bible, praying, and attending church help. Each assists you in hearing His voice and knowing His character."

Evelyn bowed her head. "Jesus, I want to know You. Thank You for dying for me, for covering my sins so I can live for You."

Marjorie embraced her, tears trailing her cheeks. "Welcome to the family, Evelyn."

Evelyn nodded, overwhelmed by the idea that she'd embarked on an adventure of faith. "Me, an engineer."

That night, Evelyn felt a fresh peace as she walked beside Mary Ellen back to her cabin. It was the kind that settled to her bones and let her know that her decision to trust Christ and seek a loving relationship with God had been right.

If only she could bottle this feeling, pull it out whenever she needed reassurance or had doubts. Tonight, she felt embraced. . .felt the burdens, hopes, dreams, and fears she'd carried had transferred to another. She felt the very real presence of the One who loved her completely.

Chapter 14

August entered with a brace of activity in Building 26 that left Mark wishing for the quieter days of 1942. Yes, it had been frustrating to design a working machine. Now the machines worked more predictably, and the number of WAVES continued to expand from the original seventy to hundreds, all working feverishly on either building components or learning how to operate the machines.

Meader continued to stress that the military needed the machines yesterday. It was a tired song. One Mark never wanted to hear again.

What more could they do? Desch's group tried to strike the balance between the need for machines and the requirement for precision in assembling them.

The lone bright spot in his days was Paige. She'd switched churches so they could spend more time together. Evelyn no longer joined the Millers, claiming to have found a church she enjoyed attending with other WAVES. He hoped she wasn't avoiding seeing him with Paige. The idea left him unsettled. And the thought that he wanted to see Evelyn outside work disturbed him even more.

John waltzed up to him as Mark reached for his hat one sultry evening. "Where do you think you're going at this early hour?"

Mark glanced at the wall clock and shook his head when he read the time. Six o'clock. Hardly an early departure for most people. "I've got an appointment."

John smiled. "Must be meeting Paige. So when are you going to give the gal a ring?"

Evelyn hadn't left yet, and she turned away as if uncomfortable.

Mark pondered the question. Paige had hinted she wanted to make their relationship permanent, but the thought still made him a bit uneasy. Until he could identify why, he'd avoid that question.

"Some things a man keeps to himself, John." Mark clapped him on the back. "See you in the morning."

"Yeah, yeah." John's muttering trailed Mark.

The sun shone, warming Mark from the moment he exited Building 26. He headed home to clean up and borrow his dad's car before picking up Paige. Tonight they'd share a late dinner and maybe a movie. He'd check her mood when he collected her. Since she taught in the morning, she might prefer dinner and dessert.

Mark whistled as he walked into the house.

"Mark?" Mom stuck her head around the corner of the kitchen. "Are you home for dinner?" A pleased smile softened her features.

"Smells good, but not tonight." Mark walked into the kitchen and kissed her cheek.

Her face fell at his words. "You have plans?"

"Picking Paige up. I'll be back later."

"I see." Those two words contained a wealth of information.

"Why don't you like her, Mom?" he shoved his hands in his pockets and leaned against the doorframe. "I've never understood that. She's a Christian. She's beautiful. She wants a family and even likes me. I'd think you'd be crazy about her and the prospect of me settling down."

Mom chewed her lower lip, never a good sign. "It's not that I don't like her."

"But. . ."

"But I'm not convinced Paige is God's best for you. Is she the woman you can spend the rest of your life with?"

"And she's not Evelyn, right?"

"Why would you say that?"

"You spend so much time with her. But *she's* not perfect."

His mother stared at him. "What does that mean?"

"She's not a Christian." Mark crossed his arms. What could she say to that? A smile creased her face. "That used to be true."

"What?" That wasn't the answer he expected. "She hasn't said anything."

"Not everybody talks about their faith. It's a new decision for her."

"That doesn't change anything." It couldn't, or it might turn his life upside down.

Mom sighed. "You're an adult. If you ask Paige to be your wife and marry her, I'll support you and welcome her into the family. Frankly, I can't explain my hesitation, but it's there."

Mark watched her, wondering if she'd say more. When she didn't, he pushed from the doorframe. "I'm not rushing into anything." Especially not after the news Mom had just unveiled.

"I know." She brushed her hands on a tea towel. "Have a good time."

Mark hurried upstairs, the shadow of his mother's questions and revelation chasing him.

Paige carried the conversation from the moment he picked her up. Teaching left her with a never-ending supply of stories that only required an audience, one he didn't mind providing especially on nights like tonight.

"You should have seen Tommy Custer with that pebble shoved up his nose." She wrinkled hers in disgust, an action Mark found charming. How many people could pull that off? "Where do boys get ideas like that? Before I taught, I would have thought events like that were isolated instances. Now. . ." She shuddered. "I know the truth. Trouble seems programmed into the very nature of little boys. If one tries something, even if it turns out badly, the other boys have to try the same thing."

Mark guffawed. "Just make sure you don't lump me in with the group."

She arched an eyebrow. "What? You didn't do crazy things like that as a boy? Never caught frogs and put them in the teacher's lunch tin? Never brought the teacher a bouquet of poison ivy—really, who thinks that's a pretty plant?"

"I didn't do anything on that list."

"No, I'm sure you didn't. Instead, you created your own list. Boys are very creative."

Mark parked the car and escorted her into the restaurant. The hostess led them to a table for two in a secluded corner. He enjoyed watching Paige take in their surroundings. He'd wrangled reservations at one of the top restaurants in Dayton, and the look in her eyes made it worth the effort and expense.

He saw the hope in her eyes.

"Is there a special occasion?"

"Do I need one?" How could he head this off before she had them walking down an aisle?

"I guess not." Her look fell a bit. "A girl can wish." She propped her chin on her hand. "So tell me about your day."

"There's nothing much to tell. Same routine."

"Really?" She cocked her head, clearly not believing him. "I'm sure you don't tell *that Evelyn* 'nothing' about your day."

"That Evelyn?" What a thing to call her. He didn't need an added reason to think about her tonight. Not when his thoughts had cycled back to her all night. He should focus on Paige, but his thoughts refused to cooperate.

Paige toyed with the edge of her menu. "You spend so much time with her. I get the crumbs."

"I work with her." That was it. Why couldn't anyone understand that? Had they all witnessed that almost kiss?

She stared at him with an "of course" look. "That doesn't mean I like it."

"So I should gripe about the men you work with? Worry about what you're doing with them?"

"Don't be ridiculous." She leaned forward on her elbows, staring at him, voice deadly quiet. "They're all married and at least ten years older than me. Nothing for you to worry about. Evelyn, however, is beautiful, intelligent, and you notice."

Mark sat back, blood pumping at her accusation. "Maybe we should leave."

"No. I need you to tell me I'm important. At least as important as your job."

"You are." The words seemed to stick in his throat. He cleared his throat and tried again. "There's no reason to be jealous."

Paige looked away, across the crowded room. The background hum of conversations and clanking dishes swelled in the silence. She smoothed her napkin across her skirt, each fidget making the silence more awkward. "I want to believe you, Mark. But I have no promise from you."

Her words cornered him. He shifted in his seat, Paige's voice warring with his mother's in his mind. "I don't know what to say."

Paige's shoulders slumped, and she hid under the brim of her hat. "You've told me what I needed to know. I'm not so hungry after all." She slid from the chair and stepped into the aisle. "I'll find my way home."

Mark watched her go, then grabbed his hat and jumped to his feet. He threw a dollar on the table, enough to cover their beverages and a tip, and followed her. What had just happened? How had a pleasant night spiraled so quickly into disaster?

He hurried out the front door, intending to offer her a ride home, but spotted her stepping into a cab. "Paige, wait."

She turned his way, one foot in the cab. She smiled sadly and settled into the cab. The restaurant's doorman closed the cab's door. Mark slapped his hat on his head and watched her leave. Uncertainty flooded him. Should he follow her? Did he want to?

※

Evelyn followed Mary Ellen into the auditorium, relieved to have the excuse to be in a group where her thoughts might focus on something other than the fact that every time she looked up at work Mark was staring at her. She felt uncomfortable around him for the first time in a long time. It didn't help that she'd overheard him tell John that his relationship with Paige looked like it was over.

Tonight's study was the perfect thing to distract her. The group filled a corner of the auditorium, but Marjorie waited for her with an open seat next to her.

Evelyn still had much to learn about her new faith, but the study and Marjorie helped her feel like she was on the right track. She tried to read the Bible on her own each morning, but sometimes the language left her confused and frustrated. It reminded her too much of days in high school trying to decipher Shakespeare. The same Shakespeare that chased her into science and math.

Evelyn listened as the evening's discussion flowed. When it ended, Marjorie turned to her, shadows ringing her eyes.

"Is everything okay?"

"It will be. My daughter Josie's husband has been drafted. I'm not sure what that means for Josie, Cassandra, and little Art Jr. Likely they will come to live with us until he returns. So many are called to serve, leaving families behind." Marjorie rubbed her forehead. "Enough about that. Is work going well? Mark seems buoyed."

Evelyn considered the question. "It is, but not in the way I expected. The problems have moderated. I'm doing what I thought I always wanted, but it doesn't seem so important."

"What do you mean?"

"Working with men, showing them my training is on par with theirs, it doesn't fulfill me like I thought." She shrugged. "But I'm glad I'm here. Someday, we'll know what our work accomplished."

"Ah, the mystery of Building 26." Marjorie smiled.

Evelyn chuckled. "Yes."

"Is there any way I can pray for you?"

"That I'd understand what God wants from me." Evelyn studied her long fingers. "Living a life of faith is confusing."

"A mystery we see only dimly. I'll pray for you, and this is the kind of prayer God loves to answer."

"Why?"

"Because you're asking to have a deeper understanding of God's purpose for you. How you follow Him in all you do."

Evelyn considered Marjorie's words. "I guess that is what I'm asking. This is still so new to me."

"And the beautiful thing about the journey of faith is that it will always have a freshness to it." Marjorie's tired eyes brightened. "His mercies are new every morning. I am so grateful it's true. I'll need to remember that in the coming months."

"Any idea where Josie's husband is going?"

"We think Art will be assigned to the European theater." Marjorie hunched forward. "Time will tell." She smiled, small and tight. "I'm grateful God is not limited to certain continents and places.

"Well, I need to head home, see Mr. Miller." Marjorie stood, then paused. "Join us for lunch Sunday?"

"I'd like that, but I've found a new church to attend."

"That's fine. How about we pick you up for lunch on our way home?"

Evelyn nodded, the thought of a meal with the Millers filling her with joy and a bit of uncertainty.

❋

The next week, rumors filtered through Building 26 that the Allies' recent success against U-boats might be related to their work. The thought energized Evelyn. Victory on the European front only became possible when supplies and men could safely cross the Atlantic.

While many pieces came together to ease the Allied losses, the longer-range B-24 airplane certainly played a role. But Evelyn hoped the rumors were correct and something they did in Building 26 had helped.

During the early days of August, the Bombes decrypted messages at increasingly faster rates. One morning, Lieutenant Meyers sent a message, summoning Evelyn to her small office. Evelyn couldn't decide whether to be excited or apprehensive. As far as she knew, she hadn't done anything worthy of a reprimand, but she couldn't be sure what the navy would focus on.

Evelyn rapped on the lieutenant's door.

"Come in."

"Ensign Happ reporting." She entered the room and paused when she saw Admiral Meader seated at the lieutenant's desk. "Sir?"

"Have a seat, Ensign." Lt. Meyers gestured to a chair in front of her desk.

Evelyn perched on the edge of the seat.

Admiral Meader observed her, the silence resting heavy. "Ensign Happ, you've participated on the project here how long?"

"Since May, sir. Came with the first WAVES."

He flipped open a file on the desk. "We've decided to reassign you."

"Reassign me?"

He arched an eyebrow in her direction. "Is there a problem with that?"

"No, sir."

"We're in the beginning stages of a new project, and with your background and experience working with the machines, you are the perfect candidate."

"Yes, sir." Evelyn reminded herself when she enlisted she'd given control of her life to the navy. However, Admiral Meader's cryptic nothings annoyed her.

Lt. Meyers watched the exchange, nodding her head.

"Ensign, you're perfect for this assignment. The lieutenant has full confidence in your ability. I know you'd like to know more, Ensign, but you'll know it on a need-to-know basis. All you need to know now is that your days here are numbered."

Chapter 15

When Evelyn returned to Adam's room, Mark noticed how quiet she was. She sank into a chair and gently shook her head.

Mark eased into a chair next to her. "Good meeting?"

She stared at Adam as if she hadn't heard a word.

"You okay?"

"Hmm?" Evelyn shook her head slightly. "Everything's fine." The machine clicked to a stop before the gears backed up. "Jackpot. Did you believe we'd accomplish this?"

"What?"

"Breaking a code as complex as the Germans'?"

Mark watched John pull the printout from the machine and take it to the Enigma. "Yeah, I did. Given enough time, American ingenuity would win out. It took a lot of work, though."

"What next?" Evelyn turned to him; the force of her gray eyes connecting with his made him hold his breath.

"I'll be here through the war."

"Must be nice." She must have read the question on his face because she hurried to continue. "To know what you're doing."

"It's a jackpot, boys and girl!" John crowed.

"Time for a break." Mark offered his hand to help Evelyn from her chair. "Let's get something to drink."

"As long as it's not the cafeteria's coffee."

Mark purchased a Coke for each of them, then they headed outside. Large flatbed train cars stood on the railroad spur behind Building 26. They hadn't been there the day before. "Wonder what they're getting ready to transport."

"We may never know." Frustration crept into her voice and lowered the set of her shoulders.

Mark searched for a change of topic. Whatever had happened in the meeting had Evelyn on edge, and she seemed unwilling or unable to tell him. "Mom said you're coming for dinner Sunday."

"Yes, though if it's easier, I can go to church with you."

"I'll let Mom know." They walked down the road a bit. "Mom enjoys your friendship."

"I enjoy it, too. She's changed my life. I'll never forget the way she's guided me to faith."

"Mom loves to answer questions."

"But it's more than that. She's good at answers. She knows what I'm thinking before I do and reaches the heart of my questions."

The only sound was that of the birds singing from a few trees. Evelyn's face had settled into an uncustomary frown. "That meeting must have been something else."

She turned toward him. "Why?"

"The confident, vivacious woman I've come to know and admire has disappeared. You are daring and fun. Someone others enjoy being around, and now you look knocked back on your heels."

"But I'm not Paige, right?" Her hand covered her mouth as if to prevent other words from escaping.

"I don't compare you to Paige." At least not more than every few hours.

Evelyn studied him then shook her head. "So you say." She took the last sip from her bottle. "We need to head back before they send the MPs. Thank you for the Coke." A shadow of a smile softened her features.

Her comment chased him that night. Paige had removed herself from his life. He couldn't blame her. His inability to commit had finally frustrated her. He hoped she met the man who would knock her off her feet. She'd probably been too patient. But now he had to confront the reality that he cared for Evelyn in a way that didn't make sense. In a way he couldn't articulate. In a way he couldn't admit.

Mark made a point over the next few days of spending breaks with Evelyn. Something still bothered her, and as they enjoyed time together, he held his feelings for her in check. She remained oblivious to what he felt or ignored it. Still, he lived for the moments she laughed at something he said—the shadows disappeared, and the old Evelyn would reappear.

Sunday, she joined his family for church and lunch. Instead of watching the service as an observer, she participated. He hid a smile as she took notes in a slim notebook. It was as if every word from the pastor watered her thirsty soul. When had he soaked in the sermon like that? He didn't know, but he felt challenged to focus on his personal walk.

While Paige had shared his faith, he'd never felt the challenge to take his faith deeper because of time with her. The thought of her still brought a pang. Investing so much time in a person to have nothing come of it was painful, but he'd acknowledged something the night Paige left him at the restaurant. She wasn't the right woman for him. He'd known it but had buried that knowledge deep in his heart.

The following week, their breaks together continued, with Evelyn relaxing more in his company. Whatever had kept her tense the prior week disappeared.

Evelyn looked at him over another Coke. At the rate he purchased the drink, maybe he should buy stock in the company.

"Do you miss her?"

"Who?"

She rolled her eyes. "Paige."

"I miss her crazy stories about her kids' antics in class. But, no. I don't regret spending my time with you rather than her."

She quirked an eyebrow at him as if she couldn't quite believe him.

"You understand parts of me that Paige never bothered to try. And you make me want to pursue my relationship with Christ." He took a breath, then wiped a tear from her cheek. "Believe me?"

"I'm trying to."

That would have to be enough until he could convince her she could rely on his word.

The first Bombes shipped to DC after being loaded onto railroad cars late at night. Mark and John had hefted a carefully packed box loaded down with rotors and connections and carried it toward the cars. They stopped when they saw the sailors with guns guarding the train.

"I guess they're taking this seriously."

"Deadly." Mark shifted his hold on the box.

John struggled with his end. "Watch it, Miller."

They strained to get the box on the train and hurried out of the way of the next box-toting pair. The night passed quickly, and Mark was grateful when the last box found its way to the train.

※

August melted into September. Though Evelyn waited for any word of her new assignment, nothing came of the meeting with Admiral Meader. She stopped looking over her shoulder, pulling away from the people around her as she waited to be shipped out to points unknown.

It helped that Mark spent so much time with her. At his invitation, she'd rejoined the Millers for church and Sunday lunches. She enjoyed the time with them and the opportunity to learn more about her new faith. One thing she'd learned was that her faith didn't make life smooth and perfect. It made the bumps on the road easier to navigate. She welcomed the peace that flowed through her days.

Marjorie continued to answer her questions, but each of Marjorie's answers generated three new questions. She hoped the woman's patience endured as she continued to monopolize Marjorie's time on Sunday afternoons.

One morning, Mark bounced into the workroom. He strode up to Evelyn, spun her around, and dipped her. She laughed at the sudden moves as her pulse raced at the warmth of his arms holding her. "Good morning to you, too." She couldn't think while he had her tipped over. "What's the special occasion?"

He eased her back to a standing position, and his touch lingered on her arms. "Come with us this weekend to watch Kat play a couple of games."

"Join who where?" He didn't make sense, but she loved the delighted grin on his face.

"My family. We're going to South Bend where Kat and her team are play-ing for the weekend." He waggled his eyebrows at her. "Join us. It'll be well chaperoned, and you'll have a great time getting away from Dayton."

"Who's 'us'?" She couldn't simply take his word on chaperones, after all. She had the WAVES image to uphold.

"Josie, her kids Cassandra and Art Jr., Mom, Dad, and yours truly." A rakish air fell over him. "You know it'll be better than any plans you could have here. Who wouldn't want a weekend surrounded by the Millers?"

She laughed. "You can be persuasive, you know that, Mark?"

"Of course."

Evelyn eased back from the circle of his arms. Her thoughts were muddled with him holding her around the waist. "Fine."

"Yes?"

"Yes. Though I have to warn you I know nothing about softball other than what I've learned from watching a couple of games at Sugar Camp."

"I'll explain it to you. We'll pick you up at six, Friday evening."

Once he had her agreement, Mark morphed into the engineer she knew. The week flew while she questioned her sanity in agreeing to go. Wouldn't a weekend excursion create more confusion with Mark?

And why did she care?

Although things had ended between Mark and Paige, that didn't mean he was free. Evelyn could list dozens of reasons they shouldn't be more than colleagues. He valued her contributions to the team, often being the first to suggest her approach be attempted. He didn't seem to care what she looked like, yet the fire of attraction sparked between them anytime they got too close. Besides, what would happen if Admiral Meader followed through with reassigning her?

Guess it was a good thing the WAVES controlled her destiny since she didn't know what she wanted anymore.

No, that wasn't true.

She wanted Mark to see her as a woman. All the time.

※

Mark tossed Josie's bag in his trunk.

Life would be a bit complicated as they headed to South Bend for the game, but he thought he'd wrangled it so that only Evelyn would travel with him. Maybe Cassandra would join them, but how much trouble could a twelve-year-old be?

Josie and her little boy, Art Jr., climbed into the backseat of Dad's vehicle. Dad walked up to Mark. "You have the map, son?"

"Yes, sir. We'll be a few minutes behind you."

"We'll connect at the hotel. Josie and the kids can share a room with Evelyn." His dad studied him a moment. "Be careful."

Mark had the distinct impression his father's caution referred to more than his driving Josie's car. Cassandra hopped into the passenger seat, a big grin on her face.

"Ready for the adventure, Cassie?"

She wrinkled her nose and stuck out her tongue. "As soon as you quit calling me that. My given name is Cassandra."

He chucked her under the chin. "Nice to see your pep is intact. Let's go get our guest." A few minutes later they pulled up to Sugar Camp. He'd barely reached her cabin when the door opened and Evelyn came out with a small bag.

Mark took it from her. "Are you ready for a great weekend?"

"Yes." A shy smile graced her lips. "Thanks again for inviting me. I could hardly wait for you to get here."

Cassandra greeted Evelyn and slipped into the backseat with a pout.

As they drove, the sky eventually darkened. The headlights made twin pillars across the pavement. Mark turned on the radio, and Evelyn sang with some of the tunes, her voice a sweet accompaniment. Mark felt settled and at peace even as the miles seemed to lengthen.

"Are we there?" Cassandra had asked the question repeatedly since the twilight had forced an end to her reading. "I can't sit another moment."

Evelyn turned toward her. "Look at all the lights clustered on the horizon. I bet we're close."

"I hope so."

"Close your eyes, Cassandra. The time will go faster." Evelyn leaned her head against the seat and turned her attention to Mark. "Tell me more about your time at MIT."

She'd peppered him for stories during the drive, and he'd cajoled a few stories of Purdue from her. They may have shared majors, but the schools couldn't have been more different. One urban, the other rural. He shrugged.

"There's not much. Study, class, study again."

"There must have been a girl." Her words fell soft in the space between them.

Something told him to tread carefully. "I took girls out on occasion, but no one serious."

"Really?"

"Yes."

"Hmm."

"Why's that so hard to believe?"

"I don't know. You seem the type to work hard, but also have fun." She paused. "At least before this assignment."

"Building 26 does drain one's energy." He tapped the steering wheel as they pulled into the outskirts of South Bend. "That's why everyone should have a weekend like this."

Evelyn laughed, a sound he wanted to tease from her again and again. "I didn't know I needed it, but I'm determined to enjoy it." She turned to look at him. "Thank you for including me."

"You're welcome." He studied her silhouette before turning back to the road. "So how about you? Any special guys?" He cringed. Why ask that? It would only make him look like a fool.

An awkward silence made him regret his question.

"No." She shrugged. "It never worked."

Cassandra sighed. "Can't you talk about anything but school and romance?" Disgust laced her voice. "I should have ridden in the other car."

Evelyn burst out laughing. "Out of the mouths of babes."

"I'm not a babe."

"I stand corrected." Evelyn looked at Mark, and he thought she winked. "We'll keep our conversation to more mundane matters. Do you have anything in mind?"

"Movie stars. Don't you think Cary Grant is amazing?" Cassandra swooned against the seat.

Evelyn kept Cassandra entertained but left Mark wondering who held her heart. It mattered very much.

Chapter 16

The weekend passed in a blur, one that Evelyn thoroughly enjoyed. Being surrounded by Mark's family wrapped around her like a blanket of acceptance. The love that flowed between them included her.

Kat didn't get to spend much time with them. Instead, her time was consumed with her team and the games. But the meal she joined held a new level of affection and teasing. Her vivacious personality rubbed off on everyone else, and Cassandra mimicked her every move and speech patterns, though tinged with her accent. The British child charmed Kat's teammates and quickly became their pet.

Evelyn tried to enjoy the games but found it hard to focus. She wanted to believe it was because she didn't understand the rules. Honesty forced her to acknowledge the man next to her provided the distraction.

She'd been attracted to her growing faith because of the example of his mother. Watching him at work each day had only reinforced her desire to see if she could share it. He worked hard but never let the frustrations wear him down, even when another failed attempt disappointed him. He'd managed to keep a light tone most days despite the constant pressure from Admiral Meader and Mr. Desch.

"Ready to head back?"

Evelyn turned to Mark, wondering how long he'd tried to get her attention. "I think we should become Blossoms followers. Trail them on the road."

Mark laughed then stretched his back. "I don't think I can handle the time on a bleacher." He twisted from side to side. "How did Mom attend my games over the years?"

"Lots of love."

"Touché." He stood. "How about another round of Cracker Jacks before we leave?"

"Add a Coke, too, and I'm in."

"Back in a minute." Mark grinned at her before disappearing up the stairs and out to the concession stand.

Marjorie scooted closer to her. "Having a good time?"

"Yes." Evelyn tried to force her features into a neutral expression, but the look in Marjorie's eyes indicated she'd failed. Miserably.

"When will the two of you quit being stubborn and admit your feelings for each other?"

Evelyn flushed at the direct question. "I don't know what you're talking about."

215

Marjorie leaned onto her arms and looked at Evelyn. "Really? I'll remember that next time I watch two people I care about avoid the truth."

"You're wrong."

"I see. Is that why you're very aware of my son?" Marjorie scooted closer and nudged Evelyn's shoulder. "Here's a life secret."

"Okay." This should be interesting.

"God cares deeply about the things that matter to you." Marjorie nodded. "It's a wonderful part about being a Christian. The things that bother and worry us can be turned over to Him with the assurance He sees and cares."

Evelyn shook her head. "He's the Creator of the universe. I doubt He cares about whether I marry and whom."

"*Au contraire*, darling. In fact, He wants us to pray about the matters in our lives. To turn them over to Him and His leading." The sound of Cassandra and Art Jr. jostling and joking with Mark reached them, and Marjorie turned to watch them. "While I might have a preference about how things turn out, God has your best interests at heart. And He wants to be your number-one focus. Seek Him, and everything else can fall into place."

Evelyn considered her words. "I have so much to learn."

"And a lifetime to figure it out."

"Special delivery for the ladies." Mark slipped into the row. "Cracker Jacks and Coke." He looked from one woman to the other. "What did I miss?"

"Nothing." Evelyn tried to smile as she took a box of Cracker Jacks and bottle of Coke. "Thank you."

The game continued around her, but Evelyn couldn't focus on it. Marjorie's words pursued her.

✳

Mark tried to pull Evelyn out of her introspective mood, but she insisted everything was okay. He settled on the bench beside her and soon coached her through softball's rules again.

Kat was a dynamo all over the infield, but he couldn't take full pleasure in that while puzzling over the woman next to him.

"Evelyn?" He touched her hand, and she jumped as if he'd trailed a lit firecracker along her arm rather than his fingers. "Are you having a good time?"

"Absolutely." A smile curved her lips. Before he was ready, the game ended, signaling the end of the weekend.

When they reached the parking lot, Cassandra opted to join Josie and the Millers for the drive back, leaving Mark and Evelyn to travel alone. The easy conversation that filled the car on the drive to Indiana reappeared as they headed back to Dayton.

After an hour, Mark's stomach growled, and Evelyn giggled. "Not enough Cracker Jacks?"

"Guess not." Mark tapped his hands on the steering wheel. "Let's stop for dinner."

Mark pulled the car into the parking lot of a small diner. He opened her door and led her inside. A waitress seated them in a booth and took his burger order.

When his food arrived, Evelyn stared at the mound of food on his plate. "I'm glad I didn't order anything. You'd need all day to eat that by yourself."

Mark stared at the burger and mound of French fries and grinned. "Guess you'll have to help me."

She snapped up a fry and ran it through the pile of ketchup. An easy silence surrounded them as he ate. Mark chewed his last bite and then swallowed. "Would you like to go on a date? When we get back to Dayton? I mean, not tonight, of course, but some other time." Where was a cork when he needed one?

He threw money on the table for their meal and tip, then pulled her to her feet. "Let's get back on the road."

Evelyn stared at him like she'd never seen him before. "What?"

"Time to finish this drive."

"Not that."

"Could I take you to dinner? Maybe a movie? Not a spur-of-the-moment, grab-a-bite-after-work, but an intentioned time with you."

"You see me most Sundays."

"I want to spend more time getting to know you apart from my family. When you're at our house, you spend your time with my mother. Don't get me wrong. That's wonderful. I love watching you probe your relationship with God. But I'd like to spend more time like we had this weekend. Alone. Getting to know each other."

She put a finger on his lips, stopping the words he intended to say.

"Don't say it unless you mean it. Words are too easy to have meaning without action."

He stared into her eyes, their gray color picking up the hint of purple in the dusky sky. "If my words aren't enough, I don't know what else I can offer."

He opened her car door but stopped her before she climbed in. Mark took Evelyn's face in his hands and placed his forehead on hers. "I would never do anything to hurt you."

Her eyes searched his, measuring his words. She licked her lips. "Those are just words, Mark."

Words? Then he'd act. He lowered his lips and claimed hers in a kiss. Evelyn stiffened a moment then relaxed. He held her smooth cheeks lightly with his hands, then started to pull back, when a honk caused him to jerk away from Evelyn.

Her eyes stayed closed a moment before she opened them and slid into the passenger seat. Mark pulled the car onto the highway, a soft silence between them. How could he tell her the kiss meant something, that he didn't kiss every girl he spent time with, without offending her like he had after the infamous almost kiss. He had to try. "Evelyn, you're an amazing woman. I hope you know what just happened means something."

He tore his gaze from the road long enough to gauge whether the words impacted her.

Evelyn stared out the side window, her face difficult to see. "It did for me, too."

The miles slid beneath the car's tires. Before long, Evelyn started regaling him with stories of her life in Washington. As he listened, Mark couldn't imagine how their backgrounds could be more different. She grew up having senators and ambassadors join the family for dinner. Occasionally his dad brought home a grad student or fellow professor, but nothing as intimidating as a senator.

As he listened, he wondered if she could be content to spend the rest of her life in a place like Dayton. If not, could he abandon a life he loved for the woman he loved? Even after he dropped Evelyn off at Sugar Camp, the questions plagued him, easy answers nowhere in sight.

The next weeks wove together in the routine of building new machines and having coffee breaks with Evelyn. Their friendship grew, built on mugs of coffee. Sunday afternoons were filled with walks and conversations, ever deepening yet cautious. Evelyn held him at arm's length as if afraid what they had couldn't last.

The weather turned colder, and October rains fell. Mark started riding home with a colleague to avoid the soaking rain. Anthony Gutling was quiet and kept to himself, the perfect companion at the end of a shift. One afternoon, Mark reached the car before Anthony and opened the passenger door to wait inside the relative warmth of the vehicle.

When he climbed in, his knees banged into the glove compartment, and the door opened. Mark groaned as bundles of papers spilled out. Nothing to do but stick them back inside.

"Evening, Mark," John Fields bellowed as he strode across the parking lot toward the bus stop.

Mark waved and turned back to his task. He groped along the floor and shoved papers back into the small compartment. He grabbed a stack of three-by-five cards. Flipping through them to see if they were in order, he paused. They contained neatly typed lists of German and Japanese individuals and organizations. Why would Anthony have these? Mark slipped them into the compartment.

Bending over, he felt under the seat and pulled out the last piece of paper. The paper felt thicker. The document opened to reveal an official seal. Mark couldn't resist scanning it. He blinked when he read the first few lines. A letter from the German embassy?

The embassy stated it could not fulfill Anthony's request. No good reason existed to contact the German embassy. Not now. A knot tightened in Mark's stomach. What should he do with this? The Germans couldn't find out about the activities in Building 26, but the letter made it clear Anthony was in contact with them.

Had he successfully communicated with the Germans before? Or was this Anthony's first attempt?

The ramifications spiraled through Mark's mind, leaving him shaken.

How to handle this?

Mark jumped from the car, paper still firmly gripped in his hand. Beads of sweat lined his brow. Start with Desch? Find Admiral Meader? Go straight to the MPs? He needed wisdom, and the navy needed this information.

"You headed somewhere?"

Mark startled and looked up to see Anthony Gutling staring at him. He'd been so caught up in his thoughts he'd missed the approach of footsteps.

"I left something in the building."

"Do you want me to wait for you?" A curious light filled Anthony's eyes. Did he suspect?

"No. That's all right. I'll walk home or catch a ride with someone else. Thanks anyway." Mark hurried back to Building 26, hoping Anthony couldn't make out the paper he still clutched. He should have shoved it in his briefcase.

As soon as he reached the building, Mark looked for Desch. He would know what to do with this information. Mark's blood pounded in his ears as he hurried down long hallways. He finally stopped one of the marines strolling the halls.

"Have you seen Joe Desch?"

The man stared through him. "No, sir."

"How about Admiral Meader?"

"Negative."

Mark grunted. He had to find them.

"I think they went home for the evening."

Then that's where Mark needed to go. Thirty minutes later, the cab he'd hailed pulled up in front of the Desches' modest home. Mark paid the man, then charged to the door. He pounded on it, more than ready to pass the incriminating document on to someone else. Let someone above his pay grade determine the best way to handle the situation.

Mrs. Desch opened the door, dressed in a simple housecoat, very different from her stylish attire during the events the Desches hosted. "Yes?"

"Mrs. Desch, you probably don't remember me, but I'm Mark Miller. I'm sorry to disturb you at this hour, but I work for your husband and need to talk to him. Now."

She must have heard the intensity in his voice, because she stepped aside. "Yes, of course. Come in." She led him to a small living room, where her husband played checkers on the floor with a small girl.

Desch looked up at Mark, a question in his eyes.

"Sir, I need a moment of your time. I'm hoping you can advise me on a sensitive matter."

"Of course. Debbie, we'll finish our game later."

"Come along with me, darling." Mrs. Desch gestured for the child to stand. The little girl obeyed and followed her mother to the hallway.

Once they left the room, Desch took a seat on the davenport. He pointed

Mark to the club chair. "What's on your mind?"

"I've been riding home with another employee."

Desch put one foot against his other knee. "Yes?"

"Today when I got to the car before him, I found this." Mark handed the sheet over, and Desch scanned the page. Furrows formed between his eyebrows. Without a word, the man bolted to his feet and headed out of the room. Mark remained seated, unsure what to do next. He heard a pounding off the hallway and shifted in his chair.

A minute later, Admiral Meader hurried into the room, Desch on his heels. "Where did you find this?"

"In a fellow employee's vehicle."

"Were you snooping?"

"No, sir. It fell out of the glove compartment. When I picked it up I noticed it was addressed to the German embassy. I knew that wasn't good news."

"Does the man know that you have this?" Meader's eyes pierced Mark, as if determined to ferret out whether he told the truth.

Mark's mouth dried up, and he tried to swallow. "No, sir, I don't believe so."

"Which is it? Yes or no?"

"I don't think he knows."

Meader settled back on the couch. "All right. Joe, would you call our guards in?"

A storm cloud gathered on Desch's brow. "You know I hate their presence."

Meader stared at Desch. Mark stiffened, uncertain what would happen in the battle of wills between the two. "Do you want me to get them?" Not that he knew where they were, but he could find them.

"No." Meader turned to him, a grave look weighing his face. "You'll talk to them in due course."

Mark didn't know what to expect, but the grilling he received in the following hours was not it. The navy security and Admiral Meader wanted to know again and again how he'd come to have the paper, how long he had known Gutling, and answers to more questions than he could answer.

His brain felt mushy, and he wondered if he could keep his answers straight. Telling the truth shouldn't be so hard, especially when he'd done nothing wrong. But as he sat in the living room being interrogated by three navy men in suits while Admiral Meader and Desch watched, he was the one under fire.

Chapter 17

A pall hung over Building 26 when Evelyn reported for duty the next morning. Security to get into the building and into Adam's room was tighter. More marines and MPs walked the halls and checked IDs.

A knot formed in her stomach and didn't ease as she hung her hat and purse on a hook at the back of the room. Adam chugged through another search, but even that sound held ominous overtones. John Fields watched the machine, but Mark didn't work next to him.

"Where's Mark?"

The bulky man shrugged. "Nobody'll say. But it's not like him to be absent."

Evelyn had to agree. In the months she'd worked in Dayton, Mark hadn't missed one day. The man was as committed to his job as anyone, even on the days he should be in bed. He'd looked fine yesterday, so she doubted poor health kept him away.

Mr. Desch strode into the room, dark circles rimming his eyes. "Ensign Happ, a word."

The knot tightened and her head began to pound. "Yes, sir."

She followed him from the room, down several hallways, and to the offices. The sun streaming through the glass walls failed to warm her.

An MP opened the door, a scowl replacing the usually blank expression. Evelyn gulped and looked at Mr. Desch.

She took a step forward, and the door closed behind her. Admiral Meader sat behind a broad desk, with a man standing on either side of him. "Please have a seat, Ensign."

Evelyn eased into a seat and noticed Lt. Meyers standing against the back wall. The woman's usually warm expression had hardened. What had happened? Whispers of panic trailed down her spine. She kept her posture stiff and perched on the edge of the seat.

"Ensign Happ, we have a few questions for you. I admonish you to carefully consider your answers."

"Do. . .do I need an attorney?"

"Have you done anything wrong?"

For the life of her, Evelyn couldn't think of a solitary thing. She glanced at Lt. Meyers, but the officer gave her no indication how she should respond. Evelyn shook her head.

"Good." Admiral Meader picked up a pad of paper. "You have been accused of spying."

Evelyn's jaw dropped. Panic colored her vision. *Spying?* Her mind couldn't embrace the word, could barely comprehend it. The word was harsh. And in a world at war, the word contained a death sentence. She swallowed and tried to form words. "I don't understand." Such a weak thing to say.

"One of your colleagues has implicated you in an attempt to contact the German embassy."

"I would never do that. I haven't done that."

"Doesn't your family frequently entertain?"

"My family?" What could her family have to do with this accusation?

"Your father is Archibald Happ, industrial lobbyist." He stated the words, but she nodded anyway.

"Yes. It's in my application."

"And in that capacity, your parents frequently entertain dignitaries." The words had a harsh edge that left Evelyn with little doubt where this line of questioning would lead. Yet she couldn't deny the truth, so nodded.

"And German embassy staff attended often."

"I suppose so." How could she make him understand that she couldn't keep track of everyone who attended? Her parents enjoyed the events far more than she did, all the talk of politics boring her endlessly. And it had been over a year. "I haven't attended one in a long time."

Everything from the tilt of his chin to the arch in his brow indicated he did not believe her. What could she do?

"Sir, I am a patriotic American who has enlisted to better serve her country. I would do nothing to compromise the missions of my country, especially one as important as this project."

"Yes, yet you managed to get around security and into Adam's room several times before being added to the list."

"I. . .yes."

"Why? Were you searching for information you could pass on to the Germans or Italians?"

"No!"

"If not, what was your purpose?" Admiral Meader leaned halfway across his desk. Evelyn refused to give an inch even though she wanted to shrink against the chair.

Her voice rose to meet his. "I wanted to be part of something bigger. Something that would impact the course of the war. It does not take someone with my background and training to understand the implications of the project housed here. We can impact this war. We already are." How else would the war in the Atlantic have shifted so dramatically? "I would never do anything to compromise anything so important to the security of my country and the safety of her fighting men."

Meader settled back in his chair. "That's what I expected you to say. You're dismissed, Ensign."

Evelyn eased from her seat, noticing Meader looking at someone hidden in the shadows.

"Well, Miller?" he barked.

Evelyn turned and stiffened when she noticed Mark Miller sitting in a corner. Everything warm in her body fled at the sight of him sitting there. Her accuser?

Evelyn flew from the room, and Mark rushed to catch up with her. "Evelyn, wait."

❊

Evelyn rushed on as if she hadn't heard him. He could only imagine what she thought after the way Meader had set him up. Mark had played right into his hands, and now Evelyn must be furious and hurt. He knew the pain he'd feel if it appeared she'd accused him.

Mark picked up his pace until he caught up with her. He grabbed her arm, pulling her to a stop. She bounced against his chest, then looked at him, gray eyes blazing.

"I never want to see you again, Mr. Miller."

"Let me explain."

Evelyn stared at him before turning back down the hall. She was poised to take off, and he couldn't let that happen. He needed her to understand what had really happened. She shook off his hand, so he hurried in front of her and grabbed her by the shoulders.

"Listen to me." His words huffed from his mouth, more forceful than he'd intended. He hung his head. When he looked up, tears hung in her eyes like crystals. Her lips were parted, and her cheeks had emptied of color. The pain in her expression pierced his heart. He leaned down and kissed her. The moment his lips touched hers, the world felt right again. This was the woman he loved. He deepened the kiss. She stopped squirming and a small sound escaped her throat. He pulled her closer, wanting to comfort her, then took a step back, placing his forehead on hers. "Evelyn."

One word. Yet it said everything. She had worked her way into his heart, and he couldn't imagine her anywhere else.

A hard hand slapped his cheek. The burning sensation sparked with pain. He pulled back and rubbed it. "What was that for?"

"You. . .have. . .no. . .right." The words spit from her mouth. "Good-bye, Mr. Miller."

❊

Evelyn hurried away from Mark. She needed to go somewhere, anywhere, to get away from him and this hideous building. Sobs hiccupped in her chest, but she forced them down. No one could see her pain. Despite her best efforts, she'd been betrayed by another man. She'd tried so hard to guard her heart but had allowed Mark under her defenses. What a fool! She knew better. And now, when her heart belonged to him, he'd handed her over as a spy.

She'd imagined the next time Mark would kiss her.

Never had she dreamed it would be in the face of his betrayal.

Oh God. The name rose like a prayer in her mind. She didn't know what else to say. Wasn't life supposed to be easier once one became a Christian? She'd never felt such pain. That kiss should have been filled with the promise of so much more. Instead, it emphasized the depths of his betrayal.

Evelyn escaped into the cafeteria, relieved to find it empty of patrons at this odd time of the morning. Too late for breakfast, too early for coffee breaks. She found a chair facing away from the door and collapsed into it. What could she do? Her mind pulsed with random ideas and questions, but she fought to pull them together into any sort of coherent plan.

"Mind if I join you?" The quiet voice caused Evelyn to turn. Lt. Meyers seemed to take that as agreement and sat at the table. "Ensign Happ, we had to interview you."

Evelyn bit back her protests.

"You gained access to a room you shouldn't have. More than once." Lt. Meyers raised her hand. "Yes, we know there were reasons each time. Still, you got in. We have to explore all avenues, even the ones we aren't convinced are right."

"What happens now?"

"You'll get a day or two off and report back to work." Lt. Meyers smiled, though it failed to reach her eyes. "You might as well enjoy them. Soon enough, you'll work long shifts again."

"What if I don't want to stay?"

The officer's eyes narrowed. "Don't forget you are a WAVES who took an oath to serve where the navy decides you are needed." Her words hung in the air. "For now, head back to Sugar Camp. I'll let you know when to return."

The next three days passed in a haze of inactivity. Each morning, Viv, Lonnie, and Mary Ellen got ready for work and left while Evelyn remained behind. Evelyn didn't know how to explain her absence to them. As soon as the others left, she pulled out her Bible and a notebook. She tried to occupy her days with study and long walks filled with prayer. A puzzling peace carried her through the uncertainty and pain. Each night, Viv brought messages from Mark, but Evelyn couldn't face him, not yet. She wasn't ready to discuss what happened. Neither the kiss nor the betrayal to Admiral Meader. Someday she'd need to hear his side, but not yet.

By Thursday night, Evelyn had decided if she spent another day in her cabin she'd go crazy. In addition to her Bible, she'd read three books in three days, a new record. By the time Viv walked into the cabin carrying a bouquet of sunflowers, Evelyn had read the same page in *Pride and Prejudice* for twenty minutes.

The bright blooms brought a smile to her face. Evelyn tossed the book to the side. "Who sent you those?"

"Oh, they aren't for me." Viv tightened her grip on the vase. "Not that I wouldn't love them. These beauties are for you."

Evelyn reached for the vase, but Viv didn't let go.

"I thought they were for me."

Viv groaned, then released the flowers. "You're a lucky woman. Extra days off and now flowers. I'd love to receive flowers from a guy smitten with me."

"I doubt whoever sent them is taken."

Viv snorted. "They say you're a smart woman? You are so nearsighted."

Evelyn took the flowers, setting them on the bedside table. A slim card hid in the bouquet. She pulled it out, hands trembling when she saw the name of the sender: Mark.

When Lonnie brought the word later that Mark waited at the cafeteria for her, Evelyn stalled.

"Are you trying to chase a good man away?" Lonnie fisted her hands on her hips.

Mary Ellen handed her a tube of lipstick. "You might want this first."

Evelyn needed to face him. Hear his side of the story. Even if it was uncomfortable. "I'm leaving."

"Oh no you don't." Viv handed her a brush. "Not before you beautify."

One glance in the mirror had Evelyn racing for the brush and lipstick. Four days of lounging while her work waited hadn't done her any favors. Ten minutes later, she crossed the camp. A whisper of air teased her neck. She shivered and quickened her pace. Mark waited on the cafeteria's front porch. He straightened and hustled down the steps.

"Evelyn." His voice caressed her bruised heart.

She stilled in front of him. Evelyn wanted to rail against his deception but held her words in check. The tentative look in his eyes made her want to forgive him. "I thought you were my friend."

"I am."

"A friend doesn't malign someone like you did!" Her chin quivered despite her efforts to still it. Heat rose up her neck as she noticed WAVES stopping and staring.

Mark touched her elbow and led her toward the parking lot. What rumors would fly around Sugar Camp after her outburst?

"I need to explain what happened." Steel lay under Mark's words. "I didn't know Admiral Meader would interrogate you."

He didn't? Then why had he sat in the room during her inquisition? "I don't understand."

Mark opened the passenger door to his dad's car and helped her in. After he climbed in, he turned to face her. "You arrived before they dismissed me. They forgot about me." He ran his fingers through his hair. "How much have they told you?"

"Just what you heard. I don't even know when I get to come back to Building 26." And she didn't know that she wanted to anymore. Her fellow WAVES had picked up on the strange treatment she'd received and that she hadn't reported to work even though she wasn't sick. Why couldn't a cold have coincided with her forced break?

"I don't know what I can tell you." Mark's grim tone made clear his frustration.

Evelyn dredged up the courage to ask the question that had haunted her. "Do they think I'm a spy?"

"They can't. Not seriously."

"Your enthusiastic support is encouraging."

Mark slipped the key into the ignition and pulled out of his parking spot. "They haven't told me much since Monday." He turned out of Sugar Camp and seemed to drive without a destination in mind.

Evelyn peeked at her watch when they passed through the light from a streetlamp. Almost 10:30. "You'll have to get me back soon. They've changed the curfew."

"I thought no one enforced it."

"It's tightened since whatever you uncovered developed." Evelyn covered her face with her hands. "They can't believe I'm a spy."

If they did, everything she had worked so hard for would disappear. She had thought becoming a Christian would make life easier, but she hadn't found any verses that supported that idea. Instead, she'd found verses about trouble filling the world. Yet God promised peace that surpassed all understanding. And in the midst of the week and its uncertainties, she'd experienced that. The trouble certainly hadn't disappeared, but she'd survived it.

"They'd be crazy if they did." Mark brushed his fingers against her cheek. "I believe you."

She needed more than that. His weak assurance didn't touch her fear. "Please take me back."

Chapter 18

The next morning, Evelyn received orders to report back to work. Without a word, the navy cleared her of any suspicion. Unfortunately, no one said anything to the other WAVES. She felt the lingering uncertainty from many of them as she walked around Building 26 and Sugar Camp. Her roommates and a few others remained unchanged—mainly the women she'd spent time with and knew well.

After a silent weekend, Evelyn found Lt. Meyers Monday morning.

The woman sat behind her desk in her closet-sized office. "What can I do for you, Ensign Happ?"

"I'm requesting reassignment to Washington DC."

Lt. Meyers considered her a moment. "The cause?"

"The navy has cast enough suspicion on me that my fellow WAVES distrust me. I need a new forum. Surely that's where Admiral Meader intended to send me months ago."

The officer reached for a pad of paper and scribbled a note. "I can't make any promises but will inquire with Washington, see if they can use your skills with the Bombes there."

"Thank you."

It was all she could expect. Now she'd have to wait.

✳

Evelyn trudged into Adam's room. Mark hated knowing that he'd inadvertently started the process that led to her questioning. She'd relaxed on Sunday, but back in Building 26 with all eyes on her, she'd retreated.

Anytime he tried to engage her, pain hid in her eyes. While he didn't point Meader and the rest toward her, he should have done more to shift their focus faster. With the disappearance of Anthony from the building, he assumed the navy had decided Anthony was the only one involved.

Yet each day, Evelyn seemed to slip away from him. Not that she said anything, but he sensed a subtle distance. By Wednesday, he needed to say something. During the morning break, he ran to the cafeteria and purchased two cups of coffee. Returning to the room, he saw her disappearing around a corner in the hallway. He adjusted course and followed.

She pushed open a side door and stepped outside. A moment later, he joined her.

"Evelyn?"

She started and turned to him. Her lips thinned.

"I brought coffee." He handed it to her, a weak offering.

"Thank you."

The cold air cut through him, enough to make him wish he'd grabbed his jacket before following her. She shivered, then took a swallow. Mark let the silence lengthen between them, waiting for her.

"I have the opportunity to join the next group of Bombes in DC."

His jaw dropped. "Why leave?"

"Life's been awkward since Meader put me on leave. Even coming back hasn't helped."

"Give it more time." She couldn't leave. Not now. Not when he loved her.

She turned, her gaze searching his face. He wanted to pull her toward him, tell her he'd be the man she needed. If only she'd stay. She swallowed, and her expression closed.

"I have to let them know today."

That soon? He needed time to change her mind. "Don't go."

"Why? I have family in DC."

"Family that doesn't care about you." She bristled at his words. "When was the last time you heard from them?"

She shrugged. "It doesn't matter."

"Yes, it does. You can't run away on the excuse of family. If they cared, they'd be in touch with you."

"If I go to DC, I'll have anonymity again. Nobody there will know about what happened here."

"Then stay so we can see what develops between us."

"More than friendship?" Her gaze searched his as if to see his soul more clearly.

"Yes." He nodded so hard his coffee sloshed. He switched the cup to his other hand and shook the hot liquid off.

"I can't do that right now." She stepped back. "A kiss isn't enough to let me think we could have more. I want forever with someone I can trust. Maybe the distance will show us if this is real."

"Forever? That's a really long time." Mark tried to infuse humor into his voice. Based on her expression, he failed.

"Yes."

Mark didn't know what to say. He wanted to believe she sensed the possibilities that existed between them. If she didn't by now, he couldn't force her to see how much he cared. He stiffened his back even as part of him whispered he would regret his stubbornness. "If you don't understand me yet, there's not much more I can say or do."

Shadows filled her eyes. He hadn't realized how much blame she pinned on him. Now that he saw things through her eyes, maybe she was right.

"I'm heading home. My family will love having me back even if I'm still in uniform."

She turned to walk away, and Mark wondered if by letting her leave, he also let the best thing in his life walk away. He stood up and placed a hand on her arm, but she gently shook it off.

"Good-bye, Mark."

✳

Evelyn hurried to Lt. Meyers's office. She had to escape Mark and the realization friendship wasn't enough. Not now.

No, she needed to get away. Start over in DC. Avoid the rumors and escape Mark. Even if she'd be more alone there than here. Her parents would be too busy to notice she'd returned, and she'd have to start from scratch with friends in the WAVES. But she'd do it.

"Lt. Meyers, I accept the reassignment."

The lieutenant's eyes looked tired. "Don't thank me yet. The Bombes leave tonight, so you leave at seven."

"Tonight?" So soon? She had so much to do if she had to leave in a few hours.

"Yes. I suggest you head to Sugar Camp and pack. I'll send a sailor at six to assist you with your bags."

"Thank you."

"You're welcome." Lt. Meyers studied her a moment. "I hope you put this event behind you and move forward. You've been an asset to this program."

Evelyn nodded. A change of scenery. That's all she needed. Once again, she could find significance in her contribution to the war effort—somewhere other than in Dayton. "Where should I report?"

"Go with the Bombes to the Naval Communications Annex. From there, they should have an assignment for you. You may have to find your own housing."

That would be the easy part since she could live at home for a bit.

Lt. Meyers handed her an envelope. "This contains your orders. Good luck, Ensign."

Evelyn saluted and backed out of the room. Once in the hallway, she shut the door and hurried to Adam's room. Mark looked up from his work when she entered, but she grabbed her hat and purse before he could say anything.

At John's questioning glance, she smiled. "I've been reassigned to DC. I leave tonight." She ignored the way Mark jolted at the words. "It's been an honor to work with you on this project." Evelyn nodded to the men and slipped from the room.

She needed this break. No sense dragging it out. Mark wouldn't offer what she needed to keep her here. And with her orders firmly in hand, she no longer had the option to stay.

Once she reached Sugar Camp, she hurried to her cabin. Who would have thought the small room would feel like home after six short months? As she packed, her gaze trailed to the drooping sunflowers. Why couldn't Mark put into words what the flowers conveyed? Mark wouldn't send flowers to just anybody. It wasn't his style. And she would not allow herself to believe what she wanted about another man. No, he'd have to say he loved her, ask her to stay, before she could do anything differently.

❉

It didn't take Evelyn long to pack her uniforms, books, and minimal personal items. She settled at the small desk to write quick notes to her roommates. Viv wouldn't understand her sudden departure, but that couldn't be helped. Orders were orders.

Next, she wrote a quick letter to Marjorie. Tears slipped down her cheeks at the thought of leaving this woman who had ushered her to her heavenly Father. She had a lifetime of growing to do, all possible because Marjorie took the time to answer each of her questions.

One sheet of paper remained.

She stared at it. It begged to be filled with a message to Mark. What should she say?

When she placed the pen on the paper, the words flowed.

❉

By Friday evening, Mark couldn't wait to get away from work. The week had dragged, Evelyn's reassignment setting him on his heels. He'd wanted to escape work, but problems had developed that required the engineers to put in long shifts. As they'd wrestled with the latest kinks, he'd missed Evelyn. They needed her different approach to problems.

Fortunately, Kat kept the dinner conversations going, laced with all the events of her senior year. And Cassandra and Art Jr. distracted his mom. She hadn't asked about Evelyn yet. Made him wonder if somehow she already knew.

It didn't matter.

The only thing that mattered was Evelyn had left, and he'd let her. What a fool!

Her absence emphasized what her presence had added to his life. Yes, she was beautiful. But her mind intrigued him. And her growing love for the Lord humbled and challenged him.

He stopped in the middle of the sidewalk.

That's what he should have done all along. Asked the Lord whether Evelyn might be the one for him.

He needed to pray. Turn her and any possibility of a relationship with her over to the Father. *Lord, be with Evelyn as she works in a new place. Give her favor and wisdom. Father, I need Your wisdom, too. She's an amazing woman. I'll confess I'm only now realizing how amazing. Help me discern whether to let go or pursue her.*

Peace eased down on him. He might not have clearer direction yet, but he'd turned her over to the One who loved her most.

When he entered the house, he sifted through the mail piled on the hall table. He found one envelope addressed to him in feminine handwriting that looked like Evelyn's. From Dayton. He ripped the envelope and pulled out a single sheet of paper.

He looked for the signature first. Evelyn. Slipping the sheet in his pocket, he headed upstairs. This letter would be read in the privacy of his room.

Once in his room, he pulled out the letter and sank to his bed. Unfolding it, he read it, then read it again:

Mark,

I hope you understand why I left. I couldn't stay, not with the rumors about me and the lack of a promise from you. I will always treasure your friendship. And wish you the best. If you ever need to find me, I'll be at the Naval Communications Annex in Washington. My time in Dayton was richer for knowing you.

Yours forever,
Evelyn

He read it again, and a flicker of hope ignited. The letter wasn't what he'd hoped, yet she'd made it clear she wouldn't be the first to declare her feelings. She might not have said the words outright, but she'd given hints. She was his forever.

He needed to make those words come true.

※

Evelyn's first days in DC settled into a routine, with Mark never far from her thoughts. Part of her wanted to believe he meant what he'd said. That he could really love her. Each time she tried to believe, her heart reminded her of another man who had said those words only to leave her days before their wedding. If she couldn't trust Paul's words, could she trust Mark?

In so many ways the two were opposites. Mark believed in God; Paul believed in himself. Mark worked tirelessly; Paul enjoyed the privileged life. Yet both confessed their love for her. And Paul had proven untrustworthy.

She wanted to believe Mark. But could she force her heart to accept what her head knew? Mark would never hurt her the way Paul had.

Work provided a refuge. The Naval Communications Annex near Tenley Square was different from Sugar Camp and Building 26. Dozens of Bombes ran around the clock, filling the rooms with heat and an amazing volume of noise. Her superiors quickly assigned her to the group charged with keeping the machines running. The design developed at NCR worked. The machines endured almost constant use at incredible speeds. If only the WAVES who worked in the rooms could withstand the heat as well.

The first time Evelyn noticed the salt dispensers next to the water fountain, she hadn't known what to think until a colleague explained the need to consume extra salt and water. After a week, Evelyn knew all too well the importance of having enough salt and fluids in her body. Without them, the heat made her faint. Fortunately, she'd left the swooning to others.

The loneliness she felt now surprised her. Even though she lived with other WAVES on the converted grounds of Mount Vernon Seminary for Girls, she struggled to build the camaraderie she'd left in Dayton. Hundreds of people surrounded her during her shifts. And when she was off duty, she shared a room with other enlisted WAVES. Instead of the rustic feel of Sugar Camp, the annex felt like a prison circled with barbed wire and guards.

What she wouldn't give to have Viv, Lonnie, or Mary Ellen here. Though her family was nearby, they were too busy to do more than invite her to the occasional fund-raiser. She hadn't expected more, but it still stung. Through it all, God never left her. She sensed His presence as she read His Word and prayed. She came to depend on the assurance He was with her.

Even so, Evelyn needed to connect with her colleagues. Her first weekend in DC, she joined a group going horseback riding in Rock Creek Park. A new roommate, Allison, chattered during the quick walk to the rendezvous point.

"Just wait until you see the park! It's like escaping completely from the city." The gal had her dark hair pulled out of her face with a scarf. She wore dungarees with a heavy jacket, boots, and gloves. "The group of us try to get away once a week for riding. As close as it is, you'd think we'd manage more often."

Evelyn tried to keep up with Allison's high-speed words and steps. "I love the park." Her parents' house wasn't far from it. "I haven't ridden much, though I've always thought it would be fun."

"Tell Pierre you need a gentle horse. He takes good care of us WAVES."

A blond gal nodded. "And wait till you see him. He looks like a movie star."

"Instead, he takes care of horses." A woman shook her head. "I don't mind, though, because we get to admire him when we're at the park."

Evelyn laughed. "And to think, I thought this was about the horses."

"Oh, that's an attraction, only a distant second." Allison tucked her arm through Evelyn's.

"Wait until you see him." The blond heaved a dramatic sigh.

"I doubt he compares to my man." Evelyn stopped walking. Her man? What was she thinking? She tucked her head and prayed. As much as she might want Mark to be hers, until he saw her as special, nothing would come of it. And she didn't need these gals to start questioning her about Mark. Their relationship was simply too complicated to explain. Colleagues? Friends? Sweethearts? If only they had bridged to sweethearts.

Allison stopped to watch Evelyn carefully. "You have a story to tell, my dear."

Heat she couldn't blame on the walk seared Evelyn's cheeks.

Allison leaned closer to Evelyn and faux-whispered in her ear, "Tell me all about it when we're alone."

The group giggled and picked up their pace. By the time they reached the park, Evelyn was more than ready to let a horse carry her. After Pierre matched them with horses, Evelyn hung back. Her horse seemed gentle, but she didn't want the others to watch while she found her balance. The gentle bump of the horse's starts and stops almost unseated her a couple of times. As she became comfortable with the horse's motion, her thoughts returned to Mark. This was the type of activity they could enjoy together.

And if she ever returned to Dayton, maybe they'd try.

Chapter 19

Six weeks since Evelyn Happ had disappeared from his life.

Mark rolled over in bed. Each day felt like a month. The knowledge settled deeper into his gut. Evelyn was the woman for him.

Did she feel the same way?

The only fail-safe method: Ask her. And *that* he couldn't leave to a letter. No matter how he tried to pen the words, they never mirrored the depth of what he felt.

No, this was a conversation that required face-to-face communication. Her response was an unknown factor, so she needed to read his face, view the depth of his love without a filter of distance between them. And he needed to see her reaction without the delay of time and the uncertainty of written words.

How could he get to DC? The navy hadn't let up on Desch, who hadn't let up on him. As long as the war raged, work would continue unabated at NCR and Building 26.

He had to know now if Evelyn loved him, if there was any way he could capture her heart.

Mark felt trapped in his room. The twin bed that he'd slept in for twenty-some years now confined. The stacks of *National Geographic* magazines he'd bought over the years teetered around him like piles of junk. Would Evelyn make room for them or toss them? He picked up the top issue and flipped the pages. He stopped at the photo of WAVES in formation in Algiers. The image of the women marching smartly in their crisp uniforms and hats made him ache to see Evelyn.

Enough.

He had to do something before he turned into a sniveling, romantic mess. He should address this logically.

He stomped out of his room and downstairs. Living in a house overrun with women and adolescents had worn him down. But he needed a strong dose of his mother's wisdom. She knew Evelyn well and might have insight he needed.

Gales of laughter—the feminine, over-the-top kind—trickled down the hallway through the closed kitchen door. Mark stopped outside it and considered retreating upstairs. He could always talk to Mom later. But the tightness in his chest every time he thought of Evelyn—and when didn't he?—forced him through the door. Besides, as overrun as the house was, it could be a long time before he caught Mom without a crowd. Art Jr. or Cassandra would surely be curled up next to her, or Kat would demand her time with the latest high school crisis.

Nope, better to do it now.

And time to consider getting a place of his own, once the war ended and housing eased up again.

The door pushed out, and Art screeched as he collided with Mark's legs. Mark took a step back and grabbed the child. "What's up, squirt?"

"Tired of girls." Art Jr.'s green eyes rounded and his mouth puckered like he'd bitten into something nasty.

Mark laughed at the child's words. "Me, too, buddy."

"Hey." Kat held the door open, hand cocked on her hip. "I thought Mama always told you to say kind words or keep silent."

"I didn't say it exactly like that, Kat." Mom peeked around the door, flour dusting her cheeks and hair. Baking turned into a contact sport.

"My most humble apologies." Mark pulled Art up on his shoulder, then swooped down into a full bow. Art giggled, a sound that made Mark smile. He righted himself and set Art back on the floor. "Off with you, Master Art."

Art grinned and tore down the hall and up the stairs, his small feet making an amazing racket.

Kat wrinkled her nose at Mark, then yelled into the kitchen, "Come on, Cassandra. I'll help you with your math homework. I know it's beyond Josie."

The mischievous glint in her eyes had Mark struggling to hold his frown. "What was that about only saying nice things?"

"That applies to everyone else, of course." She shrugged her shoulders and made an angelic face before waltzing into the dining room, Cassandra following. The girl had latched onto Kat from the moment she returned home. Probably did her good to have someone like Kat to follow around as she worked her way through American schools. Nothing affected that kid's rosy take on life.

Only Josie remained in the kitchen with Mom. As Mark entered the room, the scents of tomato and spices made his stomach rumble. "Josie, could I have a few moments with Mom?"

Josie looked up from the pile of potatoes and peels in front of her. "I'm almost done."

Mom turned from the stove to look at Mark. Something in his expression must have caught her attention. "We'll go down to the basement. I could use your help bringing some wood up. A fire in the fireplace will be perfect tonight."

"All right." Mark followed her down the wooden stairs, the clack of her heels against them sounding like the rapport of guns.

"What's bothering you, Mark?"

"I need your advice."

Mom sat on the edge of a sheet-covered chair. "Of course."

"What do you think of Evelyn?"

"You know I love her. She's a dear friend."

Mark rubbed his hands over his hair. Time to get another haircut, especially if he visited Evelyn. "I mean more than that." His tongue felt twisted into knots and refused to cooperate. "I. . .I miss her."

A soft light filled Mom's eyes. "I know."

"What do you think I should do?"

"Have you prayed?"

"It seems I've done nothing but pray. Ever since she left. Even before."

"And what is God telling you?"

Mark slumped against the wall. "That's the problem. No matter how I ask, silence is all I hear."

Mom reached out and stroked his arm, much as she had when he'd been a frustrated boy. "I've rarely heard God speak in an audible way. Often it's more of an impression. A certainty that something is right. A peace that doesn't make sense but is unshakeable. A knowing a certain path is the one for me."

Mark nodded. He could relate. "I get that kind of certainty when I pray about Evelyn and me."

"Is there anything about your relationship that doesn't line up with scripture?"

"Now that she's a Christian? No."

"If I hadn't walked her through that process, I might caution giving it more time." Mom held up a hand to prevent his protest. "But I've watched her closely, Mark. Her faith may be new, but she's committed and growing."

"But what do I do?"

Mom stood. "That, I can't tell you. You're an adult and have to make these decisions yourself. But I will pray for you. I have no reservations about you and Evelyn. She is a wonderful young woman. One I would be proud to add to our family." A teasing smile tipped her cheeks. "Though that would only make you more outnumbered."

"It would be worth it." So very worth it.

Mom must have read his mind because she laughed. "Enough. Your dad and I will pray. You do the same and act as God leads. We'll support you either way. Now get some of that wood and take it upstairs before one of the others comes looking for us."

Long after their conversation, Mark's mind continued to spin. His mom would bless their marriage. A similar talk with Dad told Mark his parents agreed on the subject. Now to pray some more. Make sure God approved.

※

Evelyn tucked her chin and shrugged her collar, trying to burrow deeper into her coat against a sharp wind. The weather forecast had made snow a possibility, and based on the clouds, it would fall sooner rather than later. She hurried to the navy vehicle, the satchel with communications strapped across her chest. She'd gladly accepted the task of delivering the missives to the Pentagon.

Her days had fallen into a pattern. The rotation of working three different eight-hour shifts over five days before getting two days off left her internal clock confused. Her body never knew when to sleep and when to wake up. Someone in the navy had decided the schedule was a good idea, but she seriously doubted that person ever worked the rotation.

She steered the car through security, exiting the annex before taking Nebraska Avenue to Wisconsin and eventually driving across the Arlington Memorial Bridge into Virginia.

Evelyn finally worked her way through several layers of Pentagon security. Acres of cars stood between her and the five-sided building. Rumor had it one could walk more than seventeen miles in the Pentagon's complex levels and layers. The building was a vast improvement over the former marshes and swamps, but big enough to leave her overwhelmed.

She parked her car, grabbed the satchel, and hiked across the parking lots and up the stairs. Finally she reached the building and worked her way through more security.

"Ensign Happ." A sailor appeared in front of her, good-looking enough to appear in recruiting materials. He saluted with a flourish. "Petty Officer Charles Stuart at your service. I'm to escort you."

"Thank you."

"Follow me."

His formal manner eased as they headed deeper into the bowels of the building. After leading her around another corner, he stopped and winked. "Join me for a cup of coffee after you drop off the communications?"

Evelyn felt conspicuous while a stream of military and civilians passed them. She cleared her throat. "I'm expected back promptly."

He lazed a grin in her direction. "Everyone has to take a break."

"I'll take mine after the war, thank you." Evelyn tightened her shoulder blades and tried to send him a strong not-interested signal. Yes, this man could turn the head of any woman, but in the few minutes they'd interacted, he'd proved he was no Mark. She took off down the hallway. "This way?"

His laughter chased her, and after twenty yards, he caught up with her. "All right. You've made your point. I'll get you to the office and back out. And whoever this guy is, he's very lucky."

"What makes you think there's someone?"

"Most gals are more than happy to take a break with me. And the annex won't miss fifteen minutes. So something else holds you back. Another guy."

Evelyn smiled, awkward at the thought this man—a stranger—could read her so easily.

Yet emptiness weighed against her. It was too late to dwell on how much Mark meant to her.

"Here we are." Petty Officer Stuart grinned. "I'll come back in five minutes to lead you out of this maze."

"Thank you." Evelyn turned over the satchel to the appropriate person and retrieved a different case. When he returned, Petty Officer Stuart tried to carry it for her, but she refused. If anything happened to that bag, the navy would have her head, not his.

"Are you sure you won't break for a few minutes with me?" He turned the full force of his blue eyes on her. Charm oozed from him.

"No. Thank you for your assistance." She nodded to him and headed toward the main doors before he could waylay her again.

Yes, he was handsome and appealing, but he wasn't Mark. And Mark was the only man she wanted.

Chapter 20

"Mr. Miller," Desch blustered his morning greeting. "You're on the next train to DC."

DC? NCR would send him to work with Evelyn? Mark stood straighter and nodded. "Of course, sir." He turned to head out of the room, ready to pack his bag. A throat cleared, and he turned back around. "Yes?"

"Aren't you forgetting something?"

John snorted. "Of course not. He's remembering that's where his girl is."

"Yeah, yeah." Desch's frown caused Mark to clear his throat.

"My assignment in Washington?"

"There's a new problem with the Bombes. Cable and phone communication isn't remedying it, so I want someone there. Fix it, and you'll be back."

His excitement nose-dived. What if he didn't want to come back? Christmas was a week away, and he could imagine a great gift for a certain WAVES.

"Well?" Desch stared at him, tapping his foot impatiently.

"Yes, sir. I'll catch the next train."

"You're booked. Collect your ticket from my assistant."

Mark turned and hurried from the room. In short order, he had his ticket and his packed bag and had hailed a cab to the station.

Once he climbed aboard the train bound for Washington, nervous energy made it difficult to sit still. He considered calling ahead, but had no way to reach Evelyn. She'd been conspicuously silent. He hadn't received a letter since the one she'd mailed before leaving. He couldn't say for sure where she lived.

He loved her—totally, completely, couldn't imagine anyone else in his life. He'd never felt this way before, even with Paige. His stomach roiled at the idea he might spend days in Washington DC at the Naval Communications Annex and not run into Evelyn.

Father, help me find her. I need to talk to her, see if she feels the same way. And thanks for the opportunity to go.

The train crawled east across the landscape. The countryside slid past the windows but never fast enough. He hunkered down with a stack of magazines but couldn't focus on any article. Instead, he imagined how a reunion scene with Evelyn would play out. The images in his mind ranged from her jumping into his arms to her walking away on the arm of another man.

He wanted to define their relationship, and he had to trust God with it. He certainly couldn't control the outcome.

A day later, the train finally pulled into Union Station. Mark joined the rush of people pushing to exit the train. His only instruction had been to report to the Naval Communications Annex. He wandered around the station until he found a taxi stand by the Christopher Columbus Statue in front. The mob of people and crush of vehicles was so different from Dayton. Dayton wasn't a small town, but DC had an energy and drive that Mark identified immediately. It reminded him of Evelyn. No wonder Evelyn pushed the way she did. Anyone who grew up here would do that.

The cab had to release him on Nebraska Avenue, and Mark walked to the fence guarding the annex. The sun's reflection glinted off the barbed wire and marines' guns.

"Can I help you, sir?" One marine stepped from the guard station, while others remained focused on the traffic outside the compound.

"I'm here from Dayton."

The marine stiffened his stance, his bulk pushing Mark back a pace. "You can't proceed without proper authorization."

"I have my orders right here." Mark reached inside his coat but stopped when the marine pointed his gun at his chest. "Whoa. Don't shoot. I'm reaching for my orders."

The man looked askance at him. Orders without uniform must not register. "Point the pocket out. I'll retrieve them."

Mark put his hands in the air and nodded. "Inside left pocket."

The marine stepped forward, reached inside Mark's coat, and pulled out the envelope. Mark put his hands down but watched closely. He hadn't gotten this close to Evelyn to get shot.

"Don't move." The man reentered the guard station and placed a call as he watched Mark.

Mark stared at the two other guards. They appeared more annoyed at his presence than anything else, but he couldn't relax and learn he'd misread them. The marine returned, his frown etched more deeply into his skin.

"What is the nature of your business here?"

How should he answer? He couldn't divulge much without revealing the project. The marines might know the nature of the machines and the work they did. Then again, they might not have a clue what they protected. He had to get into one of the red brick buildings before him where he'd find Evelyn.

"If I told you, the navy officers in Dayton would have me shot. Either you've confirmed my orders or haven't. If you have, let me pass."

The marine stared him down, then waved him through. Mark kept his back stiff until he got beyond the guards. He looked around. Almost a dozen buildings dotted the landscape in front of him. Which was the one he needed?

"Mr. Miller?"

Mark heard the voice and hesitated before turning back to the guard shack. "An escort will take you to your building and get you any passes you need."

Mark nodded and turned around to wait. People walked across the campus in front of him, all with the determined strides of having work to do. He felt out of place as he idled with a briefcase and bag. A short man hurried across the area toward him.

"Mr. Miller?"

"Yes."

"Follow me." His guide double-timed it toward a building Mark could barely see. "We're glad you've arrived. The machines are falling to pieces again for no apparent reason. Ensign Happ suggested someone from your team at NCR could identify the problem."

At Evelyn's name, Mark tuned everything else out. He'd see her. Soon.

※

The Bombes whirred around Evelyn. Even though it was the middle of December, the machines generated enough heat to keep the room stifling. The constant noise sounded better than the sudden quiet that had almost deafened her a few days ago.

One by one, the machines had broken down. The silence had been eerie.

The noise that replaced it never sounded so good.

The WAVES had jerry-rigged a system that worked. But she'd feel better when someone from NCR approved it. It should be harder than brushing the rotors off carefully to remove any shavings or other debris from the faces.

The more she worked with the machines, the more delicate they became. Keeping them operating was enough to drive a girl crazy. Evelyn wiped her forehead off with a damp handkerchief.

A gentle touch on her arm caused her to gasp, then spin around. "Mark!" She jumped into his arms before she could think.

A twinkle filled his eyes. "I take it you missed me."

The gals around them laughed.

She ducked her head against his shoulder, enjoying the strength and feel of him, and pulled back as a couple of whistles added to the noise. "Back to work, ladies."

Mark held her a moment longer, then eased away. She drank in the sight of him and enjoyed watching him do the same with her. He grinned. "Maybe I should walk out and come back in. Would I get another welcome like that?"

Annoying heat filled her face. He rubbed a finger across her cheek in a caress she leaned into. "I've missed you, Evelyn."

"And I you." She looked about the room. Everyone pretended to be focused on anything but them, but she knew it was an act. In no time, word of her welcome would float all over the building. "Let's talk later."

Mark glanced around and straightened. "Of course." *Sorry,* he mouthed. He tucked his bag and briefcase against the wall. "How can I help?"

"I hoped NCR would send you. I think I've reached a solution—at least a tentative one—but would like your take." She walked him around the machines and explained what had happened. "So we've given the rotors an extra brushing

241

with that brush Mr. Desch recommended. I think the maintenance lightened a bit after the machines were here awhile. Routine and all that."

"Are the other WAVES careful when changing the rotors?"

"Yes. There are the occasional near misses when one flies off and lodges in the floor or a wall, but so far, no one's been hurt."

Mark stopped and watched a Bombe run. "It may be time for refresher training. Reinforce how dangerous these machines are. How delicate to operate."

"You're the expert."

"You are, too."

"No, I'm another WAVES who's telling them what to do—one who hasn't been here long, at that." Evelyn wanted to retrieve the words and the edge they contained. Mark eyed her with concern. "Never mind. We'll discuss that later. You need to get settled."

"Have dinner with me tonight."

Evelyn considered him a moment. How she'd longed for more time with him. "I'd like that."

"Great. If you show me where I'm staying, I'll figure out how to pick you up."

Laughter bubbled up from inside her. "I don't think you need to worry about that. We'll walk somewhere close. Maybe even stay at the cafeteria since that's our usual pattern."

"Oh no. You've been gone for weeks—"

"Six."

"It felt longer. We're going somewhere we can celebrate being together again."

It sounded like he'd missed her almost as much as she'd missed him. Maybe that old saying about absence making the heart grow fonder wasn't crazy. She wouldn't argue with him if he wanted to spoil her. No, she'd enjoy every moment until he returned to Dayton. And she refused to let that impending reality destroy her enjoyment of this moment.

※

Several hours later, Mark wondered if he'd been crazy to come. His quarters were with the commander, who lived in the old headmistress's home. A hotel would be less awkward, though this allowed the navy to monitor his comings and goings efficiently.

At least he had his passes and a pillow to lay his head on. Evelyn had told him hotel rooms were hard to come by in the war-inflated town.

Getting time alone with Evelyn might prove more difficult. He'd already had to send a message canceling his plans with her when the commander had insisted on hearing his initial thoughts and how he wanted to proceed. Would she understand he didn't have a choice about canceling and realize how disappointed he was? He came to spend time with her, not some officer.

All he wanted to do was talk with Evelyn.

A knock sounded on his door. Mark sat up on the twin bed. "Yes?"

"Time for dinner, Mr. Miller."

"Thank you."

Mark pulled his shoes out from under the bed and put them on. With a quick look in the mirror, he headed out the door and down the stairs.

A sailor waited at the bottom of the stairs. "Follow me."

Soon he sat at the table with a handful of other men, the commander, and his wife. The conversation flowed around him, until the woman leaned toward him. "Mr. Miller, do you have special plans while you're here?"

"No, ma'am. Perform my job and return to Dayton."

"If you're here long enough, I invite you to accompany us to the White House on Christmas Eve for the Christmas tree lighting and program. It's usually quite the event. Surely you'll stay two more days."

"Thank you."

She turned to the man on her other side, and Mark took another bite of roast. As he did, a plan formed in his mind. It might work, and if it did, he'd be the happiest of men. It would take a bit of doing, though. As Mark took another bite, he mulled the developing plan. He had to try. Two days until Christmas Eve. Would it be long enough to find a ring and pull it together?

Chapter 21

Evelyn stifled the disappointment that zinged through her as another day closed. Mark had worked closely with her, but other than a quick apology for canceling their dinner plans the night before, he had said nothing about rescheduling.

Maybe the magic of their reunion had already died.

She caught him watching her and smiled. No, the connection had only intensified.

In a few minutes, her shift would end, and unless he said something, she'd leave. Without him. She'd gladly get away from the curious looks from the gals in the room—they all continued to watch her as if waiting for the next installment in a drama. But it also meant leaving Mark. What should she do? The Bombes had worked perfectly after her recommended adjustments. Maybe that would shorten Mark's stay and he planned to go home for Christmas. If so, he'd leave in the morning. He'd have no reason to stay—other than her.

"Why the heavy sigh?" Mark studied her.

"Who, me?" Evelyn looked around the room. "I didn't realize I sighed."

"Do you have plans tomorrow night?"

"It's Christmas Eve, Mark. I'll have dinner with my parents. You're welcome to join us, but you'll be on your way home, right? Back with your family?"

"I'd like to stay here. Spend it with you. If that's all right."

Evelyn bit her lip. She wanted nothing more but didn't want to be his charity case. "I'm sure your mom will want you home."

He paled as if she'd said something that pained him. "She knew when I left I likely wouldn't be back in time. Do you want me out of here?" Mark edged closer until Evelyn could smell his musky aftershave. "I want to spend the time with you."

"I would like that." A smile curved her mouth. "Very much."

"Great. Bundle up tomorrow."

"Why?"

"We'll go to the Christmas tree celebration at the White House."

"That's perfect. We'll have time afterward for dinner and a Christmas Eve service with my family."

He looked like a kid in the middle of planning a surprise.

She leaned close and whispered in his ear, "Do we have to wait until tomorrow?" Had she been that forward? Not something she'd normally say, but she couldn't let him leave DC without knowing she wanted to spend time with him. After all, she couldn't tell him anything meaningful while surrounded by women waiting to spread the information through the gossip mills. No, she needed time alone with him, out of sight of the others. They could talk, and maybe she'd learn if he felt the same way she did.

※

A tinge of relief flushed Mark at the hint of panic flecking Evelyn's eyes. It pained him to see the edge of desperation, but it also made him think she would accept when he asked her to marry him tomorrow.

This woman he loved remained an enigma in so many ways. They'd known each other a number of months, but the separation had left him wondering. When she hadn't communicated with him at all, he'd wondered if she'd washed her hands of him. Now he believed she mirrored his feelings.

"Dinner tonight? I don't think the commander expects me." He could make time for Evelyn and still pull his plans together.

A radiant smile curved her lips. She looked around the room then leaned back in. "We might even be able to sneak out now."

Mark laughed and shook his head. "Oh no. We'll work hard and finish our shift. Then we'll get away."

"All right." She slipped away, walking among the Bombes. He watched her glide between them, each step as graceful as a dance.

He needed to follow his own advice. He turned to the pages in front of him, reviewing Evelyn's detailed notes of what had happened as the Bombes broke down and how she'd responded. Her work impressed him. She'd done everything he would have done and appeared to have successfully resolved the problem. He couldn't think of anything to add. Desch would be glad for the report. One more crisis averted through hard work, engineering prowess, and common sense.

As soon as their shift ended, Mark helped Evelyn into her coat and guided her down the hall. "Where do you recommend?"

"Some of the WAVES speak highly of a place about a mile from here."

"Want a taxi or exercise?"

Evelyn grinned at him. "A walk takes more time."

"Walk it is." Mark turned up his collar and edged her against him. After they discussed a training program he could do after Christmas, he filled her in on his family, telling her all about the chaos in his parents' home. She laughed as he spun story after story starring Art Jr. The kid was an active, engaging three-year-old. Mark couldn't wait to have one of his own. He tucked Evelyn closer, shielding her from the breeze. "So how's your time here been?"

She kicked at a clod of snow on the sidewalk. "I never thought I'd say this, but I miss Dayton."

"The city?"

"I don't know how much of it is the city. I probably miss the people more. You, your family, my roommates, and fellow WAVES. I can't believe how eager I was to leave, because now I'd like nothing more than to return."

"Would the WAVES let you?" Mark hadn't thought about that angle.

Maybe he'd need to move to DC.

"I haven't asked. I may not have any choice. If the navy thinks I'm more valuable here, this is where I'm stuck."

"That sounds bleak."

"It's not all bad." She sighed, her breath frosting in the air. "I've enjoyed being back in the city, seeing my parents a couple of times."

Light flooded the little diner she indicated. The food was good, the service brusque in an East Coast kind of way that reminded him of Boston. But the companionship with Evelyn made the night. He escorted her to her dormitory at the close of the evening. Her nose and cheeks were tinged with red, courtesy of the cold.

"See you in the morning, Evelyn."

She leaned toward him, lips parted. He wanted to kiss her with every fiber of his being, but he stepped back. Not tonight. Not until they had a promise.

❄

Evelyn shifted on the hard bed. The walk and dinner with Mark had been magical. Such simple things, but the time with him had filled her heart.

The next day passed in a blur. It might be Christmas Eve, but the war hadn't slowed. The last holdouts of the Warsaw Ghetto had been wiped out, the push into Italy had stalled, and action was prevalent on the Pacific front. She had to keep the Bombes operating. Any sliver of a broken code could make a difference.

Maybe someday she'd know how much of a difference.

As time raced toward the end of her shift, she found it harder to focus. Her thoughts turned to Mark. It would be fun to wow him with a dress fit for Christmas Eve festivities and services. Instead, she'd wear a fresh WAVES suit. Again.

"I'll pick you up at your dormitory in twenty minutes." Mark bounced on his heels as he talked with the same pent-up energy of his nephew.

"See you then." Evelyn let Mark hold her coat as she shrugged into it. She'd barely have time to freshen up.

A tingle of excitement coursed through her. Tonight she'd celebrate the birth of her Savior with the man she loved. Tears filled her eyes at the thought. Her first Christmas after acknowledging Christ as her Savior. She couldn't wait to attend a Christmas Eve service and participate with eyes newly opened to the full significance. Emmanuel. God with us.

❄

Mark slipped the small square box into his coat pocket. It seemed to grow in size and bulk as it hid there. He played with its velvet edges as he walked across the annex to get Evelyn. The cab would meet them at the gate in five minutes.

Evelyn must have seen him walk up because she hurried out. He pulled her into a hug.

"Hello, beautiful."

246

"Hi." She eased back, and the lights reflected in her eyes.

"I wish I had Cinderella's coach for you. Instead, our cab should arrive in a few moments." He led her down the steps and along the sidewalk.

Evelyn tugged on his arm. "If you're looking for the front gate, we go this direction."

"Thanks." He shrugged. "Should have known I'd get turned around."

A cab idled at the curb when they reached the gate. He helped her in and gave the cabby the address: "1600 Pennsylvania Avenue."

Once they reached the White House, they followed a stream of people through the southwest gate onto the grounds. A large spruce of some sort had been decorated with hundreds of ornaments sent in by the schoolchildren of DC. They walked closer, and he suddenly understood the reason for the middle-of-the-afternoon ceremony.

"No lights."

Evelyn snuggled next to him. "Yes. Security and all that."

At the sound of "Angels We Have Heard on High," they turned to see a group of WAVES on a stage. "I'm glad you're next to me and not up there. Not that you wouldn't be a great addition."

"Nice save." Her smile faltered a bit.

Mark tugged her around the Christmas tree, away from the crowd now focused on the stage.

"Where are we going?"

"I've got a surprise for you."

She bit the side of her lip as if trying to bite back a smile. "Full of surprises, aren't you?"

"One or two."

"I didn't get you anything."

Mark tilted his head as he processed her statement. "Anything?"

"A present. I didn't know you were coming. Didn't get you anything." Her words picked up speed. He needed to slow her down somehow.

Mark slid her a step away from him. Her brow quirked, and she half-stepped toward him. He backed up another step until a branch of the spruce brushed his hair. She giggled and reached up and picked something off his shoulder. "Is this yours?"

A circle of decorated paper dangled from her fingers.

"No. Guess I should move away from the tree." He took a deep breath. This was it.

Mark eased down on one knee, not caring that it sank into a patch of snow. Evelyn gasped then covered her mouth with a gloved hand.

"What are you doing?" Tears filled her eyes, trickling down her cheeks and shimmering like crystals.

He hadn't expected her to cry. Should he continue? As cold liquid seeped through to his knee, he knew he had to. He needed to know her answer.

"Evelyn Happ, I love you." He took a deep breath. "I love the way your mind works and challenges me, the way you've given your heart to the Lord and are building your relationship with Him. I love the way being with you makes me happy." He pulled the box from his pocket and opened it then lifted it toward her. "But I hate being separated from you. Will you marry me?"

Evelyn nodded, tears coursing down her cheeks. Mark slid the ring from the box then stood. She pulled her glove off and held out her left hand. He slid the ring on her ring finger and then leaned down and kissed her, one meant to seal the birth of their future. . .the birth of their promise.

A PROMISE
FORGED

Dedication

To my uncles Rick and Bruce Kilzer, both great baseball fans. And to my aunt Laurie Kilzer, who has always made me feel like an amazingly special person. My life has been so much richer because of you.

Much thanks to fellow author Cindy Thomson for ensuring I had the softball scenes right—a task since I'm a football lover! And to Scott Shuler, archivist at the Center for History in South Bend, Indiana, which houses the archives of the AAGPS/BL, for opening the archives to me and helping me navigate the wonderful files and resources the center has accumulated.

Chapter 1

May 1943

The taxi rolled to a stop, and Kat Miller wanted to pinch herself—make sure she really sat outside the Chicago landmark. Wrigley Field. Women streamed through the gates in ones and twos, some swaggering but most staggering a bit as if starstruck by their location.

Wowzers.

When a man showed up at a softball game she played in a few months ago, she never dreamed it would lead to an invitation to play for the nascent All-American Girls Professional Softball League. She'd heard rumors of the forming league, but she hadn't dared to hope that someone would consider her or that her parents would give their blessing.

No, Kat was many things. But dreamer never topped the list. She had a strong head on her shoulders. Knew what to expect from life. This was not it.

"Calm down, Katherine Elizabeth Miller." She mimicked her mother's strong tone that talked her out of many a crazy phase. "Get out there and do what's needed. You received a letter, and you belong here as much as the next girl."

The driver looked at her through the rearview mirror. "You done talking to yourself? Ready to pay and get out of my cab?"

"More ready than you can imagine." Kat fished a bill from her pocket and handed it to the man. Grabbing her glove, she slid to the door and opened it. "Have a great day, mister."

"Yeah. You, too, kid." The man shook his head with a slight grin creasing his face.

She stepped out, and the cabbie peeled away, already intent on his next fare. Kat stood rooted like a tree planted in concrete, stomach churning at the thought she was this close to the home of baseball greats. Now that she stood closer, the others walked with shoulders back, heads high, ready to take the field and use her to clean it up. Why had she come all the way from Dayton on the basis of one letter?

Simple words. Yet words that had launched a dream she hadn't realized she'd harbored. *"We invite you to the tryouts for the All-American Girls Professional Softball League."* The rest of the letter contained a list of details: when to show up; what to bring; what was at stake; the salary range if she landed a contract.

Her breath heaved in and out until she saw black spots. She wanted this.

A chance to spend the summer traveling the region. And a team that would pay her to play a game she loved. She had to succeed this week at tryouts. She refused to go home with her head hanging.

Kat took a step toward the stadium.

Ready or not, she'd arrived.

Mom and Dad hadn't discouraged her, and she'd spied a shadow of pride on the face of her big brother, Mark. Get paid to play softball? Why wouldn't she try out? She'd loved the sport since the moment Mark had let her tag along to his games. Over time she'd badgered him enough to make him show her the basics. Hitting, bunting, throwing, catching, sliding, she did it all. Did it well enough that eventually Mark's team put her in when one of the guys didn't show.

Even Mom supported her, despite many of her mother's friends seeing the activity as less than feminine and downright questionable. What girl would choose to play in the dirt and bruise and batter her body in the pursuit of a small ball?

Someone jostled past Kat, bringing her back to the present. The uniforms the gals wore were as varied as the women. Some wore short skirts with leggings that made her long pants appear out of place. Others wore shorter pants, reminiscent of men's teams. Most wore their team jackets, the different hues creating a kaleidoscope of colors. As she walked through a turnstile at one of the gates and into the stands, Kat tried to absorb it all.

A woman with cropped curls, a baseball cap shoved on top, slammed into her. "Whatcha gawking at?"

Kat wrinkled her nose. Was that chew in the woman's mouth? Maybe it was a good thing her mother hadn't accompanied her after all. "Excuse me."

"Excuse yourself. See ya on the field. May the best one win." The gal grinned, revealing crooked teeth. "That would be me." She scampered down the stairs, not turning to see if Kat followed.

Father, help me. I want this. Oh, how she wanted this. If she was selected maybe her friends would realize she really did excel at softball, that it wasn't merely a strange obsession to be tolerated with a grin. *But even more, Lord, I want to be Your light. Show me why You have me here.* Surely He had a reason.

As she stared at the more than two hundred assembled women, she prayed He did.

✳

Jack Raymond shook his head. Of all the harebrained schemes, this latest from Chicago Cubs owner Philip Wrigley took the cake.

All-American Girls Professional Softball League. Seemed like a misnomer of the worst kind. He'd always imagined himself covering baseball for a major newspaper, and here he was—in Chicago, granted—but covering. . .*girls.*

The cherry on top of the sundae proving the world had gone crazy.

How would this launch him from small-town Cherry Hill, Indiana, to the big leagues with a bona fide Chicago paper? He shook his head, disgus roiling his stomach. He could not imagine staying in Cherry Hill any longer than required. He'd love to have moved on yesterday. Somewhere he'd find the story that launched his career to a real paper with real articles about real sports.

This wasn't it.

Jack pulled his hat lower over his eyes and slouched in the bleachers. The handful of other reporters who'd showed up looked as ready to fall asleep out of sheer boredom as he did.

One snorted and roused from his nap long enough to shift in his seat.

Yep, this was the assignment to make him consider a career change. Maybe he should convince the draft board that, even though his knee had been destroyed in a college baseball game, he could soldier with the best of them.

Jack clamped his jaw. He hated acknowledging he couldn't do something. Even more, he hated *being told* he couldn't do something. Ha, he hated weakness of any kind.

Maybe that's why he despised the idea of covering weak women playing a sport designed for men. He only had to ignore the thousands of semiprofessional women's teams playing across the country. At least that's what his publisher told him, and since Ed Plunkett signed his checks, Jack had no choice. To an extent. He'd write the stories. But it didn't mean he had to turn into one of those hacks who said whatever the publisher wanted.

Wrigley and a few other men walked to the center of the playing field. Saved from his thoughts, Jack pulled his notebook from his jacket pocket. Maybe Wrigley had something newsworthy to say. Wrigley clapped his hands and beckoned the girls his way. It looked like a brood of hens flocking toward the thin man with his dapper fedora clamped tight on the top of his head. The women milled around. Many pushed close to the cluster of men, but a few hung around the edges, appearing uncertain. Jack leaned forward to scan the group.

"Ladies, welcome to Wrigley Field. You are competing for a limited number of slots in the All-American Girls Professional Softball League. Show us the best you have. The evaluations begin now and will be rigorous. Each team has fifteen slots, so less than one third of you will find a spot on a team. And lest you think I overstate myself, the cuts begin tonight."

Jack heard a sharp intake of breath, and several of the women shuffled where they stood. Shoulders tightened, backs stiffened, and feet shifted. The tension hung thick over the diamond.

"Never forget you're here to show us women can play like men, while never letting us forget that you're women."

A lanky reporter next to Jack groaned. "Did he just say that?"

"Yep." Jack stuck out his hand. "Jack Raymond."

"Paul Barton, South Bend. Nice to meet ya." The guy shook his head. "I doubt these *ladies* can play."

"I don't know. I watched a kid play a couple of years ago in Ohio. I thought the team was crazy to have her out there—the only girl on a roster packed with guys. But you should have seen her." Jack shrugged. "She flew all over that diamond. I haven't seen many like her." That girl had almost made a believer of him, but he didn't expect that kind of magic here. Wouldn't it be something if she'd made the trip? The odds were too slim. These girls would play a little ball and head home without an impact. The league would implode within the year, and Wrigley would move on to his next crazy idea.

Another man leaned in. "You haven't watched the right women play. Some of them are amazing." He must have noticed Jack's skepticism. "Watch and see. I think you'll be surprised today. Rick Daley, down from Racine."

"Rick." Jack shook his hand then turned back to the diamond. The women listened in varying stages of attentiveness as the speeches continued.

"After practice tonight, you'll start charm school."

A murmur rose from the field, some of the women gesturing. Charm school? For softball players? This got better all the time.

Most of the gals looked like they only wanted to prove they could play. Charm was the last thing on their minds.

How could one pound around bases while running on tiptoes? The image made him chuckle. A girl switching between running and holding back so she could dance to home. Not what one normally equated with the game.

Jack looked down and stopped when one gal caught his eye as the sun bounced off her red curls. Based on the freckles dotting her face, she'd spent a fair amount of time outside. Must play on a grass field rather than on concrete. She looked like a young kid, not old enough to have graduated from high school. A ball played easily through and around her fingers as she stood there. She looked at ease; then he noticed a slight tremor running up her back.

The kid had some kind of spunk even if her body betrayed her nervousness.

Her willowy form didn't have the size of some of the gals. The first time someone charged the plate she defended, she'd get knocked across town. Bet she played in the outfield somewhere.

She scanned the stands, connected with his gaze, and winked. A wide grin crossed her face as if she couldn't imagine standing anywhere else. He shook his head. A perfect demonstration of what was wrong with women in a sport. How could you maintain feminine decorum while sliding, throwing, and running around bases? *Guess Wrigley thinks charm school is the answer.* A ripple flowed through him as he watched her.

Maybe joy bubbled from her for no other reason than that she stood there. Maybe the invitation to tryouts satisfied her.

No. She wouldn't be here without a deep desire. Only someone filled with pep or a dream would make the effort to come to Chicago for tryouts. Only a few of the gals down there held contracts. The rest would practice, wait, and pray. There weren't many slots, so most would go home disappointed after their time in the Windy City.

He hoped to join them. Even returning to Cherry Hill, the small town where he'd been banished after an article riled a powerful reader, would be an improvement over covering a women's league. The town was fired up about having its own team. He didn't understand the city fathers' enthusiasm for the scheme, but they'd raised the necessary funds to join the other five inaugural cities. And his editor had sent him to cover tryouts and get the local community even more excited with stories about the players that would form the heart of the Cherry Hill Blossoms.

He could imagine the headlines now: SALLY SMUTHERS THRILLED TO LEAVE THE COWS AT HOME AND PLAY BALL ALL SUMMER.

Ugh.

Human-interest nonsense.

There certainly wouldn't be enough action happening for sports pieces. Unless they covered a column inch or two.

Watching the girls mill, Jack snorted. He'd watch and report. If they couldn't play, he wouldn't sugarcoat.

He pulled a pack of gum—Wrigley's of course, though its inferior Orbit brand—from his pocket and shoved a piece in his mouth. He chomped hard while watching the coaches run the girls through drills. A few looked like they knew what they were doing. They slid into base with no thought for the bruises that would form, leaped for balls, chased ground balls, threw each other out. Pitchers wound up and threw underhanded pitches with a speed that made his arm ache.

After a couple of hours he couldn't watch another drill. Especially when a few of the players appeared more tentative and unsure of themselves as the day wore on.

"Leave it all on the diamond or go home. This isn't powder-puff baseball."

Paul slapped him on the shoulder. "You've got it. Some of these gals won't make it to tomorrow playing like that."

Jack grinned. "It's tough to powder your nose while running to home, isn't it?"

"I wouldn't know." Rick patted his cheek. "I've never needed the powder. Maybe some blush though."

They laughed, and Jack enjoyed the moment. Then he looked down and caught the redhead staring at him, heat flowing from her gaze. The girl looked as mad as an editor with empty space on the front page.

She stomped closer. "Who gave you the right?"

"What?"

"Who gave you the right to make fun of us?"

"Miller, get back over here." A manager bellowed his command, bringing her steps to a halt. Jack jotted down her last name along with a note to track down her first. She might make a good subject for his first piece. Profile her movements through training camp.

She stared at him a moment longer then pivoted. "Yes, sir." She marched back to the drill, throwing a look over her shoulder at him, the breeze playing with her curls.

Rick shook his head and chuckled. "She got your number."

Paul nodded. "Let's see if she can play."

Jack settled back and watched. The girl moved through the drill as if fueled by her frustration. A fluidness to her movements reminded him of that kid from Ohio. What were the odds?

Nah.

But as he watched, he had to admit she played just like that kid. In fact, the way the ball played through her fingers like it was an extension of her made him certain it was the same girl. She was a dynamo on the field, and she wasn't the only one. Some of the women played well. Quite well. So they might know a thing or two about the game.

Didn't mean people would pay to watch.

Without that, the league would flop before it launched.

Chapter 2

The day's drills might have ended, but the lectures hadn't.

Sweat caked Kat's body after a day of hard practice. Some of the gals had collapsed on the ground, wrung out by the work. Kat tried to keep on her feet but longed for a soaking bath and large meal. Lots of fruit and meat. She hadn't been this hungry in a long time.

"If you are selected to join a team, you will dress, act, and carry yourself in a manner that befits the feminine ideal." Mr. Wrigley stood back in his spot near the pitcher's mound.

"Blimey. What's that mean?"

Kat glanced at the gal next to her. The girl's nose twitched as if she smelled something unbecoming.

"I don't know." The uncomfortable image of sliding into a plate in a skirt edged through Kat's mind. "I'm sure they have a plan. We'll find out when we're selected."

"Maybe I don't want to be selected."

"Sure you do. I wouldn't have made the trip from Dayton if I wasn't willing to do what it takes to play. Within reason, of course."

"That's just it." The gal shrugged. "We don't know if their 'within reason' matches ours. I'm Dolly Carey."

"Kat Miller." She scanned the women in front of her. "As long as they don't ask me to do anything immoral or indecent, I'm open to considering it."

"I suppose."

"Each evening after you clean up, you will head to the Helena Rubinstein Salon for lessons." Wrigley rubbed his hands together and bounced on his heels.

A salon?

"Your courses will include walking, sitting, speaking, clothing choices, applying makeup, and other skills essential to representing the best of the feminine ideal." Wrigley smiled at the girls.

"He ain't looked too closely at me, has he?" Dolly rolled her eyes. "I don't fit anyone's feminine ideal."

Kat looked the girl over. Short and stout, Dolly had a pretty smile and eyes that danced with glee. "Oh, I think you do."

"Tell that to my mother. She swears there's not a lick of femininity in me or I'd be at home, hunting for a husband, rather than standing here determined to play ball."

"My mom's glad I'm here rather than chasing a boy. I'm seventeen, an age she thinks is way too young." Kat laughed. She could imagine the look on the face of her big brother, Mark, if she marched home wearing a guy's ring. At least things hadn't gotten that serious with Bobby, a guy from her school. Besides, he didn't understand baseball. Any man who wanted to be interested in her had to like the things she did. "My family thinks I have to finish high school first." She rolled her eyes. "Like I'd do anything else."

Dolly looked away. "Wish I'd had that option."

"You didn't?"

"I needed to help at home. It happens when you're the oldest of ten."

Kat couldn't imagine not finishing school or having that many siblings. Even if she married young and started a family like her older sister, Josie, she wanted to learn all she could so she could be the best wife and mother possible to her family. There was too much out there she didn't know yet. And the thought of attending the University of Dayton where her father taught seemed like the logical next step after she finished her senior year of high school.

"Before you leave, we want to show you something." Mr. Wrigley's words pulled Kat from her thoughts. "This is the uniform the teams will wear."

A woman stepped onto the diamond. She twirled a bat over her shoulder and preened as she walked in front of the assembly. Kat's jaw dropped as she stared at the outfit. "We're supposed to play in that?"

That was a dress. No other word described it. A short skirt in an ugly shade of peach, with a top that buttoned to the side.

Dolly sucked in air through the gap in her front teeth. "It's awfully short. Can you imagine sliding into base?"

Kat shook her head, wincing at the image of the rash and bruise she'd get. A general murmur rose as the player up front continued to pirouette.

"That looks more like an ice-skating outfit than a softball uniform." Kat bit her tongue rather than say what she really thought. Only a fool would design something like that and think women could play ball in it.

"Enjoy charm school. You report there in an hour."

An hour? Kat groaned. So much for a soaking bath. She'd be lucky to get a shower and a meal.

Kat joined the flood of women headed to the hotel. She unlocked the door to her room and stumbled on a packet on the floor. She picked it up, back muscles protesting.

Charm school and dresses. Just wait till she wrote Mother a letter with those details. Maybe Mother's friends would approve when they heard what was required after practice. What did charm school have to do with softball? Kat collapsed on the bed, packet in hand, and closed her eyes. A nap sounded so good, but there wasn't time. Not if she wanted to clean up before dinner and charm school.

The scratch of a key in the door forced Kat to a sitting position. Nobody else should be in here. She scanned the room again. Nope, no unfamiliar luggage hidden against a wall or under furniture.

The door opened, and a suitcase pushed through, followed by a woman.

"Aren't you cute?" A stocky woman with crazy, curly hair smiled at Kat as she wrestled the suitcase into the room. "Where are you from?"

"Dayton, Ohio." Kat smiled at her. "My name's Katherine Miller, but all my friends call me Kat."

"Well, Katherine 'Kat' Miller, I'm Lola Leoppold from southern Indiana." A soft twang peppered her words. "It's a pleasure."

Kat smiled. She might not have a room to herself, but Lola looked like the kind of person who'd make a good roommate. "What's your position?"

"Whatever will get me on a team." Lola hefted her case onto the second twin bed. "Wooh! Guess I packed too much. I'd think it contained rocks if I didn't know better. I've got to get away from home for a while, and the pay's good."

Fifty dollars a week or more. Great wages for a girl who hadn't finished high school. "It would be nice."

Lola snorted. "Doesn't look like you need the money."

Kat looked down at her sweaty outfit. She'd worn this uniform all last season, and it had lost its new shine awhile ago. If Lola thought this made Kat look like she was made of money, there wasn't much Kat could do to change that perception. A shiver traveled down her spine. Would everyone look at her so critically? Maybe she hadn't prepared for the cutthroat environment.

"What's in that envelope you're holding?"

Kat looked down at the packet. "I don't know. It was on the floor when I arrived."

"Aren't you curious?"

"Suppose I should be." She didn't open it. Instead Kat stared at it, imagining what it contained.

"You afraid it's a letter sending you home?" Lola snorted. "It's too early for that."

Maybe, but still. . . Kat took a deep breath and tore back the flap. She slipped out the sheets then scanned the first. "It's a handbook."

"See, nothing to get worked up about. Let me see it." Kat tossed the pamphlet to Lola, who opened it. "Here you go. 'Your mind and your body are interrelated, and you cannot neglect one without causing the other to suffer. A healthy mind and a healthy body are the true attributes of the all-American girl.'" Lola batted her eyes then laughed. "What a bunch of hooey."

"Regardless, this"—Kat waved a letter in the air—"says we need to be in the lobby in ten minutes for the walk to charm school."

"Then you'd better run through the shower fast, sister." Lola sniffed the air. "Or the charm will end before it begins."

Kat grabbed a change of clothes and hurried to the bathroom. With her rough edges, Lola might not be the person she would have picked for a roommate, but she'd certainly keep the training experience interesting.

After a quick shower, Kat dressed and headed downstairs to join the group walking to the charm school. Mother had always stressed manners and acting like a lady. What could Kat possibly learn?

✳

Jack slouched in a chair against the wall. He'd picked it because of the tall fake palm tree tucked next to the seat. Maybe if he was really good and lucky, the evening would pass without many of the players noticing him.

That he sat in the Helena Rubinstein Salon was proof positive he needed to keep his mouth shut. The next time he thought something mildly entertaining, he'd keep it to himself, not give Ed the opportunity to send him to the wolves, er, salon.

This did not qualify as sports reporting any way he looked at it.

It might make the society page if he were unlucky. The best hope was that Ed came to his senses and realized what a horrible idea it was to give column inches to charm school.

A primly dressed young woman ushered the players into a large room. She glided across the room like a pro, while many of the players clomped into the ballroom. Jack covered a smile. The instructors had their work cut out for them if they planned to remake all these ladies in less than a week.

"Are you always this impertinent?"

The soft, musical voice pulled Jack from his belief that no one could see him. He turned, and his gaze collided with the player from that morning. She was even younger than he'd thought, with an innocence that belied the fact coming to Chicago was probably the biggest thing that had happened to her.

Her jade eyes arrested him. They seemed to pierce through him, weigh him, and find him wanting. No woman ever did that.

Jack stood and found the girl was as petite as he thought. With creamy skin, red curls, and those green eyes, she looked like an Irish doll, one that barely reached his chest.

"Not really talkative, huh?" She crossed her arms and stared at him. "I can't wait to see what you write in the paper. I'm sure each word will perfectly represent what is actually happening here."

"Slow down. Take a breath." He held up his hands. "I doubt you'll see the article, and I only write what I observe."

"A casual observer. Non-partial, no agenda at all." She jutted her chin out, stubbornness oozing from her.

"Claiming you haven't formed an opinion about me?" Jack flashed her his most charming smile. "I'm Jack Raymond."

"Katherine Miller. And yes, I already know what I need to about you."

"Ladies, if you'll all find a chair." The older lady at the front of the room, Helena Rubinstein maybe, clapped her hands as other staff shooed the players to seats.

"Time's up."

Katherine stared at him another minute. "Guess you'll have to prove me wrong later." She strolled to a vacant chair. The gals on either side highlighted her delicate beauty.

Jack chuckled and rubbed the back of his neck as he considered her words. He could think of a dozen ways to show her how her pulse could race in the presence of the right person. Katherine Miller was no different from the other women who succumbed to his charms.

The women stood to their feet, scraping hundreds of chairs across the floor. He shuddered and wondered how to escape the torture chamber.

About the time he didn't think he could watch one more person walk across the room or endure another player being told everything wrong with her appearance, the session ended. The women left the building, many rushing out the door, all decorum taught in the last hours abandoned. A few stayed in their chairs, talking in small groups.

Katherine sat by herself, stiff and unyielding. He wondered what bothered her.

Only one way to find out. Jack walked over to join his star. "Molded to the chair?"

She frowned at him. "What?"

"Most people flew out of here the moment they were free, but you're still here."

"I guess I am. Your powers of observation astound me, Mr. Raymond."

One point for the kid. "Jack. Call me Jack."

"Maybe." She grinned at him, a cute dimple appearing in her chin. "Are you hungry?"

"Sure. What did you have in mind?"

"A huge slab of pie."

He could imagine she was hungry after the day of exercise, but as her gaze flitted about the room, something more underlined her request. "Let's find you something to eat. Can't have you melting away."

One of the chaperones stood at the door, watching the women leave. When Katherine saw her, she groaned. "I guess we'd better forget the pie."

"Why's that?"

"Rule number three. All social engagements must be approved by a chaperone. I can't give them any reason to think I won't make a good player or follow their silly rules." She chewed a fingernail and her shoulders sloped, all hints of perfect posture from minutes ago displaced.

Watching her he wanted to do something to take her mind off whatever had her tense. "Let me walk you back." At least then he could try to entertain her.

A shy smile teased her lips. "I think that works in the rules."

As they walked, he told her stories about different events he'd covered. He did his best to make every city hall meeting sound exciting or ridiculous.

Ridiculous wasn't too hard when he mentioned the feud about somebody's goat eating the neighbor's prize roses. Her laugh surrounded him, and the tension eased from her body.

They reached the door of the hotel, and she turned to him. "Thank you."

"For what?"

"Helping me forget that I could be cut tonight." Her dimple reappeared for a fleeting moment. "Good night." She slipped through the rotating door and disappeared into the lobby.

She might make this week interesting after all. He'd make certain of that.

Chapter 3

The next morning Kat stalked to Wrigley Field. Her body ached, each movement emphasizing the nonstop activity of the day before. It didn't matter. Kat would leave everything on the diamond. No way would she be sent home without knowing she had done all she could to prove she could play.

Pandemonium reigned as the managers organized the girls into groups. Kat glanced into the stands and found Jack. This time he looked bored out of his mind as he slouched on the bleachers. A pad of paper sat next to him, pages fluttering in the wind, but a pen remained tucked behind his ear. He couldn't write a story if it stayed there. Jack caught her watching him and winked. Heat climbed her neck, reaching her cheeks. She longed for a tan that would cover the color.

He leaned forward and motioned for her.

Kat sneaked a look at the coach and sidled toward the bleachers. "Yes?"

"Just wanted you to know you're an even better player now than you were the first time I saw you play."

"The first time? Yesterday?" What was the man talking about?

"No, several years ago I got to watch you back in Ohio. The only girl on a team of men."

"That's what I'm used to."

"Not after this week." He leaned back again, taking on a bored air. "You'll be busy playing with the gals after this week."

She wanted to believe he was right. But. . .too much could still go wrong. And too many other women here were too good at softball.

"Miller."

Kat startled as her name was barked. "Yes, sir?"

"You here to play or watch the reporters?" A burly manager frowned and pointed back to the diamond.

"Here to play, sir."

"Then get in line with the rest of 'em. This is worse than herding cats."

Kat laughed at the image. She could just see the man trying to organize her tabby and calico along with another three hundred or so cats. A project destined for failure.

She gave the manager her full attention and soon fielded balls along with the rest in her group. Her field of vision narrowed until the white balls were all she could see. She anticipated where they'd roll and flew around her area, determined to catch each one.

The next time she caught her breath and looked in the stands, Jack had disappeared.

Her heart sank. She shook off the sensation. Why should she care if he sat there or not? Reporters didn't understand softball anyway. When had one ever gotten the story right? No, in her experience, reporters undervalued any sport girls played. Why submit to more of that?

She didn't need anyone to tell her she played well. Especially not a reporter who couldn't play the game if his survival depended on it.

The morning passed in a blur of running, sliding, catching, and throwing. By the time lunch was served, Kat felt like she'd done everything she could on the diamond. Already she felt her muscles tightening. If she didn't stretch, she'd stiffen too much to play in the afternoon. Kat gulped water as she sat at a table with Dolly and other exhausted players. Subdued conversation flowed as they ate and introduced themselves.

Some had journeyed from as far as Canada and Florida. The common consensus was that each of them had to make a team. The options back home didn't satisfy any of them.

Kat looked around and noticed several people who hadn't made appearances. "Where is everybody?"

"Didn't you hear?" Dolly groaned. "Some got calls last night. They were sent home. Already. They really made cuts after the first day."

Kat gulped. "Cut? Already?"

"Yep." Dolly shivered. "Can you imagine? They must be serious about finding the best players. And quickly!"

That settled it. Kat would play so hard she couldn't move if that's what the managers expected. Guess it would prepare her for what she would face if she made a team.

No. Not if. *When* she made a team.

※

Jack rubbed his head then slapped his hat back on. The sun pounded down, and he wished for a bit of shade. What he wouldn't give for a desk back in the newsroom. The comfortable chaos sounded wonderful compared to the boredom of watching yet another day of drills. Spring training only accentuated his inability to play the game he had loved.

A breeze ruffled the newspaper on the bleachers next to him. He'd hunted and found a copy of this morning's *Cherry Hill Gazette*, all for the spunky redhead. He couldn't wait to toss her the issue and watch her reaction. There would be one. He had no doubt of that. Whatever it was, he'd wager it would entertain.

The managers ran the women through more drills. Jack winced each time he watched a gal throw herself into a slide toward home plate. He could only imagine the bruises forming under their shorts and pants. Nothing compared to what would happen once they wore those ridiculous uniforms Wrigley's wife had designed.

He enjoyed sports as much as the next person, but the intensity on the field was mind-boggling. A couple of women almost came to fisticuffs over catching a ball.

Jack shook his head and waited for the practice to end.

Fortunately he didn't have to cover charm school tonight. The images from last night still haunted him. Each gal had been evaluated, sometimes brutally. What had started as entertainment left him feeling bad for some of them. They couldn't control what God had given them to work with. Tell that to the salon staff who took it as a personal affront.

Yet another reason to be glad God made him a man. No one cared if his hair was thick, thin, or spotty. His eyebrows remained untouched, and thank goodness he didn't get told what cosmetics to use and where.

A shudder coursed through him at the thought.

This was supposed to be about softball. If last night was a realistic reflection, "powder-puff" accurately described the nascent league.

"All right. You're done, ladies. I'll see you in the morning." One of the managers dismissed the gals. "And don't forget your schooling tonight."

Groans rose from the crowd. Many turned and shuffled out of the park. A few collapsed on the field. Jack scanned the group for one with hard-to-miss auburn hair. He'd watched her off and on, and now when he wanted to talk to her, it figured he couldn't find her.

There.

He leaped to his feet and bounded down the last few steps, ensuring his path intersected with hers. "Hey, kid."

She stopped, the weary slump of her shoulders making him wonder if he should leave her alone. "Yes?"

"Thought you might like to see the article I wrote." He tossed the paper at her, and she caught it with sure hands.

"Thanks." Katherine flicked the paper at him in a wave and resumed her march to the exit.

He crossed his arms, waiting to see how far she'd go. "Aren't you going to read it?"

"What? You afraid no one will notice your name in print unless you force them to read it?" Her sharp words seemed to surprise her. She took a step back and exhaled. "I'm sorry. I'm not usually so. . .snippy. Forgive me?"

What did one say to that? "Sure."

"Thanks." A faint smile etched her drawn face. "I promise to read it if I can before heading to school." She sniffed the air playfully. "I think they'd appreciate it if I cleaned up first."

Jack decided to play along. "I wondered where that aroma started."

"Yours truly. Good night, sir."

"Good night." He should let her go on her way. Practice had ended, and he was free as a bird. Draft tomorrow's story, and then he could see some of

Chicago. If he followed her, he'd end up at the salon, watching instructors teach the fundamentals of feminine sitting. What was so hard about it? Cross your legs and smile. Seemed straightforward.

But he found himself following then catching the beautiful Katherine Miller. The lingering thought of Polly, the girl he'd seen a few times in Cherry Hill, teased his mind. She wouldn't be thrilled to learn he'd spent time with another woman, but surely she'd agree Katherine was too young for him. He'd been out of college a couple years, and Katherine hadn't graduated from high school.

He almost believed those words himself. Almost.

"Want some company?"

Her steps slowed down, and she turned to him. "Mr. Raymond, are you always this incorrigible?"

"Mighty big word for a sixteen-year-old."

She pulled herself to her full height—maybe all five feet, two inches. "I'm seventeen, for your information, and well educated."

He stopped short at her words then burst into laughter. "You are something."

"My brother agrees." He leaned in to catch her mumbled words. "If you don't mind, I'm really too tired to banter." She rolled her neck. "I pray I don't get a phone call."

Jack frowned. What was she talking about? "Pardon?"

"You know. A call from the manager."

"Telling you what?"

She rolled her eyes like he didn't have a clue. "The one telling me to catch the next train home. That I'm wasting everybody's time and don't need to come back in the morning." Her words rushed faster and faster out of her mouth until they practically came out as one long word. Sweat dotted her forehead and upper lip.

"Look, kid, you don't have to worry about that. You were all over the field again today. You play as well as any woman out there."

She closed her eyes and seemed to drink in his words. "I hope you're right." Smile lines creased around her eyes. "The good news is, God knows what I'm supposed to do next. I hope that includes playing softball here, but if not, He has something else for me."

"You seem pretty confident." Oddly so for someone so young.

"Absolutely. Some things never change, and God's promises are one of them."

✻

Despite her words, Kat felt the strain of the day's drills as she bantered with Jack. Instead of resting in her room, she joined the others back in charm school. Kat grabbed a seat with Lola and Dolly on either side.

Even after their conversation on the walk to the hotel, Jack had waited for her outside the hotel when she left for the walk to charm school. The man was relentless. "Any comments about your day?"

"Other than it was filled with drills? No."

"Come on. Just a sentence or two." He turned puppy dog eyes on her, and her heart flopped.

"I–I'm sorry." She'd stammered, trying to get her tongue to cooperate as she drowned in his gaze.

"Just a word."

She shook her head.

A slow grin had transformed his face. "Don't tell me."

"Tell you what?"

"I stop your heart, make your pulse race."

She snorted. "Those are mutually exclusive."

He shrugged. "Your point?"

Kat *harrumphed* before sliding away. *That insufferable man.* Who did he think he was to insinuate he affected her? With a look or a word? Nobody did that.

She took a deep breath and then eased it out. Repeated. And she would repeat it over and over until her heart got the message and slowed its dramatic gallop.

Dolly leaned against her shoulder. "Are you okay?"

A chaperone glanced their way and frowned. Kat nodded but didn't answer. Suddenly she wasn't in the mood for anyone to tell her how to sit or stand. She didn't need instructions on how to make conversation with strangers.

Unless it was with that aggravating Jack. Maybe he needed tonight's lesson.

What she longed for was a long soak in a bubble-filled bathtub, dim lights, and a tall glass of Coca-Cola. Add a huge sandwich and platter of fruit, and she'd be a happy girl. Sounded like the perfect antidote to the long day and the stress of wondering if she'd made enough of an impression to stay through another day of camp.

Instead she stood and glided across the room with a book on her head—a book!—time after time after time. If she didn't know how to glide versus march by this time, she doubted a book and repetition would make a difference. Finally the taskmasters released them after three hours of walking, standing, and sitting.

That reporter hadn't stopped watching her the whole time. In a room filled with women, many more beautiful than she ever hoped to be, why focus his attention on her? It was enough to drive her to distraction.

※

Each morning that week Jack strolled to Wrigley Field, wondering who would be left. Each day the field of prospective players shrank, but the one he had his eye on remained. The shadows under her eyes darkened until he wondered if she bothered to sleep.

The morning of May 26 dawned. This was the day the remaining girls would find out who had made it—who would fill the rosters for the six teams.

When he arrived at the park, the women were gathered around home plate.

All gazes were focused on a blank easel that had been propped up near the pitcher's mound.

"Morning, Paul, Rick." Jack sidled past them onto the bench. "What are they waiting for?"

"Nothing's been posted yet." Paul leaned back with his arms crossed on his chest.

"It's one nervous group." Rick jotted a note. "The conversation keeps falling off, and you'll see every nervous habit known to man—er, woman, exhibited out there."

"So this is it. The new teams." Jack grinned. "I bet I know one of the members."

Rick guffawed. "We all know who that is. A certain redhead."

"You don't think she's qualified?"

Rick put his hands up in front of him. "I didn't say that. There's a bunch of women out there who are qualified but still won't have a slot at the end of the day. Most of them *are* qualified."

True words. These women could play when they weren't checking their makeup or teeth.

Regardless, right now each one looked as nervous as a cub reporter in a newsroom full of Pulitzer Prize winners. Katherine stood at the edge of the crowd. The two next to her chattered like their mouths didn't have an OFF switch, but she chewed at a nail and waited. She held her body at stiff angles.

A man walked out onto the field with two sheets of paper. It felt as if all the oxygen disappeared from the area as the women waited for him to post the information.

"Glad I'm not them right now." Paul pulled out his skinny notebook and scribbled in it.

Jack nodded. His gaze kept returning to Katherine Miller. What explained this attraction? Did it stem from that one game years ago that he had watched her play? He remained unconvinced there should be a professional league for women. But there was no doubt she'd earned the right to play in it.

The man stepped back from the board, and a flood of women approached. They pushed and shoved in an attempt to get close. A woman ran her finger along the list then screamed in delight. Another walked away, shoulders hunched and head down. By threes and fours they reached the list and shrieked or cried. Some hugged each other, while others stood in shock. Most whose names weren't on the list slunk away, alone.

Katherine, however, remained to the side. Did she have any fingernails left? Why not push into the fray and discover if she'd made a team? The group got smaller until there was no reason she hadn't moved to the list. Unless she couldn't bring herself to check.

Poor kid.

Her nerves probably couldn't stand the suspense of not knowing or wouldn't allow her to propel her feet to the board so she could check.

This he could do something about.

"Catch you gents later." Jack stood and made his way to the aisle. He hopped the short wall at the edge of the bleachers and strode to Katherine.

The barest shadow of a smile graced her face when she saw him. He wanted to take her hand and rub the jagged edges of her nails, tell her whatever the result, she was a great player in his book. Instead he shoved his hands in his pockets.

"Ready to find out if you made the team?"

She shook her head. "I can't do it."

"The fireball who threw herself all over this field all week to prove she'd earned a spot can't find the courage to read the board?"

A momentary fire flashed in her eyes before she shook her head.

"May I?"

"I don't know. . . ."

"The answer won't change if I'm the one looking."

"Go ahead. And thank you."

Jack sauntered up to the board as if he didn't have a care in the world. In his opinion, she'd make a great Rockford Peach or Kenosha Comet. Yep, as long as she was far from him, she'd make a great addition to any team. He didn't need the headache of following her career, not with this strange way he couldn't stop thinking about her. Imagine explaining that to Polly. Adorable, sweet Polly Reese, who looked like a grown-up Shirley Temple and liked to spend her free time with him. Didn't hurt that his press pass gave them access to lots of places and events.

Kat cleared her throat.

He jerked his thoughts back to the moment. "Sorry."

Jack ran his finger down the list. It was in alphabetical order, but he wanted to make sure he didn't miss her.

"Let's see: Anderson, Andrews, Bartholemew. . ."

"Oh, please."

"All right, all right. I won't read the list." He chuckled. "You could do this yourself, you know." He looked at her and noticed how pale she was. "Let's see, where was I?"

She pushed past him. "Enough. Grange, Jackson, Lyle, Miller. Katherine Miller." She sagged as if her muscles collapsed from relief. He put a hand under her elbow to support her. The surge of electricity that shot up his arm forced him to step back.

"Congrats, kid. What team are you on?" *Far away. Far away. Far away.* He silently chanted the words.

Her grin split her face. "Looks like I'm a Cherry Hill Blossom."

Chapter 4

I'm a Cherry Hill Blossom. *Thank You, Lord.* Kat wanted to yell the words to the world. Instead she spun around and hugged Jack.

"Oh, I'm sorry." She tried to step back but found his arms wrapped around her. Tight. And it didn't feel so bad. In fact she might like his embrace if she let herself. What had gotten into her? She pushed against his solid chest.

"Congratulations, kid." His words were right, but as she looked up into his face, it looked pasty. Like he'd eaten something bad.

"Are you okay?"

He released her as if she'd become a hot potato and stepped back, tucking his hands firmly in his pants pockets. "Sure. Congrats. I'll see you around."

The insufferable man spun on his heel and disappeared before she could say anything. A tremble coursed through her. Fatigue? Adrenaline? The feel of his arms around her?

She didn't have time for this. The train transporting her to her new team left in a few hours. She needed to return to the hotel and pack her belongings as well as place a call home to share the wonderful news.

But first, she had to see who else made the team. She scoured the list, smiling when she noticed Dolly had made the Racine Belles team and Lola would join her as a Blossom. She'd welcome the familiar face.

Soon she'd be transported to her new home away from home.

When she reached the lobby of the hotel, Kat passed groups of players. She stopped to hug a few who'd packed and were on their way home. Why had she been selected while others who played as well got sent home? She didn't know, but the sense of celebration stayed with her.

She slipped into the phone booth in the lobby. With trembling fingers she asked the operator to connect her with her parents' home. It took forever for the call to connect, and with each click she expected to hear a dial tone. Finally a ring.

"Hello, this is the Millers' residence."

"Mom?" Tears coursed down Kat's cheeks.

"Kat, are you okay?" An edge of worry tinged her mother's voice.

"Great, actually." Kat took a deep breath and swiped her cheeks. "I made a team."

"Honey!" her mother squealed. "That's wonderful news! I wish your father or Mark were here so you could tell them. Which team?"

"I'm a Cherry Hill Blossom."

"That's close to Chicago, isn't it?"

"Yes. We'll be on the circuit playing the other teams."

"Can you come home before you go to Cherry Hill?"

"No." Kat looked at her watch, and her pulse jumped. "In fact, our train leaves for Cherry Hill in a couple of hours. I've got a lot to do before then." She hugged the phone against her ear. "I had to let you know before I got swept away." If only softball were the only reason she felt breathless. She'd have to slug that reporter the next time she saw him.

"Please let us know your playing schedule. Then we can plan to come to a game or two."

A lump formed in Kat's throat. How could she already miss her family so much? "I'd love that. And I'll let you know as soon as I know game dates."

"I love you, honey. Know we'll be praying for you. Stay close to God no matter how crazy your schedule gets."

"Yes ma'am." Kat wanted to tell her mom she'd done that all week but couldn't. She'd let the crazy schedule and fatigue interfere with her prayer and study time. She wouldn't let that continue. She'd need God to walk with her through whatever the next days and weeks brought. "Love you."

She hung up then leaned against the phone. An emptiness settled over the excitement. Here nobody knew her. She'd never felt so alone.

A fist pounded the phone booth. "Let someone else have a turn."

Kat jolted then slid back the door. "Sorry."

She tucked her chin and hurried to her room. If she didn't move faster, she'd get left. As she packed, she came across the paper that Jack had thrust at her days before. In the rush of practice and charm school, she hadn't made time to read it. Pulling it out she flipped until she found an article he'd marked. Yep, his name sat on the byline.

A rather short article, it didn't take long to read. But she stopped when she saw her name.

"Katherine 'Kat' Miller is a great example of the women who have traveled to try out for the teams. A fireball at barely seventeen, she flies all over the field then stops to powder her nose." What! She'd never done that. Well, other than that one time.

"Quite subtly these women are told how to look good for a man at charm school. Not so subtly they are told how to whack the stuffing out of a ball, bump some chum-peine on her derriere should said player block a base, and other fine points to technique. All in a day's work as they look for a good man after playing all day."

Look good for a man? Powder her nose? Is that what he thought she was here to do? Play ball until she could ensnare a man? She balled up the paper and threw it across the room, where it bounced into the trash can. Insufferable man.

Why did his words sting?

✳

Jack threw his things in a satchel and zipped the bag. He needed to get a grip. The fact one little girl had made the Cherry Hill team should not catapult him into a tailspin.

What did it matter to him? After all, she'd be in town a few months and then go back to wherever she'd come from. Too bad his editor wanted him to follow one of the new team members and the manager had suggested her. He must have guessed that the two had connected. Wait until Katherine learned of the assignment. He could see her response now. Either she'd launch into his arms or slap him. Either would be deserved. And neither sounded good.

A short taxi ride later Jack climbed out at Union Station. The train ride would give him the time he needed to polish the next article, as well as finesse a few special-interest pieces. Ed was determined to launch the team in style. Might have something to do with the money he'd invested in the idea.

Jack wove through the maze of people, past the canteen packed with servicemen and servicewomen, and finally worked his way to the tracks. His train puffed as it strained at the brakes. Jack broke into a run. He couldn't miss it. The next one wasn't until the following morning, and he'd never hear the end of it from Ed if he didn't get those stories turned in, along with an in-person account of training camp.

The sheer number of military uniforms present made Jack nervous. He didn't want to get bumped. The thought of sleeping in his bed sounded wonderful. But first he had to get on the train, find a seat, and file a story.

High-pitched laughter caught his attention. Jack froze. Surely the Blossoms wouldn't be on his train. Not tonight.

Jack turned slowly, hoping it looked casual and unrushed. There they were. Fifteen women and their chaperone, giggling like they'd won the biggest prize of their lives.

Katherine caught his eye and stonewalled him. A hard edge came over her face, and then she averted her gaze. What was that all about? She shifted her suitcase to her other hand and hurried past him to catch up with another gal, a gal who had the leggy look made so popular by Marlene Dietrich. She also had an air of experience that contrasted with Katherine's innocence. Jack had a bad feeling watching the two.

The conductor leaned out the last car. "All aboard."

The team picked up their pace, shuffling toward the car, with cases banging against their already-battered legs.

Jack hefted his satchel and hurried to join them. He should act the gentleman, help with the luggage. At least the cases he could. Before he could reach them, a porter sauntered up and started tagging the bags.

"I'll see that your bags reach Cherry Hill along with you." The porter grinned at the ladies and accepted the tips they pressed in his hands. He turned to Jack. "Help you with your bag, sir?"

"No, I've got it." He'd shove it in the rack above his seat or between his legs. It was small, and keeping it close ensured he could get out of the depot quickly once in Cherry Hill.

Katherine watched him from the side. "You needn't be so abrupt. He only did his job."

Jack considered her, hearing the ring of truth in her words as well as the heaviness of fatigue. "You're right. Looks like he's burdened enough with your bags. I'm only trying to make his life easier."

She eyed the stack of bags. "I hope he gets them on in time." She rubbed a shoulder. "That's all I have for the summer. There's no time to go home, and who knows when I'll have time to shop."

"Isn't that what women do?" Jack grinned at her, trying to tease a response from her. "Shop at the drop of a hat?"

"We're in the middle of a war, Jack. It's tricky to find things I like."

"Kat Miller, plan to join us?" The chaperone stood in the doorway to the car, a frown engraved on her face. The woman had pulled her hair back in a bun that rested at the nape of her neck under a prim hat. Her suit was conservative and fit the look for a woman tasked with keeping those entrusted to her in compliance with the myriad rules the league had established.

"Yes ma'am. Good-bye, Jack." She followed the woman onto the car.

Jack watched a moment then turned and went the opposite direction, looking for a seat on another car. He needed as much distance as he could find between himself and the enchanting Miss Miller.

Once he found a seat and settled his bag overhead, Jack pulled out his notebook and went to work.

> *There's a powder-puff plot under way to take over the smelly old game of baseball. What once was the standard image of baseball—the tobacco-chewing, rough-around-the-edges, paunchy baseball player—is being replaced in towns like Cherry Hill with the reality of women who've attended charm school and training camp.*
>
> *No one better represents this new group than young Katherine "Kat" Miller. A teenager from Dayton, Ohio, Kat played ball with her brother and other boys on teams around the city. Now she's a member of the Cherry Hill Blossoms.*
>
> *A whiz on the diamond, Kat's pretty enough for a role in the movies. Feisty and dramatic, she has a flair for the game and hits a zone that makes balls fear her.*

He smiled as he reread the beginning. Yeah, this was the stuff Ed wanted. Too bad it was so syrupy it made him sick.

※

"Looky here. It's the new darling of Cherry Hill."

Kat roused from her hotel bed, waves of exhaustion washing over her. The train had been delayed time and again in the short trip to Cherry Hill as military transport trains sidelined theirs. When they finally arrived in town around 2:00 a.m., she'd collapsed in the nearest bed.

She rubbed her eyes. "What time is it?"

"Time to read the paper." Lola tossed a crinkled section on her bed. "Don't let it go to your head. He's obviously got a crush on you."

"Who?"

"That reporter you talked to last night. Jack what's-his-name." Lola sat on the edge of Kat's bed and picked at the edges of her red fingernail polish. "Looks like he's decided to make you a star."

A star? What was the woman talking about? Especially after the things he'd said in the article he'd given her. Snagging a man indeed. "I doubt that."

She scanned the article, grimacing at the photo. She'd hated every moment of having her photo taken. The photographer had insisted she be in her uniform but checking her makeup in a mirror. Why couldn't he snap a photo during practice? No wonder they called it "powder-puff." An image the reporters had created. She was sick of that phrase, and it had only been a week.

As she reread the article, she slowed. "Whiz on the diamond"? "Feisty and dramatic"? With each word, her heart pounded faster and heat climbed her cheeks.

"See what I mean?" Lola grinned, but a hard edge filled her gaze. "He's in love."

"I highly doubt that. He's too old for me. Why, he's twenty-five, and I'm not interested. I'm here to play softball, not get a boyfriend." Besides, Bobby back home seemed to think they should spend their senior year together. Though she didn't think they were that serious.

"Sure. Well, if you get your privileged body out of bed, we have breakfast and meetings. Oh, and something called practice."

Lola disappeared out the door. What had Kat done to her? Maybe they wouldn't make good roommates, after all. For a moment, she wished Dolly had made the Blossoms instead of Lola. Oh well, there was nothing she could do about that.

Kat pulled on her robe then dug through her bag for her Bible. She'd need to find a church for those rare Sundays she was in town. Maybe her host family would let her join them. Regardless, she refused to start the day without first reading a psalm and praying. If the last week was any indication, she'd need all the fortification she could get to survive. But she wanted to do much more.

God had her here for a reason, and she wanted to be prepared. The only way to do that was to stay in communication with Him and make sure she fed her heart on a daily basis.

Be ready in season and out of season. She might not know exactly when He would call on her to represent Him, but she'd better prepare now.

Once she finished reading and praying, Kat got ready and hurried to the lobby.

"Everyone's eating at the diner next door." Faye Donahue sat in a stuffed chair, leg bouncing at a frenetic pace. "You're the last one, sister. Let's move before all the food's gone."

"I didn't realize anyone waited for me."

"Our chaperone says we have to stick together."

Kat swallowed hard around the sudden lump in her throat. This was not the way to make a good impression on the incredible pitcher. "I'm sorry."

"Don't worry about it. Let's move now. I'm starved."

Kat's stomach rumbled in answer. "I guess I am, too."

"They've got a busy day for us. Practice. Meet the local supporters. Meet our host families. Practice. Prepare for our first road trip."

Road trip. That made it all real. Ready or not, she'd play her first game in only a couple nights. The thought made her chest tighten. She could hardly catch a breath.

"Are you okay, kid?"

"Yeah. Pinch me, okay?"

Faye leaned over and gave her a good squeeze.

Kat jumped back. "Ouch. Guess I'm really here."

Now she had to prove to herself and the community she'd earned her spot and wasn't merely a pretty powder puff.

Chapter 5

L et's go see this team you've written so much about." Ed Plunkett slapped a battered felt hat on his head and tugged up his suspenders. Excitement reverberated from the guy as he rubbed his hands together.

Acid bubbled in Jack's stomach. "Sir, they might not be what you expect."

"Sure they will be. Angels who play like the boys. What's not to like?"

Plunkett had ordered all the staff to take their lunch break at the diamond. Memorial Field didn't hold any of the prestige of Wrigley Field, but it served the small city well. Blocks off Main Street, it usually hosted a constant run of Little League and community baseball games. This summer the Blossoms would dominate. All other games would be worked in around their aggressive schedule.

Just looking at the unending run of games made Jack tired, and he didn't have to play them. Once the season kicked off, the girls would play eight games most weeks. When they'd eat and sleep remained a mystery, especially when they traveled to away games.

"Come on, come on. No time to waste, girls and boys." Plunkett shooed the handful of reporters, salesmen, and secretaries out the door. Jack hurried to keep up, ignoring the hitch in his steps. Lousy day for his knee to act up.

By the time they reached the field, Jack tried to hide the way he huffed. Plunkett had powered up the street as if Rommel and his troops lurked behind. Jack pulled his handkerchief from his pocket and swiped his forehead. When he looked up, he froze. The townspeople had filled the bleachers.

It might be a routine practice to the players, but to the town it was the birth of their team.

Lunch boxes sat open, the contents consumed almost as an afterthought as everyone focused on the fifteen women on the field.

The team had dressed in practice clothes so did not have their fancy-schmancy dresses on. He couldn't wait to see the fans' reaction to those silly concoctions. The manager could field a team of nine, so practice looked lopsided. Katherine Miller hovered in the shortstop area, intent on the ball. The kid concentrated like nobody's business when on the field.

Faye Donahue wound up on the pitcher's mound, her underhanded pitch hurtling toward the batter. Jackie Smarts held her stance and popped the ball at the perfect moment to send it hurtling through the air, right into Katherine's glove.

"Did you see that!" Plunkett pumped his fist in the air. "Mark my words, boys, this was what the town needed. The Blossoms will put us on the map. Give the factory workers something worthwhile to do in the evenings after their shift. Woo-whee!"

"Sure you don't want to write the articles, sir? Your enthusiasm would be a great addition to them." Jack crossed his fingers. Maybe he'd get to do real stories on real topics. . .like rubber drives. What was he thinking? This assignment was the best thing that had happened to him.

Plunkett frowned at him, lines creasing the man's balding dome. "Raymond." The growl caused Jack to perfect his posture. "You will cover this team, and you will do a good job. Or you can hunt for a job on some other paper. Good luck with that in these times."

"Yes, sir. I mean, no, sir. I love writing about the powder puffs."

Plunkett rolled his eyes. "I'm going to watch my team play. In peace. I suggest you look for your next story. You'll find plenty on that diamond."

Jack inched away from Plunkett, all too glad to avoid the man's attention for a while. When would he learn to keep his big yap shut? His dad had always warned him that a fool made his identity clear every time he opened his mouth. He'd sure done enough of that lately.

Did he want to report or not? If he did, then he needed to buckle down and focus. His pride would kill his career before he established it if he didn't guard his thoughts.

He wanted to do a good job. So why couldn't he focus where he needed? His dreams of bigger things would never happen if he didn't do what was required here.

The crowd jumped to its feet with a roar.

Jack stood and searched the field. What just happened?

Ah. Katherine took a quick bow in center field. Her eyes sparkled, and her cheeks flushed. The girl was stunning and having the time of her life. She waved then handed the ball to Faye. With a blown kiss and last wave, she hurried back to her spot and regained her focus.

※

Concentrate. The roar as the crowd jumped to its feet rang in her ears. Kat hadn't expected the enthusiasm for a simple practice to be so complete.

"Ready to play rather than be a prima donna?" Lola's words rasped with a hard edge. Standing at second base, the woman seemed even more competitive in the twenty-four hours they'd been in Cherry Hill.

Kat tried to smile, but her face felt frozen in a mask. What had she done wrong? She'd played to the crowd. Wasn't that what the team wanted?

Manager Addebary motioned them to the dugout. "Nice job, ladies. You've already got the locals eating out of your hands." Lola shoved a sharp elbow in Kat's side. She jumped away, rubbing the tender spot. "Go clean up at the hotel. We have a meeting in the lobby in an hour to match you with your host families. Then another practice. We leave for our first game tomorrow."

"Tomorrow?" Jackie groaned. "We won't have time to settle."

"That's not what you're paid for." Manager Addebary softened his words with a smirk. "You're here to play ball, and we'll play a lot of it this summer. Brace yourselves."

An hour later Kat walked into the lobby, insides quaking, and realized she was the last arrival again. She hoped her smile held steady, though she feared everyone could see through her. So much for the competent gal who belonged. Instead she felt the lack of each of her seventeen years. The others were older, more experienced. They'd know how to handle any situation thrown at them. She'd always lived at home in the same room with the same bed.

Older couples sat in the chairs set up in a semicircle. Kat edged next to Lola. "Have they told us anything yet?"

"If you can't get here on time, why should I tell you? I'm not your babysitter."

Kat stepped back, eyes wide. "I'm sorry." Did the woman handle stress by barking at anyone unfortunate enough to be near? Kat edged away and leaned against the wall behind a potted plant.

She sucked in one breath then another. *Father, please send me a friend. I don't know who to trust and if anybody cares.* She swallowed against the lump of tears that threatened. Time to "stiffen that upper lip" as Cassandra, Josie's foster daughter from London, liked to say.

Where had the confidence gone that flooded her on the field? There had to be more to her than a ball flying into her glove.

Addebary cleared his throat and stepped to the middle, his ample stomach hanging over the front of his belted slacks. "Thanks for coming. I'm delighted to introduce you fine folks to the women who make up the Cherry Hill Blossoms. Although they will stay with you, I think you'll find they'll be busy and on the road much of the time. The season is short, intense, and packed with games. Joanie Devons here is our team chaperone. The girls already know her, and she'll work with each of you to make sure the girls follow the strict league rules. If you have any questions or need any interference run, Joanie's your gal."

With a prim smile Joanie stepped to the front. As the chaperone matched the team with families, Kat struggled to pay attention. Looked like Joanie had pulled her hair back so tight that her ears stood at attention. Did she get headaches from the tension? Kat shook her curls against her neck, glad for the freedom.

"Katherine Miller." *Oh, time to focus.* "Katherine is our youngest player, but I think you'll find her an easy addition to your home."

Kat pasted a smile on as she wondered whether Joanie had meant that as a compliment.

"Katherine, you'll be living with Mr. and Mrs. Wayne Harrison and their children."

The smile wavered as Kat counted heads. Several small ones peeked from behind the parents. Maybe road games wouldn't be so bad after all.

She looked away and stopped when she saw that insufferable Jack Raymond.

The reporter seemed inclined to stalk her every move, and the wicked guffaw he unsuccessfully stifled made her face twist as if she'd just eaten one of Grandma's tart apples before it ripened. She tried to smooth the river of wrinkles from her forehead but couldn't. She forced her attention back to her hosts.

"Pleased to meet you." Kat looked into Mrs. Harrison's tired eyes, and the urge to ease the woman's burdens overwhelmed her. "I so appreciate you offering me space in your home for the summer."

"It's not much, but you're welcome to it." The thin woman shrugged. "We'll give you as much peace as we can while you're in town."

They were just children. Surely she could handle living with them. "It will be fine. I'm sure of it."

The child with long blond braids stuck out her tongue at Kat.

Maybe this wouldn't work after all. But Kat didn't have a chance to say anything. With a clap, Addebary dismissed them.

"Thank you again for your hospitality, folks. Girls, don't forget practice begins in thirty minutes. Then you'll move to your new homes, and tomorrow we leave for our first games."

Mr. Harrison grabbed Kat's arm. "Would you like me to take anything to the house for you?"

"That's kind." Kat thought about what was in her room. "There's not much, so I'll bring it with me." Mrs. Harrison frowned, her gaze on his hand. Kat stepped away from his touch and hoped her smile softened the action. "Thank you. I'll come as soon as I can after practice."

"That'll be fine." Mrs. Harrison's expression softened. "We have dinner at five thirty sharp." She bit her lower lip. "If you can join us then."

"I'll get there as soon as I can. It depends on what Manager Addebary has planned at practice." An unsettled feeling made Kat want to clutch her stomach.

Lola brushed past her, and Kat startled. "Keep standing there, and you'll be late."

The Harrisons stared after the gal. Mrs. Harrison shook her head. "Sorry to keep you. I've written our address down for you. Anybody can direct you."

"Thank you. I hate to run, but I can't be late for practice." Kat nodded at each of them. A tightness stilted her breathing. *Father, I don't have my mother's skill at welcoming people. Yet. Please help me be Your light in their family.* Her thoughts traveled to Lola. *And with Lola and the rest of the team. I feel so out of my element and alone.* A calm descended on her, and her breathing eased. She pushed the elevator button and savored the relaxed feeling.

God would not have asked her to do this if He wouldn't provide what she needed. He'd never promised this would be an easy journey. A good thing, since so far she felt more like a player suddenly surrounded by the opposing team during play-offs than someone confident in her skills.

As long as God went with her, she could do this. Somehow she could be His ambassador.

"Miss?" The girlish voice caused Kat to turn around.

"Yes?"

"Could I get your autograph?" A girl stood a few feet behind Kat, her stance tight, brown hair tugged into a tight ponytail. Dust coated her pants as if she'd slid into home a time or two that morning.

"Mine?" The girl must be looking for someone else.

"You're Katherine Miller, right?"

Kat nodded.

"Then you're who I want." The kid handed over the morning's paper and pointed at the photo.

Kat took the paper then looked up to see Jack watching her from the corner, a cocky grin on his face. She grabbed the pen the girl offered then scrawled a signature across the bottom of her picture. The girl walked off, whistling as she clutched the paper to her chest. An unsettled feeling squished Kat at the sight. The child was entirely too happy to have her signature. The elevator doors swooshed open. A hand held them open.

"See." Jack's word whispered against her hair, and a shiver shimmied down her spine.

Kat closed her eyes, trying not to enjoy his woodsy scent. "See what?"

"I can make you a star."

Chapter 6

This was it. The first game of her professional career would begin in fifteen minutes. Kat pulled on the cream uniform for the Cherry Hill Blossoms. Her fingers tingled, and spots dotted her vision, part of her usual experience before a game started. She took deep breaths to push through the nerves.

"Who thought cream made a good color for a softball uniform?" Disgust laced Rosie's voice.

Lola guffawed. "They'll be tan before the fourth inning."

"Not if we dance from base to base." Jackie bounced on her toes, arms held in front of her in some ballet position.

Laughter swelled in the clubhouse, and with it Kat felt like she could take a deep breath for the first time since arriving in Racine. This wasn't the first game she'd played, but it felt like it. Someday she'd lose the voice in her head repeating all the times men had told her she didn't belong on the diamond. Then she'd lose the need to prove to everyone she'd earned a spot on the team. Maybe she'd believe she had the talent to contribute.

"Ladies, let's focus on the game rather than the uniforms." Joanie Devons, the always-perfect chaperone, clipped each word off precisely. The tittering died off in the face of her stiff words.

"Everyone decent in there?" Addebary's voice boomed into the room.

A girl squealed in one of the corners and yanked her uniform the rest of the way up. "Someone help me."

Kat moved over to help her button into the uniform. "We're set."

"Man coming in." Addebary eased into the room, a hand over his eyes. He peeked through his fingers. "All right. Gather round." He waited while the team complied. "Ladies, tonight we have our opening game against the Racine Belles. You've practiced hard and are as ready as I can make you. Now it's time to go out there and become a team. You have to work together and focus on what we need to do to win.

"I'm proud of you. Now let's pray and go play ball."

Everybody took off their caps and bowed their heads. "Lord, we ask You to go with us. Help us do our best. Amen."

"And help us beat the Belles."

Kat smiled at Lola's addendum. That girl had vinegar flowing through her veins.

Kat's fingers trembled as she put her baseball cap back on. She needed to get a grip on herself, lose this sense of unease and uncertainty.

"Are you gonna stare at your belly button all day or come play?"

Some days Kat wished she could smack Lola and her harsh attitude. Instead she smiled. "Let's play ball."

The women whooped and ran from the clubhouse. Kat stopped as soon as she reached the diamond. "Where are the fans?"

At most a couple hundred people sat in the stands, scattered around the bleachers.

"Guess we'll have to wow them with our playing prowess." Jackie smacked her gum, gloved hand propped on her hip.

"You're supposed to spit that out." Joanie frowned at Jackie.

"Miss Charm School isn't here, and I like playing with gum."

"Looks too much like chew. Hand it over." Joanie stuck out her hand, and Jackie spit the gum into it.

The girls marched onto the diamond and formed the victory formation with the Belles. They placed themselves in a V shape, proceeding from the point of home plate, and stood at attention while a Racine resident sang the national anthem. As visitors, the Blossoms were at bat first. Kat rode the bench as other players took their turns at bat. Lola was up first. After a strike, she hit a ball along the third baseline. Up next, Rosie got a pitch low and inside and drove it into left field. After them, two players struck out.

"Come on!" Lola yelled from second base. "Someone give me a hit to work with."

Faye marched to the plate, bat held firmly over her shoulder. She planted her feet and swung hard at the first pitch.

"Strike one!" The umpire held up the count.

Faye squared her shoulders and stared at the pitcher. The ball sailed toward her, and her bat connected with a resounding *whack*. Faye took off as her ball sailed into the outfield. Lola tore off the base and ran around third to home. She crossed home plate, Rosie sliding in behind her with a grimace.

The bench erupted. Two runs, two outs for the Blossoms.

Faye stood on second, ready to run with the next hit. Kat took a breath, slapped on a cap, and grabbed a bat to take a couple of practice swings on deck. This might be her first professional game, but she could do this. She'd spent a lifetime preparing. One more player stood in front of Kat, then she'd get her chance to knock one out of the park.

"Strike one!"

Kat focused on controlling her breathing as she took practice swings. In. Out. In. Out.

"Strike two!"

Kat looked up and noticed a line of sweat on Claudia's cheek. "Come on, Claudia. You can hit it." Kat's pulse quieted. She took a few more practice swings.

"Strike three!"

Claudia grimaced then marched from home plate.

"Better luck next time, Claud." A couple of players slapped her on the back as she walked by them and they headed out to the field.

"Get on the field, girls."

Kat dropped the bat against the fence, collected her glove, and then moved to her shortstop position. A calm settled on her. She could guard this slice of the diamond in her sleep.

The first Belle stepped to the plate and took her stance, bat held over her shoulder. Kat tried to watch her but found her gaze wandering around the stands. If the fans didn't pick up, the league couldn't last long no matter how deep Mr. Wrigley's pockets were.

Focus, Katherine Miller. Keep your eye on the ball.

Kat took a deep breath and sank deeper into her stance. She shifted her weight from side to side as she waited. The batter swung at a ball that sailed into the strike zone.

The umpire pumped his fist. "Strike one!"

The player whiffed another ball. "Strike two!"

"Come on, batter." A fan stood and leaned over the barrier. "Can't you see the ball?"

Fans around him shushed him, but the player grimaced. She squared her jaw, and fire lit her eyes. Kat watched her closely. Maybe she was mad enough now to hit the ball.

The batter swung. The bat connected. The ball sailed straight toward Kat. Kat leaped to the ball, expecting it to land in her glove. They always did. It flew past her mitt, and Kat turned to watch the left fielder and center fielder race for it. Her stomach clenched. She should have had that ball. Instead the batter made it to first base, and the fans cheered.

The man grinned. "See. I told ya you could do it." He dropped onto the bleachers with a grin.

Faye walked toward her, a ball playing through her fingers. "Come on, Kat. Get your head in the game."

Kat nodded. She had to get this right.

✳

By the fifth inning Jack felt as restless as the fans. The teams played well, but it really didn't seem much different from watching a church league, other than the fact the gals played in those ridiculous short skirts. He stood and made his way to the concession stand. A box of Cracker Jack and bottle of Coca-Cola later, he returned to his seat, not bothering to stifle a yawn.

What he wouldn't give to get a redo on the article he'd biffed, the one that got him fired from the Chicago paper and had him now covering titillating games like the one before him. He'd learned his lesson the hard way. Always double-check sources. Especially when the story involved a politician and a scandal.

He was a better reporter than this. His old editor knew it, too. Maybe he'd decided it was finally time to stop punishing him and let Jack return to the big leagues of Chicago.

Kat's playing disappointed him. The zest and magic she'd exhibited in team tryouts and practice had evaporated like the dew. All that remained were wispy hints that somewhere inside her the ballplayer lurked.

She'd have to improve under pressure before he could make her a star. And only then would he have the articles that would get his former editor's attention. That man wouldn't care about the girls' league without something more. No, he'd require a human-interest story that gripped readers and tugged them to games. Then he'd acknowledge that Jack's words had regained their power.

Jack shifted on the bench. The bench had left a permanent impression on his backside. Too bad they didn't have padding.

The game ended, with the Belles winning 4–3. The Blossoms looked deflated, but Addebary smiled as if content with the outcome.

"Come on, gals. Back to the hotel. We'll get you settled and do this all over again tomorrow."

Jack groaned. He didn't need the reminder that this was an away series. How would he kill time in Racine, Wisconsin? An idea hit him.

If he stuck close to the team, he could see if they lived by the strict rules.

No smoking or hard alcohol in public.

All social engagements approved ahead of time by the team chaperone.

No fraternization between players of different teams.

Just thinking through the never-ending list made him feel constrained. Jack doubted the players would last long with the laundry list.

It might be too early in the season, but at some point, the gals would resist the strict policies and be ready to find some fun. And when they did, he could be there ready to help publicize those slips.

His conscience pricked. He shouldn't go around looking for the worst in people. And his last attempt at investigative reporting had gotten him booted from Chicago. But the reality remained that people bought papers to see how others failed. He'd never succeed in shaking the dust of Cherry Hill from his shoes unless he gave readers the stories they wanted—no, expected.

Katherine Miller walked past, limping with dirt marring her skirt. She looked like she'd been bloodied by a neighborhood bully.

She'd fight back, find her footing.

※

Kat groaned as Joanie doctored her leg.

"You've managed to give yourself a fine strawberry, Kat Miller." The woman tsked as she painted the wound with iodine, her touch surprisingly tender. "I don't know why you girls do this to yourselves."

Pain surged down her leg, and Kat bit back a scream.

"You'll have to rehem your skirt. Looks like you didn't do too tight of a job."

"I've never liked sewing." Kat gritted her teeth and groaned.

"Maybe your host can help, but I'll see what I can do before tomorrow's game." Joanie patted her arm. "I think I'm done. Next."

Kat swung her legs over the side of the table and pushed off gingerly, favoring her bandaged leg.

"Coming to the hotel?" Lola waited inside the doorway, gear bag slung over her shoulder.

"Go ahead. I need to clean up a bit more."

"We may leave for dinner before you get back."

Kat nodded. "That's fine."

Right now all she wanted was a hot bath and bed. Maybe she'd wait to clean up until she got to the hotel. Several of the girls left as Kat eased around the clubhouse, collecting her gear.

She grabbed the last item and waved good-bye to the stragglers. "See you back at the hotel."

Joanie looked up from her latest victim and nodded. "Remember the rules."

"Yes, ma'am." This could be a long summer if she heard about the rules every time she turned around. She'd never needed so many rules before. Her parents expected her to obey them and honor her heavenly Father. That had always been sufficient. Now it looked like the regulations and monitoring would never end.

Jack Raymond lounged against the outside wall of the field house.

She tried to walk past him with a small wave. Right now she didn't want to weigh each word against how it would be construed in the newspaper. She also didn't want to pretend she was a model or movie star sashaying from the building. The thought of stiffening her back and holding her head erect with perfect posture like they'd preached in charm school hurt. She was too tired to do any of that. Instead slouching the few blocks to the hotel sounded wonderful.

Jack pushed away from the wall and stepped toward her. "Let me take you to dinner."

Kat stopped in her tracks, gear bag weighing heavy against her shoulder. "What?"

"You know...dinner, you and me. We have to eat, right?" He grinned, a smile that quirked up on the side. Kat imagined it stopped many girls in their tracks, but she bristled to think that he assumed it would work on her.

"I am not your typical woman, Mr. Raymond." Kat barreled past him.

"Hey, wait a minute." Jack picked up the pace to match hers. "I've never claimed you were a woman. You aren't even eighteen."

"No, but you'll make me a star, right? All I have to do is fall all over you and act like I can't think of anything better than spending time with you." Heat flamed in her face, and Kat wanted to bite her tongue before it got away from her. But she couldn't. She turned, planted her hands on her hips, and watched him crash to a stop. "I've no interest in whatever you have to offer."

"You think I'm propositioning you." His neck turned a dangerous red, and he clenched his fists against his waist. Kat tried to ignore the power of his stance and the hard lines that planed his face.

"Aren't you?"

He stomped away from her and back. "What rock did you climb out from under? It is possible for a man and a girl to have dinner without ulterior motives."

Did he mean it? Kat eyed him, unsure what to do. A wave of fatigue swamped her. She swayed, and he steadied her arm. A shock wave of electricity bolted up her arm. She tugged free. "I have to go." She raced down the block toward the hotel, fatigue washed away by the sense she had to get distance.

What had happened?

As her heart pulsed, she didn't want to answer the question. *God, help me.* She'd never felt such an intense emotion from one touch.

She couldn't allow her heart to follow the feeling. Jack Raymond was older—and couldn't possibly see her as anything other than a story. Why he even saw her that way, she couldn't understand. Faye was certainly prettier. Lola more confident. Anybody a better player.

Kat steeled her heart. She was here to play ball. She couldn't open her heart to a summer romance with a man she wouldn't see after the season ended. Not when she'd guarded it carefully so far.

Pushing through the hotel's door, she raced through the lobby and up the stairs to her room. She unlocked the door and collapsed on the bed.

"What got into you?" Lola gaped at her from her bed. "You're white as a new softball."

"Nothing."

A knowing expression crossed Lola's face. "Does that *nothing* go by the handle *Jack Raymond*?"

Kat shrugged.

"Watch yourself with him. You're too innocent to spend time with a man."

Chapter 7

"Raymond, this isn't good enough." Ed tossed the sheets of paper on his desk. "I've had you follow the Blossoms all over a tristate area so you could tell the good citizens of Cherry Hill why they should spend their hard-earned money and rare free time at Memorial Field, watching the girls play. This"—he gestured at the paper—"drivel doesn't hack it."

Jack stood in front of the editor's battered desk, pressure building at his temples. How long would the tirade go on this time?

"I could keep you here covering town hall and let Meredith over there follow the team. Bet she'd find the human-interest stories. Or better yet, I'll get stringers in each town. Save the paper a boatload of money we're throwing away on you and your outlandish expenses."

A muscle tightened in his jaw. "I've written good stories covering the games."

"Sure. Play-by-play is exactly what our readers want. Has them racing to the stands to buy the paper. They can get that on the radio." Ed shook his head. "We've got to offer them something they can't get anywhere else. There's too much competition for anything less." He crossed his arms and leaned over his desk. "Look, kid, I know this isn't your final destination. But if this is all you've got to pour on the page, it will be. Now get out there, and find me something I can print."

Jack strode from the room, easing the door shut behind him rather than slamming it like he wanted. He walked across the small newsroom to the reporters' bays, strides hamstrung like his writing. Four desks set in a square formation, phones and piles of papers marring each surface. He grabbed the gray fedora from his desk, slammed it on his head, and headed out the door.

"Where you headed?" Doreen Mitchell, the receptionist and gal-of-all-trades, queried before he could sneak away.

"Out."

"Told you couldn't find a story again?" The light of sympathy in her gaze was the last thing he wanted.

"Research."

"Uh-huh."

"I'll be back in an hour."

"You'll need this." She tossed him a pad and pen. "Good luck."

"Thanks."

What he really needed was every bit of luck he could get.

Main Street didn't look alive, not in between festivals. The Cherry Blossom Festival had ended in April, and with it the tourists had abandoned the town until the next festival in July. Now the regulars focused on work—long shifts at the factories on the outskirts of town that the town fathers had turned into munitions shops. All civilian activities had morphed into something that aided the war effort.

Then there was him. Stuck hunting for a ridiculous series of human-interest stories about girls playing softball. Good grief. Made him want to hunt for another line of work. Until he considered his options, that was. Spending all day standing and sweltering in a superheated factory wouldn't work with his knee any better than combat.

His was in a lose-lose situation. No getting around it.

So write stories about the girls he would. Even that was better than covering another town hall meeting.

He continued down Main Street, looking for anything that would prompt a story idea. The suits in the haberdashery's window looked outdated. Nobody had parked cars in front of the First Bank of Cherry Hill. He walked past more establishments. Jorgenson's Furniture. Behr's Soda Fountain. The five-and-dime. He stopped to scan the five-and-dime's window, but nothing caught his eye.

Jack Raymond did not struggle to find topics. But the Jack Raymond of old also didn't have women unaffected by his presence.

He stopped cold. Where had that thought slunk from?

He needed to clear his mind of one Katherine Miller. She was practically in diapers. Hadn't even graduated from high school.

But he couldn't clear his mind of her when her profile languished in his notebook.

Ed was right. Each of his reports focusing on the game alone fell flat. They were accurate reflections of the game but missed the heart. With a girls' team, that should be easy to capture. The way they gave their all to every play. The way they raced around the bases, tongues caught between their teeth as they determined to make it to home regardless of what stood in their way. The way they played hard after the game.

There was a thought.

He shoved his hands in his pockets and started walking, head down in concentration. His mind played with the idea. Some of them played mighty hard. In violation of the rules. . .

The sound of heels clicking along the sidewalk registered right before he collided with someone. He looked up and stopped. Looked like he'd conjured up a Blossom, just not the one that filled his thoughts with her athletic form and smile.

A woman sat on the ground shaking her head. For a moment he hoped he'd see auburn curls under the sporty hat. Instead a soft brown bob peeked out.

Faye Donahue shook her head then stared at him with doe eyes. "Mr.

Raymond, would you mind assisting me to my feet?" A flirty smile had him grinning in reply.

"Certainly." He pulled her to her feet, surprised by how light she felt. "Are you okay?"

"I'm a softball player. It would take more than your tap to hurt me." Faye brushed off her skirt. "Well, good day."

"Wait." Jack tapped his pad of paper. "Would you like a cherry Coke at Behr's? I wondered if I might profile you, the team's dazzling pitcher, in my next article."

"Any plans to highlight my 'tomboy antics'?"

Jack winced as she threw his words from the prior article back at him. "Or should I tell everyone you performed in a circus?"

"I thought you might focus on the beauty kit. You know, 'Avoid noisy, rough, and raucous talk and actions. . . .'"

"I like your sense of humor. Looks like I'll need to be more over the top." He opened the door to Behr's and let her proceed. "How about a banana split?"

✳

Kat didn't think she could take another moment. When awake she practiced or played in games in Cherry Hill or on the road, always surrounded by her teammates. When at home, the Harrison children kept things hopping at the house. The only place she could relax was church. Even there, she sensed people watching her—mainly with curiosity, but some looks bordered on hostility. She went to worship and remember the great sacrifice made for her.

Right now she needed peace and quiet away from others. Even an hour would do.

She hurried down Main, a tote slung over her shoulder, wearing a simple skirt and blouse. Just once she wished she could wear shorts or pants in public, but this summer she had to follow the rules. At all times. The consequences of not obeying—being sent home to Dayton—were unacceptable. She might long for some peace and quiet, but she loved every moment on the diamond. That magical experience of playing a game she loved in front of fans who wanted to see the AAGPSL teams play continued to make her feel alive.

Ahead of her a group exited the drugstore, and she slowed to let them past. A laugh caught her attention. Faye leaned on Jack Raymond's arm, giggling as he gestured while they left the store. Kat's heart stalled, and she quickly turned to look into the store's plate glass window. Her heart tightened, and she struggled to pull in a breath. The crazy reaction only reinforced her need for time alone.

The couple strolled past, but Kat kept her focus on the window. After they'd walked down the sidewalk, she turned to watch and caught Jack looking over his shoulder at her. He tipped his hat, and heat crawled up her neck.

Argh. She turned and stomped toward the park.

"Stupid girl," she muttered as she marched. This had to stop. Time to get a grip on her zigzagging, roiling emotions.

Kat reached the park and slowed her pace. A picnic table sitting in a pool of dappled sunlight pulled at her. A breeze blew through a stand of elms a few feet away, taking the edge off the heat. Children ran around a merry-go-round, their laughter filling the air. She sank onto the bench, and a bird tittered from a branch overhead.

Stillness settled over Kat as she soaked in the atmosphere. She closed her eyes, breathed deep, and quieted her heart.

Father, I'm sorry I've let so many days pass without making time with You a priority. Forgive me? Make me hungry for You. Prompt me until I can't let a day end without seeking You.

She kept her eyes closed and waited. The silence and peace enveloped her. Something rubbery plunked against her thigh. She opened her eyes, looked down, and found a dodge ball next to her.

Chucking it to a young boy who stood a few feet away watching her, she then opened her bag and pulled out her Bible. Kat opened it to her favorite passage, Psalm 40.

As she read yet again the words she'd memorized, they resonated in her spirit.

"*I waited patiently for the Lord; and he inclined unto me, and heard my cry.*" Her eyes scanned down to verse four: "*Blessed is that man that maketh the Lord his trust, and respecteth not the proud, nor such as turn aside to lies.*"

She tilted her face toward the sun. *Lord, help me to always trust in You, first and foremost in my life. I don't want to live like the proud and find myself pulled away by any god other than You.*

Any god other than Him. What did that mean? It wasn't like she would walk away and abandon God or stop going to church. What was a god? Something people exalted in their lives. That made the possibilities almost endless.

Softball?

Kat cringed. Softball was a game. Not something she worshipped. Then she considered every day that she'd made time to practice, rushed to pack a bag and catch the train that would take her to the next city and the next game. Maybe the thought wasn't as far-fetched as she'd like. *Father, forgive me.*

Verse by verse she meditated on the psalm, celebrating the way the words came to life with meaning. When she reached verse ten, she stopped and read it again. "*I have not hid thy righteousness within my heart; I have declared thy faithfulness and thy salvation: I have not concealed thy lovingkindness and thy truth from the great congregation.*"

The words stabbed her.

How many times had she failed to speak up when given the opportunity to share the goodness and faithfulness of God? To explain the great kindness He showed in His efforts to draw people to Him?

Maybe the reason she played on the Blossoms was to reveal His righteousness and faithfulness. She studied the thought, let it penetrate her heart.

Had she ever bothered to help her hosts beyond the basic role of a guest? Mrs. Harrison lived on the edge of poverty, overwhelmed with her household of children, yet had opened her home anyway. Kat vowed to find ways to help her. She needed to live beyond her comfort and take advantage of each opportunity God gave her.

God had her in Cherry Hill for a reason. One that extended far beyond playing a game. She knew that to the core of her being.

Now she needed to live like she believed it.

"Ah, so this is where you hide."

Kat started, hand placed over her heart, at the sudden deep voice. She spun on the bench and found herself staring into Jack Raymond's dark eyes. "What are you doing here?" She refrained from asking where Faye had gone.

"Thinking." Jack shrugged, his hands tucked firmly in his pockets. "May I join you?" He sank beside her before she could protest, even if she'd wanted to. "You are a puzzle, Miss Miller."

"I am?"

"Yes. You seem so above the competition that pushes so many of the girls on the team. But you're still filled with passion."

"I love softball."

He nodded. "That's clear from the moment you step on the diamond. Why? It's a game."

Kat shrugged. "I'm here for a reason."

The look he shot her told her exactly what he thought of that statement. A bit too obvious. "Everybody is."

"No. I mean I believe God has me here. I'm not sure exactly why, but I intend to play as hard as I can for as long as I can."

"With a war raging across the world, I doubt He cares all that much about your softball games. He's a bit distracted by weightier matters."

"Do you really believe that?" Kat studied him, longing to know the answer.

"Yes. I can't see how things could be different."

"Do you go to church?"

"Sure."

Kat considered him a moment. Was this one of those times God wanted her to say something? Or should she let it drop? His face seemed open, as if he wanted to hear what she'd say. *Please don't let it be one of his reporter tricks designed to get a rise out of me to give him plenty of information for one of his articles.* "If God cared enough about each of us to send His only Son to die for us, then I think He cares about what happens in our day-to-day lives. I just read a psalm that talks about God listening to us when we cry to Him. It didn't say anything about the request needing to be a certain level before He notices."

The words settled in the air around them for a minute. The silence felt comfortable, nonthreatening. As if she were talking to her brother, Mark, about a weighty topic.

"You know this won't last." Jack broke the silence, his gaze gauging her reaction.

"Why do you say that?"

"If more fans don't fill the seats, the league won't make it past this season. Simple economics at play. If there aren't enough tickets sold, there isn't enough revenue to cover the costs, let alone make a profit. The town fathers can't support it for long without some financial payback."

"It'll come." It had to.

Chapter 8

"D o you think he meant it?" Rosie lolled against the bench in the Blossoms clubhouse.

"Of course he did." Lola chomped on her gum, the grimace pasted on her face. "It doesn't take a genius to figure out there aren't enough people in the stands most days."

"Ladies, please watch your tone." Joanie paused in doctoring a strawberry on Faye's leg and gave Lola and Rosie the evil eye. "You needn't worry about the business structure of the league."

Kat listened to the exchange between the players and chaperone but didn't agree with Joanie's conclusion. If there weren't enough spectators, there wouldn't be a team. Much as the experience stretched her, she didn't want to return to Dayton and spend the rest of the summer playing an occasional game with the boys and helping Mother around the house.

With her older sister, Josie, and her kids back home while Art served in the army, home felt cramped. Add in Mark and his crazy hours at the National Cash Register Company working on his top-secret project, and she might have a bit more privacy living with strangers. Well, not actually.

No, this summer formed an opportunity to stretch her wings and fulfill a dream.

There must be something they could do to keep the league viable. "Are we active enough in the community?"

Her teammates turned and stared at Kat.

"I think my photo's in more than enough ads." Faye posed, arm pulled back as if to throw, big grin plastered on her face.

"Well, I think you're a beast, not sharing more of the camera time with the rest of us." Claudia stuck her tongue out at Faye. "Do you have to hog so much?"

"Some days you girls are too much for a body to handle. Worried about who has the most pictures in the paper. Good night." Joanie shook her head. "Y'all need to pack and be at the train station in two hours. I'm taking a break. See you at the station." She grabbed her hat and purse and huffed out of the room, letting the door slam behind her.

Lola plopped down next to Kat. "You're a cute kid, but what on earth do you think we could do?"

"Make more community appearances, maybe?"

Faye shook her head. "We're already running all the time. If we're not practicing, we're packing for a game. If we're not in town trying to humor our host

293

families, we're on a train headed to another small city that looks an awful lot like Cherry Hill. I barely find time to sleep as it is."

Others nodded and murmured among themselves.

Maybe she should wait until she had a well-formed idea to share with them. Kat stood but sat down again as Addebary barreled into the clubhouse.

"Girls, if all goes well with our trains, we'll play the Rockford Peaches tonight. They're a good team, so I want to see your best. All of it. Every slide you've held back, make it tonight. We've got three games to beat one of the leading teams.

"And we've got company on this trip."

Excitement rippled through the room. Kat couldn't imagine who would join them and why the others would think company was what they needed.

"Jack Raymond will join us on this trip. He'll be with you all the time, except when you're sleeping, of course." Addebary stared at each of them. "No fraternizing with the reporter in any kind of intimate way. He is here to learn more about each of you for a series of special stories he's writing. If it'll get more fans here to watch you play, it's a good thing. Now get going, and don't forget your gear."

After a mad scramble, the room emptied, except for Kat. She remained rooted to the bench, leaning against the cold metal locker. Jack Raymond. Traveling with them. That annoying, self-absorbed reporter. She wouldn't have a moment's peace with him there determined to make her a star. She couldn't take it. Not now.

All the peace she'd clung to since her time with God in the park threatened to abandon her. *God, help me cling to You and Your peace.*

※

Traveling on a train with that gaggle of girls. He must be desperate for a story. Jack had written a puff piece on Faye Donahue and left it along with his profile of Katherine Miller on Ed's desk. The man would have to be satisfied with them for now.

In his small apartment, really just a room behind a garage, Jack busily stuffed clothes and underwear in a satchel. Three days. Then he'd return to his abode if Ed didn't send him on to the next road series with the Blossoms. Some American dream. A twelve-by-twelve space with a bed, dresser, and hot plate. At least his dreams exceeded the scope of this town. Someday he'd shake the dust from his shoes and return to a real city. He could already smell the Windy City's unique deep-dish pizza and numerous hot dog stands.

Yep, that was the ticket.

A knock sounded on his door, and Jack looked up from his packing. Who could it be? No one ever visited him, and as he looked at the piles of laundry on the floor and dirty dishes in the sink, he hoped it wasn't anyone important. Whoever it was knocked again. "Just a minute."

Jack grabbed an armful of dirty clothes and shoved them in the bottom drawer of the dresser where they'd have to wait until his return. He strode to the door and opened it. "Polly."

"Hi, Jack. Can I come in?" Her gaze searched his face, her curls playing across her forehead and tempting him to brush them away.

"Sure." He stumbled back to let her pass. "I've got to get to the train station."

"Ed warned me." Polly glanced around, as if looking for a place to sit then leaned against the wall instead. "Jack, what's happened?"

"What do you mean?"

"I know we didn't spend all our time together, but since the Blossoms came to town, I never see you." She crossed her arms, a pretty pout playing on her mouth. "Has one of them captured your attention? Become your girl?"

Jack ran his fingers through his hair and avoided eye contact. It wasn't like he had a serious relationship with any of them. "Ed's had me traveling with the team."

"So. . ."

"Polly. . ."

"Are you leaving me, Jack?"

"I don't plan to live in Cherry Hill a minute longer than needed."

She turned her back to him. "That answers my question."

The pain in her voice made him wonder if he should backpedal. "I've never said I wanted this to be my only job."

"But I've been part of your future, haven't I?"

"Polly, I sent a letter to the United Press this week. One of these days I'll get an assignment with a news service or paper in a bigger city. I don't know when or where, but that's my goal. Things are too uncertain to make any promises to you." He shoved his hands in his pockets. Should he walk over to her? But he didn't want to give her the wrong impression, and it sounded like she'd already had them walking down the aisle—something that had never been his intention. "I'm sorry, Polly."

She held up her hand to stop him then swiped under her eyes. "I'll leave now." She thrust her chin up and stepped to the door. "You might consider a maid. Good-bye, Jack."

Jack watched her walk away, surprised that he had no desire to follow her. He glanced at his watch and startled. He needed to be at that train station now.

He shoved another pair of socks into the bag then zipped it shut. Jack grabbed the bag and headed out. After locking the door, he walked to the train station. This time the Blossoms were off to Rockford, then they'd be home for a week.

Team members had entered the station a few minutes before he arrived. Kat leaned against the wall looking tired, dark circles discoloring the area under her eyes. She must have lost her powder puff.

Kat fit the bill for a good kid. The cuteness element played heavily in her favor. From the freckles dotting her nose, to the dimple in her chin and the sparkle in her green eyes, she magnetized guys' attention without thought. She probably walked around town oblivious to her power. A good thing, too, or she'd lose some charm by wielding it as a tool. Guys would do a double take at her photo, and young women wouldn't feel threatened by her since she played such an unfeminine game, skirts aside. Jack only wished she weren't so boring. Her favorite activities revolved around church. Choir. Youth activities. Mission board. Yawn. Where was the newsworthy story in all that goodness? She'd never do anything that would make her look like anything other than the Goody-Two-Shoes life she led.

Still, she was human. Eventually he'd find her Achilles' heel.

Everyone had one. Some required more digging than others, but it always existed.

His grandmother would be horrified if she knew the direction of his thoughts. The woman believed everyone could be a saint and anyone who confessed faith in Christ would live a life above reproach. He used to believe she was right.

Now he wasn't so sure. He'd seen too much of the underbelly of life. People who wanted to take from others all the time, who thought only of themselves and did for others only when it suited them.

Everyone had an angle.

Kat wouldn't be any different. She yawned so wide he waited for her jaw to pop. When she rubbed her jaw, he stifled a grin. Her frown let him know she'd caught him.

How could he be so cynical about someone as cute and wholesome as Kat?

Time to get on the train and away from his thoughts. Maybe today he'd join one of the card games. Chat it up with the team. He'd find the angles. Write the articles Ed wanted. Get back to Cherry Hill as soon as the series ended. Watch Kat.

Lola plopped into a seat and patted the one next to her. Kat sank onto it like an obedient kid. He hadn't figured Lola out yet. A great ballplayer but with a definite chip on her shoulder, one that she directed toward Kat. Why the kid followed Lola around, he didn't understand. If Kat slipped, it would be thanks to that woman.

The girl pulled out her bag and grabbed a book. Black leather cover worn around the edges. Had to be her Bible. Jack tucked his bag overhead and walked toward them. She'd buried her nose in the book and read it like it absorbed her attention. Poor thing, though he remembered days he'd read it with the same intensity.

Everyone had an angle.

A ballplayer's angle had cost him his first job in Chicago. He wouldn't let that happen again. The longer Kat stayed on the team, the more likely she'd step away from her faith and the real girl would come out.

Nothing against her. That's just the way it worked.

Get out, stretch your wings, and decide if faith was yours or your parents'.

Man, he'd turned into a cynic. Part of him hoped he was wrong. He liked what he'd seen.

A few days on the road provided the perfect opportunity to see if Katherine's faith held up when she thought no one watched.

Part of him hoped she'd withstand the temptations. The other part knew it'd create a great story if she fell.

And he hated himself for that.

"Get a grip, Raymond." The train lurched, the motion throwing him into a seat. Girls tittered as he righted himself. Time to get this show on the road and his thoughts under control. It wasn't like he had a right to worry over Kat.

He needed to focus on what he did best. . .writing.

✳

The train jostled from side to side, and Kat swayed with it, a second-nature action after several weeks on and off the passenger cars. She watched as four of the girls played poker for pennies. Another foursome had set up a game of bridge. Jack Raymond had edged toward them and watched the action from a seat toward the back of the car. Every once in a while he wrote something on his ever-present notepad. He caught her watching and winked.

Heat crept up her neck, and she knew he had to see. A curse with her fair skin. Enough of this silliness. If he wanted to play that way, she'd join him. His eyes flashed with surprise as she sat next to him. "Ready for another round of games?"

"Have plans to slide into home again?" He grimaced as if reliving her last slide in his mind.

Kat rubbed her thigh, where the bruise had eased to yellows and greens. "I never plan to do it, you know. But I have to make it home."

He shook his head. "I still think you're crazy to do that in that dress."

"What choice do I have? I want to play, and that's the only way to do it." She turned toward him and grinned. "Though I've considered adding a pillow under the skirt. What do you think about that?"

Jack belly laughed. "You are a piece of work, Miss Miller."

How was she supposed to take that? She hadn't said anything wrong, had she?

He pulled a pack of cards from his jacket. "How about a card game?"

"I don't gamble."

"That's fine. How about pitch or euchre?"

"I think softball is more my style." His brow wrinkled at her words. "I mean, I don't know how to play either."

"That's a problem I can fix." He watched her a moment. "There's a lot you don't know, kid."

Her pulse hiccupped, even as she tensed at his word choice. She didn't want him to see her as a kid. The realization stopped her, and she scooted back on her seat. Maybe spending time with him, even in a group like this, was a terrible idea.

He must have seen something in her face because he leaned closer, his breath warm on her neck.

"Someone's going to update your education. Be careful who you trust." He opened the box of cards and flipped them around. He shuffled them without breaking eye contact.

Kat jumped up, the book falling from her lap. "I—I need to do something." A dumb thing to say, but she couldn't think of anything coherent.

He leaned over and grabbed her Bible. She cringed as he carelessly tossed it onto the seat. "This'll be waiting for you when you come back."

She couldn't think but knew she had to break the sudden connection with Jack. Spinning on her heel, she fled down the aisle, colliding with Joanie. The woman ricocheted off a seat back, but Kat didn't stop. If she did, she might not get away.

They arrived in town in time for a quick practice before it got too dark. After practice everyone scrambled to change before heading out to find dinner.

"Come on, you slowpoke. We're going to the place across the street to eat." Rosie grinned at her. "If you don't hurry, you'll miss out."

The train had arrived too late for the game. A night of freedom was so rare that the clubhouse buzzed with excitement.

"You'll join us, won't you, Kat?" Faye smiled at her, seeming to want her to join them. "We'll be back in time for curfew."

"Sure. I'll be there in a bit." Kat started tugging off her dirty practice uniform as the first group of Blossoms headed out the door. She savored the warm shower before slipping into clean clothes. Part of her longed for the quiet of her hotel room. She'd enjoy a few minutes of solitude before her roommate returned, but it felt good to be included by the others. What would it hurt to pop over and join them for a bit? She walked across the street but stilled when she reached the establishment. Harry's Pub and Grill.

A stone settled in her stomach. This wasn't what she'd had in mind when she'd agreed to stop by the restaurant. She'd imagined a mom-and-pop kind of place.

Kat stood at the door of the "restaurant." What should she do?

If she didn't go in, the others would never let her live it down. If she did, she'd be breaking every rule and could be sent home. And that didn't begin to address the way it would reflect on her faith.

Sighing, she sank to the stoop outside the door. She couldn't go in.

Clouds rolled across the moon, and Kat shivered. How long would the others be in there? Music started, and she could hear the beat of dancing feet. Crazy laughter bounced out the open windows. Maybe she should walk to the hotel. It couldn't be that far.

Kat squinted into the darkness. A creeping chill stood the hair on her arms on end. So much for being brave. The longer she looked at the shadows, the more sinister they turned.

She lurched to her feet and then hurried inside. Cigarette smoke filled the crowded establishment. Kat coughed to clear her lungs.

"There you are." Rosie giggled as she danced by in the arms of a whiskered man. "You're missing all the fun."

"Maybe." Kat shrugged. "Are y'all ready to leave?"

Rosie danced away, as if she hadn't heard.

Most of the tables were occupied without an open chair. Kat squinted, trying to find a seat then eyed the door. Maybe she should leave. The oppressive darkness kept her rooted in place. She glanced back around the room then stopped, spine stiffening. Jack Raymond sat at a table, Lola practically in his lap.

He winked at her, motioning to the vacant chair on the other side of him. If he thought she would subject herself to his company, he was sorely mistaken. She'd rather brave the unknown out there than watch him.

Kat spun on her heel and pushed through the door. Irrational pain sliced through her.

She needed an escape. Before this man wormed his way deeper into her life.

Chapter 9

The series with the Rockford Peaches behind them, the team moved to Joliet for another away series. For the first game Jack settled onto the bleachers, bag of popcorn and bottle of Coke tucked under an arm, a clump of hair spilling over his forehead into his eyes. Kat pulled her attention from him and shoved her right hand deeper into her glove. She had to focus on the game. The Blossoms led the game five to four in the bottom of the ninth, but the Jewels could turn the game around. One hit: That's all it took to tie and send the game into extra innings. She refused to imagine the Joliet team scoring more than one run.

As sweat dripped between her eyes, Kat prayed they'd avoid extra innings. The June heat and humidity had turned brutal.

She needed a tall glass of water to replace the buckets she sweated while the sun beat down on the field. She tugged off her hat, swiped her hand across her forehead, then replaced it and focused on the game. The league paid her to play, not complain.

Kat leaned forward in her position, eyes locked on the hitter. Ruth Maines, the Joliet Jewels star, took the batter's stance and focused on Faye. Faye wound up then released the pitch. The ball sailed right at the bat. Ruth stepped into it and connected with a *crack*. The fans leaped to their feet with a roar that Kat silenced as she jumped into the air and snagged the ball. Adrenaline pulsed through her, and she tossed the ball to Lola at third base who continued throwing it around the horn until it was returned to Faye.

"Great job, Kat!" Rosie yelled from second base, a huge grin on her face. "Two more like that, and we're home free."

The few loyal Blossoms fans who'd trekked from Cherry Hill whooped and hollered from their spots in the stands. Two more outs and the Blossoms would sew up the game. Kat wanted this win. Their lopsided losses ensured the Blossoms needed every win from here to the end of the season if they wanted any real chance in the play-offs.

Two Jewels had base hits that got them to first and second. Kat watched as their balls sailed into the outfield where she couldn't do a thing except grit her teeth and pray her teammates had sure hands.

With two strikes on the next batter, the runner on second broke for third. Kat had been caught off guard. If she'd crept up behind her and signaled to the catcher, they could have picked the runner off. The runner on first took second. Now the Blossoms were in hot water.

Kat shot a look at Lola who groaned on the ground next to third base. The player had raced into her, knocking Lola off her feet. Kat brushed her hands against her thighs then gave Lola a hand up. Lola swayed a moment then waved that she was okay.

That was one tough woman.

Kat shook her head and focused back on the hitter. Dolly? Had she already been transferred from Racine to Joliet? Kat knew some teams had traded players, but the Blossoms had avoided that so far. Dolly could hit a ball out of the park, so Kat wouldn't be able to do much if she connected with the ball. Faye must have remembered Dolly's skill because her first two pitches were off the plate.

If Dolly walked, the bases would be loaded. The next batter for the Jewels had a reputation for being an easy out with lots of pop flies. With two outs, walking Dolly kept her from hitting a home run and gave the Blossoms an opportunity for an easier out with the next hitter.

Two more balls, and Dolly moved to first.

Kat rolled her neck, tension pushing a headache from the back of her neck to her forehead. Faye wound up, a frown on her face but not the usual one that reflected her intense concentration. Instead it looked like something bothered her. Faye shot the ball across the plate, but the Jewel connected with the ball, sending it straight at Kat. Kat moved to grab the ball with her glove, but in the muggy air she felt like she was pushing through molasses. The ball whizzed past her glove and sailed by her.

She scrambled to turn around, but her foot caught on a divot of some sort. Kat landed on her rear end. Rosie slipped in from her spot filling in at left field and flung the ball over Kat to Ruth at home. Despite Rosie's efforts, the gal from third base slid into home. Kat hung her head and groaned.

"I should have caught that." Kat glanced at the scoreboard: 5–5. Thanks to her botched effort. She fought the sensation that a sack of practice balls had dropped in her stomach. A torrent of sweat poured from her forehead. She swiped at it and tried to pull her thoughts back to the moment. Nothing she did would change what had happened. But she could impact what came next. She had to.

The next batter hit a home run, and the game was over.

The air rushed from Kat's lungs, and she struggled to stay on her feet. They'd been so close. She trudged in to join the rest of the team as they congratulated the Jewels. She mouthed the right words but had a hard time putting her heart into them. Just once, she'd like to win more than one game. It had been awhile since the Blossoms had managed that much.

Dolly grinned as she slapped hands with Kat. "Meet me for dinner?"

That sounded wonderful, but the rules said she couldn't. No fraternization between teams. What did it matter? Would the players really lose their desire to win if they became friends with opposing players? Kat sighed. It didn't matter what she thought. "You know I can't, Dolly."

The gal's face fell. "You're right. I hoped to spend a few minutes with a friendly face, that's all."

"I'd like it, too." Kat hugged Dolly. "I didn't know you were a Jewel."

"I didn't either until two days ago. One day I'm in Racine; the next I'm on a train to Joliet. I didn't even know such a place existed until this season." She tried to act nonchalant, but the slump in her shoulders told Kat the change was lonely.

A throat cleared behind Kat, and she turned to see Joanie standing there, arms crossed and a frown on her face. "Joining us, Miss Miller?"

The tone in her voice irritated Kat. She made a decision and turned back to Dolly. "Where are you going for dinner?"

Dolly's eyes widened, and a spark filled them. "The gals picked a favorite hangout across from your hotel. Maybe it's strategic for times like this."

"I'll see if I can slip away."

"Katherine Miller. The team is leaving. Now."

Kat squeezed Dolly one more time then stepped away. "I'll try to make it."

Dolly winked at her then hurried to join her teammates.

✳

The kid was scheming. It was as clear as the score on the scoreboard that Kat was up to something with that Jewel. He vaguely remembered seeing them together at spring training.

The chaperone really should temper her harsh edges, because Kat bristled each time she issued a demand. He couldn't imagine living under the rules, especially with the strict limitations. Kat's age seemed to keep her separated from her teammates, and Joanie didn't help matters any. He hadn't figured out her angle yet, but he would. Maybe it was as simple as being a frustrated ballplayer.

Whatever the cause, he followed Kat for a bit before deciding he'd rather walk with her.

"Miss Miller."

She spun around at his words. "Please don't call me that. She's"—Kat jerked her chin toward the chaperone—"the only one who calls me that."

"Bad connotations."

"You could say that."

"Sorry about the loss, kid. You kept it close."

She snorted. "Until the last inning. How do we do that? We're so close to winning, and then we self-destruct. It's so frustrating."

"How about dinner? I'll distract you from your loss." He raised his hands before she could protest and put on his most charming smile, the one Polly used to liken to William Holden's. "We can call it an interview if that makes you feel better."

Kat stopped and studied him a moment before a gleam appeared in her eyes. "If you can talk Joanie into it, I'm in. And you have to take me to the restaurant near to our hotel."

"Why?"

"Let's just say I have my reasons."

Jack considered her words. An angle. Somewhere in them. Suddenly he knew. "So you can meet Dolly."

"Shh." Kat looked around, probably not realizing how guilty her actions looked.

"All right. You've got a deal. Clean up and meet me in the lobby. I'll talk to Joanie." His charm always worked on her. "We'll get you out for some fraternization."

Jack cooled his heels in the lobby while Kat changed. As he waited, he scanned the newspaper. The Joliet outfit wasn't much bigger than Cherry Hill's but seemed to have more true news stories. The war had heated up in Africa, and he longed to cover the story. He imagined hot sand pelting his face as he hunkered down behind a sand dune. There had to be a way to get to the real action, stop covering the foolishness of the AAGPSL, and cover something that mattered.

Maybe the letter he'd sent off to the United Press International would amount to something this time. A guy had to hope.

Kat swept down the stairs, gorgeous in a fitted blouse and billowing skirt. Delicate slippers encased her feet, and the curls on her head dripped at the edges. She had no idea she stole his breath. When was the last time he'd felt this way about Polly? Maybe it was a good thing—a very good thing—that she'd ended their tentative relationship. Kat's eyebrows shot up as she caught his gaze. He wiped his expression of surprise and offered her his arm.

"You look great." Her hand rested lightly on his arm, so he tucked his hand on top. He wouldn't let this bird fly away.

A soft smile touched her lips, easing the shadow that rested under her eyes. "Thank you."

He cleared his throat and ushered her to the door. "I hear the restaurant across the street is good."

"Let's go." She grinned at him, an impish look. "I hope you brought plenty of cash. I'm as hungry as a horse. Losing does that to me."

Having her on his arm, he didn't care about a job overseas or the state of his cash. He only wanted to prolong the moment. They teased each other as they walked across the parking lot.

"The crowd seems enthusiastic." Kat's steps stuttered as if she had lost her footing. He glanced at her, surprised to see her cheeks devoid of color.

"Are the rumors true?" She licked her lips. "Will they close the league if attendance doesn't improve?"

They reached the restaurant, and Jack opened the door. "Mr. Wrigley's got his eye set on making money. That's the ultimate goal of any venture like this."

"I wish playing a good game were sufficient." Kat bobbled through the door then waited for Jack. "He's changing the league's name. Like substituting the word *baseball* for *softball* will suddenly draw hundreds of people."

"What could it hurt?" Something had to change. Today's game had more fans than most. He wondered if that was a feature of Joliet or meant a positive change for the league as a whole. For Kat's sake, he hoped it signaled a league-wide change.

Kat remained silent, and he glanced at her. In an instant he realized he might as well disappear. Her attention focused on a table in the back. "Dolly!" Kat squealed and hurried to join the girl at the table.

He'd been a means to an end.

Too bad he wanted more.

Much more.

The realization stopped him. Cold. It would never work. He had to distance himself from this kid before he forgot she was too young and his cynical self was no good for her.

"Are you joining us, Jack?" Her dimple appeared as she grinned, all worry about the league seeming to evaporate as she joined Dolly and her teammates at the table. "There's even a seat by me."

"No thanks. I'm not interested in being a fifth wheel." His pride couldn't handle it. A few of the Jewels batted eyelashes at him, and he reconsidered. What would it hurt? Jack grabbed the chair, flipped it around, and straddled it as Kat's eyebrows shot up.

"What are you doing?" she hissed.

"Accepting your invitation after all."

She turned her back on him and launched into an animated conversation with Dolly. After a few minutes of trying to follow their banter, he gave up and focused on the cutie next to him. He was the only man at the table, surrounded by women. Even if Kat avoided him the rest of the evening, he liked the odds Jack reviewed the small menu. Looked like ethnic food—Slovenian—filled the options. Good thing he was ready to try something new.

"So what are you doing with her when you could be with me?" A brunette winked at him.

He wanted to laugh at her brashness but decided to play along. "I'm her ticket to break free."

The woman considered his words. The candles flickered, sending shadows flitting around the table. A waitress came along and took their orders.

"I can't understand why she's more interested in Dolly than you. Her loss."

"Dolly seems like a good kid."

The woman snorted, charm school forgotten or abandoned. "It'll take awhile for her to fit in with the team. I don't know why they decided to shift players at this point in the season. Not great for team unity."

"They're trying to keep the teams balanced."

"So they say."

The candles flickered again, and Kat stiffened next to him. "Oh no."

Jack turned to see what had her on edge. Joanie strode toward them, a grimace fixed on her face.

"Katherine Miller, you know the rules. There's no fraternizing with another team's members. Come with me."

Kat's chin jerked up, and he sensed her turmoil. Would she acquiesce or let the woman have it? He knew which he rooted for, but Kat didn't have it in her.

Chapter 10

Two more games, split between a win and a loss, and the Blossoms headed back to Cherry Hill. Not a moment too soon. Kat didn't know how much more of living under Joanie's microscope she could handle. If she'd understood how quickly one simple dinner would put her on Joanie's list, she might have followed the rules. Instead she now had to check in with Joanie first thing in the morning and clear all of her nonpractice and nongame activities.

But it had been worth it. She'd needed the time with a friend. Someone who cared about her and not about how she played that day.

Kat didn't think this string of games would ever end. She didn't want to spend another night trying to sleep on a train as the team traveled to the next city. Instead she'd end up watching one or two groups play cards, while another group belted out song after off-key song. Then they'd stagger from the train in Cherry Hill with one day to recover before hitting the grind again with home games—and that only if she didn't count the late-afternoon practice.

Her bed at the Harrisons' home was all she wanted. The privacy of a room, no matter how small, that she shared with no one and could close the door of sounded so wonderful she almost cried.

Yet another sign the stress of travel and the game schedule had hit home.

She tried to stifle a yawn that threatened to break her jaw.

"Come here, kid."

She looked down at Jack, his look inviting her to sit down even as his nickname grated. Joanie jumped to her feet, and Kat shuffled forward. The leash had tightened since her escapade with Dolly. Why couldn't Jack find another car filled with new passengers to annoy rather than allow his presence to remind Joanie of Kat's transgressions?

"Good night, Jack." She whispered the words as she stumbled down the lurching car, settling in a vacant row. For once she wouldn't fight a losing battle with a dozen soldiers for a seat. Tucking her purse under her head, she curled up on the seats. Not as comfortable as her bed at home. She closed her eyes against sudden moisture. What she wouldn't give for one night at home, familiar food, and people who loved her for who she was, not what she did.

This was not the time to break down. Not where her teammates could watch. They didn't need ammunition reinforcing the fact she didn't have their level of sophistication. Some days she didn't want their maturity. Other times she wished for the hard shell some of them wore. Its protection worked for them.

A weight plopped in front of her, rocking the seat back. She prayed it wasn't

Jack. No matter how much she pretended, he wasn't one of her brother's friends, someone she could pal around with and not wish for more. No, Jack had worked his way deeper.

Kat opened her eyes and relaxed when she caught Manager Addebary watching her. "Sir?"

"How you doing, kid?"

She pushed up to a sitting position, pulling on her A-OK face. "I'm fine."

He studied her in a way that suggested he saw through her words. "I hope so. Anyway, I have news for you."

"You're shipping me home." She bit her lower lip to steel herself against tears.

"No. Not this time anyway. Too many escapades like you had with the Jewels and my hands might be tied." He held up his hand as she started to protest. "Listen, kid, I understand. It's been lonely for you. But rules are rules.

"Anyway, we got the list for the all-star game next week at Wrigley. You're on the team. Just keep Joanie happy for a week, and you'll play. You might volunteer for the USO dance, too. You know how she feels about those."

"Yes sir." She rocked on the seat. "Can I tell anyone?"

"I'd wait until it's in the paper in the morning. No need for them to hear about it from you. Let others share the good news for you. Should keep things simpler around here." He pushed up. "I've got a few more to tell. Keep up the effort, Katherine."

Her eyes misted at the proud, paternal tone in his voice.

※

Good for her. Jack wouldn't pretend that he hadn't overheard the news. Instead he enjoyed watching wonder fill Kat's eyes. She looked at him with a *Who, me?* shrug of her shoulders. Jack considered moving to the seat next to her and hugging her but kept his distance. She'd be embarrassed by the demonstration— even if he meant it in celebration.

He winked at her and left it at that as soft color flooded her face.

She half turned away, as if to avoid seeing him, but not fast enough. Jack saw the grin and knew she enjoyed the mild flirting as much as the next girl. But since he'd met her in Chicago last month, there'd been no one else for him. He didn't even miss Polly, which felt a little odd after spending time with her most weeks since he'd arrived in Cherry Hill. Still, her appeal had dimmed in Kat's light. Kat fascinated him from the top of her curly head to the tips of her toes that knew how to slide into base as well as the next guy.

What a paradox.

And she was headed to the USO dance. Jack smiled. He couldn't wait to see Kat in that environment. Surrounded by red-blooded American men headed to one of the fronts. Should be a shock to her system. It was one thing to do a victory formation at each game. An entirely different thing to be hounded by men who might not see a woman for months. Okay, that was a slight exaggeration since these men hadn't shipped out yet.

The train slowed in jerks and starts. Jack rocked with the train and looked out the window. The northern Indiana landscape that surrounded Cherry Hill pulled into view. The town's grove of cherry trees looked wilted under the intense heat, but the leaves fluttered. He hoped the breeze would cool him once he stepped off the train.

A glance at his watch showed he had time to swing by his room before hurrying to the newspaper to write tomorrow's stories. Maybe that all-important letter from UPI waited.

He edged to the front of the car and detrained as soon as the last shudder swept through the cars. He tipped his hat at Kat and hurried down the platform toward the depot. As the sun blazed, Jack rolled up his shirtsleeves, juggling his satchel all the while.

By the time he reached his apartment, sweat rolled down his back. He'd need a shower before he worked his way to the office. His landlady had stacked his mail on the table as usual, and he grabbed it before collapsing on his bed. He flipped through the envelopes, stopping only when he found the one with the UPI logo. Tossing the rest of the mail on the floor, he ripped open the envelope.

Dear Mr. Raymond,

Thank you for your letter of inquiry. At this time we have no openings for reporters whose experience is focused on sports, and women's sports at that. We wish you the best in your future endeavors.

Sincerely,
The Editors
United Press International

Jack crumpled up the letter.

The contents shouldn't surprise him. Why would a service like UPI take him seriously? He remained a small-town nobody covering a nonexistent sport. If things didn't change soon, he wouldn't even report on the league.

He needed to make something happen.

He wouldn't leave his destiny in the hands of anonymous men sitting in some high-rise in a big city. No, he'd do what he did best. Write stories that garnered their attention. The kind of stories that made them sit up and notice his skills. And he'd ask Ed for a new assignment. One that better positioned him to leave.

In a rush he cleaned up, changed, and headed to the *Cherry Hill Gazette*. If he was in luck, Ed would be there and he could tackle the last item on his list.

He winked at Doreen. "That's a smart outfit."

The woman blushed to the tips of her gray hair.

"Is Ed in?"

"Gulping an antacid. Be forewarned."

Jack patted her desk. "Thank you, ma'am." He strode across the newsroom to Ed's office. The door stood closed with the blinds drawn. Usually that signaled it was a good time to give Ed space. Right now Jack didn't care. He rapped on the door and opened it before Ed answered. He sauntered into the room and plopped into the chair in front of Ed's desk.

A fizzy glass bubbled on the corner of the battered desk. Ed had his back to the door, phone pinned by his shoulder against his ear. "Fine. Keep me updated." He spun around and slammed the phone down. "Bureaucrats." He looked at Jack. "What are you doing here?"

"Writing your lead article for tomorrow's paper."

Ed snorted. "Doubt that. You've got to give me more than these blow-by-blow accounts of the games." He rubbed his hands across his balding scalp. "We'll never fill the stands this way."

"I wanted to talk about that. How about running a contest?" Jack laced his fingers and leaned forward. His mind raced as the idea came to him. "We could have a kiss-the-player contest. Sell war bonds in the process. A direct link to helping the war effort. More than the V formation and an occasional USO dance."

"How do you get the players to agree?"

"The typical spiel about doing their part for the war." Jack could even think of a player from whom he'd buy a war bond in order to kiss.

Ed cleared his throat. "I don't know."

"Marlene Dietrich and other stars have done it across the country. Why not our stars? Let's paint them as the stars we want them to be. More than hawking groceries for Bill's Market. Maybe it could be a campaign that culminates with the Cherry Hill Festival at the end of July."

"Maybe." Ed launched forward on the edge of his seat. "Put together a plan, and see if the players will agree."

"Done."

"And get me some articles I can use. More like those features on Faye and Katherine Miller. Readers ate those up."

Jack nodded. What else could he do? "I've got a few ideas from this last trip. Some day-in-the-life kind of things."

"I don't care what they are as long as they get people to the games. Get out of here."

"Yes, sir." Jack stood as Ed held his nose and picked up the bubbly drink. "Bottoms up."

Jack glanced at his watch and hustled to his desk. If he hurried, he could still make it to the USO dance. First he had to write the articles filling his mind.

❋

"Can I come in?" Victoria, the Harrisons' eight-year-old, waltzed into the room without waiting for an answer.

Kat turned from her vanity with a smile, amazed at how the child had grown on her since her arrival. "Whatcha up to, kiddo?"

Victoria rocked her foot back and forth, as if drawing a picture in a sand dune with her toes. "I wondered. Can I come with you tonight? To the dance?"

Kat bit her tongue to keep from laughing. "That would be fun, wouldn't it? I'm not much of a dancer. I bet you're better than me. But you're not old enough."

"I'll never be old enough to do anything." The child planted her hands on her hips, a perfect mirror for her mother's frustrated stance.

"I'm sorry. How about a special outing on my next free day? Just you and me."

"Really?" Victoria shrieked. "Get an ice cream? Maybe see a movie?"

"Victoria Rose Harrison. You do not invite yourself into Katherine's life. She's plenty busy without spending time with you." Mrs. Harrison sighed, an apology in her eyes. "I'm so sorry."

"I don't mind. Victoria is a delight."

The little girl stood straighter at the words. "See, Mama. She likes me." She skipped from the room, humming a tune.

"I appreciate the ways you help. Please don't feel obligated."

"I don't mind." Kat looked into the mirror, patted her cheeks, and frowned at the multiplying field of freckles. "Well, nothing I can do about these dots."

"No one notices them. Trust me. If they do, it's only because they enhance your looks."

"Yeah, the perpetually cute one."

Mrs. Harrison laughed, and the lines around her eyes eased. "You have plenty of time to find the man who captures your imagination. When you find him, you'll never let him go. Just look at us. When I met Wayne ten years ago, I never imagined I'd leave my home state or have four children in such short order." She turned to leave. "I'll leave you to your preparations."

"Do you ever regret it?"

"Regret what?" Mrs. Harrison leaned down to pick up Eric, their youngest.

Kat searched for the right words. "Regret getting married young? Following your husband to a new place?"

"No. It's challenged me at times, but that's okay." Eric whimpered, and she jostled him on her hip. "You need to finish dressing. Wear your emerald dress. I'll prepare a snack for you in the kitchen."

Kat turned back to the mirror. Her slip felt silky against her skin, a forgotten feeling after weeks of softball uniforms. She painted her legs with the leg cream—a necessity since hose had become impossible to find with rationing—then examined them. Almost as good as hose, though she doubted even that could cover all the bruises. She powdered then slipped on the emerald dress. Its simple lines settled over her as if it had been tailored for her, and the color brought extra attention to her eyes. The length of the dress didn't hurt anything either. She applied lipstick but avoided the other cosmetics. Even after the charm lessons, she didn't feel comfortable using many of them. The sailors wouldn't care.

She grabbed her purse and slipped from her room. After retrieving her snack from the kitchen, Kat went to the front porch. The shade kept the temperature bearable as she waited for her ride.

After a few minutes a car pulled up to the curb. Faye hopped out, beautiful in a navy dress with a gossamer scarf floating around her shoulders. "Ready, Kat?"

"Yes." Her voice quavered on the word. Why did this feel so important? She'd grown up around Mark's friends. But that had been in comfortable surroundings with no pressure. Tonight felt different.

Rosie and Lola waited in the car. Kat tried to stifle her reaction to Lola's shocking, heavy makeup.

Lola smacked her gum and examined Kat. "I guess I was wrong. You actually are coming. You'll have a good time with the boys."

Kat hoped so but had doubts. She couldn't be further out of her league if she tried. She almost said something then decided Lola wouldn't understand that she wanted a man who understood how to promise her forever.

Chapter 11

A swing band played radio favorites from a dais at the front of the room. The packed bodies had heated the ballroom long before Jack waltzed into the room. He tugged down his sleeve cuffs and entered the fray. He didn't care about the crush, the sailor and military uniforms mixing with a sea of colorful dresses. He wanted to find one person—see if Miss Katherine Miller relaxed in an environment like this.

It had to be a far cry from the high school dances she might have attended in Dayton. He doubted she'd done that. She seemed the type to alternate between studying, playing ball, and drills.

But even Katherine needed an opportunity to relax, let down her hair, enjoy the moment.

As long as he shared the moment. The guys outnumbered the gals two to one, leaving a tight sensation in his gut—something he'd never experienced with Polly. Jack didn't want to imagine any number of these men pawing Kat. Would she even know what to do? Playing with guys on the field was different from this scene. She needed someone to step in and protect her. Whether she knew it or not.

He scanned the room, looking for the spitfire. She stood against a wall, surrounded by sailors. Although the lines of her body suggested she was relaxed and enjoying the attention, Jack detected a small furrow between her eyes, the one that only appeared when she felt outmaneuvered. Faye danced by on the arm of a grunt, while Lola swayed entirely too close with an officer of some sort. It looked like GI Joes had grabbed all of Kat's teammates, leaving her to fend for herself.

Would he be a hero or a dog if he stepped in and swept her onto the dance floor?

Her laugh, soft and hesitant, reached his ears. That settled it; he couldn't leave her alone, not with those men.

Jack ambled toward the group, clearing his throat when he reached it. "Miss Miller, you look radiant tonight. You promised to save a spot for me on your dance card."

A spark filled her eyes. "Why, Mr. Raymond, I wondered if you'd stood me up. I would like that dance very much." She turned to the boys around her, a lilt in her voice as she played along. "If you'll excuse me. I'll look for you later."

"If she has time." Jack extended his hand and relaxed when her small hand slipped into his. How did she manage to snag so many balls with hands that delicate?

"You can't keep her to yourself, bud." A soldier thrust his chest out and took a step toward Jack.

"I hear you. We'll leave it up to her." He turned Kat toward the dance floor and away from the men.

"You are a welcome sight in this sea of strangers." Kat edged closer to him as they squeezed through the crowd. "Could we go outside rather than dance?"

"Don't you know how?" He'd meant it as a tease but, at her silence, realized she really might not have any moves. "Charleston? Jitterbug? Waltz?" She shook her head as he ticked through several additional styles of dancing. "Well, I'll teach you at least the waltz. Everyone needs to dance a waltz or two at a wedding or anniversary celebration."

As they talked, he eased her toward the door. He pushed through one side of the double-glass doors, breathing deeply of the fresh air that didn't feel so stifling in comparison to the hall. Notes of a clarinet wailing a Tommy Dorsey tune filtered from an open window. Kat cocked her head as if wanting to absorb every note.

"Isn't that beautiful?"

The saxophone shrieked a sour note, and Jack rubbed the back of his neck and winced. "If you like your beauty with a big side of melancholy and squeak."

Kat laughed. "Thank you again for rescuing me."

"My pleasure." Jack studied her a moment, until he knew his only options were to turn away or kiss her. He turned.

Twilight shadowed the cityscape as he walked Kat toward his car. He leaned against it and studied the sky.

"What are you doing?" Her breath tickled his ear as she settled next to him.

He took a steadying breath, keeping his gaze locked on the sky. "Waiting for the first evening star."

Silence followed, broken only by the rustle of leaves as the breeze brushed through the trees. Would she say anything? Most women fidgeted at the first moment of stillness. Yet Kat seemed to absorb the peace, unhurried.

Mercifully the song ended, and the bandleader announced a break. The *pop* and *hiss* of a record took the place of the saxophone. As the easy three-four time of a waltz slipped through the open windows, Jack stood. "May I have this dance?"

Kat considered him, a slight tension squeezing her shoulders. After a moment she nodded her head and stood. He slipped his right hand around her waist, sensing the catch in Kat's breathing as he did. He took her right hand in his left and eased into the three-step waltz. "One, two, three. One, two, three." He crooned the words in time with the music. "Do you feel the rhythm?"

She nodded, and he looked down at her. Her lower lip was caught between her teeth, and her steps stuttered a half count behind each of his.

"One, two, three. One, two, three." She'd settle down as she felt the music. Everyone did.

A tremor vibrated up Kat's spine. Jack looked down at her again and slowed. "Are you okay, Kat?"

If she bit her lip any harder, blood would stain her glossed lips.

"Katherine Miller, are you out here?" Joanie's high-pitched whine pierced the darkness. Kat jumped in his arms, putting space between them. "I see you, young lady. You're here to dance with the boys, and certainly not alone with a man."

She tugged her hand free and pushed away. "I—I'm sorry. I can't do this."

Before he could say anything, probe for a reason beyond Joanie's sudden appearance, Kat turned and fled into the building.

He took a deep breath, the warmth of her body lingering in the empty space. Katherine Miller was nothing more than a child. Her flight proved that fact. Yet he had never felt the way he did about her. He wanted to prolong their interactions but had to admit it had nothing to do with the fact she served as the subject for his ongoing reports on the Blossoms.

No, it had everything to do with the fact Katherine Miller was a woman. She might not realize it yet, but everyone else did. And he couldn't imagine watching her with anyone else.

✳

All week, softballs roiled in Kat's stomach. She couldn't seem to avoid Joanie's censoring or Jack's presence. When she'd headed outside with Jack, it had never occurred to her that Joanie would add it to her list of wrongs. Her request to step outside had seemed like a simple solution to avoiding Joanie. She couldn't have been more wrong. And she was flummoxed about how to change Joanie's view of her. Nothing wrong had happened with Jack.

Every time she caught Jack watching her, she flushed as hot as a Sunday afternoon at the hint of promise and desire in his eyes. That had never appeared in the eyes of any of the high school boys.

Maybe nothing had happened at the dance, but part of her wondered what might have if Joanie hadn't appeared. All Jack had wanted to do was teach her to dance. So why had she felt so vulnerable through each word murmured in her ear and every second his hand touched her waist? She tried to tell herself Jack was simply another of Mark's friends, but her heart refused to accept the words.

In the end, Addebary sent her to the all-star game over Joanie's objections. Said it would be good for the team. But the uptight looks and cold shoulders her teammates sent her way left Kat wondering if the team wouldn't be better served by Faye going to the game instead of her.

The calendar read July 1. Another hotel. Another day. Another city. This time Chicago.

Tonight she would play in Wrigley Field.

Kat rolled over then grimaced as she shifted across her latest strawberry. Just once, she wished she could slide into base without destroying her thigh. At this rate she'd have permanent black, purple, and yellow blotches long after the season ended.

An all-star. The idea seemed preposterous. So many Blossoms played as hard or better than she. But she'd been selected thanks to Jack's articles that a wire service had picked up. She didn't want to think popularity rather than skill had led to her selection, but. . .

Come on, Kat. Just accept it as an honor and enjoy the experience. She could hear her mother's advice as if the woman sat on the bed next to her. Sound advice, as always. Yet so hard to implement.

Whatever the reason she'd been chosen, she'd play shortstop for one of the teams. Maybe the stands would be full. Even if they weren't, she'd still play in Wrigley Field, something girls simply didn't do.

This was an honor. One she should enjoy to the maximum.

Soon enough the game would end, and tomorrow she'd rejoin her teammates in South Bend. Back to the grind of games, doubleheaders, travel, and more games. It might be July 1, but it felt like the season had already lasted much longer than one month.

Surely Jack hadn't made the trip.

Her heart skipped at the thought.

It shouldn't matter whether he had. She longed for one friendly face—one person to reassure her she belonged here. That it wasn't a fluke her name made the list. A pain shot through her. She couldn't look to Jack for those assurances.

Father, I'm sorry. I want You to be my source of security. I've done such a lousy job lately of keeping You in my thoughts. Tears pricked her eyes then slid down her cheeks. She swiped at them with the coarse comforter she had wrapped around herself. *Be my security. Help me find my identity in You and not in those around me.*

She wanted to be a light for Him but felt like such a failure. It seemed no matter how hard she tried, her efforts only made things worse.

Today she was Joanie-less, since a different chaperone had made the trip to Chicago. For today she didn't have to worry about how her every action and intention might be misinterpreted. She should focus on that, enjoy the momentary freedom. And revel in why she was here.

Wrigley Field.

Kat glanced at the bedside alarm clock and jumped out of bed. If she didn't hurry, she'd miss the press lunch. Then practice and the game. In no time the day would be behind her.

She pulled on her Blossoms uniform and hurried to the lobby. The concierge gave her directions to the luncheon. She thanked him and turned to leave. A familiar face peered at her over the top of a newspaper. Jack stood with a lazy smile and ambled over to her.

"Ready for the big day?"

Kat pressed a hand on her stomach. She opened her mouth, but nothing came out.

"Don't worry. You'll be great."

"The press will have me for lunch."

"You'll have them following you around like love-struck kids by the end of the hour."

A shudder shook through her at the thought. "You mean they'll all be like you?" She clapped a hand over her mouth. "I'm sorry."

Jack grimaced then put an arm around her shoulders. "You might want to watch the comments like that. I understand that arrow, which pierced my poor, vulnerable heart." She rolled her eyes and he laughed. "But the press here in the Windy City is more. . .cutthroat. They'll gladly take any information you give them and twist it." He gestured like a knife had plunged into her heart.

"You certainly know how to encourage a person." She slipped from his arm and put space between them. Jack kept pushing under her guard, something she couldn't allow. At the end of the summer she had to go home and finish school, and he couldn't be truly interested in a high school senior. Not when he could have any woman he wanted. Certainly any number of her teammates would take him on as a charity case.

And she still wasn't sure about his faith. If he had ever had any, something had turned him highly cynical.

She couldn't imagine sharing forever with someone who didn't value his relationship with God as much as she valued hers.

Her breath caught in her chest.

Forever?

※

Jack straightened his fedora and edged into the stands. Fans sat around Wrigley Field, but the stands weren't full. He could stretch out and take a nap without fear of someone brushing by him. Still, there were more spectators than at any game he'd covered so far. The smell of hot, buttered popcorn made his stomach growl. He massaged his forehead, the remnants of last night's outing with college buddies pulsing in his temples. His stomach might think it needed food, but he knew the first bite would have him running for the facilities.

A cheer erupted from the stands as the women streamed out of the dugouts. They wore standard skirts—white for one team and yellow for the other—but the blouses came from their regular team uniforms. They formed a sherbet-colored rainbow.

Real ballplayers didn't wear pastels.

He must be hungover.

It had been awhile since he'd felt that way about the AAGPBL. He pulled a program out of his pocket. Kat's friend Dolly had made the same all-star team. He imagined the two having a great time for the day they'd be together.

Although the idea of an all-star game sounded great, the reality was brutal for the players. Their teammates had a day off, but the all-stars had traveled to Chicago, would play the game, and then rejoin their teammates in time for the next game.

The announcer introduced the players, his voice crackling over the public address system. Kat stepped forward with a big grin and wave when he announced her name. Her steps bounced, and energy radiated from her.

His star.

Jack settled in, waiting for the moment she would snag the ball or make the play that solidified her stature in the game.

She might be seventeen, but that wasn't too young—just look at fifteen-year-old Dottie Schrader, who had locked in her place in the league's history books. Time for everyone outside Cherry Hill to realize that Katherine Miller had the same playing ability and star quality.

The first six innings had Jack fighting to pay attention. The play inched along, with the focus being the contest between the pitcher and batter. The powers that be should have selected Faye Donahue for one of the teams. She at least would have been easy on the eyes while time faded.

During the seventh-inning stretch Jack jerked to attention.

"My special guest today is Miss Katherine Miller," the announcer spit into the microphone. "What are you here to tell us about, little lady?"

Jack laughed, drawing curious stares from the few people seated around him. "She hates to be called that."

"It's all about war bonds." Kat's voice sounded honey-dipped, so much so he could imagine the furrow between her brows. "Today the players have agreed to sign autographs for those who buy a war bond."

"One war bond equals one autographed picture?"

"Yes, sir."

"So if a fan wants everyone's photo?"

"That's more than twenty war bonds, and the buyer's a real patriot."

"For that many, I'd think people would expect more than photos."

Jack cocked his head, wanting to catch her reply.

There was a slight pause. Had her mouth fallen open in shock? Was she considering slapping the guy? Jack rubbed his jaw, imagining the impact.

"Well, sir, what exactly do you have in mind?"

The man cleared his throat, and Jack smiled at his discomfort.

"I'm not sure what's going through your mind, sir, but this is America's wholesome pastime. We're delighted to provide a great example to younger girls who hope to someday play ball themselves. So the players will be happy to sign one photo for each war bond."

"Yes!" Jack pumped his fist in the air.

Kat's quote would lead all the articles about the all-star game. His star had just grown.

Chapter 12

The train rocked from side to side as it raced to Kenosha, Wisconsin. The Blossoms had started the second half of the season on fire. Did it have something to do with the fans filling the seats at games? It seemed that in every town they played, enthusiasm for the league had improved. Even in Cherry Hill the stands had reached capacity a time or two.

Now the Blossoms must find a rhythm that led to the playoffs. To do that, they needed to at least split the series, or their season might as well be over.

The longer Kat played with the Blossoms, the more life evolved into something complicated. And the more the thought of her final year of school welcomed her. She knew what to expect there. The role to play. Here nothing made sense anymore. Everything sucked the energy from her as she tried to please all those around her and failed miserably.

There's only One you need to please.

The words whispered through her soul. But how could she honor everyone while focusing on Him?

"It would be easier if everyone else served You."

Addebary stumbled up the aisle, and she looked away. Maybe he'd go somewhere else. She didn't have the energy to pretend right now.

"Kat Miller. You had a great series, kid," he said as he took a seat.

"Thanks, sir." Kat glanced across the car and caught Rosie staring at her, frown lines etched into the grooves of her face.

"You're coming back next year, aren't you?"

Kat shrugged. "Probably. But we'll have to see how school goes. My parents are pretty keen on me finishing and looking at college."

The man rubbed his paunch and nodded. "Understood. Keep playing like you have the last few weeks, and you'll have a spot on any team. With the stadiums filled they're expanding the league. They'll need even more players to fill all the spots."

"I'll pray about it."

"That's all I ask, kid. I'd love to have you back. Well. . ." He launched to his feet. "I'm headed to the dining car for some food. Need anything?"

"No, thank you."

After he left, Kat pulled out a paperback. She didn't know much about the book, but it had been inexpensive at the station's newsstand. She'd barely turned to page four when someone plopped down next to her.

"You are something else, you know that?" Lola crossed her arms and glared at Kat.

Kat wrinkled her forehead, trying to figure out what Lola meant.

"You know that double play from the other day?" Kat nodded. "Guess who got all the credit for it? Yep, your boyfriend made it out like you whizzed around the field getting both outs. Must be nice to have someone color the world rosy for you."

"I don't understand."

"Guess what. I'm tired of the innocent act. It doesn't do a thing for me anymore. You're working the angles like the rest of us. Only thing is, you get all the breaks. The good press. The all-star game. Not content to leave any crumbs for the rest of us. Not that I want your crumbs."

Kat fought the surge of heat that colored her vision. She should let Lola's words go. Turn the other cheek. But she couldn't. Not anymore. "I have done nothing to you. I haven't asked for any of this. Faye should have been at the all-star game. Not me."

"You've got that right."

"But guess what? I wasn't the one making the selection. I just went where they sent me. Like I do every day." People turned toward them. She needed to lower her voice, but it was like a valve had been released. She couldn't stop herself.

"I never asked for the newspaper coverage either. All I want to do is play ball. That's it. I'd love to make a few friends, but that doesn't even seem possible. So excuse me if life isn't the way you wanted it or imagined it. But it hasn't turned out that way for me either." Kat stood then stumbled as the train swayed. Her gaze locked with Jack's. Her cheeks flamed. When had he entered the car? It didn't matter. His gaze searched her with a knowing expression. She had to get away and protect herself from him. Kat grabbed her purse and ran.

✳

Jack watched Kat go. Listening to her, a flare shot through him.

She deserved better.

"Son, never fail to treat others the way you'd choose to be treated." His mother's words echoed through his heart. She wouldn't understand his need to do whatever it took to climb to a better paper in a bigger city. Instead, if he bothered to ask, she'd probably tell him to do right and trust the Lord to handle the details.

Those words used to make so much sense.

Then the world fell apart, and he'd struggled to find his footing ever since.

Maybe that was the crux of the issue. He'd struggled. Maybe he needed to step back and trust again the One who had planned his life long before he drew his first breath.

He'd have to think some more on that. But right now he needed to apologize for the way he'd set up Kat. Although he hadn't foreseen the way the other players would react, he hadn't changed anything once he became aware of their attitudes either. And he wouldn't want to be treated that way.

Sure, he hadn't done anything intentional. Who wouldn't like starring in the articles? But he'd never stopped to ask her. He'd rolled over her like everyone else.

He needed to follow her, but glue must have adhered to the seat of his pants. Rosie looked at him with a glint in her eyes.

"Can't do it, can you?"

"Huh?" He'd play dumb. Nobody else needed to know his thoughts.

"Remorse is a terrible thing."

"Don't know what you mean."

"Hmm." She looked at him, a calculating set to her face. "Isn't she a bit young for you? There are plenty of women on the team. You don't have to settle for a kid. She's sweet, but that's not what you want."

Her words wove around his mind, a glaring counterpoint to the direction his thoughts had just taken. He needed to leave. Get out of Dodge.

"I know someone who's interested, but not while you moon over a kid. So if you're ready for a real woman. . ."

A warning screamed in his mind. He needed to get away from Rosie before he acted on her offer. "Let her know I'm not interested now. Life's too busy."

That had to be the weakest excuse he'd come up with in a long time, but it gave him the gumption he needed to move. He hightailed it out of the railcar before her siren call wove an unbreakable spell.

A moment later he entered the dining car and froze. Kat huddled at a corner table. He hesitated. She was a kid. But that didn't change the truth. He wanted to be with her but couldn't let himself. Before she could see him, he turned and hotfooted it out of there like a coward.

※

Kat tugged her suitcase into a Kenosha hotel lobby. This one didn't look so different from the others she'd walked into this summer. Faded carpet, a couple of stuffed chairs, bored desk attendant. Kat accepted her room key from Joanie, found the room, and deposited her suitcase. Then she joined the rest of the team on the walk to the ball field. She strolled next to Faye but stayed silent as she listened to the chatter around her. Many of the gals talked about the dates they'd had during their last quick stay in Cherry Hill. Kat didn't have anything to add to that conversation. Most of the time she was glad, but today, for some reason, it left her feeling hollow.

They reached the clubhouse and changed into their practice uniforms before grabbing their gear.

"You with us, Kat?" Manager Addebary stared at her as if waiting for her to blow over in a stiff breeze.

"Yes, sir." Tired as she was, she'd do what it took to help the team. Since the all-star game, little risk remained of being sent home before the end of the season. Unless her stamina gave out.

"Then get out there."

Kat hurried to her position.

"If it isn't the princess." Lola chomped on a wad of gum. Kat tried to keep her gaze straight ahead and avoid the thought that Lola chewed like a cow on cud.

Rosie snickered. "Glad you could join us."

"Too bad some of your swarming fans didn't make the trip."

Kat tightened her jaw against the words she wanted to spout back. She wanted to play her best for whoever showed up to watch. And that required focused practice. "I'd really like to get ready for tonight."

"Oh, is that a command? Having money wasn't enough for you? You have to command the rest of us while you're here?" The hard edge to Lola's voice brought Kat up short. What was the story? Something had to make the woman so hateful.

Kat opened her mouth then closed it. Someone had to be the adult and do the mature thing. And that meant letting Lola's words go. *Lord, help me bite my tongue, and give me abundant grace for Lola and Rosie. Please.*

"Shouldn't you gals warm up something other than your mouths?"

Not that annoying, wonderful voice. If she wasn't careful, Jack would finish the transformation into the knight sent to defend her. Her heart tripped at the image of him vanquishing her foes and freeing her from their torment.

"If it isn't Jack Raymond. Defender of all helpless, underage maidens." Rosie rolled her eyes. "Don't forget there are real women out here."

Heat flashed through Kat at the blatant invitation in Rosie's words. How could someone be that brazen? In public?

"Miss Miller, could I have a moment of your time?" Kat had to shield her face to see the tight lines around Jack's eyes.

"What do you need, Jack?" She turned her most syrupy smile his way while trying to avoid eye contact. She did not need the jolt of looking into his eyes and the following confusion. She was too tired today to get her heart to cooperate.

"A quote from Cherry Hill's favorite softball player."

"Then you're in the wrong place. We're baseball players now."

"That's just a name change."

"Don't reporters pride themselves on getting the facts right?"

"Touché." Jack pushed off the bleachers and hiked down the stairs till he stood three or four rows above her. The annoying man forced her to keep her eyes shielded from the sun. "I still need that quote."

"And I need to get back to practice, or Cherry Hill's most popular player will lose her contract. If you'll excuse me." Kat took a step back.

"Duck!"

Kat turned around in time to see the softball blazing toward her. Then everything went black.

⁂

"Come on, kid."

Why was something tickling her neck? Kat tried to move but stopped as pain pulsed through her head. Was she lying down? That didn't make sense. And why was someone slapping her cheeks? Kat held a hand to her head. "Stop."

She'd meant the word to be forceful, but it trickled out in a whisper.

"You took a softball to the head." Jack's voice came from overhead. Did his breath brush her cheek? She tried to open her eyes, but the lids felt so heavy. Too heavy. Instead she rested.

"Katherine Miller. What have you done now?" Joanie clucked her tongue. "And I thought strawberries were painful. Looks like you'll have a goose egg before that swelling stops. Someone get some ice for the girl's head."

A murmuring in the background built until it sounded like a swarm of mosquitoes.

Kat licked her lips. "Could you tell everyone the show's over?"

"Hmm? All right, gang. Back to practice." Addebary shouted instructions and soon Kat felt movement vibrate through the ground.

"Here, this will feel cold." Joanie thrust something frigid against her hair. "We'll hold it in place for a while. Give the bruising a chance to ease. Do you think you can sit up?"

"I can try." Kat screwed her eyes shut as someone tugged on each arm, pulling her upright. Gingerly she eased one eye and then the other open. The world didn't shift, but a headache pounded from the egg at the back of her head.

"You won't play tonight, but it looks like you'll live."

"Thanks, Joanie." It wouldn't be the last time a ball beaned her, but Kat appreciated seeing the softer side of the chaperone. The side that cared more about the players than enforcing all the rules.

"I'll call a cab for you. No need for you to wait here while everyone else practices."

"I'll get her there."

Joanie eyed Jack, clearly skeptical and with a hint of mama-bear protectiveness. Maybe she really just wanted to shield Kat, and that explained her strictness. Then Joanie looked at the field. "I guess that would work this once. Don't try anything funny."

He looked at Joanie with an innocent expression that said, *Who, me?* Kat would have laughed if she hadn't feared it would hurt.

"Really, I'm fine."

"Sure you are, kid. Let's get you on your feet." He hauled her up, and she closed her eyes against the sudden swaying sensation. "Yeah, I'd say you're ready to get around by yourself. Come on."

Kat leaned against Jack and opened her eyes long enough to catch the uncertainty in Joanie's eyes. Maybe the woman wasn't so hard after all. Just unsure how to best protect her charges.

"Remember, no men in your room."

Chapter 13

The article Jack wrote about the series of Kenosha games highlighted Kat's ball to the head yet somehow managed to make her look heroic.

He thought she'd thank him. Instead she'd avoided him. So much for his good intentions. He didn't understand women. That couldn't be clearer.

But as the team crept back into Cherry Hill early Monday morning, a surprise awaited them. Fans packed the train station's platform.

"Way to go, girls!"

"Win some while you're home."

"Glad to see you're okay, Kat."

The appearance of a hundred or more fans seemed to jolt the team. Faye grinned and waved as if she'd morphed into Marlene Dietrich. Rosie sidled and disappeared into the arms of a waiting plant worker. Kat looked at Jack, a befuddled expression on her adorable face.

He leaned in next to her. "I think they want a speech."

"Then they'll have to wait for Addebary."

"He doesn't seem like the speech type."

"Neither am I. Good day, Mr. Raymond." Before he could stop her, Kat slipped from his side and through the crowd, stopping periodically to sign a program or other piece of paper some fan thrust in her face. She seemed to do so with good humor but a touch of speed. Then she disappeared.

The middle of July had arrived and with it a shortening season. It wouldn't be too many more weeks before the season ended, most of the girls leaving with it. That didn't bother him until he thought of one player.

He needed to maximize his time with her. Jack hurried after Kat. She couldn't have gotten too far. He stopped when he spotted her half a block from the depot. A young man stood in front of her, blocking her path, but she didn't seem to mind. Jack picked up his pace, in case she needed his help.

"We've—I've missed you at church."

Kat shrugged. "I can't help it when a game takes us out of town."

The kid shuffled his feet. "I guess I'm trying to say..." He cleared his throat. "I'd like to see you, if it's all right. Outside of church, I mean."

"Oh." The word popped out, and she clamped a hand over her mouth. It would be cute, if Jack didn't want to wring the neck of the acne-covered kid in front of her. "I'd enjoy that. If we can find time."

"Tonight? Dinner at Mary's Diner. Maybe a movie after that?"

Jack groaned. Tonight was a rare break for the Blossoms. Maybe he'd have to find a way to tag along. Make sure Kat was okay.

"I'd enjoy dinner but have to talk to the chaperone first." Kat took a step back. "I need to get home. It'll be a short night and practice comes early."

"I'll stop by at six, see if it's okay?"

Kat shrugged. "I'll look for you then." She hurried past him, her satchel thrown over her shoulder. The kid couldn't even stop and help her with her luggage. What a hero.

※

Kat's mind spun as practice came to an end. Larry Chalmers had invited her to dinner, and Joanie had approved it. Part of her had a jumpy feeling, while the other part wanted to hide somewhere. He seemed nice, but uncertainty floated through her. "Anyone want to field some balls with me?"

Lola laughed at her. "Practice is over, kid."

Kat longed to tell Lola she'd never get better without the extra practice, but it was clear anything she said would be ignored. Besides, she desperately needed the distraction while her mind wrestled with Larry.

"I'll stay." Kat looked up to see Annalise Fairchild stepping toward her. "I could use the extra work." A wistful tone touched her voice. The newcomer to the team in a trade that week, maybe she felt as lonely as Kat.

"Thank you."

The two pitched a ball back and forth, taking a step back each time they caught it until someone dropped the ball. Then they'd start all over again. As they worked, Kat teased the pertinent information from Annalise. An only child, her first foray out from under her parents' protective care came when she joined the league. She loved the experience but seemed jarred by the abrupt move.

"One morning I was a Peach, the next a Blossom." She sighed. "I really enjoyed Rockford."

"You'll like Cherry Hill, too, if you give it a little time."

"It's easy to see why you like it." Annalise rolled a ground ball her way.

Kat shuffled to the side and leaned over to capture it in her glove. "What do you mean?"

"A certain very handsome reporter has his eye on you. If I had someone like that watching me all the time, I'd think the town special, too."

Kat crossed her arms, stance firm as she stared at Annalise. "You're joshing."

"And I think you protest too much."

"Jack's older than my brother!"

"Jack?" Annalise crouched to field a ball. "Then you *are* close. Tell me you never had a crush on one of your brother's friends?" Annalise's chin lifted as if daring Kat to deny it. Something she couldn't do.

"There was Jason Summers."

"See." A delighted grin played on the girl's oval face. "Jack seems like a nice guy."

"He delights in teasing me."

"A sure sign of affection."

"Fine if you're a puppy." Kat tossed the ball hard. "I'm not. I want to be treated like a woman."

"Then start acting like one, rather than everybody's kid sister."

"It's what I am."

"But not the way to convince him you're a woman worthy of his love."

Kat wondered if she should smack her head. Why was she in the middle of a conversation like this?

"Come on, Kat. A man won't watch every hour of your practice and all your games if he doesn't care about you. They simply don't do that."

"I'm his assignment. And even if you're right, then he sees me as one of the guys. That always happens."

"Maybe back home, wherever that is."

"Dayton."

"Maybe in Dayton where they're used to having you around, but not Jack. He's only known you this summer. No images of a girl in pigtails to clutter his mind."

Kat tugged at a curl that had slipped out of her baseball cap. Maybe cutting her hair before the summer started had been a better idea than she'd originally thought. Otherwise she would have spent the last couple of months wearing her hair exactly as Annalise described.

Annalise laughed, the bell-like sound fresh. "You didn't."

"What?" Kat thought she pulled off the innocence.

"Wear pigtails? No wonder Jason whatever-his-name-was didn't notice you. Maybe you're the reason we had charm school." Annalise stood. "Well, time for this girl to get back to her room."

Annalise traipsed to the clubhouse, leaving Kat in a whirl of emotions that collided inside her. Could Jack really look at her that way? Did he have an interest in her that extended beyond being good story material?

Kat hurried to the clubhouse, grabbed her gear, and headed to her host home. The family was gone for the week; the quiet was exactly what she needed.

Jack was too old for her. She could imagine her parents' reaction if she came home with a serious relationship. Daddy would never let her leave the house again. In fact he might tutor her through the final year of school.

The image of sitting in a corner of her father's university office for a year made her laugh. The room overflowed with books, and if one fell, the rest would topple on top of her. She'd be buried alive and lucky if anyone found her before she turned into a skeleton. Kat's steps slowed when she reached the Harrisons' block. Some man sat on the front steps, elbows resting on his knees. She squinted against the sun, which formed a halo around him and silhouetted his features.

Kat hesitated. Should she proceed or go somewhere and wait until whoever this was disappeared?

"Larry." How could she forget he'd be there in fifteen minutes to pick her up? She squared her shoulders and marched toward the home. Whoever it was would have to get out of the way. She had a lot of work to do to get ready for an evening out.

Her steps slowed when the man stood. His features came into focus as Jack stepped toward her. "Afternoon, Kat."

"Jack." He'd never come to her home before. Why now? "What are you doing?"

"I thought you might like to join me for dinner." A smile tugged the corners of his mouth, giving him a William Holden air. His smile grew, as if he could read her thoughts.

Heat flashed across her cheeks. Why did she have to have her mother's porcelain skin?

"Come with me. Let's go have some fun. Relax a bit." Jack waggled his eyebrows. "All work and no play make Katherine Miller a very dull girl."

She pulled her gaze from his lips and shook her head. "I've already got plans for tonight."

"What? Dinner with one your teammates? You don't seem to enjoy their company that much." He took another step toward her, and her breath hitched.

"No. A young man is calling for me soon." Kat took a step off the sidewalk to get around him. She had to get away from Jack before the combination of Annalise's words, her imagination, and his presence did her in. Her imagination wanted to fly away with her, picture what it would be like in his arms, but she couldn't let it.

Jack stepped in her path. The intensity in his eyes stole her thoughts. "Kat Miller, has anyone told you that you are an incredible woman?"

Woman? Had he just called her a woman? Not a kid? Not a tagalong? A woman?

She shook her head, trying to loosen her suddenly frozen words.

He took another step closer to her. Her breath hitched again, and she forced her lungs to expand.

"You are. And I want to show you that tonight."

Wait a minute. What did that mean?

Kat shook her head and stepped back. "I have a date." *With a nice, safe, young man.* At least Larry seemed safe, especially when compared to Jack, who looked like he wanted to eat her for dessert. Maybe those times pitching a ball back and forth hadn't been so smart after all. Did he think she'd do anything for him?

"I have to go. Larry will arrive any moment. Excuse me." Kat slipped past him but was spun around.

"You can't go without this." A fire burned in Jack's eyes. Something shifted inside Kat as if he really did look into her and see her as more than she could see in herself. She suddenly felt beautiful and desirable. . .as a woman. The thought sucked her mouth dry.

Jack placed his hands on her waist and studied her face. Time froze in place as Kat wondered what Jack was thinking. She didn't dare ask him, certain she'd be shocked by his answer.

He lowered his mouth until it landed on top of hers. She stayed stiff for a moment then melted against him.

What are you doing?

A simple thought, but it had the effect of a bucket of ice water thrown on her. She gasped and pushed away from Jack. "You. . .can't."

Jack licked his lips, not letting go of her.

"Kat, is that you?"

She didn't want to look back and see Larry standing there. What must he think, seeing her like this? There was no way to explain this away.

Jack's dazed look quickly slid into his usual arrogant mask. "Are you sure you want to keep your plans with that kid when you could have me?"

She nodded. Anything had to be safer than spending time with Jack. The world felt tilted on its axis. She pushed away from Jack; this time he let her step back. She turned to Larry. "Give me a minute to get ready."

"All right." He hesitated, his gaze questioning her. "I'll—I'll wait here."

Kat hurried into the house then leaned against the door, cheeks blazing. She would go out with the safe option while her heart yearned for time with Jack. She had to get out of Cherry Hill. Soon.

Chapter 14

Another day, another train, this time to South Bend. Kat felt like she'd fallen from the train and rolled over a few times. Her muscles screamed for relief as she lay on top of the scratchy comforter on her hotel bed.

A knock came at the room's door. Kat rolled onto the floor and between the beds. "Yes?"

"There's a party waiting for you in the lobby, Miss Miller."

A party? Kat couldn't imagine who would seek her out in South Bend. "Thank you. I'll be down in a bit." Whoever it was would have to wait until she freshened up and dressed.

She considered climbing back onto the bed and ignoring whoever waited. In the end, she couldn't do it.

After a shower and quick application of approved cosmetics, Kat hurried to the elevator. Mirrors lined the walls, and she grimaced at her reflection as she stepped into the car. Even powder couldn't hide the purple smudges under her eyes. She had to find a better way to get sleep when traveling. Her mother would be horrified to see her like this.

The elevator doors slid open, and Kat stepped out. She scanned the lobby, curious to learn who waited.

"Katherine Miller, come over here."

A squeal bubbled through Kat at her mother's voice. She located her parents across the lobby and ran over. "Mama!"

Before she could do anything, Daddy engulfed her in a bear hug that pressed her face against his seersucker jacket. She inhaled the familiar musky scent that meant safety and love.

"Let me hug on her." Mama edged closer. She held Kat by the shoulders and studied her as if memorizing her face. "Honey, what have they done to you?"

"Let me play softball—I mean, baseball."

Mama patted her cheeks. "We'll see if we can't get you some rest then. Come here." She led Kat to a couch. The lobby had seen better days, but Kat wanted to savor every unexpected moment with her family, as Joanie sat in a corner of the lobby, her eagle eyes trained on Kat. Again.

Kat sighed, wishing she understood the woman's antagonism. Someday she'd get to the bottom of it, but right now she wanted to spend the time with her parents. "Could we walk instead? Get some fresh air. I can't believe you're here."

"We wanted to slip up and surprise you. We drove up last night with the rest of the family. We left them at our hotel so we could see you first. You know how Cassandra will shadow you." Kat smiled at the reference to the girl from England whom her older sister, Josie, had taken in.

Daddy opened the door, and Kat let the tension bleed from her as she stepped into the sunlight. "They all came with you?"

"We felt bad about missing the all-star game, but it was too far. South Bend, however, was the ticket. Mark managed to slip away, so here we are."

Kat hugged her mother. The bone-deep loneliness eased in that embrace. Kat nestled against her mother and soaked in the moment.

"Are you all right, Kat?" Daddy's rich voice soothed her as surely as if he were holding her like he used to when she was a girl curled up on his lap, listening to him read.

"I'm so much better now that you're here."

"Your last postcards sounded down." Mama stroked her hair, a movement that had eased Kat's anxiety since she was a toddler.

"I'm all right." Her mother's look forced the truth from her. "The constant movement and lack of a real home tires me. But I'm okay. It's only for a season."

"And when you're invited back for next year?"

"That's already happened. Maybe I want to spend the summer after graduation in a different way." The August sun felt hot, so hot that even the birds stayed silent in their trees. Kat turned the corner so they could loop back to the hotel. Time to get back in the shade. "I don't know though. I love the games. It's all the travel I'm not used to. Maybe the second season would be easier because I'd be prepared."

"Like you said, we'll evaluate later." Mama linked arms with Kat, their heels tapping against the sidewalk. "Just remember you're coming home in a few weeks."

"The season won't end until the first week of September, but I'll be home after that."

There certainly wasn't anything to hold her in Cherry Hill. Even as the thought formed, she knew it wasn't true.

When they reached the hotel, Daddy led her to the car. A few minutes later they pulled up in front of her family's hotel. Mama looked back at her, a bright smile on her face. "In addition to everyone else, Mark's girl, Evelyn, is with us. I think you'll like her, Kat."

"Are they serious?"

"She's one of the WAVES, and they work together. She's an engineer, like Mark, on that top-secret project Mark can never talk about."

"Your mama's had the pleasure of leading her to the Lord."

"A real honor."

"What happened to Paige?" Kat couldn't imagine Mark with anyone who wasn't the perfect picture of femininity like Paige. That woman could grace any fashion magazine's pages. And to think she'd chosen to spend time with Mark. That still befuddled Kat.

Mama shrugged but didn't look disappointed. "They've gone their separate ways."

Kat had anticipated a different reaction if Mark and Paige ever moved on. Before she could probe deeper, Cassandra launched from the hotel.

"Katherine, you're finally here!" Kat barely had time to exit the car before Cassandra jumped into her arms. "I've waited ever so long to see you. Why'd you have to leave? Right when we moved home with you?" A pretty pout puckered Cassandra's lips.

"Cassandra, leave poor Kat alone." Josie trailed out of the room, Art Jr. balanced on her hip. "Hey, kiddo."

Kat rolled her eyes then set Cassandra down. "Hi, Josie. How's the little man?" She chucked Art under the chin. "He's grown a foot while I've been gone."

"Almost."

Mark joined the group, a pretty woman trailing him. Kat tried to focus on Mark, but she couldn't help her interest in this woman. And Mother and Daddy didn't mind. In fact, they seemed excited. That wasn't typical for them. At all.

"Kat, I want you to meet Evelyn Happ. Evelyn, this is my kid sister." He wouldn't. Kat stepped back but not quickly enough to avoid a hair-ruffling.

"I'm not a six-year-old child, Mark."

"You'll always be my kid sister."

"Maybe I should stay with the team after this. At least they treat me like an adult." She crossed her arms, trying not to be annoyed but failing. She'd forgotten what it felt like to be perpetually seen as the baby of the family. For goodness sake, she was seventeen and had lived on her own all summer.

Evelyn winked at her. "You should hear how Mark brags about you. It's fair to say he's very proud of his kid sister."

Maybe she liked Evelyn after all.

Three hours later, Kat exhaled when her father dropped her off at the ballpark. All this family togetherness might kill her. Evelyn acted so perfect, with manners and speech that were flawless. No wonder her mother loved her. Even Josie had embraced her. And watching the look in Mark's eyes when his gaze followed her around the room left an empty feeling in the pit of Kat's stomach.

Love was in the air, and that meant change. Once he had a wife, Mark wouldn't have time for her. She felt petty even admitting that to herself.

He shouldn't need her. She was the baby in the family after all. But it felt different knowing he wouldn't follow her every game or encourage her in baseball.

And even in her WAVES uniform, Evelyn exuded glamour.

Kat studied her image in the bathroom mirror. What man would ever be attracted to her?

She was a tomboy, with freckles dotting her nose and cheeks. Her short curls often looked matted from having a baseball cap clamped on top of them. Even when that hadn't happened, they rioted around her face in an out-of-control manner.

Nobody would ever want her. Jack's attention would disappear when he no longer needed her for his stories.

⁂

A family filled one corner of the stands. The girl yelled encouragement to the Blossoms in a British accent. "Wallop the ball, Kat."

Jack watched them a moment. One of the women looked familiar. She must have been present when he had that conversation about Kat years ago at that game. She'd been a regular mama bear.

Kat shielded her eyes and searched the stands. When she found the group, she waved, a big enthusiastic sweep of her arm. She smiled, but a cord of tension stretched across her shoulders. Something bothered the young player, something very few would notice. Jack settled back, content to know he understood her. His gaze found her lips, and the memory of their kiss warmed him. Then he thought of that kid she'd left with instead of him.

Ed dropped onto the seat next to Jack, eyes dancing as he enjoyed his first road game with the Blossoms. "Our all-star brought some fans along."

"Yep, probably her family."

Ed rubbed his hands together. "Great! You can get some quotes from the proud parents for an article. Looks like her streak will continue. That girl's been a regular pay dirt of stories and quotes for you. The picture of innocence who plays like nobody's business."

A prickle poked Jack's conscience. Maybe Ed had nailed it. He used Kat, plain and simple. He'd never bothered to ask if she wanted to become a star. Instead he'd assumed she would. After all, who wouldn't? He'd decided she was the perfect candidate for it. She went along, while Faye and others worked for attention with a much more proactive approach to their publicity and articles. Jack dug into his box of Cracker Jacks, ready to get his mind off that track.

"The readers love her." The words didn't make him feel better.

"True. Or maybe they like the image you've painted for them. All-American girl come to play ball. Fulfill a lifelong dream." Ed swigged his Coke. "I wonder if she has other dreams." He shrugged. "Doesn't really matter as long as readers keep buying the paper. You've done a great job with her, Jack."

Then why didn't it feel that way? What did he really know about Kat?

And what did he really want from a kid who was leaving in a few weeks?

The more the question rattled around his brain, the more he realized he didn't know her at all. He'd focused on the external, the easy-to-see parts of her. Though those were plenty fine, they didn't begin to delve into the woman lurking beneath the surface. The woman he'd kissed so thoroughly the other night.

"Go, Kat!" Jack shielded his eyes as he searched the stands for the source of the boisterous shout. There, a petite girl of about ten, sitting next to Kat's family. What were they like? Must be pretty amazing to have raised a girl like Kat. Maybe someday he'd know.

"That's it. Keep 'em coming, Kat." A man—her brother?—pumped his fist.

Ed chuckled. "You missed the play of the game. Good thing I'm here to fill you in on Kat and Lola's double play. The two combined for two outs, my boy." Ed swiped at a bead of sweat sitting on his bulbous nose. "Stars. All of 'em are stars."

The game ended with a win. Ed left with a jig in his step, and Jack headed to the field. He slowed his steps so he'd exit right after Kat's family. No need to rush, and maybe he'd learn something.

"Kat, you darted everywhere. I don't know how you do it, girl, but I'm proud of you." The man bear-hugged Kat and she beamed, pure joy sparking in her eyes.

"Thanks, Daddy."

"Just remember you're coming home after the season."

Kat rolled her eyes. "I've promised, Dad. You know that. I'll come back, finish school, and then we'll see."

The man tweaked her nose. "I know. Call me foolish, but I need assurance this hasn't swept you away from us."

Her brother sidled up to her. "Give her a break, Dad. She's a good kid." He slugged her shoulder—quite the physical family. "Way to play. You must have learned from a pro."

"You know it, Mark." Kat wrinkled her nose at him. "See what I have to put up with, Evelyn? I do something well, and he wants the credit."

"Fishing for a compliment?" The gorgeous woman hanging on Mark's arm needled him.

Jack cleared his throat. "Good game, Katherine."

Kat jumped and spun in his direction. "Jack." A breathless quality accented the word. "I'd like you to meet my family. This is the man who decided it would be a good idea for all the players to trade kisses for war bonds. I helped him see the error of his ways."

"Be fair, Kat. Everyone thought it was a good idea."

"Which is why it got dropped from the festival." Kat rolled her eyes then grinned at her daddy. "See, you taught me well."

In a moment she'd introduced him to everyone, and Jack prayed there wouldn't be a quiz. Too many names, from too large a group.

"Would you like to join us for dinner, Mr. Raymond?" Kat's mother smiled, but a definite question lay in her eyes, the kind that made him wonder what would be grilled at dinner: the steak or him?

Chapter 15

J ack, my boy, I've got the ticket for you." Ed rolled out of his office in his chair, pleased with himself over something.

Jack didn't really care what it was as long as it got his mind off the memory of watching Kat leave her house with that kid. Since returning to Cherry Hill, he'd worried there'd be a repeat event. The image remained locked in his mind. He needed to face the music. He had it bad for Kat.

If her kiss were any indication, she felt the same way he did but refused to acknowledge it. Her actions sure hadn't shown him she cared.

"Are you with me?"

Jack looked up from his typewriter, the one he hadn't typed a word on all day. "Sure."

"Tomorrow night you'll emcee the war-bond event. Your star ballplayers will sign autographs and do other things to encourage the fine folks of Cherry Hill to give their hard-earned dollars to the war effort."

"That doesn't sound too bad."

"It's not. Should be a piece of cake for a refined man like yourself." Ed shook his head, as if disgusted with Jack. "This is your chance to do something for the war. At least pretend a little enthusiasm."

"Yes, sir!" Jack saluted Ed, who batted his hands at Jack and walked away.

"Always the kidder, aren't you?" Ed muttered as he headed to his office. "Maybe I should have kept this job for myself. You try to give a guy a break, a plum assignment, and he acts like he's too good for it."

Ed's door closed, blocking his words. Jack rolled his chair away from his desk, leaned back, and locked his hands behind his head.

"You'd better get your tux out, Jack." Meredith leaned on his desk, one shapely leg crossed over the other.

"Yeah?"

"I've heard we'll have a movie star or two in town. Part of their war-bond efforts."

Jack sat up. That might make things more interesting.

"Thought that would get your attention." Meredith studied him until he had to fight the urge to squirm. "I don't know why you always have to play the hard guy. Ed's done nothing but give you breaks. So this isn't Chicago. What's the big deal? At least you've got a good job doing what you're good at. And you're safe while you do it. The least you can do is show some appreciation and a little enthusiasm on occasion."

"So you don't want my job after all. I'm touched."

Meredith stared at him then launched from his desk. "You are a piece of work."

Jack laughed as she stormed to her desk, grabbed her hat and purse, and headed to the door. "I need some fresh air."

With the room emptied, Jack leaned back again. Maybe he was the one who needed fresh air. Or a fresh perspective.

Ever since he'd accosted Kat—that word still made him cringe, but it best fit the situation—he'd felt bothered. Nothing could distract him from the fact that he hadn't shown himself to be a man worthy of her affection. Let alone worthy to hope that someday she could love him.

He treated everyone around him as if he were a porcupine, and none of them deserved that.

"Doreen, I'm headed to lunch."

"It's ten o'clock." She wrinkled her nose at him. "Didn't you have breakfast?"

"I'm hungry now." Jack bit back a growl. He didn't need an inquisition, just space.

"Okay." Doreen eyed him, as if checking for claws. "You might try the farmers' market."

"Thanks." He strode from the building and stopped as the sun blinded him on the sidewalk.

What was that story? The one he'd learned in Sunday school? Some guy traveling on a highway only to be blinded by a bright light and hearing Jesus speak to him?

Jack turned right and wandered down Main Street. That encounter had changed the man's life. Hadn't the man persecuted believers and then become a chief proponent of the gospel? Jack didn't know why it had entered his mind, but the story remained firmly embedded in his thoughts. He reached a church, hesitated, and then walked in. Coolness embraced him when he stepped inside its shadows.

Paul? Was that the man's name?

A Bible sat on the back pew, and he picked it up. The leather cover felt rough but settled in his palm like it belonged there. He made his living with the written word but couldn't remember the last time he'd picked up a Bible. Must have been years earlier, before college.

"Can I help you, young man?"

Jack looked up to find a man standing in front of him, clad in jeans and a short-sleeved, button-down shirt. "Do I need to leave?"

"Oh no." Wire-rimmed glasses perched on the man's nose couldn't hide the curiosity and openness in his face. "I make it a practice to see if there's anything I can do to help those who find their way inside these doors."

"You don't need to worry about me. I'm fine." The man hesitated a moment, his smile never faltering. The longer he waited, the more Jack felt the compulsion to ask him a question. "Isn't there a story in here about a man blinded on a road? Maybe Paul?"

"You're on the right track. Paul was headed down one path, and God blinded him in order to get his attention. It worked. Paul left his dramatic encounter with God changed and then revolutionized the world for Christ." The man gestured to the space next to Jack. "May I?"

"Sure."

He settled onto the seat, hands loose in front of him as if he had all the time in the world to sit and contemplate with Jack. "What brings Paul to mind today?"

"Honestly? I'm not sure. It's been a long time since I've spent much time in church."

"Church is important." The man laughed. "But you could say I'm biased. I pastor this body, and I'm sure they'd be shocked to hear me say this, but church isn't the most important thing. The thing that matters for eternity is the state of your relationship with Jesus Christ. If He is the Son of God and Savior of your soul, then you've taken the first step. But He wants more. He wants to be the Lord of your life, the One you follow in all you do. If the church can help you learn how to do that, how to live for Him, then we've done our job.

"But if all you do is come to church because you think it's what you're supposed to do, then you could end up like your friend Paul. A man with tons of head knowledge but no real relationship with the Lord. And in trying to do what his knowledge told him was right, Paul worked in direct opposition to God. Not a position I ever want to find myself in."

Jack chewed on that a minute. "I'm still not sure why this came to mind now."

"Maybe it's God's way of getting your attention." The man considered Jack. "I've always been encouraged by the fact that Paul did horrific things to God's people, yet God still used Him mightily."

"Yes." Jack leaned back and considered the stained glass rising above the pulpit. The image of an empty tomb, with the stone rolled away, glowed in multihued color. He felt the tug of truth—that he had slipped away from something important and foundational to life. Jack ran his fingers over the Bible's surface. "Thank you for your time. You've given me something to chew on."

"Then I've done my job." The man slapped his hands on his thighs and pushed to his feet. "My name's Don Harrison. Feel free to take that Bible you're holding. We've got plenty more. And come by anytime to sit and contemplate or look for me, and we can chat more. The doors are open most of the time."

The man slipped up the aisle and then through a door off to the side of the pulpit. Jack sat a moment more before standing, the Bible held firmly in his grasp.

※

The next evening Jack stood in front of his mirror, twisting his tuxedo bow tie back and forth. It didn't look right, but he couldn't figure out how to fix it. The clock on his table donged. Six o'clock. "Rats. I can't waste any more time on this."

He grabbed his hat but hesitated to put it on. No sense messing up his oiled hair.

Jack hurried outside, and the heaviness in the air felt like a wave of hot water had hit him. Blasted humidity. He'd be a sweaty mess before he reached the dance hall.

What had gotten into him?

He'd read the Bible the night before, reconnecting with the faith instilled in him as a child. Then today everything felt off. The time had come to make a decision, and that reality made him a bear.

Turning down the street, Jack mumbled to himself. He knew he had to get a grip before he reached the event. The charm would need to ooze from him in a thick, realistic way if people were going to buy war bonds. And that meant removing the weighty stone on his back that put him all out of sorts.

Fine. Jack stopped and planted his feet. Time to do what he knew was right.

All right, God. I know what You want. And I know it's the right thing. I want You in control of my life, but I admit I'll fight You for it on occasion. No need to restart our relationship with lies. But teach me how to submit and live a life that honors You. Turn me into a Paul who can transform the world for You. Even here in Cherry Hill.

He waited but didn't feel the earth shift. "What did you expect?"

A lady weeding her victory garden looked at him with a half fearful expression.

"Good evening, ma'am."

She nodded then watched as he walked past.

※

Addebary had forced Kat to play a leading role tonight. No matter how she protested that anybody else would do a better job emceeing the war-bond dinner, he'd insisted the role was hers.

He certainly hadn't understood how much she hated public speaking. Playing in front of a crowd was one thing. She could hide inside her uniform. Speaking was completely different.

The butterflies stampeding through her stomach highlighted that fact.

Kat ran her hand down the emerald chiffon floor-length gown she'd purchased for the event. She hoped she didn't look a fool, but she'd had to buy a dress to play the part. It wasn't like she'd brought an evening gown to Cherry Hill. Times like this, she wished Mama or Josie lived closer. But a couple of the other players had gone with her and had at least given her feedback. Though when Rosie had held up the black gown, Kat had put her foot down.

It was a fundraiser, not a funeral.

Kat glanced in the mirror and practiced her smile. Her lips twitched at the edges, but no one would notice that from a distance. If she were lucky, her mystery fellow emcee wouldn't notice either. And her nerves would remain her secret.

Mrs. Harrison knocked on her door. "You look lovely, Kat."

"Thank you." She looked in the mirror one last time, practiced her smile, then turned. "Am I missing anything?"

"Just this." Her landlady stepped in with a strand of pearls in her hand. "These will be the perfect touch."

"I can't wear those."

"Yes, you can. My little contribution to the effort. I don't wear them often now that I have children to yank on them." She chattered while she affixed the strand behind Kat's neck. "Let's see. Your hair. We need to sweep it up. Then you'll have the perfect look."

A few minutes later Kat looked in the mirror and had to admit Mrs. Harrison had been right. The pearls and upsweep transformed her into a woman she hardly recognized. She suddenly felt like Cinderella headed to the ball. Maybe she'd find her Prince Charming. Her cheeks warmed at the ridiculous thought. "Thank you."

"You're welcome. Have a great time, and tell me all about it in the morning." Mrs. Harrison's smile didn't quite hide the shadow in her eyes. "Mr. Harrison's ready to give you a ride. And don't forget to get a taxi to bring you home. You can't traipse through Cherry Hill in that gown and those shoes."

Kat smiled at the mothering. She might not have Mama here, but God had surrounded her with a family who cared.

Mr. Harrison opened the door for her with a bow. And the night only grew more magical as she stepped from the car and entered the country club. Someone had spent hours decorating and had transformed the entryway with strung lights and more tulle than she'd seen since Josie's wedding.

She waltzed up the stairs and through the doors.

The buzz of at least a hundred murmuring voices filled the hall. She didn't want to think about how many people attended. Instead she focused on the rainbow of gowns. Hers fit right in with the elegant yet simple note most of the women had hit.

"There you are." Ed Plunkett, the editor of the paper, slid next to her. "Our own Cherry Hill Blossoms star."

Kat felt heat climb her neck at his words. "I'm not really a star."

"Tonight you are." He took her arm and guided her through the hall. "We've got a couple B-list stars here including Victoria Hyde and Robert Garfield. But don't worry, you'll outshine them all."

"Do you really need me?" *Please say no.*

"Of course. Local talent and all that." He slowed and scanned the crowd before taking off again. "Ah, here we go. Your fellow emcee."

A man turned and looked at her, his gaze taking in every inch of her, a slow smile growing on his face.

Chapter 16

Katherine Miller took his breath away. From the red curls piled on top of her head to the tips of her black shoes peeking out from the hem of her green dress, the girl had metamorphosed into a woman.

The shortstop had disappeared, hidden in a gown designed for a princess.

Jack bowed and offered his arm. "Mademoiselle."

A pinch of color appeared on each cheek. "Jack."

The way his name slipped off her tongue, he wanted her to say it again.

"All right, you two. You have a job to do tonight. Once that's done, you can stare at each other all you want."

Color rushed up her neck in a manner that made Jack want to slug Ed. All he could do was deflect the attention from her. "I'll get Miss Miller up to speed." She shot a look at him—probably from the use of her formal name. But he had to do something to create a distance between them. Otherwise his emcee duties would fall to the side as he swept her into his arms and danced the night away.

"I wouldn't mind the overview." Her voice had an edge to it. So she didn't appreciate his efforts. He'd make a note of that.

Ed ran them through the lineup then left to find his movie stars.

No way Victoria Hyde could look as good as his Kat.

Whoa.

His Kat. He needed to rein that thought in. . .fast.

Before Jack could do or say anything to reveal his thoughts, the mayor stepped up to be introduced to Kat. In mere minutes men surrounded her, and Jack found himself on the outside of the circle. It was as if all the men recognized that Kat was a beautiful flower ready to be picked. The thought unsettled him. He didn't know which was worse: watching her like some grouchy sentinel or recognizing that he might have competition from real men for her attention and affection. That kid didn't stand a chance now. . .but Jack himself might not either.

And how did all this fit in with his new commitment to a life of faith?

His head hurt just thinking the questions.

She looked over the crowd until their gazes connected. He read her silent plea and slipped through the assembled men.

"I think you promised me this dance." The thought of her in his arms made him giddy.

A soft smile tipped her lips. "If you'll excuse me, gentlemen."

The men grumbled but parted, allowing the two to pass.

Kat's shoulders relaxed. "Could we get a glass of punch instead?"

Jack changed directions and led her to the punch and hors d'oeuvres. "Are you ready for tonight?"

She shook her head. "I hate speaking." She put her hand over her mouth, as if to stop more words from escaping.

"A fear?"

She nodded.

"I'm not so fond of it myself." Jack shrugged and tucked his hands deep in his pockets. "Guess it's a part of life."

"Yeah. Thanks for making me a star." Sarcasm laced her sentence.

"Here to serve."

The band ended the song, and the bandleader invited attendees to take their seats. "I think that's our cue."

She glided through the crowd to the head table. As he watched her, Jack forgot about the age difference. All he saw was a woman, one who had captured his interest and his heart.

❋

Kat's heart beat wildly in her throat. A waiter swooped her salad plate away, replacing it with the main course. Jack sat next to her, playing the perfect gentleman. It seemed like a switch had turned in him when he saw her on Ed's arm. As if tonight he saw her as more than a ball-playing high school student. The ember that occasionally appeared in his gaze had flared to life. The thought both excited and terrified her.

What had she experienced of life? Not enough to cause a man like Jack to love her.

And to tell him her fear without a thought? She'd lost her mind.

And her heart.

That thought made her drop her fork, and it clattered to the floor. So much for appearing the sophisticated woman. What a fraud.

Victoria Hyde sat to the left of Jack and smiled at her. "Don't worry. It happens to the best of us."

Robert Garfield nodded. "All the time. Don't let it bother you."

The evening could only get better. After all, she'd only embarrassed herself in front of movie stars and the man she loved. She longed to sink through the floor.

The band struck a few quick notes, the cue to begin the program, and she launched to her feet. The chair tipped behind her and would have fallen if Jack hadn't caught and righted it. "You okay?"

She nodded fiercely, sure she looked even more like an idiot. "Can we get this over with?"

"Only if you take a deep breath and look at me."

"No." She didn't need him to see the terror that burned through her like a white-hot fire. Couldn't risk him seeing her fight the nausea that threatened to reject her salad. That humiliation would topple her after everything else.

Jack grabbed her hand and caressed her fingers, the sensation pulling her thoughts from her stomach. "You can do this, Kat."

"Because I'm your handcrafted puppet?"

"No, because you're an amazing young woman. You have the poise and ability to do this with grace and style. Now get up there and show everyone what I already know—that you are a fascinating person they'll be blessed to meet."

If he kept talking like that, she'd walk to the moon. "Yes, Jack."

She followed him to the podium, suddenly feeling like Katharine Hepburn when she followed Cary Grant's character in *Bringing Up Baby*. She needed to be more than his shadow, even if he was the reason she could find the strength to stand there. People had come to buy war bonds and support the war effort, so she needed to do her part and get them excited. If only she knew how.

※

Kat transformed in front of Jack. Her chin came up, her fingers stopped twitching with the fabric of her gown, and a real sparkle bubbled in her eyes. It was like watching Snow White come to life when the prince kissed her. Jack took a step back and let her precede him to the podium.

"Good evening, Jack." Her gaze embraced him before she turned to the audience.

"Kat." He looked at the crowd, a blur in the haze behind the spotlight that engulfed them. "And good evening to all you fine folks out there." A roar erupted from the crowd. "Tonight we're here to raise money for the war effort."

Kat leaned in, and he paused. "With a little help from two movie stars come all the way from Hollywood to spend the night with us." The crowd tittered, and flames erupted in her cheeks as she must have realized what she'd said. "I mean—"

"Please welcome Victoria Hyde and Robert Garfield." Jack gestured toward each star, and the crowd welcomed them with all the warmth he expected from Cherry Hill's residents. He even heard a few wolf whistles mixed in with the applause. The stars stood, waved, and then bowed and curtsied. "They'll join us up here in a few minutes." Jack looked at the cards Ed had left on the podium for them. They might not need the prompts at the rate they were going. "Katherine Miller, you look splendid tonight. Let everyone see how lovely you look."

Kat stepped out from behind the podium and posed for the crowd. "Why thank you, Jack. It is a bit different from my usual uniform."

"Mm-hmm." The crowd laughed with him. "So what brings you here?"

"Other than getting to play dress-up for an evening?" She batted her eyelashes at him. She had no idea how fetching and magical she looked. "Here to do my part for the boys." She looked him up and down for a moment, and he wondered what was running through her mind. "Jack, you wear that tux like it was made for you. Not quite what the boys in uniform wear."

The crowd laughed with her, but Jack froze. Her eyes remained guileless. His head knew she hadn't meant anything by the remark, but as laughter rolled across the auditorium, he didn't care. He felt the reality of it.

Everyone here would think he'd shirked his duty to fight. Just another pretty boy. And none of them would ever care to know the truth: that the military wouldn't have him.

※

A wall slammed into place between Jack and Kat, but she didn't know why. As the crowd laughed, she searched her mind for a reason. The laughter died down but Jack remained silent. Kat hurried through the next particulars then invited the stars to the podium. Their job was to launch the bond sale with a flurry of support.

While the stars worked their magic, Jack and Kat returned to their seats. He acted the perfect gentleman, but he'd disappeared. He sat next to her, back ramrod stiff.

"Jack, what is it?"

He chewed on his lower lip but didn't turn in her direction.

"Please, if I said or did something, you need to tell me. I can't apologize for what I don't understand."

"It's nothing, Kat. Really."

The words were right, but she didn't believe him. Should she push to get an answer from him? Was this the place? As he fiddled with his cuff links, she knew she had to try. "I'm sorry."

He sighed, still not looking at her. "I know."

"Are you going to tell me what I'm sorry about?"

"Do you really think I'm hiding rather than fighting?"

"No." Her fingers played with her purse strap where it lay in her lap. Suddenly it hit her. "Jack, I'm so sorry that you think I meant that with my comment. See? This is why I hate speaking. Things always come out wrong."

"Not quite what the boys are wearing." His tone mocked hers.

"I'm sorry."

He took a deep breath then blew it out until there couldn't be any air left in his lungs. "I know."

"So get up there and make fun of me next. You can even be intentional about it."

"No, thank you. No one would believe me. And I'd be a terrible emcee."

"Well, aren't you?" She giggled as he shot her a look that should have made her squirm. "Look, you're stuck with me for the night. Let's make the best of it. Then I'll write a formal apology that your paper can print."

He grimaced.

"Fine, you come up with the mea culpa since all my ideas give you indigestion."

The embers reignited in his eyes.

"On second thought, I revoke that offer. Just forgive me."

"Already have. But I think it's too late to revoke your offer, little girl. I like the idea of writing the retraction."

As he said the words, for once she didn't protest. Instead she let them settle over her like a term of endearment.

"We have unfinished business." He grinned at her like he wanted to sweep her out of the chair and into his embrace. "But that can wait. Until I take you home tonight."

The way he said the words made her stomach jump with anticipation touched with fear.

Kat tried to focus on her hostess duties as the night wore on. The citizens bought war bonds like it was a contest to see who could give more. The stars autographed photos as part of the incentive to buy. Kat slid to the background and allowed Jack to cajole the crowd to give more and more. Almost as if the more he talked, the more they'd forget her offhand comment.

Finally the night ended, and Ed released them to go home. Addebary walked up to her as she hit the door.

"Good job, kid. I knew you had it in you. See you in a few hours for practice." He ambled off, a baseball cap slammed on his head—a definite oddity in the crowd.

"I think I have you to myself now." Jack swung her around then pulled her tight to his side. He groaned when a group of local businessmen stopped them for congratulatory remarks. "Thanks, gents. Time to get the star home before practice." He led her to a waiting taxi. After settling her into the cab and sliding in next to her, he rattled off her address.

An awkward silence settled over the cab. After a few minutes the taxi pulled in front of the Harrisons' house, and Kat opened her mouth to thank Jack for the ride. He placed a finger against her lips, stilling her words.

He studied her face, seeming to memorize every feature. She fought the urge to look away. She wasn't a child and needed to act the part of an adult.

"You kids getting out, or do I keep my meter running?"

Kat jerked back and laughed as Jack pulled out money for the fare. "Thanks, Gramps."

"Just helping young love along."

Jack helped Kat from the cab and walked her to the door. "I don't think we need any help."

She stood, back against the door, mesmerized by him. Her breath hitched, and then he leaned forward. His lips brushed hers, and an electric shock charged the air. "Good night, princess."

He walked down the sidewalk whistling an off-key tune, while Kat tried to catch her breath.

Chapter 17

Jack grabbed a copy of the paper as he strode through the door. A photo of Kat and him in full emcee role blazed across the top of the front page, the crowd laughing and Kat grinning in that irrepressible way of hers.

Princess. That's what he'd called her, but last night he meant something completely new. It wasn't the fact she'd been dressed up and looked like a princess. No, something deeper had settled inside him as he watched her fight her fear.

"Here comes the conquering hero." Ed grinned as he swaggered from his office. "I told you you'd be great."

"I guess you did."

"Record numbers raised last night. Good work."

"I don't know that we had anything to do with it."

"Maybe not, but I wouldn't bet against you." Ed rubbed his hands together. "We may have to bring that kid back for other events. The two of you were total magic. Fire and ice."

Jack didn't need to ask who filled which role. No, he hadn't warmed up until the night ended. Then it had taken an ironclad act of will to walk away from Kat with the warmth of her kiss scorching through him.

"Well, back to the Cherry Hill Festival." Ed shook his head. "You sure know how to kick one off." Ed headed to his office then stopped just inside the door. "Come see me once you're settled. I've got something to run by you. Something I think you'll like."

Jack tossed his hat on his desk and grabbed a pencil. He didn't like the way his thoughts cycled back to Kat at any unguarded moment. If she ever figured out the trend, he'd be exposed. Vulnerable.

Could he handle that?

Could he entrust his heart to her?

Did he want to?

The pencil broke in Jack's grip. Whatever Ed had for him had to be better than this.

Jack strode into the office and plopped into the battered chair in front of Ed's desk. Ed had his back turned to him, phone pressed to his ear. "Yeah, he just barged in. I think he'll be excited to consider your offer." Jack leaned forward at the words. What kind of offer would involve him? "We'll be in touch."

Ed hung up then ran his fingers through what was left of his hair, ending with a shaking motion at the base of his scalp. "Still eager to leave Cherry Hill?"

Jack considered his words carefully. "Maybe."

"Thought that might be your answer, seeing how a little woman is here."

"That can't go anywhere."

"Really?" Ed watched him like Jack had turned into prey he couldn't wait to devour. "I expected you to stonewall, but I'm no fool. There's something special between the two of you when you aren't denying it."

Jack started to protest, but Ed stopped him. "Hear me out."

"All right." Jack settled back and crossed his arms.

"Would you be more or less interested in this certain someone if you weren't bound to be separated in a few weeks?"

"More, but what's the point? There's no way her parents will let her stay here. Cherry Hill isn't as important as finishing high school." And he couldn't blame them. That's why he couldn't do anything to make his feelings official. He rubbed his neck. Though he'd let his emotions leap ahead last night.

Ed rubbed his hands together like a boy ready to get the gift of his life. "What if I had the solution for you?"

"When did you metamorphose into a matchmaker?"

"I'm a romantic at heart."

Jack snorted then coughed to cover it. "I'm listening."

"Good." Ed pulled a paper from beneath a stack on his desk. He tossed it at Jack, who read the masthead.

"*Dayton Times?*"

"Yep. A buddy of mine from college is now managing the city desk for the paper. He's short staffed, thanks to the war. Asked if I knew anyone who could tackle the city beat without a lot of training. You came to mind." Ed grinned like he'd handed Jack the holy grail of journalism.

"It isn't exactly Chicago."

"Nuts." Ed batted his hands at Jack. "Why this crazy fixation with Chicago? Move to Dayton, do a good job, and you'll find yourself a step closer to that city."

Jack considered the idea. "What's the salary?"

"You'll have to ask Pete. If you like the idea, he wants you in two weeks."

That fast? "It's been years since I spent one day in Dayton."

"What's to know? It's a small city. In the Midwest."

As if that explained everything. "I'll think about it."

"Do that. And when you're ready, here's Pete's number."

Jack took the piece of paper and tucked it in his pocket. "Are you that eager to get rid of me?"

Ed shook his head. "Just a—"

"I know. . .a romantic."

He left the office, mind spinning. Maybe this was something he should pray about. What if Kat didn't want him to follow her? Had he imagined her response to his kiss last night? Doubts assailed him.

The next day Jack walked up the steps of the Cherry Hill Community Church. He couldn't think of a time he'd attended church for anything other than a wedding or funeral. While he nodded at people he knew, a certain redhead sat halfway up the sanctuary by herself. He eased onto the pew next to her.

"Mind if I join you?"

She shook her head, the ghost of a smile turning up her lips.

Chords of music poured from the organ, and he turned his attention to the front. The peace of worshipping crested over him.

To think he'd turned away from this. He'd been a fool to pretend he didn't need God. As the hymn ended and the pastor walked to the podium, Jack leaned forward. What wisdom would this man impart during the sermon?

❋

Another road trip then a quick series at home. The pace wouldn't ease before the playoffs. In the moments she had to herself, Kat couldn't believe her time with the Blossoms would end in mere weeks.

Jack showed up at the clubhouse, did the routine interviews, but through all of them seemed distracted. He might have sat next to her at church, but he hadn't said much to her afterward. And now he read a Bible on the train, too. Kat almost didn't know what to make of the change. Still, he seemed distant. He hardly looked at her, while her lips tingled each time she saw him.

She didn't know whether to shake him or hit him.

But any time she tried to get him alone to ask what was going on, he disappeared like he'd turned into a vapor.

One day she must not have covered her consternation when she watched him from across the diamond. Faye sidled next to her, hand and glove on her hips. "Get your head in the game, Kat."

"Sorry." Kat fluffed the curls that perspiration had adhered to her neck.

"We need you focused if we're going to win and move up in the standings." Faye glanced at Jack where he hunched on a bench. "Don't worry. He'll come around."

Kat tried to push the thought from her mind before it led to the next. Did she want him around? The answer was a resounding yes. But what if he didn't want her? Argh, she couldn't do this. Not now.

She forced her attention back to the game, what they paid her to do. Catch that little ball and prevent scores. She might not be able to interpret Jack's silence or force him back to her, but she could control her efforts. The rest she had to leave to God. She must silence her fears and trust Him to know what was best for her future.

The crack of a bat connecting with a ball brought her attention sharply to focus. She sidestepped toward the ball, reaching it just as Rosie did. They collided, but Rosie came up with the ball. She waved it at the crowd while Kat stood and dusted off her uniform. Rosie grinned then tossed the ball to the pitcher. She turned her back to the stands, huffing. "Don't make me run like that again."

Kat bit her tongue. It wasn't her fault Rosie hadn't stayed in her area.

"Next time you're daydreaming, I may not reach the ball in time."

"I'll keep that in mind."

Addebary signaled the umpire and trotted out to where they stood. "Is there a problem, ladies?"

"No, sir." Kat shook her head.

"Then let's play the game, if you don't mind. That's what our fans paid to see."

Rosie walked away with a flounce of her skirt. A man in the second row whistled, and Kat blushed for Rosie.

"Come on, Miller. Get in the game."

"Yes, sir." Kat squared her shoulders. Thoughts of Jack and the confusion he generated in her had to wait.

After the Blossoms squeaked out a win, Jack disappeared again. Somehow he managed to write articles that included highlights of what she did during the game. But if he did it again, he would do it without talking to her since all she saw was his back as he left.

Fine! If that's how he wanted to be, she'd cooperate. No more wasted thoughts on him, especially when they interfered with her playing. No one had ever done that. Before Jack.

※

Jack walked through his thinking one more time. He couldn't make this change without knowing he did it for the right reasons. Would he resent it if he moved and then Kat forgot about him? He had a feeling he'd make sure that didn't happen, but what if?

He'd prayed the best way he knew how. He'd read his Bible. He'd talked to the pastor.

Nothing seemed to stand in his way. Instead everything pointed toward the move.

Even his landlord was eager to have him break his lease so she could relet the apartment at a higher rate. It almost felt too easy.

Was that a sign?

The pastor had told him to pray, read the Bible, and ask for peace. If he had peace and couldn't find reasons to stay, then he should step out in faith. Easy for a pastor to say. After all, he was paid to have faith.

Jack's recent steps of faith were new enough that he didn't know if he could trust them. Would he even know if God told him to stay?

The questions pained his mind, stretched his understanding.

All he knew was he had to make a decision.

Jack marched into Ed's vacant office and picked up the phone. After a few attempts, Doreen got him connected with the Dayton paper.

"Jack Raymond calling for Pete Hodges."

After several minutes, a gruff voice answered, "Hodges."

"Sir, this is Jack Raymond."

"About time you called."

"Yes, sir."

"So, are you taking the position? Ready to work harder than you ever have?"

"You certainly know how to sell a man on the job."

Rough laughter carried over the line. "Blunt, aren't you? I like that in a reporter. You'll need that around here. This isn't Cherry Hill."

"That's what I'm counting on."

They talked details, and when he hung up, Jack wiped sweat from his forehead. He'd done it. He was Dayton-bound. Now to tell Kat. He needed to think of the right way. A way that would make it a memory worthy of a promise he hoped would last forever.

※

A rare day arrived that week. The Blossoms had a day without a game. Kat lounged in bed for an extra hour while the sun lit patterns on the patchwork quilt, then got up to help Mrs. Harrison with her children. A series of clouds brought a brief rain shower, perfect for creating puddles for the three oldest children to splash in when she took them to the library late that morning. After corralling them home, a bit soaked but grinning, Kat wondered how Mrs. Harrison found the energy to umpire them every day. Mothering was exhausting work.

When Kat stepped into the kitchen, a fragrant sweetness tickled her nose.

"These came while you were out." Mrs. Harrison pointed her chin at a bouquet of flowers while she continued to chop carrots.

"For me?" A pounding filled Kat's ears at the thought someone had sent her flowers.

"Yes, but you'll have to read the card to see from who. I didn't open it."

"Thank you." Kat grabbed the card and rushed to her room. Flouncing on her bed, she opened the note. *"Will you honor me by joining me for dinner? Jack. P.S. Joanie Devons gave her approval."*

The last words brought a smile. How thoughtful that he checked before asking.

She returned to the kitchen to call to accept before she could think too hard. After a few moments the operator connected her to the paper. "Is Jack there?"

"No, honey. Can I take a message?"

Kat hesitated. What could she leave in the message? Besides, the petty part of her wanted to punish him for his weeklong silence by saying no. But she had three weeks left in Cherry Hill. She didn't want to waste them apart from Jack. Not if the possibility of more lingered between them. "Yes, if you could tell him—"

"Oh, wait a minute. Here he comes." There was a muffled sound then scattered words. "Here he is."

"Jack Raymond." At the sound of his rich voice, Kat's mind blanked. "Hello?"

"Um, hi." *Way to sound like a sophisticated woman.* Kate Hepburn would have said something—anything!—better. "This is Katherine. Katherine Miller."

"Hey, princess."

With that word her pulse slowed, and her thoughts ordered. "Hi. Thanks for the flowers. They're beautiful."

"You're welcome." She didn't know why, but she'd expected more.

"So. Are you still free tonight?" If he hadn't thought she was a kid before, he certainly must now. Could she be any more tongue-tied?

Silence filled the air. She knew it. He regretted sending the invitation. She dropped her forehead to her hand and stifled a groan.

"Only if you can join me." She could sense his smile over the wire.

Her heart began to race. "I can."

"Good. I'll pick you up at seven."

Just like that they had an official date. A moment later Kat hung up and leaned against the counter.

"Good news?" Mrs. Harrison smiled as she watched Kat.

"The best. I think." She chewed on a fingernail. How should she dress for the mystery date?

Tonight might answer some of her questions. She needed to learn if they could ever have more than friendship before she moved home. That much she had to know.

The rest could wait.

Chapter 18

It had to be a rule somewhere that you didn't take a woman out to dinner in your shirtsleeves. Jack strolled up the Harrisons' sidewalk, the muggy weather making him wish he'd broken that rule and left his suit coat at home. He felt rings of sweat at his neck and underarms. Not the suave image he'd tried to achieve.

He certainly wasn't William Holden.

But he didn't want a Hollywood life filled with glamour and fame. He couldn't stand glitz and fakeness. What he wanted was a relatively simple life. Work hard. Play hard. Love hard.

And every time he pictured the love hard part, a certain redhead with springy curls and lots of freckles dotting her pert nose played the starring role. He couldn't imagine anyone else in that role. Frankly he didn't want to.

He hoped the flowers he held didn't tip the scales over the top. The fresh-faced daisies were different from the fancy bouquet the florist had fashioned earlier for Kat. Jack wanted Kat to know he saw the woman lurking beneath the surface. But he also knew the fresh-faced girl—she was the one who'd captured his imagination. His attention. His heart.

Hopping the last two steps, Jack rapped on the door. A few moments later, Mr. Harrison came to the door. "Should I ask what your intentions are, young man?" His words were harsh but softened by a smile.

"That might be taking the pseudo dad role a bit far."

"Agreed." Mr. Harrison opened the door. "Come on in. I'm not sure, but I think she's doing something last-minute, like powdering her nose. I'm relieved my girl's not old enough yet for scoundrels like you."

"Yes, sir." They passed the minutes talking about the latest news from the front. The Italians were abandoning Sicily while the Solomon Islands were under attack. The men agreed they were ready for some good news. "Let's hope the Allies keep the Italians on the move."

The soft clomp of heels sinking into carpet finally reached his ears. Jack struggled off the davenport and onto his feet. Kat wore a soft blue dress with flared skirt that emphasized her tiny waist. He could get used to seeing her in real clothes rather than her uniform and practice clothes.

"Hello, Jack." A flash of something—expectation?—filled her doelike eyes.

"Katherine. These are for you." He held out the daisies and enjoyed the soft blush that colored her cheeks.

"They're beautiful. Thank you."

"Almost as pretty as you."

"Let me put them in some water." Katherine hurried from the room, returning a minute later.

"Are you ready to head out?" She nodded, and he turned to Mr. Harrison. "A pleasure talking with you, sir."

"You, too, Jack. It's not every night I get to talk with someone as up on the wires as a newspaperman. Now don't keep the girl out late. I'd hate to have to chase you down with my shotgun."

The soft color in Kat's cheeks deepened. Jack offered his arm and then ushered her outside. "Do you mind if we walk the few blocks downtown?"

"If I did, it'd be a bit late, wouldn't it?"

"Touché, mademoiselle."

"It's a good thing I like exercise." Kat did a shuffle step around him as if she'd transformed into Ginger Rogers. Too bad he wasn't Fred Astaire. "Thank you for the flowers. They're beautiful."

"Not as beautiful as you."

She stopped and looked at him, searching past his walls. "Is that a line?"

Jack matched her gaze. "No, Katherine Miller, it's not."

"Good." She turned so she was shoulder to shoulder with him, and he instantly missed the connection. "I'd hate to have to evaluate every word you say tonight."

Jack snorted. "You are something else."

"That's what my brother tells me."

They strolled downtown, the conversation light and easy. How did she manage to do that? She gave no indication she tried to impress. Instead Kat was who she was. Did she understand that's what made her so incredibly special and unique? They passed the Italian restaurant with its rich, spicy aroma then sidestepped a couple exiting a Chinese eatery. The ginger twanged his nose. Kat didn't seem interested in either. Instead she kept up a steady flow of stories about her family and home. They came to life as she mimicked voices and gestured with abandon. She swung an arm, and he ducked.

She stopped, giggling behind her hand. "Sorry about that."

"You are nothing if not enthusiastic about life."

"That's one way to describe it." She shrugged. "I talk with my hands when I get nervous. If people are ducking for their lives, then they aren't watching me."

Jack stopped and brushed a soft curl that had escaped her hat. "I like watching you."

"Why?" He almost missed the whispered word.

Here it was. That all-important moment to convince her he saw to the heart of her.

"I mean, there are so many women around here who would love your company. Why not Faye or Rosie? Or anyone else?" She took a breath then forged ahead. "Why me? I'm nothing but a kid compared to them."

"I don't want to compare you to anyone, Kat. God's made you into an amazing young woman with the promise of a lifetime of depth and character." That didn't sound quite right. He worked with words, for goodness' sake. Couldn't he get this right? "Doesn't 1 Timothy talk about not letting anyone look down on you because of your youth? So shouldn't you stop doing that? Sure you're younger than me. It's not the first time in history that's happened. Let's try this, see where it leads."

A cloud formed on her brow. That definitely hadn't come out right.

So Jack tipped her chin up and communicated in a way that words couldn't destroy.

❋

His lips settled on hers, and Kat momentarily forgot where she was. She longed to forget everything—to trust Jack's words at face value, but she had to guard her heart. In his kiss she sensed a commitment, but he hadn't said the words yet. Until he did, she had to put distance between them. Especially when chances were it would all end in a matter of weeks anyway.

Someone wolf whistled behind them. Kat startled and pushed against Jack's chest. The kiss intensified, then he stepped back.

Kat sucked in a breath. "You—we—we can't do that, Jack." She pressed a trembling hand into her stomach, trying to calm the riot of butterflies storming inside. A hooded look cloaked his eyes as he searched her face.

He nodded. "Of course, you're right."

"I'm missing something." She waggled her fingers in his face, emphasizing the ring finger. "I have to be careful until I'm wearing that special something."

Jack shook his head and laughed. "You are the most amazing woman, Katherine Miller."

As they continued down the sidewalk, she hoped he meant it. Because all she wanted was to be the woman he could never forget.

They circled downtown, and Kat wondered if Jack intended to take her somewhere for dinner. Her stomach rumbled, and he must have heard.

"Ready for some food?"

She nodded. Maybe she should lower her hopes from the candlelit dinners she read about in all those dime-store novels. Maybe reality didn't match the images she'd read.

Jack glanced at his watch. "We've got time for dinner before I take you to the movie. Let's eat here." He opened the door and ushered her into a diner. From the first glance it didn't look like much. Kat hoped she wouldn't find cockroaches in the corners if she looked closely. Maybe she'd better keep her eyes half shut.

"Are you sure it's okay?"

"Don't let the look dissuade you. They put all their effort into the cuisine."

"Cuisine. I hope it lives up to the label."

"It will, or I'll eat my hat."

"Anything has to taste better than that."

"Are you kidding?" Jack tapped the top of his hat. "This is premium straw, princess."

A waitress walked up. "Table for two?"

"Yes, and a quiet corner, please."

Kat closed her eyes as the waitress led them to a small table. *This would be good. This would be good. This would be good.* Jack wasn't trying to kill her. Kat opened her eyes and settled onto a bistro chair. The waitress handed them single-sheet menus and left after reciting the daily specials.

"Recommend anything?"

"Trust me, it's all good." Jack ran a finger down the menu. "Try the steak or pork chops."

Kat's stomach lurched then grumbled. "I guess it doesn't care what I eat as long as it's food."

They shared a laugh and chatted as the waitress took their orders and brought Cokes. By the time their entrées arrived, though, Jack had retreated. He still participated in the conversation, but something weighed on him. Should she ask or wait him out? This was so different from the group outings she'd had with other high schoolers back home. Maybe that was it. She'd done something to remind him she was too young for him. It was one thing to quote a Bible verse to her. Another thing completely to spend concentrated time with her.

Kat chewed a bite of the perfectly cooked steak, savoring the flavor and choosing her words. She swallowed and took the plunge. "Jack, I understand if you want to cut tonight short. Feel free to take me home after dinner."

"What? Is that what you want?" Confusion tightened his posture.

"No, but you're so quiet I thought I bored you. I mean, I understand if I do."

"No, Kat." He reached for her hand and stroked it with his thumb. "It's not that. I have something to tell you. Something I hope will make you as excited as I am."

"Are you headed overseas?"

"No–o–o–o." He drew the word out, turning it into multisyllables. "I didn't think you'd be eager for me to go that far away."

"Isn't that what you want?"

"A bigger paper would be nice, but I've found one a lot closer to home. A lot closer to you."

"To me?"

"I've accepted a job with the *Dayton Times*." His smile stretched from ear to ear, while her thoughts raced.

"You're moving to Dayton?" She felt like a parrot, echoing his words.

"Next week."

"Next week?" She shook her head, trying to dislodge the echo.

Jack nodded, a wary expression crossing his face. "Next week. I thought you'd be glad to hear this."

Her eyebrows drew together and her mouth opened; she tried to relax her face. "I am. You surprised me. That's all."

Jack leaned toward her, elbows planted on the table, tie dangerously close to landing in his mashed potatoes. "Kat, we can't test the future if I'm here and you're in Dayton. It's too far, and you have to finish school." He stated the words matter-of-factly, starkly. "There's something here." He gestured between them. "I sense it and know you do, too. I want to see where it leads."

"I do, too." Kat licked her lips and tried to swallow around a sudden mountain blocking her throat. "Moving. Jeepers. That's serious."

"Yes."

That single word hovered between them. Kat shifted, fingers of discomfort climbing her spine. Yes, she wanted a deeper relationship with Jack. More than friendship. But this? Now she squirmed at the thought of what he'd done for her. "You didn't have to."

Jack ran his fingers through his hair and leaned back. "I already did. I had hoped you'd like this."

Kat pushed a smile on her face, knowing it didn't hide the storm of confusion in her eyes. "I'm surprised. That's all." Jack started to push back from the table, but she grabbed his hand, silently begging him to stay. "Thank you."

"You're welcome." He slouched. "I don't want to pressure you for more than you're ready for, Kat. But you are the girl who waggled her fingers at me earlier. The only way that can happen is if we're in the same town and can try a relationship without the craziness of the baseball season. We need to see what we're like in normal life." He took a breath and considered her. "There's something special between us. You liven my life in a way no one else has. I don't want to lose that before we see what God has for us."

"I love how you've dived into your relationship with God."

"That's thanks to you. I want to be the man you can love."

"You already are."

Jack glowed at her words. "Then you aren't upset that I'm coming to Dayton?"

"No." She really wasn't. And as she looked at him, she knew she couldn't say anything else. And she really was excited, wasn't she, under the layers of shock and wariness?

Chapter 19

The jitters wouldn't leave Kat alone.

She'd always expected to feel ecstatic after reaching an understanding with a young man. Isn't that what happened to the heroines in most romances? Instead she felt trapped in a screwball comedy and couldn't figure out how to escape.

Jack was attentive but distracted. And then he moved, with promises they'd see each other often once she returned home.

Would that happen?

There'd be the added scrutiny of her father, a welcome occurrence, but few boys withstood it long. Would Jack be different?

And then there'd be their schedules. She doubted he'd eagerly escort her to homecoming. And would he proudly take her to his work affairs? It would be a far cry from him shadowing the team.

His move brought a wave of pressure she'd never anticipated.

Kat prayed about it. It was all she knew to do. Ultimately it remained the best thing she could do. Much better than continued fretting.

What if Jack was the one?

Wasn't it the perfect example of something only God could orchestrate? How else could a girl from Ohio meet a man living in Indiana and fall in love? The thought brought a peace she clung to. And if God wasn't in it, He'd let her know. If she somehow missed God's direction, she had no doubt Mama would get the message and clue her in. If anyone had a direct line to God, Mama did.

Someday Kat hoped she had a faith that mirrored Mama's. And just maybe this was an area worthy of diving into God and praying with the tenacity and fervency Mama exhibited. Maybe Kat could develop that closeness in a relationship of her own with God.

The thought excited her.

If that was the only reason she went through this with Jack, it was reason enough.

The final home game for the Blossoms had a bittersweet note to it. Even if they won, it wouldn't be enough to elevate them to the playoffs.

The season would end.

The locker room didn't ring with the banter and good-natured joshing that usually filled it before a game.

"All right, girls, gather round." Addebary gestured for them to circle around him. The players obeyed, some kneeling and others grabbing a bench.

"It's been a good season. We're not heading where we'd hoped. But I want you to go out there and leave Cherry Hill with a game it won't forget. One they'll talk about all winter and that will draw the locals back to the very first game of the season.

"It's an honor to be your manager. I couldn't be prouder of another team. Let's play ball."

Joanie cleared her throat.

"Right. Let's pray first." Everyone whipped their caps off and bowed their heads. "God, thank You for the season and for each of the players. I ask You to keep them safe for one more game. Give them a good off-season with their families. And if it's not too much trouble, could we have one last win? For the fans? Amen.

"Now let's play ball."

Kat followed her teammates to the dugout. They formed the victory V one last time, and tears clouded her vision. She needed to go home, but she'd miss this. Would she be back? She didn't know. She couldn't focus on that question right now, or the tears would escape.

After a local school chorus sang "The Star-Spangled Banner" and the crowd recited the Pledge of Allegiance, it was time to play. The Blossoms batted in the bottom half of the inning. Kat sat on the bench, yelling encouragement to Annalise.

Annalise missed a ball right down the heart of the plate. "That's okay, Annalise. You can hit the next one."

Lola shook her head. "You'll always be a Goody-Two-Shoes, won't you, kid?"

"Probably."

"I've never met anyone quite like you."

Kat grinned at her. "You'll miss me. Might as well admit it."

"Sad thing is, you're probably right."

The first five innings passed in a draw. Neither team could pull ahead. Instead the game turned into a pitchers' duel.

In the bottom of the ninth, Kat stood and made her way to the on-deck circle. She felt the pressure tighten her shoulders as she grabbed a bat and took a couple of practice swings. She wasn't a bad batter, hitting .264 over the season. She didn't like that the seventh-inning stretch came and went with the scoreboard showing zeros. Now in the ninth, time was running out.

Sweat trickled down her forehead and streamed down the small of her back. Lola swung hard but missed.

"Strike three. You're out." The umpire pumped his arm while Lola muttered and stomped back to the bench.

"Come on, Kat! Keep your eye on the ball, and swing for the fences!" Rosie's shout carried over the crowd noise.

"Sure thing." If only it were that easy: Tell her body what to do, and it'd happen.

"You can do it." Annalise's encouragement calmed the tremor shuddering through Kat.

Kat tried to imagine Jack in the stands, encouraging her to make it happen. He'd say she was a star and look at her like she had no choice but to hit a home run.

God, help me do my best.

She closed her eyes, took a deep breath, opened her eyes, and stepped up to the plate. A coolness settled over her. She'd found the place where all of life narrowed down to that small ball. The stands faded to a softened blend of color and noise. She could almost feel the pitcher's breathing.

The pitcher wound up and let loose a ball that sped toward the plate, but it sank low. Kat held her stance, not taking the bait.

"Ball!"

One down, three more to come.

The next pitch whizzed toward her ear. Kat spun in an attempt to avoid getting hit in the head again. She righted herself and turned to glare at the pitcher.

"Ball two! Two and oh!"

"Come on, Kat." Rosie's voice carried from third base. "Just give me a shot. That's all I need."

Kat nodded, never taking her eyes off the pitcher. The next pitch seemed to bob and weave as it flew toward her. Kat stepped into it and swung with all her might. She thought she'd missed, when the top of the bat connected, tipping the ball into the air. Rosie took off from third, head down, and barreled toward home. Kat hesitated a moment, trying to see if the ball was foul then took off down the baseline. Her legs pumped as she turned toward second. The crowd whooped and hollered. Kat reached second base and watched Rosie collide with the catcher and the ball roll from the catcher's hand.

Addebary raced to Rosie and spun her around.

Kat smiled. Finally Rosie had her chance to be the star. How fitting that it came in the final game of the season.

The Blossoms stormed from the dugout, surrounding Addebary and Rosie. Kat jogged the rest of the way around the bases, and Lola pulled her into the celebration. Soon Kat and Rosie bounced across the field on their teammates' shoulders.

The fans raced down and joined the party. They seemed eager to celebrate the win, even though the season had ended. The team went to Addebary's home to celebrate. Kat's teammates bubbled with plans for the rest of the year.

"I'll head back to Wisconsin and teach my first-grade class again." Annalise smiled as if she couldn't wait to get back to the room full of noisy six-year-olds. "There's nothing like watching their faces brighten when they understand addition or first read a book."

Rosie grimaced. "You can have the wee ones. I'll spend the year back at my dad's dairy. Doing the same things I've done every day since I learned to walk." Her face soured further. Guess the excitement of her starring role in the game had expired. "And each morning I'll count down to how many days are left before I come back."

"So you decided to come back to Cherry Hill after all?" Lola eyed Rosie over the top of her glass of tea.

"You bet. What else would I do?" Rosie nibbled a cherry.

Addebary caught Kat's eye and motioned toward his tiny kitchen. Kat stood and followed him into the room. "Have you reached a decision? I don't want to spend spring training looking for a new shortstop."

Kat stared at the tips of her shoes. "I'll need to talk to my parents when I get home."

"They let you come this year."

"True. I'm just not sure what next year holds."

Addebary crossed his arms and leaned against the counter. "What more do you need, kid? You know we want you back."

"I know. I guess I need to figure out what's after school."

"Sure. But all of that can include coming back next summer."

Kat laughed. "You are one persistent man."

"That I am—especially when the town fathers have ordered me to bring back our star player."

"You're kind, but others can do what I did."

"Not in a way that fills the stands."

"I'll keep praying about it." Kat slipped out of the room, hugged her teammates, and then headed home. She needed to pack, but first she needed to clear her head, remove the confusion and lingering cobwebs from the season. Frankly she was so tired from the pace of the season and the thought of returning home and jumping straight into school that the idea of repeating the season drained her.

✳

Dayton didn't have the energy and excitement of downtown Chicago, but it certainly wasn't as sleepy as Cherry Hill. As Jack explored the city for the perfect apartment, he'd settled on a charming neighborhood blocks from downtown and near the National Cash Register Company. Near the University of Dayton, trees lined the sidewalks and the homes were old and substantial. He lived over another garage for another widow, but he liked the sense of independence, coupled with the role of protecting guardian.

The September morning had a chill to it as he headed toward the *Dayton Times*. The newsroom was bigger with more stringers running in and out, giving it a pulse that made the Cherry Hill paper look empty.

But then he had spent a summer covering girls' softball there.

Here his days and nights were filled with covering various government meetings, interspersed with teas and social events. Truly eclectic and very different from the sports page.

One thing he hadn't planned with the move was how to reconnect with

Miss Katherine Miller. Thoughts of her haunted his days and lonely nights. He'd seen on the wire the Blossoms had won their final game. . .not enough to get them in the playoffs but enough to leave them feeling good. A positive springboard for next year.

What if Kat wanted to play again next year?

There were so many things he could worry about if he let himself, but what was the point?

He could generate a list of experiences he and Kat needed to have before he spent too much energy on next year. But first, he had to find out if she was home. And if she had time to see him. Or was the life of a high school senior too intense to hang out with a geezer like him?

During his next break he grabbed the nearest phone and asked the operator to connect him to Kat's number.

"Hello?"

"Is this Mrs. Miller?"

"Yes?" The warmth in her voice didn't hide the question.

"This is Jack Raymond, a friend of Kat's. I wondered if she'd made it home yet from Cherry Hill."

"Yes, she's back and in school. Working hard to catch up on the days she missed."

"Good." Jack worried his lower lip.

"Can I take a message for her?"

"Just let her know Jack called."

"Oh, Jack. Are you the reporter she talks about?"

"Yes, if she says nice things about me."

The woman laughed. "Yes, she does. I remember meeting you in South Bend. Why don't you join us for dinner if you're in town?"

Jack quickly accepted, curious to know what Kat's expression would be when she saw him. He'd know a lot with that glance, though he wondered why she hadn't mentioned to her family that he'd moved to Dayton. After getting directions and realizing he lived in the neighborhood, Jack hung up, anticipation pumping through him.

In a matter of hours he'd see Kat again. Maybe she'd missed him as much as he'd missed her. A man could hope.

Chapter 20

By four o'clock Kat wanted to catch the next train headed west. The day had passed slowly at school, but at least her friends seemed to have a new respect for her ball-playing. Unknown to her at the time, the *Times* had run some of Jack's wire articles during the season.

Amazing what a difference an article could make.

Still, the thought of nine months filled with days that mirrored this one horrified her. The summer had spoiled her with its constant activity. It may have worn her out, but she'd felt alive. She wouldn't miss the strawberries sitting in classes, but her body already felt dormant, legs slack, arms useless.

It didn't take much effort to hold a pencil and scribble a couple of notes.

The final bell sounded, and Kat launched from her chair.

"See you tomorrow, Kat." Joanna, her constant companion last year, waved as she hurried out of the classroom. She stopped in the doorway. "You want to join some of us at the dime store for a Coke?"

"Can't. I'm supposed to help my sister with her kids tonight." Another change from when she left. It was odd not being the youngest in the house anymore. "See you next week." Kat stuffed her last assignment into her satchel and closed the flap. She walked to the door and collided with a solid chest. She looked up, up into Bobby Richardson's smoky eyes.

"Welcome back. I wondered if you'd decided to stay away."

"I agreed to come home before I signed the contract." Kat shrugged. It had certainly taken him long enough to track her down.

"Did you see the article the paper ran on you?" Was that admiration in his eyes? "Jeepers, Kat. You made an impression on somebody. Being selected out of so many trying out."

"I guess."

Bobby starred on the high school baseball team, and their friendship had slowly developed last year. Then, she would have done anything to have him look at her in such an assessing way. Now his eyes weren't the right color. She wanted someone else to show the interest in her.

"Can I walk you home?"

Kat cocked her head and considered him. "Isn't that out of your way?"

"It's not a problem. I'd like to hear about your season."

"All right." What could it hurt? Even if he wasn't the man she wanted to be with, he'd help the blocks pass.

During the walk, Bobby coaxed stories from her, until Kat wearied of talking and tried to turn the attention back to him. Finally they reached the walkway to her home. "See you Monday, Bobby."

He handed her bag over after a moment. "See ya." He saluted her and sauntered down the sidewalk as if he didn't have a care in the world. Kat watched a minute, empty from the assurance that boys like Bobby held no interest for her anymore.

No, a certain man had stolen her heart with his ability to see into her heart and coax her to believe in herself. Jack had known she could contribute in a real way to the Blossoms. His belief had transformed her.

Boys like Bobby couldn't compare. Not anymore.

Jack Raymond had ruined her.

Kat turned to her house, dreading a night filled with the noise and activity that had invaded with the return of Josie and her children. After her summer, she needed some peace and quiet, but this wasn't the place to find it. She took a step up the sidewalk but stopped when she noticed a figure sitting in Mama's rocking chair.

And it wasn't Mama.

In that instant every stifled hope surged to life.

He'd come back.

Just like he'd said, Jack hadn't forgotten her.

The future was theirs, filled with the hope of a promise.

❄

A rumble of thunder sounded, one that matched the clanging in his head as Jack watched the kid saunter off. He wanted to read Kat's mind. She hadn't appeared engaged, keeping a couple of feet between her and that boy.

Maybe he should leave now, before he did something crazy that revealed how insanely, over-the-moon, crazy-in-love with Kat he was. Especially since Kat stood on the sidewalk, white as a sheet, still as a statute, her gaze glued to him. She licked her lips but still didn't move. Guess he'd hoped for a different reaction. Anything more than this.

He pushed out of the rocker, sensing it whiz into motion behind him. He grabbed his fedora, slammed it on his head, and danced down the stairs. No way he'd let her see how her lack of emotion impacted him like a head to the chest in a brawl. He drew closer then stopped. Twin tears trailed down her cheeks.

Tears?

He hated tears. Didn't know how to respond to them. Always did and said the wrong thing. Why did women have to cry so much? And couldn't Kat provide a clue as to whether they were good or bad tears?

He took a hitched step forward and stopped two feet from her. Kat's chin dipped as if she wanted to hide her tears. "Kat?"

She took a step forward and was in his arms before he could move. "Where have you been? Why did you leave before I did? Do you have any idea how lonely it was in Cherry Hill without you? And then you weren't here?" Her words blubbered on top of each other, and all Jack could do was circle her with his arms and put his chin on top of her head. She fit so well next to him.

How could he have thought of walking away a minute ago?

A throat cleared, and though Kat tried to step out of his embrace, he tightened his hold.

"Katherine Miller?" The tone was firm as it questioned.

Jack looked into her father's eyes. "Sir."

"I believe you have an introduction to make."

Kat settled against Jack's side. "Daddy, I hope you remember Jack Raymond from your trip to South Bend. Jack, this is my daddy."

"You can call me Louis." The man shook Jack's hand with an extra-firm grip. Message received. No one could hurt his baby girl without going through him. Jack respected that. "Darling, let's get Jack inside and reintroduce him to Mama."

"I've already met her. In fact, she's the one who invited me."

Kat's head bounced off his shoulder as she turned to look at him.

Jack studied her. "What?"

"Mama's intuition working overtime again."

Louis laughed. "You know better than that, Kat. I'd call it her prayer life."

"Yes, Daddy." Kat looked at Jack. "You've only got one more person to survive."

He quirked his eyebrows.

"My brother. He's a typical big brother. Loving. Picks on me. Overprotective."

"That worries me."

Kat grinned, the last shadow of tears clearing from her face. "He should." She looked Jack up and down. "Remember, he's bigger than you."

Jack puffed up at the challenge. "I can take him."

"I hope you don't have to." A wistful quality lengthened her words.

"Me, too, Kat. Me, too." Jack squared his shoulders and led her to the door.

Dinner was a loud affair, the table surrounded by Mr. and Mrs. Miller; Kat's sister, Josie, and her kids; and Kat and Jack. Mark didn't make his appearance until dessert. The conversation bubbled around them, chaotic and scattered while all Jack wanted to do was take Kat to the side and hear about how the season ended and learn where her heart was now that she'd returned home.

After Kat helped clean up the supper dishes, her mother shooed them out the door. "Why don't you two walk a bit?"

"Don't be too long." Her daddy didn't even look up from his newspaper.

A soft smile brightened Kat's expression. "Guess you passed Daddy's inspection."

That was good. Now he wanted to pass hers. Kat grabbed a small bag that sat tucked in a corner of the porch. He reached for her hand as they strolled down the street, deeper into the neighborhood.

"Let's turn here." Kat led him around a corner.

"Why do I get the feeling you've got a plan?"

"Maybe I do. Don't worry. It's a spot we can catch up but also do something fun."

"Lead on." He grinned when she led him to an open field. Mature trees dotted it, but lines in the grass delineated a baseball diamond. He should have known she'd bring them to a spot where she could be completely comfortable. If she was, then he would be, too.

She opened her bag and pulled out two well-worn baseball gloves and a ball ready to come apart at the seams.

"Do you think the ball will last?"

"I'd be more concerned about the glove. It's Mark's." She winked at him over her shoulder as she sashayed away from him. She had no idea what she did to him. "Ready?" She whipped the ball his way before he had the glove on.

He sidestepped out of the way, and Kat laughed while he pulled the glove on and crab walked to the ball. "This is why I cover sports."

Kat sobered instantly. "Do you regret it?"

"Regret what?" He had to hear what she had to say.

She plopped down on the grass, her skirt billowing around her. "Moving here. For me."

"Katherine Miller, I could never regret that. You are the most amazing woman I've ever known. And I knew I didn't want to stay in Cherry Hill. Dayton's a good move."

"But what if I go back to Cherry Hill next summer?"

There. That was the crux of the issue. "Addebary still trying to get you to commit?"

She nodded, chin wobbling. He sat down next to her, leaned over, and kissed her before she could succumb to more tears. She clung to him, returning his kiss. He pulled back, staring into her eyes.

"Are you listening to me, Kat?" She nodded, but he couldn't tell if she really heard. "You need to get this, though I'll say it as often as you need. I want to be with you. You're the woman I want to forge my future with. If that means we return to Cherry Hill from time to time, I'll go gladly as long as you're with me."

"Do you mean that?"

"Absolutely."

"Good." She smiled at him in a way that made him sit back, wondering what was coming. "Because you've spoiled me for all the high school boys. And everyone else is off fighting." She tried to slip away, but he wouldn't let go.

"I think that comment entitles me to another kiss."

A sweet smile lit her face from the inside. As the ball and glove dropped to the ground, Jack leaned closer. And in that moment, he sensed the power of a future forged on a promise of forever.

A Letter to Our Readers

Dear Readers:

In order that we might better contribute to your reading enjoyment, we would appreciate you taking a few minutes to respond to the following questions. When completed, please return to the following: Fiction Editor, Barbour Publishing, Inc., P.O. Box 719, Uhrichsville, OH 44683.

1. Did you enjoy reading *Ohio Brides* by Cara C. Putman?
   - ❏ Very much. I would like to see more books like this.
   - ❏ Moderately—I would have enjoyed it more if _____
   _____
   _____

2. What influenced your decision to purchase this book?
   (Check those that apply.)
   - ❏ Cover   ❏ Back cover copy   ❏ Title   ❏ Price
   - ❏ Friends   ❏ Publicity   ❏ Other

3. Which story was your favorite?
   - ❏ *A Promise Kept*   ❏ *A Promise Forged*
   - ❏ *A Promise Born*

4. Please check your age range:
   - ❏ Under 18   ❏ 18–24   ❏ 25–34
   - ❏ 35–45   ❏ 46–55   ❏ Over 55

5. How many hours per week do you read? _____

Name _____

Occupation _____

Address _____

City _____ State _____ Zip _____

E-mail _____

MY

CONNECTICUT WEDDINGS

THREE-IN-ONE COLLECTION

by KIM O'BRIEN

Three modern-day Connecticut women are confused by the changes their lives have taken and wonder if they can risk new romance during times of trial.

Contemporary, paperback, 368 pages, 5.1875" x 8"

HEARTSONG
PRESENTS

If you love Christian romance…

$12.⁹⁹

You'll love Heartsong Presents' inspiring and faith-filled romances by today's very best Christian authors. . .Wanda E. Brunstetter, Mary Connealy, Susan Page Davis, Cathy Marie Hake, and Joyce Livingston, to mention a few!

When you join Heartsong Presents, you'll enjoy four brand-new, mass-market, 176-page books—two contemporary and two historical—that will build you up in your faith when you discover God's role in every relationship you read about!

Imagine. . .four new romances every four weeks—with men and women like you who long to meet the one God has chosen as the love of their lives—all for the low price of $12.99 postpaid.

To join, simply visit www.heartsongpresents.com or complete the coupon below and mail it to the address provided.

Mass Market, 176 Pages

✂ -

10/15

YES! Sign me up for Heartsong!

NEW MEMBERSHIPS WILL BE SHIPPED IMMEDIATELY!

Send no money now. We'll bill you only $12.99 postpaid with your first shipment of four books. Or for faster action, call 1-740-922-7280.

NAME_____

ADDRESS_____

CITY_____ STATE _____ ZIP _____

**MAIL TO: HEARTSONG PRESENTS, P.O. Box 721, Uhrichsville, Ohio 44683
or sign up at WWW.HEARTSONGPRESENTS.COM**